Davis Country

Davis Country

H. L. Davis's Northwest

Edited by Brian Booth and Glen A. Love

Oregon State University Press
Corvallis

A Northwest Reader
Robert J. Frank, Series Editor
The Northwest Readers Series presents collections of writings by notable Northwest authors and anthologies on provocative regional themes.

The paper in this book meets the guidelines for permanence and durability of the Committee on Production Guidelines for Book Longevity of the Council on Library Resources and the minimum requirements of the American National Standard for Permanence of Paper for Printed Library Materials Z39.48-1984.

Library of Congress Cataloging-in-Publication Data
Davis, H. L. (Harold Lenoir), 1896-1960.
Davis country : H.L. Davis's Northwest / edited by Brian Booth and Glen A. Love.
p. cm. -- (Northwest readers)
Includes bibliographical references.
ISBN 978-0-87071-577-8 (alk. paper)
1. Northwest, Pacific--Social life and customs--Fiction. I. Booth, Brian. II. Love, Glen A., 1932- III. Title.
PS3507.A7327A6 2009
813'.52--dc22
2009016583

Oregon State University Press
121 The Valley Library
Corvallis OR 97331-4501
541-737-3166 • fax 541-737-3170
http://oregonstate.edu/dept/press

Dedication

For my wife, Gwyneth Booth,
and in memory of the Booth family of Douglas County

For my wife, Rhoda Love,
and to the memory of Edwin R. Bingham

Contents

Introduction

Harold Lenoir Davis, generally known as H. L. Davis (1894-1960), was the Oregon country's first major writer, one who challenged the region's lackluster literary history. By the force of his own talent, he gave the Northwest its first distinctive voice, and thus jolted Northwest literature into the twentieth century.

He was born in a now-forgotten hamlet called Rone's (or Roane's) Mill in the western foothills of the Cascade Mountains in Douglas County, Oregon. The nearest identifiable present-day community is Nonpareil, northeast of Roseburg. Both places suggest something of Davis's targets and effects as a writer: Nonpareil, literally "without parallel," breathes the air of shameless pioneer boosterism that Davis was to capture and poke fun at in his fiction and essays. And Roseburg had its moment of national fame in 1959 when a truckload of ammonium nitrate and gelatin caught fire and exploded, destroying much of the town's center, a blast something akin to the cultural ruckus that Davis's writings in the 1920s and 1930s stirred up in what had pretty much always been a politely dull Northwest literary scene.

Davis's parents, James Alexander and Ruth Bridges Davis, raised Harold and his three younger brothers in a succession of backwoods and rural communities in the Roseburg area. Harold, for some reason, later took for his own birth year (1894) that of his younger brother Percy (1896), after Percy's death in 1910. James Davis was a country schoolteacher; though he had lost a leg in a sawmill accident as a boy, he was well known as an effective teacher and disciplinarian, an active outdoorsman and horse trainer, despite the encumbrances of crutch and cane, and the best rifle shot in that part of Oregon.[1]

The family moved across the Cascades to the high-plateau town of Antelope, Oregon, in 1906, when Harold was twelve years old, and from there two years later north to The Dalles in Wasco County on the Columbia River, where James Davis became principal of the high school from which young Harold graduated in 1912. That was the end of his formal education, but he was from the start an omnivorous reader and a quick study who picked up foreign languages, folklore and folksongs, and the guitar. (According to promotional copy from his publisher, William Morrow & Company, "Mr. Davis is a fine guitarist and his classical repertoire includes works of Pergolesi, Boccherini, Mozart and Tarragona. He sings from memory 1,312 American folk-songs,

High school graduation, The Dalles, 1912

including French-Canadian, Louisiana Creole, Hispano-American and Negro.") He also quickly mastered the multiple occupations—printer's devil and typesetter, sheep and cattle ranch hand, packer, Deputy County Assessor and tax-notice server for Wasco County, etc.—that he mentions in the first article in this anthology, "Davis on Davis," his own short overview of his life. There may be a few "stretchers" in it, as Huck Finn says in commenting upon his creator, Mark Twain, and *The Adventures of Tom Sawyer* at the start of his (Huck's) book, but "he told the truth, mainly." Readers may look to "Davis on Davis" for further biographical details, while this introduction surveys some reasons why H. L. Davis is worth our attention, why he may be the greatest Northwest writer, and why those who haven't read him, and especially those who consider themselves Northwesterners, are in for a treat.

The reference to Mark Twain is not out of place in relation to Davis, who was, in several respects, the Northwest's Mark Twain, the first writer to represent this far and isolated corner of the country as an authentic voice, the sort of startlingly new and unused voice that Twain was for an emerging and distinctively American literature. Ernest Hemingway famously remarked, in his *Green Hills of Africa*, that "[a]ll modern American literature comes from one book by Mark Twain called *Huckleberry Finn*." What Hemingway meant was that Twain had laid claim to the American vernacular, the words that people used in common speech, as the basis for American fiction. H. L. Davis brought that truth home to the Pacific Northwest, whose written language up to that point had been mostly bookish and consciously literary.

Davis was native-born in southwestern Oregon and experienced the place with a fresh, Twain-like sense of its special qualities. Like Mark Twain, his roots on both sides of his family were southern; Davis's people were from eastern Tennessee. He shared some of the opinions and prejudices of his time and heritage, though he admired courage and craft and personal responsibility wherever he found it. Like Twain, Davis made great use of regional folklore and the understated humor of the American frontier. And like Twain, Davis took great delight in language, in the choice of the right word over the almost-right word; the difference between the two, as Twain once said, was the difference between the lightning bug and the lightning.

Davis was, however, no national (or even regional) public celebrity like Mark Twain. Davis, at times, could be a difficult person. He rejected most social life and had contempt for literary politics. He did not go to New York to receive his Pulitzer Price in fiction, "because he did not want to place himself on exhibition." Reportedly a New York editor travelled to California to talk to Davis and took a long taxi ride up to the Napa Valley, where he climbed through a barbed fence and knocked on the door of Davis's ranch home. Davis refused to open the door and the editor returned to New York.

Davis's niece, Barbara Davis Kroon, said he was hard on other people—but just as hard on himself. His behavior sometimes cost him friendships and strained family relationships. His disputes with publishers after his first novel was published resulted in a twelve-year delay before the appearance of his second. Still, Davis had some close friends and assisted younger writers with their careers. After a first marriage that ended in divorce, his second marriage in 1953 was an apparently happy one, lasting until his death in 1960. If he had little inclination toward a genial public persona, he seemed content to be evaluated by the worth of his stories, novels, essays, and poems. Trust the work, not the author, might have been his personal credo.

Davis's childhood home near Roseburg was among rural whites and Native Americans on the edge of a tribal Indian land grant, and he spoke the local Indian patois, along with English, as a child. He had a keen sense of Oregon's seasons and climate, of the unique qualities of its many regions and ecological niches. Wherever he lived, the Oregon country was exhilarating for him. He was all alive to what was around him. Like no writer before or since, he captured the landforms and colors and texture of the country. He knew the names and habitats and qualities of the region's native plants and animals, the sounds of its valley streams and big rivers, of the wind in the tops of tall firs. He knew the feel of places, right down to the air touching his face, or the smell of it in his nostrils. He knew the country's people, their traditions, their behaviors. And he could get it all down on paper, in the sounds and the distinctive shadings and colorings of the local speech.

All that Davis wrote—substance and style—was new to the Pacific Northwest. Although it was not the most recent section of the continental United States to receive what Mark Twain sardonically called The Blessings of Civilization, the

Northwest was probably the last to develop a written literature worthy of the name. With a few exceptions from the pioneer era, such as Theodore Winthrop's *The Canoe and the Saddle*, Frances Fuller Victor's *The River of the West* or her *The New Penelope*, and Joaquin Miller's *Life Amongst the Modocs: Unwritten History*, not much literature written before 1920 in the Northwest is still readable today. While the early Northwest did face many physical and cultural barriers to creating a body of literary work, other regions of the nation had produced, at much earlier stages of their development, a considerable written literature of lasting interest and importance. Yet the Northwest remained, into the twentieth century, largely silent and unstoried.

True, there was a rich mine of oral literature in the Northwest from the original, indigenous Oregonians, an ancient tradition of storytelling, such as has been gathered in collections like Jarold Ramsey's *Coyote Was Going There: Indian Literature of the Oregon Country*. But these Indian stories remained for the most part buried in languages unknown to the new white inhabitants. The newcomers possessed no such long and deep integration into this place, and they turned away from it, strangers in a strange land. When they attempted literature, which was seldom, given the hardships of frontier life, they were likely to produce imitations of what they retained of their former education and lives "back East."[2]

Even into the twentieth century, strong new writing did not emerge. Why this abnormally long period of arrested development in Northwest literature? Looking back, one could conclude that Northwest writers held themselves aloof from the actual primary conditions of frontier and post-frontier life that surrounded them. To begin with, the evangelical influence of the early missionary settlements in the Oregon country seemed to combine easily with the Victorian gentility and refinement of polite American society to produce what became a characteristic tone of uplift and preachiness in the Northwest. This was perhaps best exemplified in Frederick Homer Balch's *The Bridge of the Gods*, published in 1890 and the Northwest's first widely read fiction, a story of the attempt of a New England minister to carry the gospel to the Indians of the Columbia Gorge. The note of piety is peculiarly Northwestern. It seemed to join easily with the region's early image as a destination for God-fearing families and homes and farms, as opposed to the lurid reputation of California to the south, with its hellish mining camps and its high-living San Francisco. Such an image of the Northwest also doubtless served well to mask the fervor with which the region's own movers and shakers rushed to convert its apparently boundless natural resources to private gain.

A second nineteenth-century book, mentioned earlier, Theodore Winthrop's account of his journey through the wilds of Washington Territory in 1853, has much to recommend it. But in one sense it adds another heavy load of moral responsibility to the Northwest's obligations to art. Winthrop's *The Canoe and the Saddle*, published in 1863, is the work of a young New Englander, himself a descendant of Puritan notables and theologians John Winthrop and Jonathan Edwards, who might have been literary surrogates for the fictional hero of Balch's *The Bridge of the Gods.*[3] What seems to have most impressed Winthrop's early readers—and what may still stir us today—was his deep attraction to the country's inspiring natural beauty and temperate climate. When he beheld the region's stunning snow-covered peaks and magnificent forests, he was moved to lofty predictions of a future higher civilization. Crossing the Cascades from Puget Sound, his route took him along the southern flanks of Mount Rainier, which the Indians called Tacoma, or Tahoma, the name Winthrop chose to use, reminding his readers that "[m]ountains should not be insulted by being named after undistinguished bipeds" (32). Winthrop believed that such sublime peaks as Tahoma somehow could inspire the Northwest's coming (white) populace to some higher achievement:

> Our race has never yet come into contact with great mountains as companions of daily life, nor felt that daily development of the finer and more comprehensive senses which these signal facts of nature compel. That is an influence of the future. The Oregon people, in a climate where being is bliss,—where every breath is a draught of vivid life,—these Oregon people, carrying to a new and grander New England of the West a fuller growth of the American Idea . . . with such material, that Western society, when it crystallizes, will elaborate new systems of thought and life. It is unphilosophical to suppose that a strong race, developing under the best, largest, and calmest conditions of nature, will not achieve a destiny (90-91).

Once again, as with the evangelical influence, Winthrop's Olympian pronouncements seemed to call for only High Moral Seriousness from Pacific Northwest writers. No "low" stuff need apply. Contrast nearly all nineteenth-century Northwest writing with lively and memorable California books like Mark Twain's *Roughing It* or Frank Norris's *McTeague* and one feels the greater appeal, for readers, of sensate California over moralistic and imitative Oregon. In poetry, there was a similar Northwest lag. The most popular poem of the pioneering Oregon country was Sam Simpson's "Beautiful Willamette," whose borrowed diction and jingling meters, lifted from Edgar Allan Poe's "The Raven," turned a distinctive frontier river into something more appropriate to a settled and pastoral English countryside.

This denial of the reality of Northwest life seems to have enervated Northwest literature through the late nineteenth and early twentieth centuries. Consequently, most of the early writing from the Oregon country suffers from a smothering moral earnestness, a yearning after refinement that effectively cuts it off from contact with revivifying earthiness, and the energy of folk traditions. "They wanted a city for home lovers, in the midst of a country of high-rollers and wild-horse peelers," wrote H. L. Davis, who was to challenge this barren respectability. He was referring to his then-home town of The Dalles in an early essay, though he generalized by titling the piece "A Town in Eastern Oregon," as if his lament could be expanded to encompass the entire region: the townspeople "could only make their town feel as if it belonged to them by making it over. The things they altered might not be any better, but at least they wouldn't feel that they owed them to the wild country in which, after half a century, they were still practically strangers." So, Davis implies, the real world, the ordinary life lived by real people from whose presence an indigenous actual literature, one with a vivid sense of local life, might have taken root, had been sanitized away. "Indians, freighters, steamboat men, saloons, bawdy houses—they had to destroy them for with them life in their town would be too loud and uncomfortable to be worth living."

By the mid-1920s, much of the Pacific Northwest literary scene seemed hopelessly uplifted. Still lacking any firm regional identity or a major writer to shape its direction, the region's official culture battened upon Writers' Clubs and Poetry Societies and even a Parliament of Letters in Seattle. The chief impresario of the latter gathering was Colonel E. Hofer of Salem, the editor of a literary journal, *The Lariat*, and the self-elected leader of the fight for "clean literature" in the Northwest, "sweet, readable songs that leave a good taste in the mouth and sweet jingling in the hearts of readers."[4]

All of this was too much for Davis and fellow-writer James Stevens, both serious young Northwest authors whose work had already appeared in national publications. Davis had also won a national award, *Poetry* magazine's Levinson Prize in 1919 for his early poems. Acutely embarrassed to be geographically linked with such folk as Colonel Hofer and his followers, and some questionable writing instructors at local centers of higher learning, Davis and Stevens, under the inspiration and example of the country's leading literary critic of the time, H. L. Mencken, issued in 1927 an outrageous little pamphlet with a ponderous title: *Status Rerum: A Manifesto upon the Present Condition of Northwest Literature Containing Several Near-Libelous Utterances, upon Persons in the Public Eye.* The pamphlet was printed on a hand press in The Dalles, evidence that Davis and Stevens were taking things into their own hands. And from the start, they weren't holding back:

> Other sections of the United States can mention their literature, as a body, with respect. New England, The Middle West, New Mexico and the Southwest, California—each of these has produced a body of writing of which it can be proud. The Northwest—Oregon, Washington, Idaho, Montana—has produced a vast quantity of bilge, so vast, indeed, that the few books which are entitled to respect are totally lost in the general and seemingly interminable avalanche of tripe.[5]

Status Rerum was only a slapdash piece of journalism, the sport of an evening's work by a couple of talented youngsters under the influence of high (and strong) spirits, but the derisive little pamphlet later proved somewhat embarrassing to both Davis and Stevens. They had smart-alecked themselves out of a place at the table of the Northwest literary establishment, and, though they spurned such a place, they had mixed feelings about having vented their spleen on literary third-raters. They would have to watch their own backs in the future. James Stevens remained in the Northwest, slowly worked his way out of the doghouse, and went on to a significant career as a Northwest writer. But Davis seemed to regard the attack as a necessary and justifiable act of separation from the region and its cultural elite, even while also allowing that *Status Rerum* left a bad taste in his mouth. He avoids mentioning it in his "Davis on Davis" autobiographical sketch, and he was uncomfortable enough with his now-curdled relationship to the Northwest literary scene that after the early 1930s he chose to live the rest of his life outside the Northwest, mostly in Mexico and California, though Oregon remained the setting of his best fiction and essays. He once told Oregon writer Howard McKinley Corning, "I can only write about Oregon when I am away from it."[6]

Still, as a cultural event of its own, *Status Rerum* seemed to accomplish its aims, blasting to rags and pulp the record of mediocre gentility in Northwest literature and signaling the region's first step toward recovery from a near terminal case of high-mindedness. James Stevens said that with *Status Rerum* and the controversy that swirled around it, "Stewart Holbrook, Richard L. Neuberger, Archie Binns, Nard Jones, and other budding writers of the day found a new excitement in the art they hoped to practice."[7] An important companion event in 1927 was the first appearance of a groundbreaking regional magazine, *The Frontier*, edited by Harold G. Merriam at the University of Montana. Davis welcomed the new *Frontier* with an announcement in its March 1928 issue, writing in support of the new journal, "We began here with a new way of life, new rhythms, new occupations. We have failed to make that freshness part of ourselves," and he called for new writers to appear on the Northwest scene.

Davis answered his own call with the publication in 1935 of his first novel, *Honey in the Horn*, a book that bolted through the Northwest literary landscape like a runaway steer through an afternoon tea party. The novel's opening lines announced immediately that the Oregon country had found itself an authentic voice for the first time:

> There was a run-down old tollbridge station in the Shoestring Valley of Southern Oregon where Uncle Preston Shiveley had lived for fifty years, outlasting a wife, two sons, several plagues of grasshoppers, wheat-rust and caterpillars, a couple or three invasions of land-hunting settlers and real-estate speculators, and everybody else except the scattering of old pioneers who had cockleburred themselves onto the country at about the same time he did. The station, having been built in the stampeding days when people believed they were due for great swarms of settlement and travel around them, had a great many more rooms and a whole lot more space than there was any use for; and so had the country behind it. Outside the back fence where the dishcloths were hung to bleach and the green sheep-pelts to cure when there was sun was a ten-mile stretch of creek-meadow with wild vetch and redtop and velvet-grass reaching clear to the black-green fir timber of the mountains where huckleberries grew and sheep pastured in summer and young men sometimes hid to keep from being jailed.

Critics and reviewers were quick to notice the resemblances to Mark Twain's writing and characters in the novel. The main character, a homeless boy who pulls up stakes from the motley crowd at Uncle Preston Shiveley's run-down establishment to find his own way of life, is often seen as a Northwestern version of Huck Finn.

And the novel's narrator, a laconic country-bred storyteller, resembles an older Huck Finn who hasn't lit out for the territories, but has stayed around and soaked up his home region like a sponge. He knows this Oregon place so intimately that its essence just rolls out of him as effortlessly as water flows out of a hillside spring. We are likely to trust the authenticity of this colloquial voice; perhaps because it is so unlike its bookish predecessors. It is easy to fall into being the reader this narrator presupposes. The understated humor at the edge of his words can beguile us into a story and a countryside that, even at this early stage, seems likely to be at the heart of that story. There is a rightness to it all, down to the ground and the native vegetation that grows on it, and the people who live on it, or pass through it on their way to someplace else, or try to make money from it, or hide from the law in its woods.

The first stage of Northwest literature, imitative, undefined, and dependent upon early models of style and expression brought in from the East came to a close here with the brash opening lines of *Honey in the Horn*. In no uncertain terms, Davis's novel announced a new level of development, unapologetic in its bold assertion of the actuality and significance of the local. Like the work of Mississippi writer William Faulkner, emerging at just this time, Davis had fastened upon a patch of American ground that he knew intimately, and given it distinctive life. The Oregon country had found a voice of its own, had shaken off its cultural cringe, and had ceased to be a poor imitation of the Eastern establishment. It had finally ceased to be "Awregone," and had become "Orygun," as Oregonians like to say it.

Honey in the Horn won the most coveted national award for a novel, the Pulitzer Prize, in 1936, and was called by H. L. Mencken the best first novel ever published in America.[8] Mencken was also instrumental in bringing Northwest literature out of the Victorian parlor, publishing Davis's colleagues such as James Stevens and Stewart Holbrook in his influential magazine, *The American Mercury*. Davis went on to write four more well-regarded novels and published two collections of his often superlative stories and essays as well as two poetry collections..

By the end of his life Davis had written well enough to break free of the trap he had always feared and avoided, the same fate scarlet-lettered on a T-shirt self-mockingly worn by Texas author Larry McMurtry, reading "Minor Regional Novelist." Davis, joined by other talented writers of the times such as James Stevens, Vardis Fisher, Anne Shannon Monroe, Hazel Hall, Stewart Holbrook, Nard Jones, Archie Binns, Robert Cantwell, Roderick Haig-Brown, Murray Morgan, Richard Neuberger, and Betty MacDonald, provided the primal energy and style to break the Northwest out of its long slumber of respectability, to make its writing vividly memorable, and, eventually, to open it up to new challenges and the influences from the wider world. Of the succession of Northwest writers who followed Davis, perhaps fellow-Oregonian Ken Kesey, especially in his *Sometimes a Great Notion*, is closest in spirit to capturing the rural locale that Davis first claimed.

When one considers some of the talented prose writers of the region today—Ursula Le Guin, Ivan Doig, William Kittredge, Craig Lesley, David Guterson, Molly Gloss, Mary Clearman Blew, Jonathan Raban, Barry Lopez, Kim Stafford, Timothy Egan, Sherman Alexie, and John Daniel, among others—it seems clear that Northwest writing has inevitably evolved and stretched out to encompass wider cultural and imaginative territories. Many Northwest literary artists have, since Davis's time, gone in these new directions, but all have as their heritage from Davis and the innovators of his time a confidence to trust and use the materials of the Northwest place in which they find themselves.

Finally, Davis's writing comes into special relevance in this time of environmental awareness and challenge. Thinking back to Theodore Winthrop's hope in the 1850s that the Northwest's astonishing natural scenery would influence future generations, including ours, to be better people, Davis offers us his own low-rent version of this possibility: not in Winthrop's romantic renderings of the dazzling mountains like Tahoma or the soaring forests of the Cascades, but in the lowliest of natural beauties. Davis reminds us of the emotive power deep at the heart of simple things: A boy who had to work hard to overcome a bad start in life, and this all given back in a forgotten homestead orchard and "the scrubby tangle of old trees in bloom . . . [that] had lived and developed courage to bring forth its clumps of perfect flowers, pink apricot and apple, green-white plum and white pear and cherry, through all the tangle of dead and broken and mutilated limbs that showed how hard it had been to live at all." Or Old Man Isbell, for whom exile from his sagebrush country would have been fatal: "the yellow-flowered, silver-green sage, the black-foliaged greasewood, blossoming full of strong honey; the strong-scented, purple-berried junipers, and the wild cherry shrub, with its sticky, bitterish-honied flowers and dark sour fruit; the pale red-edged ridges, and the rock-breaks, blazing scarlet and orange and dead-black—to lose them would have killed him. By these things, an old sagebrusher lives."

Such moments of natural oneness—integrating character with setting—are everywhere in Davis, and may be the strongest of his gifts as a writer, recalling Twain's masterful rendering of Huck's simple and unconscious celebration of the great, rolling Mississippi River that is his life. Ecological consciousness inevitably follows love of a place. It may be that we are, after all, the inheritors of something of Winthrop's prophecy of an environmentally graced Northwest. With environmental concerns thrust before us with increasing urgency, it is not surprising that they appear in most contemporary Northwest writing.

The Northwest has become, since Davis's time, the once-hopeful American West's own West, the last good place. Looking back, we can regard Davis as the first native-born Northwesterner to bring such an awareness of the primacy of the elemental natural world to prominence in his work.

Having taken into our minds and hearts the beauty of the Northwest, we are also responsive to the threats it faces. We can hold fast, like Davis, to what bonds us to this place. And to keep us steadfast to our personal Northwest, through such a pleasure as reading, is a hidden reward for those who discover H. L. Davis.

Notes

1. Biographical information on Davis, for which we are grateful, is provided by Paul T. Bryant's valuable study of the author, *H. L. Davis* (Boston: Twayne, 1978).
2. For four representative views of the history of Northwest literature, see George Venn, "Continuity in Northwest Literature," in *Northwest Perspectives*, Edwin R. Bingham and Glen A. Love, eds. (Seattle: University of Washington Press, 1979); Harold P. Simonson, "Pacific Northwest Literature-Its Coming of Age," *Pacific Northwest Quarterly*, 71:4 (October 1980); Glen A. Love, "Finding Oregon in Short Fiction," *The World Begins Here*, Glen A. Love, ed. (Corvallis: Oregon State University Press, 1993); and John M. Findlay, "Something in the Soil?: Literature and Regional Identity in the 20th-Century Pacific Northwest," *Pacific Northwest Quarterly*, 97:4 (Fall 2006).
3. A recent edition, including an excellent introduction and notes by editor Paul J. Lindholdt, is Theodore Winthrop, *The Canoe and the Saddle: A Critical Edition* (Lincoln: University of Nebraska Press, 2006). Page references here are to this edition.
4. "How to Get Into The Lariat," *The Lariat*, 6 (1925), 318.
5. Original copies of *Status Rerum* are a rarity. Fortunately, the text has been reprinted in Warren Clare's article, "'Posers, Parasites, and Pismires': *Status Rerum*, by James Stevens and H. L. Davis," *Pacific Northwest Quarterly*, 61 (January 1970), 22-30. Clare's essay is reprinted in H. L. Davis, *Collected Essays and Short Stories* (Moscow, Idaho: University of Idaho Press, 1986), but the text of *Status Rerum* there is not wholly accurate. Glen A. Love's essay, "Stemming the Avalanche of Tripe," dealing with the influence of H. L. Mencken on Davis, Stevens, *Status Rerum*, and Northwest literature, originally published in *Thalia: Studies in Literary Humor*, 4:1, 1981, is also reprinted in the Idaho Press edition.
6. Corning, Howard M. "All the Words on the Pages, I: H. L. Davis." *Oregon Historical Quarterly* 73 (December 1972): 293-331. Unless otherwise indicated, all subsequent Corning quotes throughout the book come from this *OHQ* article.
7. James Stevens Collection, University of Washington Libraries. Unless otherwise indicated, all subsequent Stevens quotes throughout the book come from the Stevens Collection.
8. *Letters of H. L. Mencken* (New York: Knopf, 1961), 394.

Davis on Davis

The following brief autobiography was written by Davis for his friend Thomas Hornsby Ferril, a notable western poet who also was editor of a Denver weekly newspaper, *The Rocky Mountain Herald*. Davis's short autobiography appeared in *The Herald* in 1951, and was later included in Stephen Dow Beckham's *Many Faces: An Anthology of Oregon Autobiography* (1993), one of the six volumes of "The Oregon Literature Series," published by Oregon State University Press. Further material by Davis that appeared in *The Herald*, and Ferril's tribute to Davis at his death in 1960, may be found in *The Rocky Mountain Herald Reader*, edited by Ferril and his wife, Helen. There, Ferril calls Davis "probably the most important writer of the modern West" (75).

Additional biographical information, including recollections from two of his contemporaries, follows Davis's brief autobiography.

Davis on Davis

Born in southwestern Oregon, October, 1986, at a place called Roane's Mill (no longer in existence) in the foothills of the Cascade Mountains—a beautiful country then, Douglas fir timber, ash and rock-maple, wild blackberries, white-tailed deer, blue grouse, speckled trout. It was on the fringe of a settlement of half-breed Indians, also no longer in existence. Their lingo was a run-down species of Hudson's Bay French. I was able to talk it before I could talk English; and still could if I tried, I think.

Ancestry East Tennesseean. One grandfather served in the Confederate Army (38th East Tennessee Confederate Infantry) and was killed at Vicksburg in 1863. The other grandfather crossed the plains to Oregon in the 1840s; a Hardshell Baptist preacher by trade, but also a skilled cabinet-maker and a fairly accomplished horse-trader. My father was a country schoolteacher; moved around from one Southwest Oregon community to another all during my childhood. At nine, I worked summers as a printer's devil on a country newspaper. At twelve I ditched journalism, and got a job on a stock-ranch in the Eastern Oregon back-country, working with sheep and cattle. There were Mexican sheep-shearing crews that worked their way north from Texas to Canada every spring, shearing the local flocks as they moved; I had to keep tab on the fleece they sheared, which usually led to arguments with them. From that, I learned Spanish. Since they were always getting into fights and stabbings among themselves and the law needed somebody who could interpret their post-mortem explanations, I got a job at seventeen as deputy sheriff out in the sheep country. Except for sheep-shearing ructions, it was mostly serving attachments and rounding up sheep-herders who had gone crazy, or at least crazy enough to attract notice. Nothing very picturesque about it, but it did require considerable diplomacy at times.

At twenty, I worked as a surveyor for the U. S. General Land Office in one of the National Forests. The survey camps had to be supplied by pack-train over mountain trails, and the packer always raised hell about having to bring in books; they were heavy, he complained, and they took up valuable space and couldn't be tied down solid and always had to be repacked whenever a horse fell over a bluff, or anything of that incidental nature. He had a point, all right, so I figured it out that foreign-language books would be exempt from most of his lowbrowed griping; they were lighter than American ones, they could be splayed out or wadded up into small corners in the packs, and they cost a lot less and took a lot longer to get through. So I turned to French and German and Spanish for reading-matter (most standard English books I haven't ever read in English, even to this day, though I've read almost all of them in French or Spanish translations). Along in that phase, I ran across some poems in German that looked interesting enough to try imitating. (They were by Detlev von Liliencron; actually they were not particularly interesting, but they did look easy to imitate). So I whiled away the long evenings writing a lot of short poems patterned after them. The patterning wasn't very successful. They looked a lot less like von Liliencron's stuff than I had expected them to. I had a half a notion to tear them up, but finally, drifting into the Army for a spell (Seventh Cavalry, Mexican border; it didn't amount to much) I sent them to Harriet Monroe's *Poetry*, just on a chance that I might be mistaken.

It turned out rather well, I think, as I look back. Harriet Monroe didn't in the least mind the poems' shortcomings as imitations; in fact, I don't think she ever suspected that they were supposed to be imitating anything. She printed them, with a considerable splurge and they were awarded the Levinson Poetry Prize for that year; 1919, as I recollect. After that, I took up poetry-writing whenever I could spare time for it. After the Army, I worked as a clerk in a bank, stock-keeper for a power and light company, time keeper for track-gangs of Mexicans, Negroes, Greeks and Japanese on the Union Pacific Railroad; also deputy county assessor, and finally, folk-song singer for a radio station in Seattle.

The folk-song job came in 1928. Toward the end of it, I sent a poem to H. L. Mencken for the *American Mercury* (he had written asking for one, I have forgotten why) and he suggested in accepting it, that I might try writing some prose for him. I tried three short prose sketches, he took all three of them and asked for more, so I deserted radio and settled down to writing stories and articles for the *Mercury*. After several months, he turned a story down (it was too long and over his readers' heads) and I sent it to a New York agent, just as an experiment. The agent sold it to *Colliers*, which paid such a fantastically vast price for it that I abandoned the *Mercury* and took to writing slick-paper fiction as a sort of career, I hoped. I kept it up till 1931, when Harriet Monroe, being worried that I had strayed so far from poetry, engineered a Guggenheim Fellowship for me to Latin America.

On the strength of that, I went down to Mexico City to live. Got together a book of poems (later published as *Proud Riders*, Harper and Brothers, 1942) and then, the Guggenheim Fellowship having run out and the United States being at the bottom of the Great Depression, decided to stay down there and start a novel. I didn't have much of an idea about what it was to be like; all I figured was that possibly some publisher would advance enough on the opening chapters for me to live on till the magazine market loosened up again. I shipped off the first six or eight chapters, and everything worked out fine, except for the usual one nasty little detail. The publishers made no difficulty whatever about advancing me enough to live on for a spell, only they insisted on dolling it out in installments as the remainder of the novel was sent in. If no more was sent in, they gently intimated, there wouldn't be any installments. So I had to buckle down and finish it. It was difficult, because I had written the opening without the faintest idea how it was all to come out in the end, but I got through it by almost killing myself at it, and it was published in August, 1935, under the title (stuck on in a moment of complete desperation) of *Honey in the Horn*. It was awarded the Harper Novel Prize for 1935 and the Pulitzer Prize for 1936. It really did have something, I guess. I still get letters about it from people who have just finished reading it. A new paper-backed edition of 100,000 copies is to be published by the Cardinal Series of Pocketbooks in December of this year.

Lived in Mexico a little over four years, all told. Then back to the United States, bought a ranch in Northern California mostly as a place to live on while I slashed off books and magazine pieces and things, and made the usual discovery, after a few years at it, that there is no middle ground about owning a ranch. You either live off it or it lives off you.

So I threw it up, late in 1944, moved down to San Francisco Bay (Point Richmond on the East Bay facing the Golden Gate) and settled down to catch up with the books I had laid out to write: *Harp of a Thousand Strings*, Wm. Morrow & Co., 1947; *Beulah Land*, Morrow, 1949; *Winds of Morning*; Morrow and Book-of-the Month Club, scheduled for January, 1952.

All my novels, sometimes deliberately and sometimes not, develop their narrative on two or three different levels of feeling and values. *Honey in the Horn* is ostensibly a story of a pioneer backwash of the final years of settlement, tinctured with picaresqueness and a lightly-colored love-story. Underneath that, it is also a guidebook to Oregon: not only its climate, scenery, topography, flora and fauna, but also its range of emotions, perceptions, traditions, behavior-patterns. *Beulah Land*, which carries a series of pioneer wanderings back to the South and West of the 1850s, also holds in its background a study (as Mr. Thomas H. Ferril has astutely pointed out in one of his reviews) of the various kinds and effects of love on human character.

The new one, *Winds of Morning*, is another of the same order: on its surface, it is the story of an Oregon pioneer returning after years of absence to the country he had known in his youth, when it was still all untracked and open to settlement. There's a murder-mystery and its solution, and a delicate and beautifully-handled love-story, on which his adventures and experiences are threaded. But underneath those reliable ingredients, there is a calm presentation of the traditional pioneer ideals, the hopes and expectations of the first comers to a new and untouched country, contrasted against the realities of the Oregon wheat-country during the money-making fever of the 1920s, and its effect not only on the country itself, but on the people who have inherited it, the children of the first settlers, and their children, what they have made of the country, what it has made of them. On this level it is both a study in sociology and a descent into disillusionment, sometimes touching close to tragedy and more often running into wild and outrageous comedy. And on still another level of narrative, it is an account of the advance of an Eastern Oregon spring into the sagebrush country, from the wheatfields bordering the Columbia River to the deep timber of the high mountains, worked out with as careful detail and sense of movement as the logistics of a military campaign.

There are other narrative levels in it, even beyond these, but probably there is no use overdoing it. I wish I could have given you something about it that might be summed up, maybe in a couple of sentences, instead of all this stringing it out. But, goddam it, it just ain't that kind of a book.

Here are remembrances of Davis by two prominent Pacific Northwest writers who were his contemporaries, James Stevens and Howard M. Corning:

In 1950, Stevens recalled that "Harold Davis was a rare and wonderful soul in those days of 1927-28. He could and did herd sheep, punch cows, skin mules, lay track, brand calves, shuck wheat, run fence, pitch hay, and do about any other job in the ranch country, but milk. And at 9, he could lecture on Shakespeare to school marms."

Stevens remembered the first time Davis had driven him "up the old trading trail from The Dalles, then stopped where the mightiest distances rolled west from the Columbia Gorge, an incredible panorama in purples at dawn." Stevens "tried to say something remotely adequate in appreciation, but Davis interposed with this information: 'I didn't stop to get a speech from you on the scenery,' he said. 'I only want to remind you that Calvin Coolidge is the President of all this.' And the Dodge rolled on."

Corning recalled Davis as having "perhaps the most beautiful eyes I ever remember seeing on a man … his complexion was clear, his hair dark, not black, though not quite brown either … it was those firm lips with the full supporting strength of the lower one and the rather narrow but strong chin, that gave command to his face. Clearly it seemed always in his desire to appear self sufficient. Only his rather slight physical build restricted any aspect of real strength. He talked with a soft steady voice." Corning felt that "Davis wasn't a person you could argue with; anyone could tell, from the set of his mouth, that his conclusions, once arrived at, were unalterable."

Davis struggled with health problems all his life. James Stevens wrote that "His bronchial sensitivities eventually took Davis into the Southwest. The God damn Bull Durham cigarettes were more hell on him than the cold and wet of Oregon." After living primarily in Mexico City and California (Napa Valley, Point Richmond, and Los Angeles), he moved to Oaxaca, Mexico shortly after his second marriage in 1953, and spent most of his last years there writing while hampered by poor health.

Davis's left leg was amputated about four years before his death and he was confined to a wheelchair. He continued to write, including essays for *Holiday* magazine, and started on his last novel. In October 1960 he suffered several heart attacks and died on October 31, in a San Antonio hospital.

Davis in Oaxaca, May 1953

Honey in the Horn

Davis's first novel, *Honey in the Horn* (1935), won him critical acclaim, the Harper Prize, and the prestigious Pulitzer Prize for fiction in 1936, and continues to find new readers today. The following selection from the book's opening chapters is a microcosm of the full story. Davis quickly establishes a group of strongly individualized characters, occupations, and behaviors. But there is an authorial wisdom working beneath these depictions that acknowledges a non-human world of weather, country, and natural history that goes its own way, and may shape human events as it will.

H. L. Mencken in his front page review of *Honey in the Horn* in *Books* of the *New York Herald Tribune* wrote that: "The noble old quality of gusto, which dribbled out of the American novel when its practitioners began to remember their duty to humanity, here returns at high voltage. It would be hard to think of another native tale, save it be *Babbitt* or *Huckleberry Finn* which testifies more gloriously to the author's delight in concocting. The thing begins to glow with joy on the very first page, and until Mr. Davis tires of it at last, and shuts it down with scant ceremony, it remains *scherzo* in the grand manner. But if you translate *scherzo* too literally and think of it as meaning only farce, then you will be mistaken indeed, for this book is in essence perfectly serious, and what Mr. Davis essays to do in it is not merely to recite an amusing story about a herd of stupid people, but to penetrate, as far as may be, to the secret of the American pioneers … It is thus history, as well as fable, and social document as well as history, and in all three aspects it is very good stuff." (Corning, 1972.)

H. L. Mencken did not speak for much of the Pacific Northwest. Davis recalled that "When *Honey in the Horn* first hit the bookstores up in Oregon, it raised the biggest literary hellaballoo the Pacific Northwest had ever seen. All the papers ran indignant editorials about it; there were whispering campaigns, abusive and threatening letters … wholesalers for the area refused to stock the book at all." (Davis letter to Mildred Ingram, see page 270.)

Howard M. Corning recognized Davis's achievement in *Honey in the Horn* but wondered, "why couldn't he find a few favorable and halfway honorable characters in the whole cosmology of man shaping the Oregon reality? Oregon, which had shaped the Davis talent, Oregon, which Davis had used to build a book so beautiful and so ugly—was there nothing about the state, except the

compelling landscape, that he could appreciate or feel grateful for?" Corning said that "deep-dyed Oregonians quickly resented its untypical portrait of the pioneer character and spirit."

CHAPTER I

There was a run-down old tollbridge station in the Shoestring Valley of Southern Oregon where Uncle Preston Shiveley had lived for fifty years, outlasting a wife, two sons, several plagues of grasshoppers, wheat-rust and caterpillars, a couple or three invasions of land-hunting settlers and real-estate speculators, and everybody else except the scattering of old pioneers who had cockleburred themselves onto the country at about the same time he did. The station, having been built in the stampeding days when people believed they were due for great swarms of settlement and travel around them, had a great many more rooms and a whole lot more space than there was any use for; and so had the country behind it. Outside the back fence where the dishcloths were hung to bleach and the green sheep-pelts to cure when there was sun was a ten-mile stretch of creek-meadow with wild vetch and redtop and velvet-grass reaching clear to the black-green fir timber of the mountains where huckleberries grew and sheep pastured in summer and young men sometimes hid to keep from being jailed.

The creek-meadow in season was full of flowers—wild daisies, lamb-tongues, cat-ears, big patches of camas lilies as blue as the ocean with a cloud shadowing it, and big stands of wild iris and wild lilac and buttercups and St. John's wort. It was well-watered—too blamed well in the muddy season—and around the springs were thickets of whistle-willow and wild crabapple; and there were long swales of alder and sweetbrier and wild blackberry clumped out so rank and heavy that, in all the years the valley had been settled, nobody had ever explored them all. When the natural feed in the mountains snowed under late in the year, deer used to come down and graze the swales and swipe salt from the domestic stock; and blue grouse and topknot-quail boarded in all the brush-piles and thorn-heaps by the hundreds all the year round.

It was a master locality for stock-raising, as all good game countries are. Why the old settlers had run stock on it for so many years without getting more out of it than enough to live on would have stumped even a government bulletin to explain. They did get a good living regularly, even in times when stock-raisers elsewhere were wearing patched clothes, shooting home-reloaded cartridges, and making biscuits out of hand-pounded wheat. But in the years when those same localities were banking and blowing in great hunks of money on hardwood-floored houses and coming-out parties for the youngsters and store-bought groceries and candidacies for the Legislature for the voting males, the old people up Shoestring went right on living at their ordinary clip, neither able to put on any extra dog in the good times nor obliged to lank down and live frugal in the bad ones.

None of the Shoestring settlers had much of a turn for practical business, probably because living came so easy that they had never needed to develop one. What they had developed, probably unconsciously and certainly without having a speck more use for it, was a mutual oppositeness of characters; and it had changed them from a rather ordinarily-marked pack of restless young Western emigrants with nothing about any of them except youth and land-fever, to an assortment of set-charactered old bucks as distinct from one another in tastes, tempers, habits, and inclinations as the separate suits of a deck of cards.

Not that there was anything especially out of line about that. There used to be plenty of communities where old residenters, merely by having looked at one another for years on end, had become as different as hen, weasel, and buzzard. But the fact that the thing was common didn't make it explain any faster, and the Shoestring settlement's case was harder because the men's characters were so entirely different and all their histories so precisely alike. They had all started even, as adventurous young men in an emigrant-train; they had gone through the same experiences getting to Oregon, had spread down to live in the same country, had done the same work, and had collogued with the same set of neighbors over the same line-up of news and business all their lives long. It looked as if they had treated the human range of superficial feelings to the same process of allotment that they had used on the valley itself, whacking it off into homestead enclosures so each man could squat on a patch of his own where the others would be sure not to elbow him.

They had, of course, done no such fool thing. It was more likely merely something that had happened to them. Whatever it was, they had all come in for it, and it made both monotony and complications of character among them impossible. As far as personality went, they were each one thing, straight up and down and the same color all the way through. Grandpa Cutlack, who lived on Boone Creek nearest the mouth of the valley, ran entirely to religion, held family prayer with a club handy to keep the youngsters from playing hooky on the services, and read his Scriptures with dogged confidence that he would one day find out from them when the world was going to end. He was a short black-eyed man with bow-legs and an awful memory for smutty expressions, which were continually slipping into his conversation in spite of him, and even into his prayers.

Next up the valley beyond him lived Phineas Cowan, whose inclinations, in spite of his advanced age, were lustful and lickerous. He had begotten half-breed children enough to start a good-sized town, kept squaws distributed around the country so that he could ride for two weeks without doubling his tracks a single mile or sleeping alone a single night, and was still willing to tie into any fresh one who failed to outrun him. Then came Orlando Geary, a tremendous man with a pot belly, a dull marbly eye, and a bald head so thick that getting the simplest scrap of information through it required the patience of a horse-breaker. Not having imagination enough to be afraid of anything, he was always retained to make arrests, serve legal papers, and sit up at night with dead people. He was also one of the several dozen early-day men about whom it was told that he had gone out single-handed after a bunch of horse-thieving Indians, and that he not only brought back all the horses, but also the Indian chief's liver, which he ate raw as a sort of caution to the surviving redskins not to do that again.

Beyond his place was a strip of open country, and then came a clearing which belonged to Pappy Howell, who promoted horse-races and gambled on them. Next to that was a deserted two-story ranchhouse where Deaf Fegles had killed himself in a drunk by jumping out of an upstairs window to get away from some imaginary snakes; and next to that a measly two-room cabin with a pole-and-puncheon roof which was Joel Hardcastle's. His passion was thrift, and he was so close and careful about saving money that he had never got round to making himself any. His was the last place up the valley except the toll-bridge station on Little River that was Uncle Preston Shiveley's.

The station was not of Uncle Preston's founding or construction. He was the scholar of the community, with a great swad of intellectual interests like writing and investing and experimenting with plants and minerals and historical research, and no concern whatever about anything so low as charging a wayfarer a round dollar to cross a river on a home-made bridge. But he had taken the station over ready-built by marrying the original proprietor's daughter, and he ran it, even when it interfered with his more serious work, as a sort of tribute to her memory. On it, by way of reminding posterity that he skirmished that ground too, he had planted an apple-orchard, built up a band of coarse-wooled sheep, and raised a couple of bad-acting sons who got drunk, fought and trained around with thieving half-breeds until, to keep from being distracted from his studies by the neighborhood rows they got into, he called in Orlando Geary and had them formally kicked off his property for good.

None of Uncle Preston's studies had ever brought him in the worth of a mule's heel full of hay, but he was death on anything that distracted him from them. He had been known, while trying to write up a pamphlet on his pioneer memories, to sit watching a coyote chase three valuable lambs right up to the barnyard fence without lifting pen from paper until the women disturbed him by yelling for somebody to do something quick. Then he got up and killed the coyote with a shotgun; and, to make it strictly fair all the way around, he also killed the three lambs for having got themselves where a coyote could bushwhack them, and for bringing their troubles in to bother him with. He was a short man with long arms and tremendous shoulders and an alert glary eye like a fighting horse, and he was full of tall principles of justice about human rights and the sacredness of privacy. Horning in on a man's time, he argued, was stealing, and ought to be punished as such; and when his two sons got drunk and decided to come back on him after he had evicted them, he got permission from the district court to buckshot the pair of them the minute they set foot on his premises. They stayed away from him after that, a matter of ten years, until one of them killed the other in a fight and took to the brush with a reward up for his scalp with or without the ears attached. Uncle Preston buried the dead son, closed up their house and hauled off their furniture and effects, and gave the Indian woman they been living with twenty dollars to go home. Then he went back to writing a history of the early statutes of Oregon, and he was still at it in the fall when a fierce flood of early rain drowned the country, hoisted the river clear up to the toll-bridge deck-planks, and caught all his sheep to hellangone in the mountains with only about a nine-to-eleven chance of getting out.

Even to a country accustomed to rain, that was a storm worth gawking at. It cracked shingles in the roof, loaded the full-fruited old apple-trees until they threatened to split apart, and beat the roads under water belly-deep to a horse. Ten-foot walls of spray went marching back and forth across the hay-meadow as if they owned it, flocks of wild ducks came squalling down to roost in the open pasture till the air cleared, and the river boiled yellow foam over the toll bridge and stumps, fence rails, pieces of old houses, and carcasses of drowned calves and horses against it. Uncle Preston sat locked in an older upstairs storeroom writing his history, and, about dark, the young housekeeping girl got tired of being scared all by herself and climbed the stairs to tell him how much of his property he had better get ready to see the last of. The sheep hadn't been heard from and were probably stuck up in the mountains to die; the toll bridge had slipped downstream two feet and promised more; a couple of apple-trees had split at the forks; the house itself was not exactly as safe as the ark, because one of the trees was liable to fall on it and cave in the roof.

"If it caves in we'll move to the barn," said Uncle Preston through the door. "If it don't, I'll finish this chapter here. Did I hear a wagon on the road toward Round Mountain awhile back?"

She said the roads were so bad no wagon could be out in them. Then a tree cracked horribly and scared her downstairs; and he went back to his writing. His chapter was about the first violation of the state statute against polygamy. The transgressor had been, not a Mormon, as one might have supposed, but an Indian in the Kettle River country who was suspected of murdering a white packer. There was no proof against him, but somebody discovered that he had six wives, so they arrested him for that, and, camping overnight on the way in with him, burned him with a red-hot ramrod till he got up and ran. Since that was legally an attempt to escape, they shot him, which was what he had coming in the first place. It proved that the old days had enforced justice strictly in spite of their roughness and offhandedness, and Uncle Preston hauled his books together and wrote fiercely to get done before the apple-tree fell in on the roof. It let out a crack like an explosion and came down somewhere with a thump that jolted the whole house, and the housekeeping girl climbed the stairs again.

"It fell," she said, breathing short. "It smashed through the granary. And they're burning the signal fire down on Round Mountain. A mile high, it looks like. But they've changed it and I can't tell what it means."

"You can, but you want an excuse to tell me about it," said Uncle Preston. Everybody in the country had been warned that a fire on Round Mountain would mean Wade Shively's tracks had been picked up and that the people in Shoestring were to look out for him. Everybody had expected that he would head back into the valley sometime because it was country he was most familiar with. It was almost a relief to know that it had happened at last. "He won't come here," said Uncle Preston. "If he does, I'll shoot him, and he knows it. You know it bothers me to hear about him when I'm writin', so what do you come hintin' around about him for?"

"There was to be only one fire if he came this way," said the girl, leaning against the door. The hallway was dark, with a lonesome smell of bitterish willow-bark that the rain had crushed outside. "There's two fires, right alongside of one another. I can't tell what they mean. And the sheep aren't in yet. I tried to send the Indian boy out to look for them, but he wouldn't go. He sassed me."

Uncle Preston said to let the sheep go to hell and let the Indian boy alone. In the old days, two fires on Round Mountain had meant that some lost youngster had been found and that all the searching parties could knock off looking for him and come in. But no youngsters got lost any more—none, at least, that anybody wanted to find again—so what it probably meant was that Wade Shively had done something else. Not but what it seemed wasteful to light fires over an ordinary course-of-nature episode like that. If people held an illumination every time his son cut another notch in his hell-stick, the country's supply of standing timber would be used up before the lumber companies got round to stealing it. "Whatever he's been up to, he won't bother us," said Uncle Preston. "You can go on back—" He stopped, and the front legs of his chair hit the floor with a thump. Two horses were wading the wet leaves under the dripping apple-trees. "Go and see who that is. If it's him, shine a lamp through the back door so I can git a sight on him when he lights down. Damn his soul, I told him I'd shoot him if he come botherin' me at work!"

She came back and reported with her voice panicky; but it was only two herders from the sheep, after all. What jumped her was that the sheep were down at the edge of the timber, drowning, and the two men had given up and come in to find out about the fires on Round Mountain. The third herder, a drip-nosed youth whom Uncle Preston had inherited from his sons' abandoned household, was staying with them through ignorance and contrariness, but it was no use sending anybody to help him. When sheep decided to go down, they stayed down, and any effort to reason them out of it would be simply elbow-grease gone to hell.

Uncle Preston took it as if dropping four thousand dollars' worth of mutton down a mudhole was an everyday operation. "Well, we won't have 'em to winter," he said. "Go get supper and let me finish this chapter before some goddamned thing does happen. You men didn't hear a wagon on the road half an hour ago, did you?"

CHAPTER II

Uncle Preston's list of intellectual interests ranged far outside the pioneer history he was muling away his time on. He knew Latin, and had books by authors like Sallust and Suetonius and Cicero and Leviticus which he could rip off by the nautical mile. He had high-toned truck by Hume and Jeremy Bentham and Volney and Gibbon as easy at his tongue's end as his own whiskers, and he could invent mathematical problems about the area grazed by a calf picketed on a ten-foot rope to a three-foot tree that nobody could work except himself. He had written a novel-length romance about that very neighborhood in which an Indian chief's daughter ran off with a high-strung young warrior from a hostile tribe, and how, when the vengeful pursuers were closing in, she hove herself over a bluff to keep from being parted from the man of her choice. It was founded on solid statistics, too. An Indian woman in the early days had gone over a promontory on Little River, though some of the older Indians claimed she got drunk and fell over, and a few mountain men told it that her parents backed her over, not to prevent her marriage, but in an effort to hold her down while they washed her feet.

Besides the romance, which was called *Wi-ne-mah: A Tale of Eagle Valley*, he had turned off a considerable raft of poetry. Most of it was for use in autograph albums, and was on the order of "May your joys be as deep as the ocean, your sorrows as light as its foam"; but there were also pieces in which he had got mad and cut loose against retail merchants in town when, to his notion, they had dealt a little closer with him than they should have:

> Oakridge is a pretty little ring;
> I say damn the whole damn thing.
> John S. Chance and R. C. Young
> And the whole damn bunch ought to be hung.

It lacked finish, but it helped his feelings. Probably it didn't miss the truth such a vast distance, either, for they were hard traders in Oakridge, bred and nourished in the faith that old settlers had been put there by Divine Providence to be trimmed. But writing was only one of Uncle

Preston's excuses to keep busy when he should have been licking lambs and midwifing ewes, and the fact that he didn't stay with it long was one reason that he pelted to it with such red-eyed devotion when he came back to it. With the same hell-bent consecration to research, he had invented a medicated soap-powder that would heal burns and poison oak. He had experimented diligently with native herbs and had discovered several that would make him sick, though none that would cure anything. He had the power, right in his own person, of charming away warts, and a man afflicted with the blasted things had only to mention the fact to Uncle Preston to have them disappear, leaving the afflicted member as smooth as a cat's stem-end. He had experimented with tobacco-culture and had produced several sample plugs of home-grown leaf, a sort of stagnant green in color and so rank in taste that even the Indians refused to risk their health by chewing it. He could play dance tunes on the violin, and call the figures with a wealth of lively new expressions that kept people alleman-lefting and do-se-doing till their ligaments atrophied, to hear what turn of phrase he had cooked up to order the next manoeuver in.

Public-spiritedness about children who had been left orphaned or abandoned was another of Uncle Preston's off-and-on interests. He hadn't been able to raise the two sons of his own get to be anything but quarrel-picking drunks and community nuisances, but that didn't hinder his streaks of adopting loose youngsters to try his system on again. Mostly it consisted of turning them loose to range his premises as they pleased, and mostly it worked pretty successfully. A couple of his adoptions were children of a hired man who had died, people alleged, of trying to chew his experimental plug tobacco. They stayed in town during the wet season, going to school and behaving themselves as pious and scholarly as a lantern-slide lecturer on the Holy Land.

Another adoption was an Indian kid of about thirteen, with less behavior and more story to him. He belonged to a little community of fish-eating Athapascans in the lower valley, and he had been born with an extra finger on each hand. Among the Athapascans of Southern Oregon, it was an article of religion to destroy all deformed children at birth, and the youngster's mother had only managed to save him out by wrapping his hands in buckskin and pretending that they had been burned. The stall worked all right until a traveling missionary showed up, convoked a sort of mother's meeting in the tribe and insisted on taking the bandages off to see what the burns looked liked and whether they needed medical treatment. He then left, after lecturing the squaw severely on the naughtiness of telling falsehoods; and she gathered the youngster up and carried him eighty miles across the mountains to Uncle Preston's station before the rest of the women could spread the news of her deception and organize a drowning-party in the interest of tribal eugenics. She never went back to the tribe, which got pretty thoroughly killed off in a measles epidemic not long after; and, though she lived with Uncle Preston's two sons until they swapped her to a sheep-shearing crew for a second-hand pistol, she never came back to see the youngster, either.

As well she didn't, for, probably because he was raised with whites, he grew up ten times more fanatical about Indian culture than any wickyup buck in the country. Everything the fish-eating settlement had ever believed in he believed, too, even to the by-law which had decreed his own extermination. He refused to have any truck with his mother because she lived with white men and because her saving his life had been in some way responsible for the tribe coming down with the measles. He wore his hair braided into a coon-tail on his chest, refused to wear shoes or go to school, and spent hours in the haymow, tootling tribal melodies into a flute made out of the drumstick of a turkey.

He was an unsociable little pint of willow-juice, with no friends among his own people because they blamed him for their tribal bad luck and wouldn't have him, and none among the whites because he wouldn't have them. One thing that made him worth keeping was his ability to handle horses, which few Indians of that country had. A colt in his charge never needed wearing down in the bucking-pen. Two days alone with the Indian youngster, during which nothing happened that anybody could see, and the animal would lead out as tame as a toy wagon and walk off under a saddle without even looking around to see what the blamed thing was. Besides horse-breaking, he amused himself in good weather by potting big red-headed woodpeckers in the brush because their scarlet top-knots had once passed among his people for money. When it rained he sat in the barn with the horses and practiced playing his flute by sniffling into it through his nose; and what happened to the station or any of the people on it cut no more figure with him than the tariff on beeswax or the new men's styles in embroidered suspenders.

The newest of Uncle Preston's adoptions was Clay Calvert, and he was the drip-nosed youth of about sixteen who had gone with the sheep to the mountains and refused to quit them and come in when the herders did. He had a knob-jointed godforsakenness of expression about him, and a mean-spoken sassiness that kept people from being pleasant to him even when they wanted to. Partly it was because he had been raised with people who didn't want to be pleasant, and partly because he had discovered that he could head off conversation about his personal history by being offensive with his personal character. His mother had borne him in some fence-corner, and when he was six years old had taken him with her while she cooked for an outfit of harvest-campers. The harvesters broke up in a row somewhere near the bush cabin where Uncle Preston's two sons lived, and she stopped off and married one of them—which one nobody had ever felt interested enough to look up. She hung on for nearly four years with them and then died, and her youngster stayed on with their fighting and helling and squaw-rolling for six years more, until the shooting. Then Uncle Preston closed the bush cabin up and took him home; and he got in a row with the housekeeping girl and the Indian youngster before he had been there two days. Both of them had taken the notion that he was only to stay there until the court decided what to do with him. He had set his head on living there a long time, and maybe for good, because it was the first place he had ever seen where things ran quietly and solidly. So, having called the Indian boy a grasshopper-eating Siwash and the housekeeping girl Pop-eyes, he went to the mountains with the sheep, where he could use all the hard language he wanted to without hurting anybody's feelings.

The housekeeping girl, who was Drusilla Birdsall, was the last on the list of Uncle Preston's adoptions. In point of time she had been on it longer than anybody else, for she was rubbing sixteen and her parents had been drowned fording a creek in the fall rains before she was old enough to talk. She was blond, round-faced, and not popeyed in the least, though she did swell and bulge a little in spots when she was excited. Another and unluckier failing was that when anything worked deeply on her emotions, her insides would register the fact by rumbling audibly. It prevented her from having anything to do with young men because the more she felt drawn to one the more distinctly she sounded as if her inwards were falling down a flight of stairs. Since it was a choice between repressing her natural instincts and feeling ridiculous, she let the instincts go over the tailboard and turned herself all over, from the heels as far up as she went, into a feeling of responsibility for the station. The loss of the sheep hurt her like a bereavement. She blamed Clay Calvert for it, because no sheep had ever been lost until he went along to help herd. That, by ordinary logic and considerable childishness in applying it, meant that he must be responsible. The two hired herders she didn't blame at all. They had never lost sheep before, and they had always done as she ordered without sassing back. She helped them guess about the meaning of the fires on Round Mountain while she rustled their supper.

The supper was all everyday victuals, but there were plenty of them. There was fried deer-liver with onions, a little greasier than it needed to be; beefsteak, excellent cuts but infernal cooking, with all the juice fried out and made into flour-and-milk gravy; potatoes, baked so the jackets burst open and showed the white; string beans, their flavor and nutritive value well oiled with a big hunk of salt pork; baked squash soaked in butter; a salad of lettuce whittled into shoestrings, wilted in hot water, and doped with vinegar and bacon grease; tomatoes stewed with dumplings of cold bread; yellow corn mowed off the cob and boiled in milk; cold beet-pickles, a jar of piccalilli, and a couple of panloads of hot sourdough biscuits. For sweets there were tomato preserves, peach butter, wild black-cap jam, and wild blackberry and wild crabapple jelly. For dessert there was a red-apple cobbler with lumpy cream, and two kinds of pie, one of blue huckleberry, the other of red. The country fed well, what with wild game and livestock and gardens, milk and butter and orchards and wild fruits, and no man was ever liable to starve in it unless his digestion broke down from overstrain. When the table was set, Drusilla went upstairs and called Uncle Preston. He was writing like the devil beating tanbark, his chair creaking like a walking-beam as he followed his pen across the paper and then reached to stab it into the ink-bottle, and he explained that he was in the middle of walloping home the moral of his chapter. He would rather eat cold victuals than look at the sheep-herders' table manners anyhow, so they had better go ahead and eat without him.

They were doing it, and he was still peeling off the snapper-end of his chapter, when a wagon pulled up to the carriage-block in front of the station. Two half-dead horses were on the pole, and they sagged down in the deep leaves, too fagged to need tying while two half-drowned men got out and came in without being asked. One was a dark, soft-featured little half-breed who was sometimes hired by the sheriff's office for hard trips because, though worthless for anything else, he could make horses go anywhere. He spread his hands to the stove, smiled apologetically as if he expected somebody to kick him, and began to steam dry. The other man was Orlando Geary. He wore a cartridge-belt with a gun, which meant that he was traveling on business, and, after a dullishly wistful invoice of the food on the table, he sloshed upstairs, mumbling to himself. Uncle Preston recognized his step and called his name and asked what was up; but he had his opening already made up, and he repeated it off as if he hadn't been spoken to.

"Press," he said. His voice was deep and mechanical, as if words were being blown through him by an outside blast of air. "This is Orlando Geary, Press. I'd like to see you downstairs a minute, if you ain't too busy."

He wanted, probably, to manoeuver the conference down within range of the victuals in the dining-room. Uncle Preston refused to be so accommodating. "I'm a whole hell of a lot too busy," he said, without getting up. "What do you have to see me about? If it's got anything to do with Wade Shiveley, you're wastin' your time."

Old Geary took a heavy breath, rattled water on the floor from his wet clothes, and dug down after another prepared speech. "We want to see you about Wade Shiveley, Press," he recited. "He killed another man last night, it looks like. We found old Pappy Howell shot and layin' in the road yesterday mornin' on the way back from a horse-race. They claim he started from the racetrack with about eight hundred dollars on him. Wade's tracks was around him, so it looks like Wade killed him and took it."

"What do you want me to do?" said Uncle Preston. The news didn't seem to faze him. "Do you want me to help you find him? Talk, damn it! I got work to do."

Prepared speech number three sounded less as if it had hit the line of conversation by accident. Old Geary delivered it with one ear leaned downstairs for fear the noise of plates might mean that the table was being cleared. "This ain't got anything to do with arrestin' Wade Shiveley, Press," he said. "We wouldn't ask you to do that, on account of your natural feelin's. We don't need to, anyway, because we caught him ourselves this mornin'."

On the downstairs section, his artless announcement had about the same effect as if he had yanked the roof off the house and galloped away with it. Drusilla backed halfway through the kitchen door with one hand held over her mouth and her eyes dilated. The two sheepherders stared at one another, and Payette Simmons, the older of them, picked up a cream-pitcher and shook it carefully over his steak without noticing that it wasn't salt. None of them spoke, and even Uncle Preston was silent for some minutes. Then he brisked up. After all, he had never been able to do anything about his son, and there was still a lot that he could do on pioneer history if people would let him. "Well, you've got him, and as far as I'm concerned you can keep him," he said. "Did you swim all the creeks between here and town to tell me about it?"

Old Geary said no, there were three creeks that it hadn't been necessary to swim, and he had supposed lighting the old-time recall signal on Round Mountain would have told everybody about the capture. The thing was that the county jail was a little bit rickety to hold a man like Wade Shiveley, and the authorities had decided to ship him north to the state pen for safe-keeping until his trial. He had asked to talk to some one of his home people before his train left, and had mentioned Uncle Preston particularly. The authorities favored the notion, figuring that, if he could talk out before a lawyer got to him, he might tell what he had done with old Howell's eight hundred dollars. Therefore, they had sent after Uncle Preston to come on the canter, and would he please get his coat and tell them where they could find fresh horses?

"I'll be damned if I go a step," said Uncle Preston. "I told Wade Shiveley a good long time ago that I didn't intend ever to see him again. You heard me, because you helped put him off the place. I've got work to do, and he's got no right to come botherin' me at it. Now you stand away from that door, Orlando, or I'll shoot the panels plumb through you!"

Old Geary stepped away from the door and stood dripping in the dark hallway. After five minutes, he tiptoed back. He hadn't been able to think up any offhanded reopening on such short notice, so he took the whole colloquy back where it had started from. "This is Orlando Geary, Press," he said, patiently. 'I'd like to see you downstairs a minute. You've got a kid here that used to live with Wade Shiveley. I'll take him, if you'll fetch him for me."

Uncle Preston explained that Clay Calvert was out cheering the last hours of a band of sheep, and they would have to wait until he came in. "He'll be all beat out when he gets here, though, and he don't like Wade Shiveley any better than I do. If you yank him out for any all-night sashay on these roads, you ought to be ashamed of yourself."

"I ain't anxious to take him," said Orlando Geary, and edged toward the stairs. "I'll take you, if you'd ruther. We'll need some fresh horses."

Downstairs, he drew up to the table where the heat from the stove would strike him and hauled platters within reach of his fork. The two herders watched him enviously and wonderingly because he had caught Wade Shiveley and because of the forkfuls of food he was able to get his mouth around. He paid no attention when they volunteered that Clay Calvert was a hard-mouthed young hellfry who would undoubtedly make trouble about going to town. They themselves had bumped heads with him when they tried to persuade him to leave the sheep and come in with them. It was pure concern for his welfare, and instead of being grateful he had cussed and drawn a knife. Old Geary swallowed and wiggled his head in a double gesture of understanding and getting down a difficult mouthful.

The second herder, a long-necked man named Moss who turned all his gs into ds after the fashion of stump-country roustabouts, inquired how the doddam they had dot onto Wade Shiveley's tracks. He had been more than halfway planning to have a stab at the Wade Shiveley reward himself. There was a certain melancholy interest in hearing how it had been pulled from under his fingers. Old Geary cleaned his plate with a piece of bread, pulled the meat-platter close, and said well: "There was some buzzards circulatin' around the oak-grub country back of Roan's Mill," he stated, turning pieces of steak pensively. He had evidently told the story before, though the presence of food kept him from putting much spirit into it. "I laid somebody had been killin' a deer out of season, so I saddled up and paced over there to see what was left of the carcass. What's in this dish, preserves? So I hadn't anymore than turned into the millroad when what did I see but the blood-curdlinest sight that—is everybody through with these string beans?—the blood-curdlinest mangled-up human corpse that a man ever laid eyes on. All shot up with a soft-nosed slug that had gone to pieces on the bone, and the rain and mud and all. Dogged if I didn't feel teetery to look at it. There ain't any hossradish to go on this meat, is there?"

Drusilla brought a saucer of fresh-scraped horseradish, and retreated to the kitchen door, anxious to hear what had made him feel so teetery, but ready to leave if the recital got too strong for her. He horseradished his steak, ate a slice experimentally, and told on. The wet clay around the dead man held tracks, and some of them had been made by a horse with one broken shoe. He had no notion who it might belong to, but it made trailing easy. So with a few mill-hands to back him up, he followed it along into the mountains and up to a deserted trapline cabin. Wade Shiveley was in it. Getting him was no trouble, because they found him asleep. The money, of course, they didn't find. It was only after they got him in jail that they learned there had been any. But it was somewhere, and it was eight hundred dollars.

There was a difference in habits of thinking between the men of that deep-grassed old sweetbrier country and the women. It came out plainly when Orlando Geary pulled loose from the subject of the strayed eight hundred dollars. The two herders cheered up and lordamercied one another and talked about the amount of high-rolling a man could do who found where it was hidden. There was plenty of imagination among those stump-country men, because they had to depend on it for entertainment; but entertainment was all they ever got out of it. Putting it to grind on the meaning of life or man's mission to the universe or the problem of putting meat in the skillet was something they never thought of. They used it instead to picture the coming true of impossible make-believes and what-ifs that an ordinary roundhead would have been ashamed to squander his fancy on even in moments of desperation. They paid no attention when Orlando Geary reminded them that the money wasn't in the least likely to be found by them, and that when found it was not going to be spent on high-rolling, but turned over to the county authorities according to the law in such cases made and provided. To hear them talk, finding it would be no job at all, and the law would need a blamed sight more than making and providing to get it away from them when once they got hold of it.

Drusilla was a different cut of character. She didn't join in the herders' conversation. Carrying out empty dishes, she thought of the lost sheep and what the station was going to run on without its regular income from wool and lambs, and about Clay Calvert, who was elected to help the authorities find eight hundred dollars in cash, whether he wanted to or not. She brought a stack of hot biscuits to the table and put old Geary a question. "Suppose Clay does find out where the money is," she inquired, "and then suppose he won't tell you or show you anything about it? Suppose he digs it up himself and gives it to somebody or puts it in his wife's name or something? You couldn't make her give it back, could you?"

The problem was a little complicated for old Geary, but he handled it cleanly. "You mean that kid I'm a-takin' in?" he said, to have everything straight. "He ain't got any wife."

"He could mighty easy git one, with eight hunderd dollars in his hatband," said Payette Simmons. "Only he won't, because he won't go with you. He'll pull in here wet and tired and stubborn, and he'll balk and contrary you. I'll bet you money on it."

"He will, too, go!" Drusilla said. She shortened her neck challengingly. "He's no good around here except to lose sheep, and if he don't go Uncle Preston will have to. He's got to go. Don't you men put him up to hang back, either. If you do you'll never work for this station again, I'll promise you that!"

It was nothing to them whether he went or stayed. They promised not to put him up to anything, and then talked about Pappy Howell and the horse-race in which he had won eight hundred dollars and Wade Shiveley's foolishness in shooting him and leaving tracks. When Uncle Preston came down for his supper, they had the whole subject about talked out, so they dropped it and he told them stories about the country as he had found it when he was a young man packing a mule-train across the mountains to the Coast. While he talked, the rain stopped and the moon came out and plastered the great spread of soaked grass with foggy silver, so swift and blinding that the cattle came out of their shed and stood in it to see what it felt like. The big apple-trees around the house dripped so loud and threw such black shadows that nobody inside noticed the turn of weather until the Indian boy in the barn began tootling a sort of cat-fight tune on his turkey-bone flute to celebrate it.

About the middle of the tune—though it didn't have any middle that was exactly identifiable as such—they heard a tired horse come dragging through the deep apple-leaves. Orlando Geary took a last thundering swallow of something and got up to go out, but the two herders shook their heads and Drusilla motioned him back. It was Clay Calvert, all right, but they knew by the way his horse walked and by the way he slammed the barn door open without announcing himself, that he was packing a chip and hunting for somebody to knock it off on. Orlando Geary sat down again, and they waited while Uncle Preston told how he had come to inherit the toll-bridge station in the early days.

CHAPTER III

On the morning that the storm hit the sheep-camp in the mountains, a shortage of bedclothes waked Clay Calvert at the exact time when a big coyote paid a before-daylight visit to the sheep to purvey himself a feed of fresh mutton. It was a lucky circumstance, though at the time it didn't seem one, because the purveying process had such an outlandish half-dreamy solemnity about it that he stood and watched it from start to finish without interfering until the sheep was killed and the coyote settled down to load up on her carcass. But merely watching it that far made the mountain sheep-camp seem new and a little disagreeable, so that he didn't feel homesick about leaving; and he learned a couple or three things about the power of intelligence over instinct that stood him in hand a good many times afterward, not merely in handling animals, but in looking out for himself.

The sheep were bedded in a high mountain meadow that was half a swale of red wild snapdragons and half blue-flowering wild pea vine. There were a couple of square miles of open ground in it, walled on three sides by a stand of black fir timber that looked solid until you got within two yards of it, and on the fourth by a grove of mountain-ash saplings, fencing a chain of springs that were the headwaters of Little River. The sheep-camp was pitched close to the grove because it was handy to water; but the sheep insisted, principally because nobody wanted them to, upon picking open bed-ground in the middle of the meadow. There was no risk in it during the summer, but in the fall bears sometimes moseyed in to feed on the bitter scarlet berries of the mountain ash, and the herders took turns sleeping out with the sheep to see that they didn't get raided.

Guard duty was not burdensome in clear weather. A man didn't have to make any rounds or do any solitary vigils with his eyes propped open and a gun across his knees. He had only to keep his upper ear cocked for any unusual flurry or scuffling among the sheep, and to remember, whenever he turned over in his blankets, to reach out and lay a chunk or two of wood on the fire so it wouldn't go out. With a little practice one could do that without even waking up.

The herders kept a kind of off-and-on surveillance themselves when it was Clay's turn at it, because he was new to the responsibility; but they didn't watch one another because they were both veterans and touchy about it. Payette Simmons had herded sheep over thirty years, and Serphin Moss, the second herder, for considerably more than twenty. Between the pair of them, Clay got reminded of his inexperience and immaturity about every other time he turned round. It wasn't as if there had been any complicated mysteries about the business. The trouble was that they had both spent a good many more years learning it than their jobs were worth, and it hurt them to let on that anybody could acquire any understanding of it in less time that it had taken them. Their fussing and nosing and volunteering childish orders and supervising childish jobs made them hard to put up with. Clay got up with a chill when there was barely light enough in the tent to see by, and stole himself an extra blanket from old Moss. Before spreading it, he looked out the tent door and saw that the guard-fire was down to a couple of coals and that Payette Simmons had gone sound asleep with the bed-canvas pulled over his bald spot. The sheep were jammed together on account of the chill, and the close-packed yellowish fleeces pitched and heaved restlessly like the top of a forest catching the wind. Outside the pack, a few strays trotted uneasily, looking for an opening to crowd into. Not a sound came from them. They weren't wide awake enough to bawl, and their hoofs were cushioned on a couple of hundred years' accumulation of meadow-grass. The strays bored their way into the herd, which settled into drowsiness, with only one old ewe left moving around them at a worried sort of amble.

She raised her gait to a jog, glanced down at her side, and then put on still more speed, like an old lady being pursued by a cheap pitchman in the street. As she circled the herd she drew farther away from it, and, when her orbit brought her past the tent, Clay saw what ailed her. An old he-coyote was trotting beside her, his shoulder pressed against hers, holding a little back so she would keep trying to get ahead and rubbing her close so her shrinking from him would carry her out of the range of the herd that she was working her best lick to get back to. He made no effort to hurry or hurt her; she was still so close to Simmons' guard-fire that he didn't dare to. If she had blatted or turned on him, and started a rumpus, she would have been saved. But she was too scared to do anything but avoid him and try to outrun him. She trotted faster, and he let out another hitch of speed and rubbed her as if to remind her that he was still there. When they rounded the herd a second time, he had worked her a quarter of a mile away from it.

The promenade lasted a long time. Clay's legs hurt with cold. The light strengthened, and the sky bloomed full of light rose places where the dawn hit the bellies of black clouds. The sheep and the coyote trotted their round solemnly, pressed close like a pair of small-town lovers on Sunday afternoon, without noticing the daylight or each other. They went behind a stand of tall blue-joint grass, and Clay leaned a pack-saddle against the tent-pole and climbed on it to keep sight of them. When he picked them out, they had stopped. The sheep stood with her legs spraddled and her head dropped so it almost touched the ground, and the coyote stood watching her and waiting for her to look up. There was still time for Clay to have scared him off. A yell would have done it. But he held in because he didn't want to face a lifetime of wondering what the coyote had intended to do next, and because if he stopped the killing Simmons and Moss would claim it was all a yarn he had made up himself. He leaned against the tent-pole and waited, knowing perfectly what was going to happen, but willing to freeze his very liver to see how.

It was scarcely worth waiting for. As ceremonious as the preparation had been, the slaughter happened with no ceremony at all. The sheep lifted her head and the coyote trotted close and cut her throat with one swift open-fanged swipe. She knelt, folding her knees under her a good deal like the Lamb in pictures of the Holy Family, and died. It was so simple and she was so quiet about it that it scarcely seemed a finish to anything. But it was one, as the coyote proceeded to demonstrate sickeningly and unquestionably. He took a good long look around, and then dropped his muzzle and lapped the fresh blood under the sheep's chin.

The motion, as far as the coyote was concerned, was merely one of cashing in on a good morning's work. But it knocked the pictorial stateliness of the preliminaries plumb in the head. Clay didn't want to watch it, but he couldn't keep his eyes off it. To put a stop to it so he could go back to bed and get warm, he reached down Moss's rifle from the tent-pole and threw down and shot.

He didn't look at the sights, because he scarcely cared whether he hit the coyote or not. All he wanted was to make the brute leave. But the gun was a specially stocked one that Moss had bought for winter fur-gathering, and it handled so beautifully that it didn't need aiming. The bullet drove center with a smack. The coyote bounced a couple of feet in the air and hit the ground with his legs jerking slowly like a piece of machinery running down. The ordinary marksman's impulse would have been to gallop across and see where the bullet had connected and what damage it had done. Clay hung the rifle back on the tent-pole and climbed down from the pack-saddle. He wished he hadn't shot at all, because, in the moment that he pulled trigger, the coyote reminded him of Wade Shiveley, whom he had imagined he was shut of for good.

Both herders woke up at the shot. Serphin Moss reared up against the tent roof and grabbed his boots, yelling at old Simmons, who he supposed had done the shooting, to inquire what the dod-damn it was and whether he had dot it. Moss was long-faced and candid-looking, with an expression which long years of herding had subdued almost to what he worked with. He looked so much like a sheep himself that when he opened his mouth you half expected him to blat, and he generally half did it. Payette Simmons was an older man with a considerably better flow of language, though he didn't use it for much except to tell lies with. On ordinary occasions he talked faster than Moss, but in emergencies he didn't talk at all. He bounced up from beside the dead guard-fire, his bald head shining in the cold light, his shirt-tail flapping on his bare stern, and his gray whiskers hackled up behind the sights of his rifle, which he pointed at the tent under the foggy-minded impression that somebody in it had taken a shot at him. Clay gave him no chance to get his head back in working order. When Simmons' thoughts were all hitting the collar together, he could lie himself out of a three-ton safe.

"You can go back under the blankets if you want to, Santa Claus," Clay told him. "It ain't Christmas yet. A coyote just got a sheep, and I got him. Lucky you had your head covered, or he'd have eat your nose off."

He would have had Simmons cured of ordering him around for life if Moss hadn't stuck himself in the tent door to take a hand in gouging it into him. "Yes, pile on back into bed, for Dod's sake," he chipped in, all hearty and sarcastic. "Dit through dreamin' about them doddam women, or you'll lose us every tockwallopin' sheep we doddam well dot."

According to Simmons' own representations, which he spun off by the mile when he felt good, he was a considerable hand as a stud. His gray whiskers didn't match up with his claims, but he explained that they had been caused by the strain of watching women try to kill themselves over him. He also had one lop-lidded eye which, by his account, had been disabled by a female lodge-organizer to keep other women from falling in love with him. He could invent windies about his stand-in with the girls faster than a turkey could gobble grasshoppers. None of them had much truth to them, probably, for he passed among the stump-country roustabouts as a man who spent his leisure in Mother Settle's straddling-house talking about sheep-herding, and his work-season in the sheep-camp talking about the women who had hung onto his shirt-tail to keep him from abandoning them. Seniority made him the boss herder, and Moss had managed, by chesting his own authority down on Clay Calvert, to get himself resigned to it; but he still didn't believe that it was right. Moss himself was too bashful to patronize Mother Settle's riding-academy, and played the more expensive game of getting himself a wife through the Heart and Hand matrimonial bureau as often as he could afford it for as long as she could stand him. It came to about the same thing when you fractioned it down; but the fact that Moss spent his money on marriage brokers and preachers and divorce lawyers meant, to his notion, that he was moral and deserving of responsibility. Simmons squandered his on Mother Settle in smaller installments, which meant that he was impure and shameless. Could anything be better proof of it than his having lost a sheep on a worn-out old coyote-trick? Moss thought not. "That's a hell of a fine fire you been teepin' up out there, ain't it?" he inquired, sarcastic and glad of the chance. "Dit back into bed or else put your pants on. You ain't on Front Street in town."

That was piling it on too thick. Instead of making Simmons meek and humble, it made him mad, and it started the day off in a row with

Moss and Simmons digging on each other, and Clay, who had started the whole thing, shoved back into the position of referee; not that his opinion amounted to anything, but because it was the only one they had handy to work on. Simmons climbed into his pants, ordered the dead sheep skinned before the meat got to tasting of wool, and added that the next man he heard any back-talk from had better get ready to draw his time and walk home. Then he winked at Clay to indicate that the threat didn't apply to him and made a vulgar gesture with his fingers toward Moss which was Indian sign-talk to denote a simpleton who ran off at the mouth. Moss didn't get that, but he muttered confidential opinions about Simmons' debauched character and crumbling intellect all the way out to the dead sheep and all the time they were working the hide loose.

They were skinning out the forelegs when a few flakes of snow fell on the warm stripped meat between them, and Simmons yelled to them to give it up and run in the horses. They were going to pull camp and more before the storm hit, and there was no time to fool around about it. The air was as dark as twilight, and tree outlines a mile away had gone out in a black smudge like something scrubbed off a slate. But even in that Moss found an excuse to bellyache, because they had been hectored off to pelt out a dad-blasted forty cents' worth of second-rate mutton when any dod-damned fool might have known that there was a snowstorm working down on them.

The horses were forehobbled and easy to catch, and Simmons had the beds rolled and the canvas *alforjas* packed by the time they came crow-hopping in. The sheep needed only to be lined out and started moving, because the coyote had bunched them as competently as any herd-dog could have done. Each man singed a mammock of mutton on a stick and ate it in the empty tent, and then they struck and rolled it. It seemed almost like stripping something naked to expose the square of brown earth where they had come for meals and sleep and rest and shelter until, because it was used for a different purpose, it had got to seem a different species of ground for anything around it. Turning it back out-of-doors showed how little difference their living on it had made, after all. None, except that they had worn the grass down so the whirl of snowflakes turned it white while the deeper-grown meadow was still only a brindlish gray.

There was a good deal of cussing and yelling and chasing around about leaving, but there was no regretfulness. The herders had done it too many times, and they knew too well what they were getting out of. A storm so near the summit of the mountains could pile up snow from six to ten feet deep. As for Clay Calvert, the place was spoiled for him. The sheep-killing and the dead coyote had turned him against it. He felt every minute as if he was breathing a wind off Wade Shiveley. Clay hadn't felt any overmastering surge of affection for either of the Shiveley brothers, but he had liked the one who got killed the best, and he felt scared and sickened of Wade for having killed him.

They got the sheep moving with an hour's spanking and kicking and screeching and throwing rocks while the snow thickened. Then they lined the pack-horses in front and plodded across the clearing into the dark wall of timber, leading their saddle-ponies behind. When they looked back at the meadow, it had turned all white, and nobody could have told that they had ever been there. Even the dead ewe and the dead coyote were white humps that might have been snowed-in bushes. There was an easy and reassuring feeling about knowing that they were being put out of sight so peacefully. Wildness had destroyed them; now it was getting to work to cover up the mess and all the messes it had made during all that year in the mountains. Deer crippled by cougars, wild cattle hurt fighting among themselves, hawk-struck grouse, stiff-jointed old dog-wolves waiting in some deep thicket for death to hit them and get it over with. The snow would cover them, more snow would fall and cover them deeper, and when spring came it would melt and the freshets would carry what was left of them away. Even the bones wouldn't last, because the little wood-mice would gnaw them down to the last nub.

Essays and Stories

The following pages, the most extensive portion of this book, contain some of H. L. Davis's best short fiction and essays first published in magazines between 1929 and 1959. "Old Man Isbell's Wife" published in *American Mercury* in February 1929 was the first story published under Davis's name. Davis published nine more stories and essays in *American Mercury* between 1929 and 1933. "The Kettle of Fire," his last story, was written for the Oregon Centennial issue of *Northwest Review*, the University of Oregon's literary journal, in 1959. Of the following selections, all but "Hell to Be Smart" (previously uncollected) are drawn from two collections of his work, *Team Bells Woke Me and Other Stories* (1953), which contains most of his people-centered stories, and *Kettle of Fire* (1959), which mostly centers upon Northwest places. All of the *Kettle of Fire* selections except for the title story were written for *Holiday* magazine as a series on the Pacific Northwest, and published in the 1950s. Davis scholar and critic Paul T. Bryant astutely observes that Davis's style and tone in dealing with humans is ironic and humorous, but when he turns to the land he is direct and serious and often filled with wonder (Bryant, 1978]). These two aspects of Davis's world-view are memorably present in the selections here.

"Oregon," the first essay in this section, resulted from one of Davis's last trips through his home state, and was published in *Holiday* in 1953. It is a moving and reflective piece touching on the various places where Davis lived in the first decades of the twentieth century. In the last sentence, Davis could have been thinking about himself: "It was Oregon, all right: the place where stories begin that end somewhere else. It has no history of its own, only endings of histories from other places; it has no complete lives, only beginnings. There are worse things."

As usual, Davis's "Oregon" did not sit well with the Oregon establishment. In their November 1, 1960, obituary for Davis, the *Oregon Journal* noted that "there was more Davis than Oregon in the account … [and] a reader would have a very strange idea of this state if it weren't for the pictures."

Oregon

It used to be a saying in Oregon that people who lived there could change their whole order of life—climate, scenery, diet, complexions, emotions, even reproductive faculties—by merely moving a couple of hundred miles in any direction inside the state. Maybe they still can, but there is not that feeling about coming back to it after a long time away. I have tried returning from three different directions now, and touching it at any point unfailingly brings all of it back on me, not a collection of separate localities but always as one single and indivisible experience. Everything belongs in it, and it all comes together: the gray high-country sagebrush ridges of the Great Basin where I once herded cattle, the rolling wheatlands fronting on the Columbia River to the north where I lived as a youngster, the greentimbered valley country between the high Cascade Mountains and the Coast Range where I was born and grew up—where people sometimes lived all their lives without having any idea what the naked earth looked like. Except for the cultivated tracts, there were not a dozen acres in the country without a stand of Douglas fir trees.

Beyond the Coast Range is the open coast, and it belongs in the experience too. I used to hunt deer there every fall. My grandfather homesteaded down one of the little coastal rivers in the eighteen-seventies, and my mother lived there as a girl. The country was not logged off then, and there were no roads. The family marketing had to be done by taking a homemade canoe down the river, and the children explored the neighborhood by walking on fallen logs where hundreds of gaily colored garter snakes collected to sun themselves during the afternoon. It must have been an intrusive kind of place to grow up in, with white-topped combers jarring the granite cliffs like dynamite blasts and the long wall of black spruce and cedar tossing and roaring in the spring gales, and swarms of huge gulls screaming and fighting over the salmon that got washed out on the sand bars in the spring spawning runs. It would be the same now, probably. Cliffs and combers and gulls are still there, and so is the timber, black spruce or fir or cedar, not bent or twisted by the sea wind but standing straight and rigid against it as the gray cliffs in which they are rooted. They do let down a little along the creeks and old clearings; there are intervals where they leave room for masses of grayish-green alder and dogwood and maple. There is not much variety of color in the country. Except when the flowers are out, it is mostly variations of green, and even autumn alters it very little: a few blots of yellow in the maples, sometimes verging on white, a few streaks of pink in the dogwoods, though hardly enough of either to break the monotony. The extremes of temperature are too small to color leaves very brilliantly. In some places the alder leaves merely die and fall off without coloring at all.

The wildflowers do make a difference. They are all through the woods and grasslands when spring opens: dogwood, wild cherry, sweetbrier, flowering currant, mock orange; ground flowers like lamb's-tongues, cat ears, blue camas lilies, red bird bills, patches of buttercups and St. John's-wort, wild violets that are not purplish like garden violets, but the intense sky blue of jaybird feathers, and yellow violets, trilliums, blue lilies of the valley and pink swamp mallow, besides skunk cabbage and water lilies, which are mostly ugly. Wild asters, foxgloves, azaleas and rhododendrons come later in the summer when the berries are beginning to ripen—wild blackberries, black raspberries, black haws, wild strawberries, red and black huckleberries.

Wild berries were a staple article of diet for farm families in Western Oregon a generation ago. Some species, like the native wild blackberry, were scarce in many sections then, because hurried and careless picking destroyed the vines. They should be taking a fresh hold now. Picking them always took hard work and time, and it is easier nowadays to buy such things at the market, so the berries are left for the blue grouse and bears, which don't object to hard work and have more time than they know what to do with anyway. People in some areas used to depend on the mountain Indians to come through the country with their pack trains every fall, peddling huckleberries and wild blackberries, as they always wandered through peddling muddy water cress out of dripping gunny sacks every spring, but those signs of the changing seasons ended a good many years ago. Indians nowadays do their wandering mostly in automobiles, the same as everybody else, and seldom with anything to sell.

The berries go on growing, nevertheless. There are places in the scrub oak and bracken of the red-earth foothills where, in late April or early May, the wild strawberries are crowded so close together under the broom grass and bracken that you will crush a handful at every step; there are huckleberry swales in the higher mountains where the bushes are bent flat to the ground with the weight of their berries, and trails show where the bears have had to fill up on bitter ashberries as a corrective against overindulgence in them; there are wild blackberry patches in the old timber burns of the back country where, in the late spring, the drumming of ruffed grouse sounds like a battery of rivet guns running full blast.

Some of the country's most common and useless-looking types of vegetation have stories back of them. The evergreen blackberry vine, which tangles itself over all the old fences and abandoned homestead clearings, was brought across the plains by the women of the first emigrant train in 1843, and watered and tended carefully during the entire journey as something to plant in their new gardens. Once it was started, they discovered that the native wild blackberry was far superior to it in size, flavor and accessibility, so it was left to run wild, and in many parts of the country it has become a serious pest. The Spanish moss, which grows in long skeins and festoons on the oak trees of the lower valleys, belongs on the opposite side of the ledger. None of the early settlers had imagined there could be any possible use for it until one winter in the early 1850's, when a deep snow buried all their pastures and they discovered that their cattle were keeping alive by eating Spanish moss from the low-hanging tree branches. Since most of the moss grew higher, the settlers took to cutting the trees down to keep a supply of it within reach. After the first few days, the cattle would come charging through the snow whenever they heard the crack of a tree about to fall, and the children of the settlement had to be stationed around it with clubs to keep the cattle from stampeding in and being crushed under the tree when it came down.

The moss has never been used for anything since, but the memory of help given in need takes a long time to wear off. A great uncle of mine, who came to Western Oregon as a youngster in 1852 and lived there till he was past ninety, told me once about standing guard in the snow with the other children during that winter, and added that he had never since been able to look at Spanish moss without a vague stir of gratitude, or at cattle without a deep feeling of dislike. He had five or six children, all born and brought up in the valley country where he spent nearly all of a long and useful life. None of them stayed there after they were grown. They all moved away, and scattered according to the usual pattern for such families: one to New York, one to Washington, D.C., a couple to Los Angeles, one to some city in the Middle West. They used to come back on visits sometimes. They are all elderly now; some may be dead.

The constant drifting away of second generations from this country, and the influx of new people from other states, may have something to do with its persistent sense of newness, of everything being done for the first time. The growth of the towns probably helps too. Many Western Oregon towns have trebled in size since the war; most have doubled. There are old buildings still left in them, but they are usually overshadowed by an environing swarm of new stucco supermarkets, car and tractor showrooms, chain-saw and logging-truck repair shops, real-estate offices, Assembly of God tabernacles, drive-in movie theaters (generally referred to as "passion pits"), country-club residence subdivisions, antique and curio shops, and places offering such out-of-the way amenities as fortune-telling, agate testing, and streamlined bull service.

Even if it were possible to account for all these new and varied enterprises in detail (what, for insurance, is there about bull service that anybody could streamline?), trying to trace out the original lines of these towns runs into all kinds of confusions and bewilderments. The local residents are usually not much help. Traveling through the lower valley country last spring, I stopped at one of the newer towns to have a surgical dressing put on an infected finger. The doctor's office was upstairs over the drugstore. From the window, there was a view of two motels, a service station, the highway bridge over a small creek, and a gaunt old three-story frame hotel, tall and shabby and narrow-windowed, shedding loose boards and patches of ugly yellow paint behind a clump of huge half-dead pear trees. The doctor saw me looking at it as he worked, and remarked that it was a real relic. It had been a kind of roadhouse for gold miners back in the early days, he had heard: saloon, dance hall, gambling house, that kind of business.

"Some rip-roaring old times there when it was new, I guess," he said. "Shootings, big-money gambling, one thing and another. Dance-hall girls, and all that. It could tell some wild old stories, I guess, if it could talk. It is a kind of an eyesore, the shape it's in; a firetrap too. It ought to be fixed up or got rid of, or something. We could have a real town here if these State people weren't so fussy with their restrictions."

He was young, sociable, and interested in a lot of things. He was originally from Wisconsin, had come out during the war as medical officer in an armored division that carried on field training in the desert around Fort Rock, and had decided to stay on afterward and grow up with the country. I asked which State people seemed the most bothersome, and whether there weren't other places where they were less stringent. He said it was the highway department, mostly, though none of them were easy to get along with if you wanted to do anything.

"All their regulations about what you can build and where, and what you can do and what you can't do, till you'd think we were some bunch of mental cases that had to be told to come in out of the rain," he said. "There are other places, I suppose. Still, I don't know. I like this one. All this new country, and seeing things to do with it. You don't get that in the older places. It's worth something. There's a kind of a feeling about it."

New country, I thought. Down the little creek that was visible from his office window was part of the old trail over which Ewing Young and ten herders drove 600 head of cattle in from California in 1837. It was something of an achievement, by all accounts. His herders quarreled among them selves so fiercely that he had to sit up nights with a loaded gun to keep them from killing each other, and he dared not attempt to reconcile them for fear they might get together and decide to kill him. He got cattle and herders in safely, despite difficulties, and other herds followed. By 1842, the trail was a main route of travel. And not over an hour away was a town on the Umpqua River where the Hudson's Bay Company had a fort and trading post in 1834, and French Prairie near Salem was all wheatfields and orchards by then. . . . What was Wisconsin in 1834? Indian country, like most of Maine, and Minnesota, and Louisiana, and Northern New York, and all of the Tennessee Valley. Oregon is not new; it is older than most of them. Its population turnover gives it an illusion of newness, that is all. However, the doctor was right about one thing: there is the illusion, the same as in the beginning, and an illusion is enough, if it can be made to last.

His ideas about the old hotel having had a rip-roaring past were all wrong, though: colored by too many moving pictures, probably, or by some older resident trying to make the country sound interesting. Merely a hotel was all it had ever been: an overnight stop on the old stage line across the mountains from the coast, with the usual accommodations for man and beast. There had never been anything rip-roaring about it: no wild times, no dance-hall girls, no big-money gambling, probably no great amount of money to gamble with, if gold mining had been its main source. There was gold mining back in the hills in the early days, and some even up to a few years ago, when high operating expenses forced most of it to close down, but none of it ever produced much. A sheep herder prodding around in a dry creek bed on the Upper Rogue River in the early 1930's took out more actual gold in a single afternoon than most of the early-day miners ever saw, or the old hotel either. My grandfather, who was a Hard-Shell Baptist clergyman, used to hold religious services in its main lobby every month or so when he was circuit rider for the district. He was not in the least rip-roaring, though he was responsible for the only shooting the place ever had recorded against it; not exactly a conventional one, though it was disastrous enough in its results.

It happened, according to family tradition, one night after a wedding in the hotel at which he had been invited to officiate. After the ceremony, he withdrew to an upstairs room and went to bed, leaving the guests to their dancing and celebrating, which usually lasted till daylight. Along past midnight, he was roused by some disturbance in the horse corral that sounded as if prowlers might be sneaking up to spring the gate and stampede the horses. Raising an alarm seemed a waste of time, in such an emergency, so he rummaged an old muzzle-loading shotgun out of a closet, rammed down a double load of powder and shot, leaned out of the window and let go both barrels at the shadows outside the corral gate. Nobody ever found out whether he hit anything or not because, loading the gun hurriedly in the dark, he had rammed the tail of his nightshirt down one barrel along with the powder, so the shot yanked him out of the window headfirst. He fell three floors into the middle of the wedding celebration with his shirttail in flames around his neck and scared everybody almost to death. Several guests collapsed, and some ran eight or ten miles without stopping. My grandfather sustained a broken arm and second-degree burns, and miscarriages were claimed by two ladies and denied heatedly by three others, including the bride.

The difference between that uncolored incident and the rip-roaring type of conventionalized fantasy is the difference between tradition and illusion. Tradition is what a country produces out of itself; illusion is what people bring into it from somewhere else. On the record, the illusions have considerably the better of it. People keep bringing them in. Those who kept the traditions going keep drifting away and scattering, to New York and Washington and California and places in the Middle West. Still, it will go on producing new ones, probably. It always has.

There used to be an old sawmill and logging settlement back in tne deep timber on the eastern fringe of the valley country, where my father taught school when I was not much over two years old. It was a small-scale sort of operation, with no prospects of expansion, because its local market was limited to a scattering of homesteaders and cattlemen around the neighborhood, and distance and bad roads made hauling its lumber out to the railroad impossible. Still, between the homesteaders and some half-breed fragments of an old Indian tribe back in the hills, there was enough to run a school on while it lasted. Afterward, the mill closed down, the homesteaders moved away, the Indians were rounded up and shipped north to the collective reservation at Siletz, and the school and settlement were abandoned for a good many years. Recently, after back-country logging had been put back on its feet by such new wrinkles as tractors, hard-surfaced roads, power chain-saws, truck transportation and a rising market for building material, a big lumber company bought up the old camp and the timber back of it, built a fence between it and the main road, and hired a watchman with experience in handling firearms to keep campers and hobos and log pirates out.

There was nothing about the old logging camp that I wanted particularly to see. I had lived in it when too young to remember it; the stories people used to tell about it afterward were associated with them, not with the place. It was the lumber company's watchman I went up there to call on. I had known him from years back, when I was on a Government survey in one of the national forests up in Northern Oregon, and he was guide and camp wrangler for a symphony-orchestra conductor from New York who liked trout fishing, or thought he did: a strutty, playful old gentleman who sang resonantly while fishing, and naturally never caught anything.

The watchman didn't have to work as a guide, being very well off from speculating in orchard lands around the Cascade foothills, but he liked the woods and would rather be working at something than sitting around doing nothing. He used to come over to our camp of an evening and tell stories about being sent out to track down people who had got themselves lost back in the deep timber. He held that anybody could get lost in the woods, there was nothing disgraceful about it, he had been lost in that very country half a dozen times himself, though he was accounted an authority on its geography and landmarks. Whether it turned out seriously or not depended on the kind of intelligence a man used after he got lost. A fool would never admit that he was lost; no matter how completely bushed he was, he always knew his location and directions exactly, and got himself worse lost trying to make them work out. The watchman said he had brought out lost hunting parties in almost a dying condition who were so positive he was taking them in the wrong direction that some of them had to be dragged to get them started. His stories were not only diverting but helpful. I have been lost in the woods a couple of times since then myself, and without them I would undoubtedly have done pretty much what he said the fools always did.

The hard-surfaced road back to the old logging camp had strung the twenty-mile stretch of adjoining country so full of small cottages and shacks and chicken-farm lean-tos that there was hardly any country left until I got within sight of the old logging-camp buildings and the lumber company's fence and padlocked gate. Beyond that, everything changed. There was a dirt road, sprinkled with dead fir needles, with a dusty spot showing where quail had wallowed. The big Douglas firs stood straight and tall and motionless up the sidehill, not crowded together as they are in the rainier mountains near the coast, but scattered out between clumps of hazel and vine maple and open patches of white-top grass and pink fireweed. There were no rusty car bodies or can dumps or barnyard manure piles in the creek. It rattled past clear and bright and untroubled, reaching back through thickets of red willow and gray alder and sweet bush to some old stump land overgrown with evergreen blackberry vines. There was a grouse clucking somewhere up the hill, in a sort of anxiously persistent tone that for some reason was restful to listen to. It was impossible to tell where it was coming from: sounds in timber country have a curious way of seeming to come from the air itself rather than from any tangible thing in it.

The old logging-camp buildings were all nailed up and deserted, except the one nearest the road. It had its windows unboarded, with a school election notice tacked to the door above a wooden-seated chair, and a tin tobacco box alongside containing a few rusty nails, a fire warden's badge, a carpenter's pencil, some loose cigarette papers, and a half-box of .22 cartridges. The watchman was nowhere around. I left my car at the gate and climbed over it and walked up the road a few hundred yards to look around.

There were deer tracks in the road, a doe and two fawns, and big-foot rabbit tracks, and a blue grouse hooting in the firs somewhere, but it was not altogether as the Lord had left it. People had lived here once, up the dirt road for miles back into the hills. My mother used to tell about some of them: an old cattleman, enormously wealthy, who kept eight squaws, one at each of his line camps, and had children by all of them regularly, though he was then past seventy, and a town named after him which is still flourishing. And one of the young half-breeds who drew a knife on my father in school, and then tried to make up for it by bringing him presents—potted plants, ornamented mustache cups, dressed turkeys—all of which turned out to be stolen; and another half-breed, a youngster of about fifteen, who used to write poems, each stanza in a different-colored ink, and peddle them around the settlement at two bits a copy. People used to buy them and never read them. And another cattleman, middle-aged and quarrelsome, was supposed to have set himself up in business by murdering and robbing an old Chinese peddler, and had a mania for giving expensive wedding presents to every young married couple in the community, even those whose fathers he was sworn to shoot on sight. . . . There were more of them. It had been a big community once. There had probably been as many people in it as there were in the chicken-farm cottages down the creek, and they had stayed there at least as long. But they had marked it less, or maybe the marks they made were the kind that healed over more easily. A few were still visible: some old stumps grown over with vines, some half-burned fence posts showing through the fir needles, part of an old corduroy wood road running uphill into the salal, with rabbit fur scattered in it where a hawk had struck. The creek had taken out some of the old marks, seemingly. A tangle of whitened driftwood piled high above a cutbank showed that it had sometimes flooded. There were scuff marks across a strip of sand below the cutbank where some beavers had dragged sticks to use in building a dam.

They had their dam finished, and the cutbank was partly undermined where they had started a tunnel to their nest. It was nothing to be proud of, as far as workmanship went. I had always heard that beavers had a sort of obsession for work, and spent all their time at it because they enjoyed doing it, but the dam didn't show it. They hadn't cut down any trees for it at all, though there were dozens of alder and willow saplings within easy reach. They had merely made it a tangle of dry sticks from the driftwood, most of them no bigger than a lead pencil. The whole thing was so childish and flimsy that they had to weight it down with rocks to keep the creek from washing it away. It was some sort of commentary on modern times, probably, but a man gets tired of having the same thing proved over and over again. It was time for me to go back, anyway.

The company watchman was sitting in his chair by the door when I got back to the gate. There is always a certain trepidation about meeting somebody you haven't seen for twenty years, but he hadn't changed much. He had always been grayish and scrawny, and he was merely a little grayer and scrawnier. He apologized for being out when I came, and said he had been down arguing with some of the chicken-farm people who kept trying to sneak through the company fence and dump garbage upstream in the creek. He didn't know why it meant so much to them to dump it upstream, and they hadn't been able to explain it very convincingly themselves. Their main argument seemed to be that it was a free country and the creek belonged to everybody, and the lumber company had no right to go around telling people what they could do and what they couldn't. It looked sometimes as if they couldn't stand to see anything in the country left as it had been before they got there. It preyed on their minds, or something.

"There's not much left for them to worry about," I said. "Not around here, anyway."

"It's no better up north," he said. "There's highways crisscrossed all through the mountains up there. A highway into the mountains lets people see what wild country looks like, if they can find room to drive between the log trucks. Nobody ever figures that the wild country might not want to see what people look like. It's like that old saloonkeeper up on the Columbia River that had himself buried in an Indian graveyard when he died, because he'd decided that Indians were better to associate with than white people."

I remembered the story. Everybody had been deeply impressed by his wish to associate with Indians after he died. Nobody had thought to find out how the Indians felt about associating with him. It turned out that they were not impressed by the prospect at all. After he had been buried in their tribal graveyard, they moved all their graves somewhere else and let him have it all to himself. Building a main highway into a wild country is like driving a red-hot poker into a tree and expecting the sap to start circulating in it. The living tissue of the tree draws back from it, and the sap goes on circulating around it; or else the tree dies.

"There's wild country left," the watchman said. "More than you'd think, from the way they've fixed things down the creek below here. It's not much different than it used to be, if you figure it right. You've got to figure it in time instead of mileage, that's all. It used to take a day for a man to drive up here from the railroad with a team and wagon. You, probably drove it in less than an hour, and you're surprised that it's all built up. If you'll take a team and wagon and take out on some of these old corduroy wood roads into the hills for a day, the way you'd have done twenty years ago, you'll run into all the wild country you want. You may have to chop some logs out of the road and fight yellow jackets off the horses, but it'll be wild. The animals and everything else."

"Not all the animals," I said, and told him about the beaver and their scamped job of dam-building up the creek.

"They're Oklahoma beavers, I expect," he said. "Moved out from the Dust Bowl back in the hard times, more than likely. You've got to remember that they've been through a lot, and that it don't do any good to stand around and criticize. What they need is help. You ought to have chewed down a few trees for 'em, to get 'em started off on the right foot."

It was not the first tribute to the Oklahoma temperament I had heard, though most were less indirect. "Are they as bad as that?" I said.

"We're none of us perfect," he said mildly. "They're not exactly the kind of company I'd pick to be shipwrecked on a desert island with, but there's points about 'em. I had a crew of sixty of 'em fighting a little brush fire in some second-growth timber on Thief Creek last fall, and they were as conscientious as anybody could ask in a lot of ways. Paydays and mealtimes they never missed. They even fought fire off and on, till it got within about three-quarters of a mile of 'em. Then they dropped everything and legged it out of there at a gallop. Well, they have to learn. It takes time."

"It sounds as if it might take a lot of it," I said. "More than either of us will ever see, probably."

"I've seen 'em come in like this before," he said. "Some as bad, and some worse. They spread back into places like this and dumped garbage and slashed trees and strung fences and tore up grasslands and fixed everything around to suit themselves. Then, they got old, and their kids grew up and moved away somewhere else and sent for 'em and a lot of 'em died out, and now they're all gone. They never last. They think they will, but they never do. They swarm in here with their car wrecks and bellyaches and litters of children, and they pile in to fix the whole country over, and it civilizes 'em in spite of themselves. Then they pick up and go somewhere else to show it off. I may live long enough to see it here yet. Hell, lots of people live to be over ninety nowadays. It'll happen, anyway."

It was looking past externals to an underlying purpose in the country, whether it was the right one or not. And it may have been the right one. Years before, when I was timekeeper for a Greek extra gang on the old Deschutes Rail road, the foreman of the outfit used almost the same terms in trying to explain about some squabble that had got stirred up among the men. The details were a little involved, and he finally brushed them aside and attacked the root of the problem.

"The trouble with these fellows is that they ain't been over here in this country long enough to know anything," he said.

He was Greek himself, from some small coastal village in the province of Corinth. He had left home when he was young, because of some parental difficulty: he had sneaked his father's muzzle-loading pistol out to see how it shot, and the load of slugs and scrap iron tore all the bark off two of the old man's best olive trees, so he ran away to keep from being skinned alive. "All these fellows know is how things are back in the old country. They think that's all they need to know, and it ain't anything. They ain't civilized back in the old country."

The idea that an expanse of Eastern Oregon sagebrush where horse-Indians still wandered around living in tepees and digging camass could represent a higher stage of civilization than the land that had cradled Sophocles and Plato was so startling that I laughed.

"Well, it's the truth," he said, "them people in the old country ain't civilized. They don't know what it is to be civilized till they've been over here awhile. It takes a long time for some of 'em."

"You ought to be civilized by now, anyway," I said. "You've been over here a long time."

"If I was, I wouldn't be out in a place like this," he said. "I didn't say this country got people civilized. I said they found out what it was like to be civilized, that's all. That's as far as I've got."

It did work out to some kind of system. The older generation found out what civilization was; the younger absorbed it, and moved away somewhere else to show it off: Joaquin Miller from his parents' farm in the Willamette Valley to Canyon City, and to England, and to his final exhibitionistic years in California; Edwin Markham from Oregon City to California and to his end in New York; John Reed from Portland to New York and Mexico and to his tomb in Red Square in Moscow. . . . Civilization? At any rate, it was something.

I got a camera from the car to take some pictures of the old logging-camp buildings. It was not difficult to pick out the one we had lived in from the stories my mother had told about it. It was the one with the high front porch; she had told about two drunk half-breed Indians rolling and fighting under it one night on their way home from town, and how she lay in bed listening while one of them beat the other to death with a rock. She was alone in the house; my father was away at a teachers' conference in Roseburg, the county seat.

The watchman looked the camera over, and said he had been intending to get one himself. He wanted to take some pictures of the country to send his son, who lived in Hollywood.

"San Fernando, I guess it is, but it's the same thing," he said. "He works in Hollywood. He's got one of these television shows, 'Know Your Neighbors,' or something like that; interviews with people, and things like that. He's doing well at it, but it don't leave him much time for anything else. He can't get away much. It'll be a big thing some of these days, but you have to stay with it. If you don't you lose out."

The country north through the Willamette Valley is lovely in the spring, with long expanses of green meadowland and flocks of sheep and dairy herds and clumps of wild apple and plum and cherry flowering against the dark fir thickets along the streams. The towns have a certain New Englandish look about them, emphasizing a difference between their culture and that of the country around them that has existed from the earliest days. The townspeople came originally from New England, and were traders and small merchants and artisans. The settlers in the rural areas were mostly open-country cattle raisers from the Mississippi Valley—Missouri, Arkansas, Tennessee, Kentucky. The two cultures have never mixed, and there has been little sympathy or understanding developed between them. Each is admittedly indispensable to the other: country people need towns, and towns have to live on the country, but there is not much enthusiasm in accepting the necessity.

A highway turns east from Salem across the Cascade Mountains by the Santiam Pass, following an old toll road built by cattlemen in the 1850's as a driveway by which to move their herds from the Willamette Valley to the open-country sagebrush and bunch-grass ranges of Eastern Oregon. It couldn't have looked like much of a move, as far as appearances went. The Willamette Valley grasslands are green, luxuriant, well-watered, and usually open for grazing throughout the entire year. East of the mountains the country is arid, colorless, baked dry in summer and whipped by blizzards in winter, its sparse clumps of whitish-green bunch grass not sodded, but spaced out two or three feet apart from each other with naked red earth showing between each clump, or sometimes hidden so close among the sagebrush roots that an outsider will wonder how cattle turned out on it are managing to keep alive, when they may have been put there to fatten for market. There is not much nutriment in grass that has had too easy a time of it; it will keep cattle alive, but not put weight on them. The bunch grass, which has had to fight for every inch of its growth, is far superior in nutritive value to any of the deep sod grasses west of the mountains. There might be some suspicion of a moral back of this, except that cattlemen are not interested in the moralistic aspects of the subject. Nor are their cattle.

Last April I drove east by the highway over the mountains through Santiam Pass. Deep snow all through the pass and in scattered drifts far down into the timber. Blue Lake down in a deep basin to the south, still and deserted; the snow roofs of the summer cabins looked peaceful and attractive. Not a living soul in any of them. Mount Washington towering back of the lake, its huge snowy peak striking into the blue sky like a spear. Snow in patches even below the level where the fir timber changes to yellow pine; salal bushes in bloom among the pines, hanging full of little pink bells like heather, the shallow drifts of old snow under them splotched with pale yellow where their pollen had shed. No wild life in the fir timber, not even birds. A few magpies among the pines, and a tiny lilac-throated hummingbird working on the salal blossoms. Near where the pine thins out into scattering juniper, a little town called Sisters, where sheepmen used to load their pack trains for the camps in the mountains; remote, quiet and dusty, a movie theater showing some tired B-Western picture. A youngster of about sixteen at the gas station gave me some directions about roads, and then said, "What does television look like?" . . .

North through the Warm Springs Indian Reservation. Open juniper and grassland, the timbered Cascade Mountains off to the west, a few cattle and some scattering wheatfields. The agency was about the same as it was twenty years ago: the store and gas station probably new. Some young Indians in a car, apparently from Klamath or somewhere south, on their way to a spring salmon festival at Celilo on the Columbia River. I noticed that a couple of them had their hair marcelled, apparently to get rid of the Indian straightness. It didn't seem much of an improvement. Until recent years there were only dirt roads through the reservation, and it was even lonelier than it is now.

. . . North to the Columbia River at Celilo. It was late afternoon, and twenty years had not changed it much: the gigantic blue shadows reaching down from the gray-black cliffs over the white sand and dark water were still enough to make a man catch his breath and forget to let go of it. No picture can do what the place itself does; the pen-and-ink drawing that Theodore Winthrop made of it for his *The Canoe and the Saddle* in 1860 comes no farther from it than any of the modern photographs. They all miss the intensity of tones, and the scale—the cliffs a thousand feet high, the shadows half a mile deep and twenty miles long, the rapids thundering spray into the air higher than a man can see. The houses scattered in the rifts of cold sunlight have a helpless look, as if the whole thing stunned them. . . .

The salmon festival appeared to be all over with. Several dozen out-of-state cars were pulled up alongside the old Indian village (a huddle of unpainted board shacks along the river, dirt-floored and completely unsanitary, which seem now to have become merely a show piece; the Indians live in some large white corrugated-iron barracks on higher ground, which look very clean and thoroughly dull) and tourists were poking around asking questions of a few middle-aged Indians, with some squaws watching from an old Cadillac sedan. They had on their best clothes, and seemed prim and a little self-conscious. It couldn't have been much of a salmon festival. In the old days, the centerpiece of a salmon festival was always a wagonload of canned heat, and the ceremonies usually wound up in a big free-for-all fight. It was a little dangerous sometimes, but the guests did have something to talk about for the rest of the year.

The river seemed muddy, possibly because of blasting downstream for the foundations of a new hydroelectric dam at The Dalles. When finished, it will back the river up so there will no longer be any rapids, or any salmon fishing either. Probably it is as well. It can't be good for human beings to live as anachronisms, and a salmon festival that has to restrict itself to merely serving salmon is too meaningless to keep on with.

. . . South through the Sherman County wheatfields to Antelope. The wheat towns remain unchanged, at least: no new buildings, the old ones all still standing, though some seemed vacant. The great divisions of color in the wheatfields were beautiful: bright green winter wheat, black summer fallow, white stubble, running long curves and undulations across the ridges to the sky line and into the gray sagebrush to the south. A flock of sheep grazing along a little creek bed at the edge of the sagebrush, with the herder's camp wagon drawn up behind a clump of junipers; not much of a camp wagon, merely a small high-wheeled trailer with a stovepipe stuck through the roof. The herder came out and stopped to talk for a minute: an elderly man, gray and stocky and taciturn. He complained of the long winter, which had been hard on the sheep, and offered to trade his high-powered rifle for my .22 pistol, because there was no longer anything around that a man could use a high-powered rifle on. He had herded sheep most of his life, he said, and didn't mind it. A man could get used to anything. It was easier nowadays, with cars and radios, than it had been. He had a radio in his camp wagon, and liked to listen to it, except the commercials, which made him want to buy things when he was miles from the nearest town and couldn't. His son was in college, he said, studying law, in Los Angeles.

Antelope had not changed in appearance since I lived there as a youngster. It was still a quiet, grayish little town with tall poplars lining the streets and a creek valley spread out below it. The only thing different was the people. They had been mostly Indians and Highland Scots: big lumbering men, some with the reddest hair I have ever seen, who talked English in a curious half-falsetto tone, when they could talk it at all. The only languages one commonly heard on the street were Gaelic and Chinook jargon. It had been a homesick experience, trying to get used to them at first. Now it was a homesick feeling not to find any of them left.

The newspapers had a follow-up story about the salmon festival at Celilo. There were a few touches of the old tradition in it, after all; according to the reports, some of the guests got drunk and got to fighting, and the venerable Celilo chief got poked in the jaw and was confined to his bed, feeling terrible. The stories gave his age as somewhere around eighty-two. It must have been all of twenty-five years ago that he appeared as a witness in a Federal-court hearing involving some old fishing-rights treaty, and gave his age as eighty-eight. Still, anybody is entitled to feel younger at a party than at a Federal-court hearing.

. . . South to Bend. The road follows the high country along the rim of the Deschutes River canyon, with a view of all the big snow peaks to the west: Mount Adams, Mount Jefferson, Mount Hood, Mount Washington, the Three Sisters, Broken Top. Sometimes, when the air is clear and the wind from the north, you can see Mount Shasta to the south. A man working in this country during the summer falls into the habit of counting these peaks from the north to south regularly every day, and watching to see how their snow lines are holding out against the heat.

In the irrigated lands north of Bend, there were ring-necked pheasants all along the road. They stay close to it, knowing that it is against the law to shoot from a public highway, but not knowing enough to keep out of the way of traffic. I counted eight that had been killed by cars, in ten miles.

The general notion about company towns is that they are ugly, spirit-destroying, and deliberately sordid and monotonous. Bend and Klamath

Falls are both sawmill towns, dominated by big lumber companies. They are the two loveliest towns in Eastern Oregon, and perhaps in the entire West. Certainly there is nothing in California that can come any where near either of them.

. . . Southeast to Lakeview. The road from the Deschutes River into the Great Basin is through two great national forests, the Deschutes and the Fremont, with pine timber for miles on both sides of it. There are ice caves off to the north a few miles, probably originally blown into some body of molten lava by imprisoned steam, and not much to see. A cave is a hole in the ground, and ice is ice. The short dark-colored underbrush among the pines is used as summer grazing by the cattle herds east in the Great Basin, its foliage being highly esteemed for its meat-building properties. The stockmen call it "chamiso"; erroneously, since it bears no resemblance to the chamiso of Arizona and California, which is worthless as forage, is pale gray instead of dark, and grows only on ground open to the sun, never in woods.

This country has never been notably accurate in picking names for things. The little blue-flowered ground plant known here as "filaree" is not in the least like the afilerilla of the Southwest, and is not even the same botanical species. Nobody could possibly confuse the two, one being a flowering plant and the other a flowerless grass, so the misnaming must have been accomplished in the dark, or maybe it was mere cussedness. There are dozens of similar cases. The Douglas fir is not a fir, but a spruce; the Port Orford cedar is not cedar, but a subspecies of redwood; the sagebrush is not sage, but wormwood. Some local breeds of trout are really grilse, what the restaurants serve as filet of sole is either sea perch or flounder, and their lobster (which has no claws, merely antennae) is probably some kind of overgrown prawn.

. . . There are a few little towns scattered along this corner of the Great Basin: Silver Lake, Paisley, Valley Falls. They are old and a long way apart, with a subdued sort of charm about them—gray poplars lining the streets, old houses set back against the willows along the creek, lilacs and bleeding heart and white iris coming into bloom behind the gray picket fences. The little creeks hurry past bright and swift and eager, though there is nothing much for them to hurry to. Since the waters of the Great Basin have no outlet to the ocean, the only end its creeks can look forward to is stagnation in some of the alkali lakes down in the desert.

One of the towns had a small roadside lunchstand run by an elderly couple who had owned a cattle ranch in one of the valleys back in the old wagon-freighting days. The old gentleman came out and visited while I had lunch. He was bright, alert, and quiet-spoken. Nobody would have guessed him to be much over fifty, though he must have been considerably past that to have been running a cattle ranch so far back. He spoke of some of the old wagon-freighters, and said he had lost his ranch in the depression, and had been in the country so long he couldn't bring himself to strike out for a new one. There was no chance of starting over again where he was; all the small ranches had been wiped out in the bad times, and the country had fallen into the hands of four or five big cattle syndicates, which ran it to suit themselves. They had everything bought up—homesteads, small ranches, Government land leases—and they hung onto it. A small outfit would not stand a dog's chance trying to buck them. They were the main reason that the town was dead. With the syndicates sitting on everything, there was nothing for new people to come in for.

"They must bring in some business themselves," I said. "You can't run cattle outfits that size without a payroll."

"It don't amount to much," he said. "Not the way they run things, with cross fences and branding chutes and trucks and tractors and everything done by machinery. When they hire a cowboy, they don't ask him if he can stay on a horse or handle a rope. What they want to know is whether he can repair a truck and dig postholes. In the old days, any of those outfits would have kept seventy or eighty men on regular. Now they get by with a dozen apiece; fifteen, maybe. They pay 'em well, I hear. More than they're worth, to my notion. Most of 'em couldn't work for me for nothing. Assembly-line mechanics, that's all there is to 'em."

We talked about men we had both known. One had started a bootlegging business in a small sheep town up north, and when things began to slow up and the businessmen began to close down and move out, he decided to take over all their businesses and run them himself, to keep the place going. Now, in addition to his bar, he ran the drugstore, the grocery, a hay and feed business and the barbershop, besides handling a small line of dry goods, notions, plumbing supplies and fuel. He also repaired shoes, sold hunting and fishing licenses, ran a branch of the county library, and was agent for a laundry and dry cleaner in one of the bigger towns.

"I hope he stands it, handling all that," I said. "He must be old by now."

"A man will stand a lot to hang on in a place he's got used to," the restaurant man said. "Anyway, he's not old. He can't be much over sixty."

. . . All the Great Basin is high country. The altitude of the flatlands around Picture Rock Pass is over 4000 feet, and the mountains are twice that. In the short timber northeast of Picture Rock Pass are mule deer; to the southeast, around Hart Mountain, there are antelope. In between, lying under the huge hundred-mile length of mountain scarp known as the Abert Rim, is a chain of big alkali lakes—Silver Lake, Summer Lake, Abert Lake, Goose Lake. Some are over thirty miles long. During cycles of scant rainfall, they are dry beds of white alkali, as they were during the 1930's, and in 1858 when Lieutenant Philip H. Sheridan camped in the area on some obscure Indian campaign. When the cycle turns, they run full of water again, as they are beginning to do now. The water is too alkaline for any use except as scenery, and Abert Lake has a pronounced odor, but it is pleasanter to live with than the dust clouds, and the uselessness seems a small thing when the great flocks of wild ducks and geese and black-headed trumpeter swans begin to come down on it in their northward migration every spring.

There is something wild and freakish and exaggerated about this entire lake region in the spring. The colors are unimaginably vivid: deep blues, ferocious greens, blinding whites. Mallard ducks bob serenely on mud puddles a few feet from the road, indifferent to everybody. Sheep and wild geese are scattered out in a grass meadow together, cropping the grass side by side in a spirit of complete tolerance. Horses and cattle stand knee-deep in a roadside marsh, their heads submerged to the eyes, pasturing the growth of grass underneath the water. A tractor plowing a field moves through a cloud of white Mormon sea gulls, little sharp-winged creatures, no bigger than pigeons and as tame, following the fresh-turned furrow in search of worms. A flock of white snow geese turning in the high sunlight after the earth has gone into shadow looks like an explosion of silver.

The black-headed swans trumpeting sound like a thousand French taxi horns all going at once. If you happen to be close when they come down, the gigantic wings sinking past into the shadows will scare the life out of you. It is no wonder that the Indians of this country spent so much of their time starting new religions.

. . . Frenchglen, Steens Mountains. Nobody hears much about the Steens Mountains. They are near the southeastern corner of the state, a 10,000-foot wall separating the Great Basin on the west from the tributaries of the Snake River on the east. There is a wild-game refuge in a creek valley along the western rim, with antelope and pheasants and flocks of wild ducks and geese scattered all through it.

. . . The little lake high up in the mountains looked about as it did when we used to ride up over an old wagon road in the late summer to fish for speckled trout. It was small, not over a quarter of a mile long, and not shown on most maps at all. The thickets of dwarf cottonwood around it had not grown or dwindled, the water was rough and dark and piercingly cold, and the remains of old snowdrifts in the gullies back of it still had the curiously regular shapes that looked, at a little distance, like spires and towers and gables in a white town. There was no town anywhere near; the closest was over a hundred miles away. It looked as quiet as it always had at sundown—the dark water, the ghostly cottonwoods, the scrub willows along the bank, a few scrawny flowers spotting the coarse grass. About dark, a wind came up, and it began to rain and kept it up all night. By morning it had eased up a little, but the wind was stronger and it was spitting sleet. Being snowed in, in such a place, was not a tempting prospect. I loaded the soggy camp rig into the car, turned it around gingerly in the mud, and headed out.

There was a sheep camp in the cottonwoods at the head of the lake where the road turned down the mountain. The camp tender was striking camp to pull out, the tent hanging limp on the ridgepole and flapping cumbrously when the wind struck it, the pack mules standing humped against the grains of sleet and gouts of foam from the lake that kept pelting them. The sheep were already on the way out; they were jammed so close together down the road that it was impossible to get the car into it. I stopped, and the herder called his dog and went ahead to clear a lane through them.

It was slow work trying to crowd them off into the cotton wood thicket and there was open ground beyond, so I waved to him to drive them on through to where they would have room to spread out. He nodded, and came back to stir up the tail-enders. It was not a big herd; three hundred, maybe, mostly old ewes, hardly enough for two full-grown men to be spending their time on. He got the tail-enders started, and stood back and dropped the cottonwood branch he had been urging them along with. I expected him to say something, but he looked away, watching the dog round up a few stragglers. He was about forty, heavy-boned and slow-looking and bashful, as if he was trying to avoid-being spoken to. It struck me what the reason might be, and I took a chance on it.

"*De Vascondaga, verdad*?" I said.

That was it. He had been trying to dodge around admitting that he didn't know English. A good many Basque sheepherders in that country didn't.

"*Si, Vizcaya*," he said. "*Aldeano de Zarauz*."

Vizcaya was one of the Basque provinces. Vascondaga was the collective name for all of them. He was from the country adjoining some town named Zarauz.

"*Hace mucho?*" I said.

"*Dos anos*," he said. "*Mas o menos*."

He was not being exactly co-operative. I would have given a good deal to be able to sling a sentence or two of Euskera at him, just to see him jump, but wishing did no good. Spanish was the best I could manage. I tried a change of subject.

"It is slow moving a camp with pack mules," I said.

"We work with what we have," he said.

There didn't seem much left to say on that. I tried the weather.

"*Que tiempo malo*," I said.

"*Hay cosas peores*," he said. "There are worse things." He was loosening up a little.

He had something specific in mind, I thought. If he had been over here only two years—"You saw the Civil War in Spain?"

He nodded, and took a deep breath. "Nobody sees all of a war. I saw people shot. I saw our house burned. My father was shot. I didn't see that, but I saw enough."

"You are *desterrado*?" I said. It was a polite expression the Spaniards used for a political refugee. It meant some thing like exile.

"A little," he said. Then he took it back. "No. I am not *desterrado*. This is my country, here. It is the only one I need."

His handful of lumbering old ewes plodded down the open slope in the wind. The mules flinched and humped uneasily as a blast rattled sleet against them. Some torn leaves from the cottonwoods skimmed past.

"Some people would call it bleak," I said. "Weather as cold as this."

"Nobody can know what is good until he has seen what is bad," he said. "Some people don't know. I do."

He went to help the camp tender with the packs. I drove out of the cottonwoods and through the sheep and on down the mountain. It was Oregon, all right: the place where stories begin that end somewhere else. It has no history of its own, only endings of histories from other places; it has no complete lives, only beginnings. There are worse things.

Open Winter

The drying east wind, which always brought hard luck to Eastern Oregon at whatever season it blew, had combed down the plateau grasslands through so much of the winter that it was hard to see any sign of grass ever having grown on them. Even though March had come, it still blew, drying the ground deep, shrinking the watercourses, beating back the clouds that might have delivered rain, and grinding coarse dust against the fifty-odd head of work horses that Pop Apling, with young Beech Cartwright helping, had brought down from his homestead to turn back into their home pasture while there was still something left of them.

The two men, one past sixty and the other around sixteen, shouldered the horses through the gate of the home pasture about dark, with lights beginning to shine out from the little freighting town across Three Notch Valley, and then they rode for the ranch house, knowing even before they drew up outside the yard that they had picked the wrong time to come. The house was too dark, and the corrals and outbuildings too still, for a place that anybody lived in.

There were sounds, but they were of shingles flapping in the wind, a windmill running loose and sucking noisily at a well that it had already pumped empty, a door that kept banging shut and dragging open again. The haystacks were gone, the stackyard fence had dwindled to a few naked posts, and the entire pasture was as bare and as hard as a floor all the way down into the valley.

The prospect looked so hopeless that the herd horses refused even to explore it, and merely stood with their tails turned to the wind, waiting to see what was to happen to them next.

Old Apling went poking inside the house, thinking somebody might have left a note or that the men might have run down to the saloon in town for an hour or two. He came back, having used up all his matches and stopped the door from banging, and said the place appeared to have been handed back to the Government, or maybe the mortgage company.

"You can trust old Ream Gervais not to be any place where anybody wants him," Beech said. He had hired out to herd for Ream Gervais over the winter. That entitled him to be more critical than old Apling, who had merely contracted to supply the horse herd with feed and pasture for the season at so much per head. "Well, my job was to help herd these steeds while you had 'em, and to help deliver 'em back when you got through with 'em, and here they are. I've put in a week on 'em that I won't ever git paid for, and it won't help anything to set around and watch 'em try to live on fence pickets. Let's git out."

Old Apling looked at the huddle of horses, at the naked slope with a glimmer of light still on it, and at the lights of the town twinkling in the wind. He said it wasn't his place tell any man what to do, but that he wouldn't feel quite right to dump the horses and leave.

"I agreed to see that they got delivered back here, and I'd feel better about it if I could locate somebody to deliver 'em to," he said. "I'd like to ride across to town yonder, and see if there ain't somebody that knows something about 'em. You could hold 'em together here till I git back. We ought to look the fences over before we pull out, and you can wait here as well as anywhere else."

"I can't, but go ahead," Beech said. "I don't like to have 'em stand around and look at me when I can't do anything to help 'em out. They'd have been better off if we'd turned 'em out of your homestead and let 'em run loose on the country. There was more grass up there than there is here."

"There wasn't enough to feed 'em, and I'd have had all my neighbors down on me for it," old Apling said. "You'll find out one of these days that if a man aims to live in this world he's got to git along with the people in it. I'd start a fire and thaw out a little and git that pack horse unloaded, if I was you."

He rode down the slope, leaning low and forward to ease the drag of the wind on his tired horse. Beech heard the sound of the road gate being let down and put up again, the beat of hoofs in the hard road, and then nothing but the noises around him as the wind went through its usual process of easing down for the night to make room for the frost. Loose boards settled into place, the windmill clacked to a stop and began to drip water into a puddle, and the herd horses shifted around facing Beech, as if anxious not to miss anything he did.

He pulled off some fence pickets and built a fire, unsaddled his pony and unloaded the pack horse, and got out what was left of a sack of grain and fed them both, standing the herd horses off with a fence picket until they had finished eating.

That was strictly fair, for the pack horse and the saddle pony had worked harder and carried more weight than any of the herd animals, and the grain was little enough to even them up for it. Nevertheless, he felt mean at having to club animals away from food when they were hungry, and they crowded back and eyed the grain sack so wistfully that he carried it inside the yard and stored it down in the root cellar behind the house, so it wouldn't prey on their minds. Then he dumped another armload of fence pickets onto the fire and sat down to wait for old Apling.

The original mistake, he reflected, had been when old Apling took the Gervais horses to feed at the beginning of winter. Contracting to feed them had been well enough, for he had nursed up a stand of bunch grass on his homestead that would have carried an ordinary pack of horses with only a little extra feeding to help out in the roughest weather. But the Gervais horses were all big harness stock, they had pulled in half starved, and they had taken not much over three weeks to clean off the pasture that old Apling had expected would last them at least two months. Nobody would have blamed him for backing out on his agreement then, since he had only undertaken to feed the horses, not to treat them for malnutrition.

Beech wanted him to back out of it, but he refused to, said the stockmen had enough troubles without having that added to them, and started feeding out his hay and insisting that the dry wind couldn't possibly keep up much longer, because it wasn't in Nature.

By the time it became clear that Nature had decided to take in a little extra territory, the hay was all fed out, and, since there couldn't be any accommodation about letting the horses starve to death, he consented to throw the contract over and bring them back where they belonged.

The trouble with most of old Apling's efforts to be accommodating was that they did nobody any good. His neighbors would have been spared all their uneasiness if he had never brought in the horses to begin with. Gervais wouldn't have been any worse off, since he stood to lose them anyway; the horses could have starved to death as gracefully in November as in March, and old Apling would have been ahead a great deal of carefully accumulated bunch grass and two big stacks of extortionately valuable hay. Nobody had gained by his chivalrousness; he had lost by it, and yet he liked it so well that he couldn't stand to leave the horses until he had raked the country for somebody to hand the worthless brutes over to.

Beech fed sticks into the fire and felt out of patience with a man who could stick to his mistakes even after he had been cleaned out by them. He heard the road gate open and shut, and he knew by the draggy-sounding plod of old Apling's horse that the news from town was going to be bad.

Old Apling rode past the fire and over to the picket fence, got off as if he was trying to make it last, tied his horse carefully as if he expected the knot to last a month, and unsaddled and did up his latigo and folded his saddle blanket as if he was fixing them to put in a show window. He remarked that his horse had been given a bait of grain in town and wouldn't need feeding again, and then he began to work down to what he had found out.

"If you think things look bad along this road, you ought to see that town," he said. "All the sheep gone and all the ranches deserted and no trade to run on and their water threatenin' to give out. They've got a little herd of milk cows that they keep up for their children, and to hear 'em talk you'd think it was an ammunition supply that they expected to stand off hostile Indians with. They said Gervais pulled out of here around a month ago. All his men quit him, so he bunched his sheep and took 'em down to the railroad, where he could ship in hay for 'em. Sheep will be a price this year, and you won't be able to buy a lamb for under twelve dollars except at a fire sale. Horses ain't in much demand. There's been a lot of 'em turned out wild, and everybody wants to git rid of 'em."

"I didn't drive this bunch of pelters any eighty miles against the wind to git a market report," Beech said. "You didn't find anybody to turn 'em over to, and Gervais didn't leave any word about what he wanted done with 'em. You've probably got it figured out that you ought to trail 'em a hundred and eighty miles to the railroad, so his feelings won't be hurt, and you're probably tryin' to study how you can work me in on it, and you might as well save your time. I've helped you with your accommodation jobs long enough. I've quit, and it would have been a whole lot better for you if I'd quit sooner."

Old Apling said he could understand that state of feeling, which didn't mean that he shared it.

"It wouldn't be as much of a trick to trail down to the railroad as a man might think," he said, merely to settle a question of fact. "We couldn't make it by the road in a starve-out, year like this, but there's old Indian trails back on the ridge where any man has got a right to take livestock whenever he feels like it. Still, as long as you're set against it, I'll meet you halfway. We'll trail these horses down the ridge to a grass patch where I used to corral cattle when I was in the business, and we'll leave 'em there. It'll be enough so they won't starve, and I'll ride on down and notify Gervais where they are, and you can go where you please. It wouldn't be fair to do less than that, to my notion."

"Ream Gervais triggered me out of a week's pay," Beech said. "It ain't much, but he swindled you on that pasture contract too. If you expect me to trail his broken-down horses ninety miles down this ridge when they ain't worth anything, you've turned in a poor guess. You'll have to think of a better argument than that if you aim to gain any ground with me."

"Ream Gervais don't count in this," old Apling said. "What does he care about these horses, when he ain't even left word what he wants done with 'em? What counts is you, and I don't have to think up any better argument, because I've already got one. You may not realize it, but you and me are responsible for these horses till they're delivered to their owner, and if we turn 'em loose here to bust fences and over run that town and starve to death in the middle of it, we'll land in the pen.

It's against the law to let horses starve to death, did you know that? If you pull out of here I'll pull out right along with you, and I'll have every man in that town after you before the week's out. You'll have a chance to git some action on that pistol of yours, if you're careful."

Beech said he wasn't intimidated by that kind of talk, and threw a couple of handfuls of dirt on the fire, so it wouldn't look so conspicuous. His pistol was an old single-action relic with its grips tied on with fish line and no trigger, so that it had to be operated by flipping the hammer. The spring was weak, so that sometimes it took several flips to get off one shot. Suggesting that he might use such a thing to stand off any pack of grim-faced pursuers was about the same as saying that he was simple-minded. As far as he could see, his stand was entirely sensible, and even humane.

"It ain't that I don't feel sorry for these horses, but they ain't fit to travel," he said. "They wouldn't last twenty miles. I don't see how it's any worse to let 'em stay here than to walk 'em to death down that ridge."

"They make less trouble for people if you keep 'em on the move," old Apling said. "It's something you can't be cinched for in court, and it makes you feel better afterwards to know that you tried everything you could. Suit yourself about it, though. I ain't beggin' you to do it. If you'd sooner pull out and stand the consequences, it's you for it. Before you go, what did you do with that sack of grain?"

Beech had half a notion to leave, just to see how much of that dark threatening would come to pass. He decided that it wouldn't be worth it. "I'll help you trail the blamed skates as far as they'll last, if you've got to be childish about it," he said. "I put the grain in a root cellar behind the house, so the rats wouldn't git into it. It looked like the only safe place around here. There was about a half a ton of old sprouted potatoes ricked up in it that didn't look like they'd been bothered for twenty years. They had sprouts on 'em—" He stopped, noticing that old Apling kept staring at him as if something was wrong. "Good Lord, potatoes ain't good for horse feed, are they? They had sprouts on 'em a foot long!"

Old Apling shook his head resignedly and got up. "We wouldn't ever find anything if it wasn't for you," he said. "We wouldn't ever git any good out of it if it wasn't for me, so maybe we make a team. Show me where that root cellar is, and we'll pack them spuds out and spread 'em around so the horses can git started on 'em. We'll git this herd through to grassland yet, and it'll be something you'll never be ashamed of. It ain't everybody your age gits a chance to do a thing like this, and you'll thank me for holdin' you to it before you're through."

II

They climbed up by an Indian trail onto a high stretch of tableland, so stony and scored with rock breaks that nobody had ever tried to cultivate it, but so high that it sometimes caught moisture from the atmosphere that the lower elevations missed. Part of it had been doled out among the Indians as allotment lands, which none of them ever bothered to lay claim, to, but the main spread of it belonged to the nation, which was too busy to notice it.

The pasture was thin, though reliable, and it was so scantily watered and so rough and broken that in ordinary years nobody bothered to bring stock onto it. The open winter had, spoiled most of that seclusion. There was no part of the trail that didn't have at least a dozen new bed grounds for lambed ewes in plain view, easily picked out of the landscape because of the little white flags stuck up around them to keep sheep from straying out and coyotes from straying in during the night. The sheep were pasturing down the draws out of the wind, where they couldn't be seen. There were no herders visible, not any startling amount of grass, and no water except a mud tank thrown up to catch a little spring for one of the camps.

They tried to water the horses in it, but it had taken up the flavor of sheep, so that not a horse in the herd would touch it. It was too near dark to waste time reasoning with them about it, so old Apling headed them down into a long rock break and across it to a tangle of wild cherry and mountain mahogany that lasted for several miles and ended in a grass clearing among some dwarf cottonwoods with a mud puddle in the center of it.

The grass had been grazed over, though not closely, and there were sheep tracks around the puddle that seemed to be fresh, for the horses, after sniffing the water, decided that they could wait a while longer. They spread out to graze, and Beech remarked that he couldn't see where it was any improvement over the tickle-grass homesteads.

"The grass may be better, but there ain't as much of it, and the water ain't any good if they won't drink it," he said. "Well, do you intend to leave 'em here, or have you got some wrinkle figured out to make me help trail 'em on down to the railroad?"

Old Apling stood the sarcasm unresistingly. "It would be better to trail 'em to the railroad, now that we've got this far," he said. "I won't ask you to do that much, because it's outside of what you agreed to. This place has changed since I was here last, but we'll make it do, and that water ought to clear up fit to drink before long. You can settle down here for a few days while I ride around and fix it up with the sheep camps to let the horses stay here. We've got to do that, or they're liable to think it's some wild bunch and start shootin' 'em. Somebody's got to stay with 'em, and I can git along with these herders better than you can."

"If you've got any sense, you'll let them sheep outfits alone," Beech said. "They don't like tame horses on this grass any better than they do wild ones, and they won't make any more bones about shootin' 'em if they find out they're in here. It's a hard place to find, and they'll stay close on account of the water, and you'd better pull out and let 'em have it to themselves. That's what I aim to do."

"You've done what you agreed to, and I ain't got any right to hold you any longer," old Apling said. "I wish I could. You're wrong about them sheep outfits. I've got as much right to pasture this ridge as they have, and they know it, and nobody ever lost anything by actin' sociable with people."

"Somebody will before very long," Beech said. "I've got relatives in the sheep business, and I know what they're like. You'll land yourself in trouble, and I don't want to be around when you do it. I'm pullin' out of here in the morning, and if you had any sense you'd pull out along with me."

There were several things that kept Beech from getting much sleep during the night. One was the attachment that the horses showed for his sleeping place; they stuck so close that he could almost feel their breath on him, could hear the soft breaking sound that the grass made as they pulled it, the sound of their swallowing, the jar of the ground under him when one of the horses changed ground, the peaceful regularity of their eating, as if they didn't have to bother about anything so long as they kept old Apling in sight.

Another irritating thing was old Apling's complete freedom from uneasiness. He ought by rights to have felt more worried about the future than Beech did, but he slept, with the hard ground for a bed and his hard saddle for a pillow and the horses almost stepping on him every minute or two, as soundly as if the entire trip had come out exactly to suit him and there was nothing ahead but plain sailing.

His restfulness was so hearty and so unjustifiable that Beech couldn't sleep for feeling indignant about it, and got up and left about daylight to keep from being exposed to any more of it. He left without waking old Apling, because he saw no sense in a leave-taking that would consist merely in repeating his common-sense warnings and having them ignored, and he was so anxious to get clear of the whole layout that he didn't even take along anything to eat. The only thing he took from the pack was his ramshackle old pistol; there was no holster for it, and, in the hope that he might get a chance to use it on a loose quail or prairie chicken, he stowed it in an empty flour sack and hung it on his saddle horn, a good deal like an old squaw heading for the far blue distances with a bundle of diapers.

III

There was never anything recreational about traveling a rock desert at any season of the year, and the combination of spring gales, winter chilliness and summer drought all striking at once brought it fairly close to hard punishment. Beech's saddle pony, being jaded at the start with overwork and underfeeding and no water, broke down in the first couple of miles, and got so feeble and tottery that Beech had to climb off and lead him, searching likely-looking thickets all the way down the gully in the hope of finding some little trickle that he wouldn't be too finicky to drink.

The nearest he came to it was a fair-sized rock sink under big half-budded cottonwoods that looked, by its dampness and the abundance of fresh animal tracks around it, as if it might have held water recently, but of water there was none, and even digging a hole in the center of the basin failed to fetch a drop.

The work of digging, hill climbing and scrambling through brush piles raised Beech's appetite so powerfully that he could scarcely hold up, and, a little above where the gully opened into the flat sagebrush plateau, he threw away his pride, pistoled himself a jack rabbit, and took it down into the sage brush to cook, where his fire wouldn't give away which gully old Apling was camped in.

Jack rabbit didn't stand high as a food. It was considered an excellent thing to give men in the last stages of famine, because they weren't likely to injure themselves by eating too much of it, but for ordinary occasions it was looked down on, and Beech covered his trail out of the gully and built his cooking fire in the middle of a high stand of sagebrush, so as not to be embarrassed by inquisitive visitors.

The meat cooked up strong, as it always did, but he ate what he needed of it, and he was wrapping the remainder in his flour sack to take along with him when a couple of men rode past, saw his pony, and turned in to look him over.

They looked him over so closely and with so little concern for his privacy that he felt insulted before they even spoke.

He studied them less openly, judging by their big gallon canteens that they were out on some long scout.

One of them was some sort of hired hand, by his looks; he was broad-faced and gloomy-looking, with a fine white horse, a flower-stamped saddle, an expensive rifle scabbarded under his knee, and a fifteen-dollar saddle blanket, while his own manly form was set off by a yellow hotel blanket and a ninety-cent pair of overalls.

The other man had on a store suit, a plain black hat, fancy stitched boots, and a white shirt and necktie, and rode a burr-tailed Indian pony and an old wrangling saddle with a loose horn. He carried no weapons in sight, but there was a narrow strap across the lower spread of his necktie which indicated the presence of a shoulder holster somewhere within reach.

He opened the conversation by inquiring where Beech had come from, what his business was, where he was going and why he hadn't taken the county road to go there, and why he had to eat jack rabbit when the country was littered with sheep camps where he could get a decent meal by asking for it?

"I come from the upper country," Beech said, being purposely vague about it. "I'm travelin', and I stopped here because my horse give out. He won't drink out of any place that's had sheep in it, and he's gone short of water till he breaks down easy."

"There's a place corralled in for horses to drink at down at my lower camp," the man said, and studied Beech's pony. "There's no reason for you to bum through the country on jack rabbit in a time like this. My herder can take you down to our water hole and see that you get fed and put to work till you can make a stake for yourself. I'll give you a note. That pony looks like he had Ream Gervais' brand on him. Do you know anything about that herd of old work horses he's been pasturing around?"

"I don't know anything about him," Beech said, sidestepping the actual question while he thought over the offer of employment. He could have used a stake, but the location didn't strike him favorably. It was too close to old Apling's camp, he could see trouble ahead over the horse herd, and he didn't want to be around when it started. "If you'll direct me how to find your water, I'll ride on down there, but I don't need anybody to go with me, and I don't need any stake. I'm travelin'."

The man said there wasn't anybody so well off that he couldn't use a stake, and that it would be hardly any trouble at all for Beech to get one. "I want you to understand how we're situated around here, so you won't think we're any bunch of stranglers," he said. "You can see what kind of a year this has been, when we have to run lambed ewes in a rock patch like this. We've got five thousand lambs in here that we're trying to bring through, and we've had to fight the blamed wild horses for this pasture since the day we moved in. A horse that ain't worth hell room will eat as much as two dozen sheep worth twenty dollars, with the lambs, so you can see how it figures out. We've got 'em pretty well thinned out, but one of my packers found a trail of a new bunch that came up from around Three Notch within the last day or two, and we don't want them to feel as if we'd neglected them. We'd like to find out where they lit. You wouldn't have any information about 'em?"

"None that would do you any good to know," Beech said. "I know the man with that horse herd, and it ain't any use to let on that I don't, but it wouldn't be any use to try to deal with him. He don't sell out on a man he works for."

"He might be induced to," the man said. "We'll find him anyhow, but I don't like to take too much time to it. Just for instance, now, suppose you knew that pony of yours would have to go thirsty till you gave us a few directions about that horse herd? You'd be stuck here for quite a spell, wouldn't you?"

He was so pleasant about it that it took Beech a full minute to realize that he was being threatened. The heavy-set herder brought that home to him by edging out into a flank position and hoisting his rifle scabbard so it could be reached in a hurry. Beech removed the cooked jack rabbit from his flour sack carefully, a piece at a time, and, with the same mechanical thoughtfulness, brought out his triggerless old pistol, cut down on the pleasant-spoken man, and hauled back on the hammer and held it poised.

"That herder of yours had better go easy on his rifle," he said, trying to keep his voice from trembling. "This pistol shoots if I don't hold back the hammer, and if he knocks me out I'll have to let go of it. You'd better watch him, if you don't want your tack drove. I won't give you no directions about that horse herd, and this pony of mine won't go thirsty for it, either. Loosen them canteens of yours and let 'em drop on the ground. Drop that rifle scabbard back where it belongs, and unbuckle the straps and let go of it. If either of you tries any funny business, there'll be one of you to pack home, heels first."

The quaver in his voice sounded childish and undignified to him, but it had a more businesslike ring to them than any amount of manly gruffness. The herder unbuckled his rifle scabbard, and they both cast loose their canteen straps, making it last as long as they could while they argued with him, not angrily, but as if he was a dull stripling whom they wanted to save from some foolishness that he was sure to regret. They argued ethics, justice, common sense, his future prospects, and the fact that what he was doing amounted to robbery by force and arms and that it was his first fatal step into a probably unsuccessful career of crime. They worried over him, they explained themselves to him, and they ridiculed him.

They managed to make him feel like several kinds of a fool, and they were so pleasant and concerned about it that they came close to breaking him down. What held him steady was the thought of old Apling waiting up the gully.

"That herder with the horses never sold out on any man, and I won't sell out on him," he said. "You've said your say and I'm tired of holdin' this pistol on cock for you, so move along out of here. Keep to open ground, so I can be sure you're gone, and don't be in too much of a hurry to come back. I've got a lot of things I want to think over, and I want to be let alone while I do it."

IV

He did have some thinking that needed tending to, but he didn't take time for it. When the men were well out of range, he emptied their canteens into his hat and let his pony drink. Then he hung the canteens and the scabbarded rifle on a bush and rode back up the gully where the horse camp was, keeping to shady ground so as not to leave any tracks. It was harder going up than it had been coming down.

He had turned back from the scene of his run-in with the two sheepmen about noon, and he was still a good two miles from the camp when the sun went down, the wind lulled and the night frost began to bite at him so hard that he dismounted and walked to get warm. That raised his appetite again, and, as if by some special considerateness of Nature, the cottonwoods around him seemed to be alive with jack rabbits heading down into the pitch-dark gully where he had fooled away valuable time trying to find water that morning.

They didn't stimulate his hunger much; for a time they even made him feel less like eating anything, Then his pony gave out and had to rest, and, noticing that the cottonwoods around him were beginning to bud out, he remembered that peeling the bark off in the budding season would fetch out a foamy, sweet-tasting sap which, among children of the plateau country, was considered something of a delicacy.

He cut a blaze on a fair-sized sapling, waited ten minutes or so, and touched his finger to it to see how much sap had accumulated. None had; the blaze was moist to his touch, but scarcely more so than when he had whittled it.

It wasn't important enough to do any bothering about, and yet a whole set of observed things began to draw together in his mind and form themselves into an explanation of something he had puzzled over: the fresh animal tracks he had seen around the rock sink when there wasn't any water; the rabbits going down into the gully; the cottonwoods in which the sap rose enough during the day to produce buds and got driven back at night when the frost set in. During the day, the cottonwoods had drawn the water out of the ground for themselves; at night they stopped drawing it, and it drained out into the rock sink for the rabbits.

It all worked out so simply that he led his pony down into the gully to see how much there was in it, and, losing his footing on the steep slope, coasted down into the rock sink in the dark and landed in water and thin mud up to his knees. He led his pony down into it to drink, which seemed little enough to get back for the time he had fooled away on it, and then he headed for the horse camp, which was all too easily discernible by the plume of smoke rising, white and ostentatious, against the dark sky from old Apling's campfire.

He made the same kind of entrance that old Apling usually affected when bringing some important item of news. He rode past the campfire and pulled up at a tree, got off deliberately, knocked an accumulation of dead twigs from his hat, took off his saddle and bridle and balanced them painstakingly in the tree fork, and said it was affecting to see how widespread the shortage of pasture was.

"It generally is," old Apling said. "I had a kind of a notion you'd be back after you'd had time to study things over. I suppose you got into some kind of a rumpus with some of them sheep outfits. What was it? Couldn't you git along with them, or couldn't they hit it off with you?"

"There wasn't any trouble between them and me," Beech said. "The only point we had words over was you. They wanted to know where you was camped, so they could shoot you up, and I didn't think it was right to tell 'em. I had to put a gun on a couple of 'em before they'd believe I meant business, and that was all there was to it. They're out after you now, and they can see the smoke of this fire of yours for twenty miles, so they ought to be along almost any time now. I thought I'd come back and see you work your sociability on 'em."

"You probably kicked up a squabble with 'em yourself," old Apling said. He looked a little uneasy. "You talked right up to 'em, I'll bet, and slapped their noses with your hat to show 'em that they couldn't run over you. Well, what's done is done. You did come back, and maybe they'd have jumped us anyway. There ain't much that we can do. The horses have got to have water before they can travel, and they won't touch that seep. It ain't cleared up a particle."

"You can put that fire out, not but what the whole country has probably seen the smoke from it already," Beech said. "If you've got to tag after these horses, you can run 'em off down the draw and keep 'em to the brush where they won't leave a trail. There's some young cottonwood bark that they can eat if they have to, and there's water in a rock sink under some big cottonwood trees. I'll stay here and hold off anybody that shows up, so you'll have time to git your tracks covered."

Old Apling went over and untied the flour-sacked pistol from Beech's saddle, rolled it into his blankets, and sat down on it. "If there's any holdin' off to be done, I'll do it," he said. "You're a little too high-spirited to suit me, and a little too hasty about your conclusions. I looked over that rock sink down the draw today, and there wasn't anything in it but mud, and blamed little of that. Somebody had dug for water, and there wasn't none."

"There is now," Beech said. He tugged off one of his wet boots and poured about a pint of the disputed fluid on the ground. "There wasn't any in the daytime because the cottonwoods took it all. They let up when it turns cold, and it runs back in. I waded in it."

He started to put his boot back on. Old Apling reached out and took it, felt of it inside and out, and handed it over as if performing some ceremonial presentation.

"I'd never have figured out a thing like that in this world," he said. "If we git them horses out of here, it'll be you that done it. We'll bunch 'em and work 'em down there. It won't be no picnic, but we'll make out to handle it somehow. We've got to, after a thing like this."

Beech remembered what had occasioned the discovery, and said he would have to have something to eat first. "I want you to keep in mind that it's you I'm doin' this for," he said. "I don't owe that old groundhog of a Ream Gervais any thing. The only thing I hate about this is that it'll look like I'd done him a favor."

"He won't take it for one, I guess," old Apling said. "We've got to git these horses out because it'll be a favor to you. You wouldn't want to have it told around that you'd done a thing like findin' that water, and then have to admit that we'd lost all the horses anyhow. We can't lose 'em. You've acted like a man tonight, and I'll be blamed if I'll let you spoil it for any childish spite."

They got the horses out none too soon. Watering them took a long time, and when they finally did consent to call it enough and climb back up the side hill, Beech and old Apling heard a couple of signal shots from the direction of their old camping place, and saw a big glare mount up into the sky from it as the visitors built up their campfire to look the locality over. The sight was almost comforting; if they had to keep away from a pursuit, it was at least something to know where it was.

V

From then on they followed a grab-and-run policy, scouting ahead before they moved, holding to the draws by day and crossing open ground only after dark, never pasturing over a couple of hours in any one place, and discovering food value in outlandish substances—rock lichens, the sprouts of wild plum and serviceberry, the moss of old trees and the bark of some young ones—that neither they nor the horses had ever considered fit to eat before. When they struck Boulder River Canyon they dropped down and toenailed their way along one side of it where they could find grass and water with less likelihood of having trouble about it.

The breaks of the canyon were too rough to run new-lambed sheep in, and they met with so few signs of occupancy that old Apling got overconfident, neglected his scouting to tie back a break they had been obliged to make in a line fence, and ran the horse herd right over the top of a camp where some men were branding calves, tearing down a cook tent and part of a corral and scattering cattle and bedding from the river all the way to the top of the canyon.

By rights, they should have sustained some damage for that piece of carelessness, but they drove through fast, and they were out of sight around a shoulder of rimrock before any of the men could get themselves picked up. Somebody did throw a couple of shots after them as they were pulling into a thicket of mock orange and chokecherry, but it was only with a pistol, and he probably did it more to relieve his feelings than with any hope of hitting anything.

They were so far out of range that they couldn't even hear where the bullets landed.

Neither of them mentioned that unlucky run-in all the rest of that day. They drove hard, punished the horses savagely when they lagged, and kept them at it until, a long time after dark, they struck an old rope ferry that crossed Boulder River at a place called, in memory of its original founders, Robbers' Roost.

The ferry wasn't a public carrier, and there was not even any main road down to it. It was used by the ranches in the neighborhood as the only means of crossing the river for fifty miles in either direction, and it was tied in to a log with a solid chain and padlock. It was a way to cross, and neither of them could see anything else but to take it.

Beech favored waiting for daylight for it, pointing out that there was a ranch light half a mile up the slope, and that if anybody caught them hustling a private ferry in the dead of night they would probably be taken for criminals on the dodge. Old Apling said it was altogether likely, and drew Beech's pistol and shot the padlock apart with it.

"They could hear that up at that ranch house," Beech said. "What if they come pokin' down here to see what we're up to?"

Old Apling tossed the fragments of padlock into the river and hung the pistol in the waistband of his trousers. "Let 'em come," he said. "They'll go back again with their fingers in their mouths. This is your trip, and you put in good work on it, and I like to ruined the whole thing stoppin' to patch an eighty-cent fence so some scissorbill wouldn't have his feelings hurt, and that's the last accommodation anybody gits out of me till this is over with. I can take about six horses at a trip, it looks like. Help me to bunch 'em."

Six horses at a trip proved to be an overestimate. The, best they could do was five, and the boat rode so deep with them that Beech refused to risk handling it. He stayed with the herd, and old Apling cut it loose, let the current sweep it into slack water, and hauled it in to the far bank by winding in its cable on an old homemade capstan. Then he turned the horses into a counting pen and came back for another load.

He worked at it fiercely, as if he had a bet up that he could wear the whole ferry rig out, but it went with infernal slowness, and when the wind began to move for daylight there were a dozen horses still to cross and no place to hide them in case the ferry had other customers.

Beech waited and fidgeted over small noises until, hearing voices and the clatter of hoofs on shale far up the canyon behind him, he gave way, drove the remaining horses into the river, and swam them across, letting himself be towed along by his saddle horn and floating his clothes ahead of him on a board.

He paid for that flurry of nervousness before he got out. The water was so cold it paralyzed him, and so swift it whisked him a mile downstream before he could get his pony turned to breast it. He grounded on a gravel bar in a thicket of dwarf willows, with numbness striking clear to the center of his diaphragm and deadening his arms so he couldn't pick his clothes loose from the bundle to put on. He managed it, by using his teeth and elbows, and warmed himself a little by driving the horses afoot through the brush till he struck the ferry landing.

It had got light enough to see things in outline, and old Apling was getting ready to shove off for another crossing when the procession came lumbering at him out of the shadows. He came ashore, counted the horses into the corral to make sure none had drowned, and laid Beech under all the blankets and built up a fire to limber him out by. He got breakfast and got packed to leave, and he did some rapid expounding about the iniquity of risking the whole trip on such a wild piece of foolhardiness.

"That was the reason I wanted you to work this boat," he said. "I could have stood up to anybody that come projectin' around, and if they wanted trouble I could have filled their order for 'em. They won't bother us now, anyhow; it don't matter how bad they want to."

"I could have stood up to 'em if I'd had anything to do it with," Beech said. "You've got that pistol of mine, and I couldn't see to throw rocks. What makes you think they won't bother us? You know it was that brandin' crew comin' after us, don't you?"

"I expect that's who it was," old Apling agreed. "They ought to be out after the cattle we scattered, but you can trust a bunch of cowboys to pick out the most useless things to tend to first. I've got that pistol of yours because I don't aim for you to git in trouble with it while this trip is on. There won't anybody bother us because I've cut all the cables on the ferry, and it's lodged downstream on a gravel spit. If anybody crosses after us within fifty miles of here, he'll swim, and the people around here ain't as reckless around cold water as you are."

Beech sat up. "We got to git out of here," he said. "There's people on this side of the river that use that ferry, you old fool, and they'll have us up before every grand jury in the country from now on. The horses ain't worth it."

"What the horses is worth ain't everything," old Apling said. "There's a part of this trip ahead that you'll be glad you went through. You're entitled to that much out of it, after the work you've put in, and I aim to see that you git it. It ain't any use tryin' to explain to you what it is. You'll notice it when the time comes."

VI

They worked north, following the breaks of the river canyon, finding the rock breaks hard to travel, but easy to avoid observation in, and the grass fair in stand, but so poor and washy in body that the horses had to spent most of their time eating enough to keep up their strength so they could move.

They struck a series of gorges, too deep and precipitous to be crossed at all, and had to edge back into milder country where there were patches of plowed ground, some being harrowed over for summer fallow and others venturing out with a bright new stand of dark-green wheat.

The pasture was patchy and scoured by the wind, and all the best parts of it were under fence, which they didn't dare cut for fear of getting in trouble with the natives. Visibility was high in that section; the ground lay open to the north as far as they could see, the wind kept the air so clear that it hurt to look at the sky, and they were never out of sight of wheat ranchers harrowing down summer fallow.

A good many of the ranchers pulled up and stared after the horse herd as it went past, and two or three times they waved and rode down toward the road, as if they wanted to make it an excuse for stopping work. Old Apling surmised that they had some warning they wanted to deliver against trespassing, and he drove on without waiting to hear it.

They were unable to find a camping place anywhere among those wheat fields, so they drove clear through to open country and spread down for the night alongside a shallow pond in the middle of some new grass not far enough along to be pastured, though the horses made what they could out of it. There were no trees or shrubs anywhere around, not even sagebrush. Lacking fuel for a fire, they camped without one, and since there was no grass anywhere except around the pond, they left the horses unguarded, rolled in to catch up sleep, and were awakened about daylight by the whole herd stampeding past them at a gallop.

They both got up and moved fast. Beech ran for his pony, which was trying to pull loose from its picket rope to go with the bunch. Old Apling ran out into the dust afoot, waggling the triggerless old pistol and trying to make out objects in the half-light by hard squinting. The herd horses fetched a long circle and came back past him, with a couple of riders clouting along behind trying to turn them back into open country. One of the riders opened up a rope and swung it, the other turned in and slapped the inside flankers with his hat, and old Apling hauled up the old pistol, flipped the hammer a couple of rounds to get it warmed up, and let go at them twice.

The half darkness held noise as if it had been a cellar. The two shots banged monstrously, Beech yelled to old Apling to be careful who he shot at, and the two men shied off sideways and rode away into the open country. One of them yelled something that sounded threatening in tone as they went out of sight, but neither of them seemed in the least inclined to bring on any general engagement. The dust blew clear, the herd horses came back to grass, old Apling looked at the pistol and punched the two exploded shells out of it, and Beech ordered him to hand it over before he got in trouble with it.

"How do you know but what them men had a right here?" he demanded sternly. "We'd be in a fine jack pot if you'd shot one of 'em and it turned out he owned this land we're on, wouldn't we?"

Old Apling looked at him, holding the old pistol poised as if he was getting ready to lead a band with it. The light strengthened and shed a rose-colored radiance over him, so he looked flushed and joyous and lifted up. With some of the dust knocked off him, he could have filled in easily as a day star and son of the morning, whiskers and all.

"I wouldn't have shot them men for anything you could buy me!" he said, and faced north to a blue line of bluffs that came up out of the shadows, a blue gleam of water that moved under them, a white steamboat that moved upstream, glittering as the first light struck it. "Them men wasn't here because we was trespassers. Them was horse thieves, boy! We've brought these horses to a place where they're worth stealin', and we've brought 'em through! The railroad is under them bluffs, and that water down there is the old Columbia River!"

They might have made it down to the river that day, but having it in sight and knowing that nothing could stop them from reaching it, there no longer seemed any object in driving so unsparingly. They ate breakfast and talked about starting, and they even got partly packed up for it. Then they got occupied with talking to a couple of wheat ranchers who pulled in to inquire about buying some of the horse herd; the drought had run up wheat prices at a time when the country's livestock had been allowed to run down, and so many horses had been shot and starved out that they were having to take pretty much anything they could get.

Old Apling swapped them a couple of the most jaded herd horses for part of a haystack, referred other applicants to Gervais down at the railroad, and spent the remainder of the day washing, patching clothes and saddlery, and watching the horses get acquainted once more with a conventional diet.

The next morning a rancher dropped off a note from Gervais urging them to come right on down, and adding a kind but firm admonition against running up any feed bills without his express permission. He made it sound as if there might be some hurry about catching the horse market on the rise, so they got ready to leave, and Beech looked back over the road they had come, thinking of all that had happened on it.

"I'd like it better if old Gervais didn't have to work himself in on the end of it," he said. "I'd like to step out on the whole business right now."

"You'd be a fool to do that," old Apling said. "This is outside your work contract, so we can make the old gopher pay you what it's worth. I'll want to go in ahead and see about that and about the money that he owes me and about corral space and feed and one thing and another, so I'll want you to bring 'em in alone. You ain't seen everything there is to a trip like this, and you won't unless you stay with it."

VII

There would be no ending to this story without an understanding of what that little river town looked like at the hour, a little before sundown of a windy spring day, when Beech brought the desert horse herd down into it. On the wharf below town, some men were unloading baled hay from a steamboat, with some passengers watching from the saloon deck, and the river beyond them hoisting into white-capped peaks that shone and shed dazzling spray over the darkening water.

A switch engine was handling stock cars on a spur track, and the brakeman flagged it to a stop and stood watching the horses, leaning into the wind to keep his balance while the engineer climbed out on the tender to see what was going on.

The street of the town was lined with big leafless poplars that looked as if they hadn't gone short of moisture a day of their lives; the grass under them was bright green, and there were women working around flower beds and pulling up weeds, enough of them so that a horse could have lived on them for two days.

There was a Chinaman clipping grass with a pair of sheep shears to keep it from growing too tall, and there were lawn sprinklers running clean water on the ground in streams. There were stores with windows full of new clothes, and stores with bright hardware, and stores with strings of bananas and piles of oranges, bread and crackers and candy and rows of hams, and there were groups of anxious-faced men sitting around stoves inside who came out to watch Beech pass and told one another hopefully that the back country might make a good year out of it yet, if a youngster could bring that herd of horses through it.

There were women who hauled back their children and cautioned them not to get in the man's way, and there were boys and girls, some near Beech's own age, who watched him and stood looking after him, knowing that he had been through more than they had ever seen and not suspecting that it had taught him something that they didn't know about the things they saw every day. None of them knew what it meant to be in a place where there were delicacies to eat and new clothes to wear and look at, what it meant to be warm and out of the wind for a change, what it could mean merely to have water enough to pour on the ground and grass enough to cut down and throw away.

For the first time, seeing how the youngsters looked at him, he understood what that amounted to. There wasn't a one of them who wouldn't have traded places with him. There wasn't one that he would have traded places with, for all the haberdashery and fancy groceries in town. He turned down to the corrals, and old Apling held the gate open for him and remarked that he hadn't taken much time to it.

"You're sure you had enough of that ridin' through town?" he said. "It ain't the same when you do it a second time, remember."

"It'll last me," Beech said. "I wouldn't have missed it, and I wouldn't want it to be the same again. I'd sooner have things the way they run with us out in the high country. I'd sooner not have anything be the same a second time."

Fishing Fever

One thing about fishing that most fishermen are not conscious of and most non-fishermen uninformed about is that it gives its devotees a slightly peculiar set of values—not distorted, exactly, but a little transfigured and elevated and outside what ordinary people might expect. The case of a friend of mine who works in the Government atomic-energy plant at Hanford in the State of Washington may illustrate how it sometimes works. He came back this spring from a fishing trip along a small creek that empties into the Yakima River a few miles from where he is employed, and reported various details about the state of the water and what flies the trout were rising to and how they had to be handled. He also mentioned that while he was fishing some of the downstream holes late one forenoon, he had happened on a couple or three buffalo grazing a strip of dead bunch grass between the county road and the creek. It struck him as unusual to find buffalo wandering loose along a main county road within picnicking distance of so modern a development as an atomic-energy plant—actually they must have been almost in sight of it—and he had thought for a moment of going back to his car and bringing a camera to photograph them, to prove that such things could happen.

It was too bad he changed his mind. The buffalo were not strays from some circus or carnival company, as might have been supposed. They were real native wild buffalo, from a small and scattered herd that had inhabited the broken country called the Rattlesnake Hills in the Big Bend of the Columbia River since long before any white men had ever seen it. Washington Irving's *Adventures of Captain Bonneville* mentions their being there in 1833, though even then they were so wild and cautious that the Indians never hunted them, and seldom even saw them. Two or three loose specimens from the only completely untamed buffalo herd in the United States might have been worth a photograph or two, at least. My friend admitted that he should have got his camera and tried it. The trouble was that they were between him and his car, and he couldn't get to it without herding them down toward the creek. If they waded into it, they would muddy the water and spoil the fishing the rest of the way downstream, and he couldn't bring himself to risk that. Fishing, after all, was what he had come out there for. Photographing buffalo was all very well, but he was not prepared for it, physically, emotionally or temperamentally. He even regretted having a camera along to feel tempted by. Next time, he had decided, he would leave it at home so he could feel free to concentrate on essentials.

Fishing fever can do that to a man's sense of proportion. It can also color his judgment in matters that have nothing to do with nature or wild life at all. In the Pacific Northwest, where I was born and brought up, it once reached far enough to have a permanent effect on the country's history. Back in the 1840's when the Oregon boundary question was in controversy between the United States and Great Britain, a British admiral was sent out by his government to report on whether the disputed territory was worth holding onto. His report went into considerable detail about its worthlessness and savagery and remoteness, and added, as a final clincher, that the salmon in the streams and coastal waters were the most worthless part of it, because the blasted things wouldn't rise to a fly. In the light of all the evidence, he recommended handing the territory over to the United States, hide, hair, horns and fins, and good riddance, which was done. There is no record that his government ever gave evidence of displeasure over his recommendation. He had reported according to his lights as an officer, a patriot and an angler. No government could have asked more.

He was a little sweeping in stating that West Coast salmon wouldn't rise to a fly, though the oversight was not very important. There are times during the spring spawning run when they will rise to a fly, or to anything else within reach that is moving, but that phase only lasts a few days out of the year, and since nobody can ever tell when it will occur, it is hardly worth counting. The Indian system of seining or dipnetting at the foot of a rapid is still the most reliable way of catching them, and it bears much the same relation to sporting fishing as the Chinese method of catching fish with a trained cormorant, or the practice among the Nevada Paiutes of circling a river-shallow and clubbing them to death. The admiral was right in disdaining such low business, and in feeling that any region where it had to be resorted to was unworthy of membership in the Empire. His moral rigidity not only changed international boundaries and shunted a good many people into United States citizenship who might otherwise have been subjects of the Crown, but it may also have laid down a tradition of picayunishness in Northwestern angling. People who acquire their first experience of fishing in the Pacific Northwest are always a little sniffish about fishing techniques elsewhere, and about any kind of fishing that does not involve either trout, steelhead or salmon. Fishing for anything outside those three species is not really fishing at all, but merely something for school kids to piddle at with a bent pin and a switch and a length of string.

It is true that there are not many other species of edible fish in Northwestern streams—a few sturgeon in the Columbia River sometimes and an annual run of eels, which used to be dipnetted and dried by Indians for their winter food supply and shunned vigorously by everybody else—but even when some other edible species turns up it is likely to be viewed with suspicion, merely because it is outside any of the accepted categories. Once I dropped in on a sheep camp on the Upper Columbia River and found the two herders arguing acrimoniously over a tin bucket half-full of some largish high-keeled fish with heavy scales, which they had snagged out of a nearby slough and were having trouble identifying. One held that they were chubs, the other insisted that they were squawfish. It was not a point that could be easily compromised, so they had got down to personalities, which was not settling anything.

One thing they had managed to agree on. The fish, what ever they were, were mud eaters and unfit for human consumption, and they would have to be got rid of when the argument was over. I took a close look at the bucket, not being quite sure what either chubs or squawfish looked like, but being willing to learn. The fish were neither one nor the other. They were small-mouth bass. There were a dozen or fifteen of them, and some must have weighed close to a pound and a half. I explained to the herders what they were and that they were considered highly edible in many parts of the country where nothing better was available, but they were not much impressed. They seemed to suspect that I was trying to stay neutral by siding against both of them, and they went on with their argument as if I hadn't said anything. I left them building up a fire to burn the fish so their herd dogs couldn't get at them, and still arguing, sometimes changing sides on each other for the sake of variety. The argument mattered more than the fish, seemingly. Sheep herding is a draggy life, and anything that will make red-hot conversation is always welcome.

Even among the three categories to which fishermen in the Northwest are restricted by tradition and prejudice, there's room for individual preferences. A really confirmed salmon fisherman will hardly ever consider any other form of fishing worth talking about. My grandfather, a Hard-Shell Baptist clergyman, was of that stripe, and once flogged one of his sons for reminding him that it was Sunday when he was stringing up his tackle to head for the creek where the chinooks were cavorting like squirrels in a brush fire. When salmon fishing is good, it is lively enough to suit anybody. Nothing gets around faster or fights harder than a chinook, once he is hooked, and a man's glands would have to be down pretty low to resist the waves of varying emotions called into action in getting him worn down and landed. Still, the skill required is only in landing him, not in hooking him to begin with. No amount of art or guile can induce a salmon to take a lure unless he feels like it, and if he does feel like it, nothing can stop him. It is the same with steelhead. A steelhead will strike anything that moves at the depth where he happens to be feeding. If you can figure out what the depth is and sink your bait exactly to it, the rest is merely a matter of hanging on and praying that the tackle will hold.

By trout-fishing standards, this is missing out on two-thirds of the fun. The best part of fishing, to a trout addict, is in figuring out a lure that the trout will fall for when they are not especially interested, or in some technique of casting or handling that will get a bait past the swarm of eager fingerlings near the surface to reach the big ones on the bottom, or some similar refinement that will make use of some idiosyncrasy of nature to circumvent the trout's sluggishness or cussedness. To such people, there is a more genuine sense of accomplishment in casting a Number Twelve fly thirty feet against a cross wind through a two-foot gap in the underbrush and hooking a reluctant trout than there is in landing a thirty-pound salmon after a fight lasting an hour and a half.

Even in trout fishing there are distinctions. Rainbow trout, because of their unusual hardiness and ability to stand transplanting, are almost the only species to be found in the Coast streams now, besides being common in the Andean lakes of South America, in New Zealand and even in some parts of Africa. They are a beautiful fish, resilient and high-spirited and adaptable almost anywhere, with a peculiar habit of changing coloration to suit their environment. In a sunlit stream with a varicolored bottom they will develop streaks and splashes of vivid scarlet against a ground of blackish-green, while in shaded mountain lakes with a heavy snow cast they breed to a pale leaf-gray with no markings at all. They are used almost exclusively in restocking Western streams, replacing the earlier speckled mountain trout, which have long since been crowded out by competition from livestock, irrigation projects, sawmills, chlorinating plants and people.

The speckled mountain trout was the species I knew earliest. There used to be nothing else in the small lakes and snow creeks of the high mountains. They were also in the upland streams of the Great Basin, where, since there was no such thing as trout transplanting then, they must have been ever since the post-glacial period. In spite of their touchiness about being crowded or maybe because of it I still think they were the finest trout to fish for that ever existed. They were not large: the biggest ones were from twelve to fifteen inches, and the average was less, but they had fire and dash and spirit, and when they came after a fly they put the whole works into it. A rainbow or a golden trout will sometimes fritter around for an hour making feints and passes at a floating object, out of mere curiosity or idle-mindedness. A speckled trout never moves till his mind is made up, and when he does move he means it. He grabs a fly before it is even in the water and is halfway to the next county before the astonished angler recovers enough presence of mind to take up slack. There is nothing shilly-shally about a speckled trout. Whatever he does, he does for all he is worth. Rainbow trout are more adaptable and easier to handle, and they afford healthful recreation for thousands of weekend sportsmen who catch them out of every creek within range of a main highway as fast as the trucks from the State hatcheries can pour them in, but there is not the same feeling about them, or about that kind of fishing, for that matter. It lacks something; you can tell it by the grim, set-featured expressions of the anglers.

This tank-truck system of delivering trout to anglers is a highly practical and efficient one, though the people who run the tourist accommodations don't always seem as appreciative about it as one might expect. In a roadside lunchroom on the Chelan River in Central Washington this past summer, I remarked something to the waitress about some fishermen who had been flycasting across a long riffle near some tourist cabins for half an hour without any noticeable result except to get their lines tangled together a few times. She said she supposed they were practicing: the truck from the hatchery was not due till the end of the week, and there wouldn't be any fish in the river till it showed up.

"It only puts in enough to last through the weekend," she said. "Sometimes they don't last even that long. These hatchery trout are half-tame anyway, and you could catch them with your hands if it wasn't for all those tourists splashing around squabbling over them."

It didn't sound very absorbing. "You'd think they'd try out some of the creeks back in the mountains, instead of just waiting around like that," I said. "It would be less crowded, and they'd get away from traffic and see some new country."

"They don't want new country," she said. "They've got what they want, right here, traffic and all. They like it."

And still, this shift from the old outdoor spirit of self-reliance and exploration to a dependence on weekly fish deliveries by truck has a bright side to it. There are a lot of small back-country creeks where the hatchery trucks never come, because of their remoteness or inaccessibility or something. In the old days, when fishing meant going where the fish were, even the smallest of them got fished out thoroughly before the season had been open a week—sometimes sooner. Under the new system of trucking fish where the fishermen are, the wilder and smaller streams are left alone, and some of them that were once hardly worth fishing at all have come back surprisingly.

There was one where I stopped for a day last spring, out in the sagebrush country in Central Oregon; a little string of rain pools at the bottom of a rimrock canyon, called Buck Creek, which joins the Deschutes River a mile or so below the old Indian salmon-fishing ground at Sherar Rapids. It is very small and shallow; a man could step across it almost anywhere, and in the old days it was not considered worth bothering with except as a source of minnows and crawfish to use for bait in the big whirlpool below the rapids. I had walked upstream along it for a few hundred yards to look at an old Indian burying ground where a few beautifully made arrowheads sometimes got washed into sight by the spring rains. There were no arrowheads, but when I tossed a cigarette butt into the creek, the shallow pool churned and came alive with trout rushing to strike at it. I had no flies, only a few small bait hooks that I had got down the Coast and nothing to bait them with, and it was too early for grasshoppers; so as an experiment I tried baiting with a catkin from some willows along the bank. They grabbed at it as if it were money from home. They would probably have grabbed another cigarette butt as readily if I had wanted to insult them with one. I caught a couple of dozen from the one small pool in twenty minutes, and could have run it up to a hundred from the pools farther up the canyon if there had been anything to do with them.

One such place could have been an accident, but there were others. There was a creek back in the desert country a few weeks later where I sat for an hour watching a pair of hawks at work picking ten-inch trout out of a hole at the edge of an old hay meadow and carrying them away to a rimrock cliff a mile or so distant where they evidently had a nest. I don't know how much of a brood they had to provide for, but in the hour I spent watching them they lugged away enough trout to have foundered three or four full-grown men, and they were still at it when I left. Shooting at them would have scared them off, maybe, but it wouldn't have helped the trout much. The creek went dry in its lower reaches every summer, and saving them to dry up with it didn't seem any more humane than leaving them for the hawks, and considerably less picturesque.

There was still another small mountain creek out in the sagebrush near the Nevada line where an elderly Polish couple used to run an overnight station for travelers, with broiled trout as the staple item on their bill of fare. The old Polish woman had never managed to learn English in the forty years she had been living there, but she could go back of the barn at any hour and in any season, with a cane pole and a dilapidated black-gnat fly with no leader, and come back in fifteen minutes with half a dozen trout running three-quarters of a pound apiece. Nobody else could catch anything out of the creek except water dogs in those days, but when I tried it this past summer there were trout in every hole, and they rose to almost anything that was thrown at them. Some of the sheep herders around the neighborhood thought the old woman had cast a spell on the creek while she lived there, and that it wore off after she moved away. But they were also prepared to argue that killing a spider would bring on rain and that food cooked by electricity introduced harmful electrons into the digestive system, so the theory didn't count for much except to give life in that part of the country a slight added interest, which it could stand. There were fish in the creek and they were biting, and it was more than they had ever done when the old Polish woman lived there, anyway.

Shifts of population have wiped out fishing in many places, but that also can work two ways. There used to be a wild stretch of burned-over hill country up the Oregon coast adjoining the Siuslaw National Forest where I went deer hunting sometimes in the fall. The only road into it then was a crooked wagon track down the open beach, with a few loose planks strung out across the worst places to keep cars from losing traction and miring down. There were small creeks every few miles that had to be forded with a rush and a prayer because of quicksand, and anybody rash enough to risk being overtaken by an incoming tide could catch a horse-load of fish out of them in a morning—trout, salmon trout, steelhead, salmon, candle smelt—depending on the season. A new main highway has gone in since then, the whole coast country has filled up with people and towns, and the creeks have been converted into logging ponds and spillways for municipal sewer systems. There is an embarrassed feeling about going back to country like that, trying to figure out old landmarks that have been built over by glass-fronted residences and realty offices, buying color film and the latest magazines in a supermarket and remembering having killed an eight-point buck deer between its front entrance and the garden-supply emporium across the street. It really was not so long ago as it sounds—twenty years, maybe. If any of the townspeople were told about it now, they would undoubtedly conclude that it must have been done with a flintlock rifle, back around the time of Lewis and Clark. Anything that happened in the country before they moved in is all lumped together as pioneering, whether it happened in the administration of Jefferson or Hoover.

Back of one of the new towns there was an old pack trail that wound up into the hills, following an almost-dry watercourse for a couple of miles and ending at a little clearing and a clump of empty cabins where a man I knew had taken up a homestead back in the early 1920's. He was middle-aged then, with a good many years of assembly-line work behind him, and he had picked the place as a peaceful and uncompetitive location where he could live out the rest of his days, untroubled by urban pressures and work schedules and hurry and people. He had put in several years of hard work clearing the place and making it livable: felling trees, grubbing stumps, clearing brush, splitting rails and shingles, building fences and cabins and sheds and lugging furniture up the trail from the road, mostly on his back. I don't know whether he ever got it completely arranged to suit him or not; the population boom along the highway drew him away from it, as it drew all the people from those little back-country homesteads, and he was running a logging-camp commissary and lunch counter somewhere down the coast and doing very well at it.

The work he had done on the place was being taken back by the wilderness. Mountain laurel had overgrown his fence and garden, the sheds and cabins were sagging and half unroofed, and his beehives had all been tipped over and ripped apart by bears. Most of the things he had carried up the two miles of trail on his back were still there, though dilapidated—the cast-iron kitchen stove, the heavy old oak dresser, some walnut rocking chairs, a big nickel-plated kerosene lamp, a set of old-fashioned steelyards for weighing deer, a wheelbarrow: all things that represented hard work and hopefulness and illusion, all thrown away, rusting and falling apart in the bracken and dwarf alder and wild huckleberry that were beginning to push up even between the floor boards of the cabin.

The one thing that kept the feeling of futility and disappointment from being unbearable was the pond he had built for his water supply. It was merely a dammed-up spring that spread back into a pool about twenty feet across, mud-bottomed and overgrown with alders, and so shallow in most places that leaves fallen into it stuck half out of the water. But there were big speckled trout in it. I counted half a dozen that must have been fifteen inches long, lying close to the surface and paying not the slightest attention to me, though I could have knocked two or three of them out with a stick if there had been one handy. They couldn't have been planted there, because none of the hatcheries cultivated speckled trout, and they couldn't have come in from anywhere else, because the pond was completely landlocked, with no intake or outlet that they could have come by. It lightened the oppressive feeling about the place to have them there, wherever they had come from, and to know that Nature, instead of merely wiping out and burying man's errors of judgment, was turning some of them to use for her own purposes. Nature is more ingenious than we sometimes imagine, and she is accustomed to working over our mistakes from having worked over plenty of her own.

The problem of how fish get into waters that are completely landlocked is always fascinating to speculate on—the native trout that were in the upland streams of the Great Basin when the first whites came to the country, the annual run of huge indigenous suckers up the Truckee River in Nevada, unlike any other suckers in the world and with no point of origin except where they are now; the tiny little semisardines in the half-alkaline Lake Texcoco in the Valley of Mexico, the golden trout in the glacial lakes of the California High Sierras, the whitefish of the lovely little Lake Zirahuen in Michoacán: none of those waters have any outlet anywhere. There is no way that fish could have got into them from anywhere else. Could they have hatched out of the rocks all by themselves, or might it have been the mud? Neither seems altogether satisfying as an explanation, and still, they had to start somewhere. Did the pre-Columbian Indians know about fish planting?

I have never been able to work out any reasonable answer for it, and I never stop trying. Once, out pigeon hunting at the edge of a small village in the desert country of Northern Mexico, I got so absorbed in studying a swarm of odd looking little yellow-and-black-spotted fish in an irrigation ditch that I forgot all about the pigeons in the nut palms overhead. Since pigeons were a regional delicacy and the fish weren't, I ruined the reputation of Americans as a practical-minded race for the entire village. The ditch was nothing but a small desert seep; it came out of the ground in one place, wandered through some gardens for half a mile, and went back into the ground again. None of the people in the village had any idea where the fish had come from or how long they had been there: always, they were inclined to think, though the subject didn't interest them much. The village was not especially interesting either, I thought. It is only because of the fish in the irrigation ditch that I remember it now. An interest in fish or fishing can communicate itself to things around it sometimes, and sometimes they need it.

Sometimes such an interest can get itself mixed into a man's individuality until it is hard to tell where he stops and it starts. I was staying for a few days at a run-down old hotel in one of the little Northern California hill towns last fall, and was sitting on the whittling bench outside the front entrance talking with the proprietor about some of the Indian reservations in the neighborhood when a man came riding down the street toward us on horseback. He was somewhere past middle age, gray-haired, trim and stately-looking, dressed in store clothes and a white shirt, with a crutch laid across his saddle pommel like the long rifle in a Frederic Remington painting of a typical frontiersman. When he got close, I saw that he had a fishing rod strapped to the crutch. The hotel man nodded to him as he rode past, and said he lived in some old mining cabin a mile or two out of town, and had been a schoolteacher until he got too old and crotchety for it. Now he didn't do much of anything: drew a small pension, trapped a little in the winter, drafted legal documents that were not important enough to hire a lawyer for, wrote letters to the county newspaper for people who liked to pop off in public and wanted some big words thrown in for style—odds and ends like that. He managed to make out. The country didn't offer much of a field for him, what with his lameness and his education.

"There's places that might," I said. "He don't have to stay here, does he?"

"He thinks he does, I guess," the hotel man said. "He's at work lining out some old mining road that hits a little creek back in the hills. He aims to have it put back in shape and start some kind of a sportsmen's resort along the creek somewhere—charge a dollar a day for fishing and camping, or something like that. He thinks there'll be money in it. It might work. He claims there's trout up there so thick you can write your name in 'em with a stick, and I guess there are. He brings out plenty of 'em."

"Patching up one of those old mountain roads can run into money," I said. I had tried it once myself. A helicopter would have been cheaper; so would a monorail railroad, or a ski run, or almost anything. "It's a long trip in here from any of the main highways too. He might not get customers enough to pay himself out on it."

"Hell, he'll never do it anyway," the hotel man said. "He gets too much fun out of keeping his damned creek to himself. There ain't a week goes by that he don't come swaggering in with a big string of trout to slap people in the face with. He gets a lot out of it. A man's got to have something to be proud of, I guess."

"It's a wonder somebody don't try to find out where this road into his creek is," I said. "You could trail him."

"I don't care where it is," the hotel man said. "Let him keep it to himself, if it's any satisfaction to him. I've got a creek of my own back in the breaks that'll beat hell out of anything he's got."

There really is a sort of sustaining feeling about having a creek somewhere that other people don't know about, or in knowing something about it that they have missed. Mine is not a creek, exactly, but the backwater of an old hydroelectric dam across a small river that runs into the Columbia from the snowfields of the high Cascade Mountains in Southern Washington. The backwater forms a lake eight or ten miles long, though there are only two or three places in it where the fishing amounts to much. The country on both sides is logged-off stump land grown back to small second-growth timber and underbrush, the old sawmill sheds and bunkhouses are buried in rhododendron and wild blackberry vines, and there are the remains of a few old orchards that were bought out by the hydroelectric company and vacated when the dam went in. The water in the lake is deep and inhumanly cold, with an odd ash-green cast that makes it look opaque, though it is clear and colorless in the shallow places or when dipped out in a bucket. It seems odd to associate age with anything as contemporary as a hydroelectric installation, but it has been there a good many years: long enough for the vegetation and wild life to have become completely adapted to it—from the marten and wood ducks nesting along the shallows and deer and ruffed grouse in the old orchards to the trout that were originally rainbow-colored and have changed to the pale gray-green of the lake water in the deep places.

The trout stay deep and out of sight during the morning low water in the lake, and it is impossible to sink a spinner far enough down to reach them without fouling it in the tangled boughs of some old orchard that got flooded under when the dam went in. Around mid-afternoon, the floodgates are closed to build up the water level for the peak load that comes in the towns down the river after sundown—the quitting-time rush, the show windows and electric signs lighting up, the electric ranges and water heaters being turned on for dinner. The water rising somehow changes the afternoon light to a luminous white glare and strikes the air over it into a silence that feels as if something had stunned it. In the middle of the hush, in an expanse of smooth water where the reflection of light is so intense it hurts your eyes, the trout begin rising, breaking the glare and the silence with little rainbows of water drops as they come out of the water and slap back into it. It is like being suspended between two separate worlds, one among the drowned cabins and dead orchards at the bottom of the lake, the other of the towns down the river with their quitting-time rushes and electric ranges being turned on and show windows lighting up, feeling and knowing them both without being touched by either.

Silence and passion. . . . The trout work best on a Number Eight stonefly trailed about an inch below the surface on a long line. Some of them run two or three pounds apiece.

Old Man Isbell's Wife

The cow-town started as an overnight station on the old Military Road through Eastern Oregon into Idaho. The freighters wanted a place to unhitch and get the taste of sagebrush out of their mouths. They were willing to pay for it, and one was built for them by the people who like, better than anything else, money that has been worked hard for—not to work hard for it themselves, but to take it from men who do.

The cow-town itself was a kind of accident. When they built it, they had no idea beyond fixing up a place where the freighters could buy what they wanted. They fixed it up with houses—houses to eat in, houses to get drunk in, houses to sleep in, or stay awake in, houses to stable horses in; and, as an afterthought, houses for themselves to live in while they took the freighters' and cattlemen's money. And money came—not fast, but so steadily that it got monotonous. There were no surprises, no starvation years, no fabulous winnings or profits; simply, one year with another, enough to live on and something over. They got out of the habit of thinking the place was an overnight station to make money in. They began, instead, to look at it as a place to live in. That, in Eastern Oregon, meant a change of status, a step up. The risk of the place being abandoned was over; there, straddling the long road between Fort Dalles on the Columbia and Fort Boise on the Snake River, was a town.

The new status had no effect upon its appearance. Ugly and little it had begun, and ugly and little it stayed. The buildings were ramshackle and old, with the paint peeled off; and, including the stack of junk behind the blacksmith shop, the whole thing covered an area of ten blocks. Two acres of town, in the middle of a cattle range of ten thousand square miles. Yet in those ten blocks a man could live his entire lifetime, lacking nothing, and perhaps not even missing anything. Food, warmth, liquor, work, and women; love, avarice, fear, envy, anger, and, of a special kind, belonging to no other kind of life, joy.

Over the ten thousand miles of range, whole cycles of humanity—flint Indians, horse Indians, California Spaniards, emigrants, cattlemen—had passed, and each had marked it without altering its shape or color. The cow-town itself was one mark, and not the biggest, either; but that was a comparison which none of the townspeople ever made. They were too much used to it, and they had other things to think about. What interested them was their ten blocks of town, and the people who lived in it.

All country people keep track of each other's business—as a usual thing, because they haven't anything else to think about. But the cow-town people did it, not in idleness, but from actual and fundamental passion. They preferred it to anything else in the world. It was not in the least that they were fond of one another—though, of course, some of them were. That had nothing to do with their preference. It was merely that what their town did was life—clear, interesting, recognizable; and nothing else was. They stuck to what was familiar. It must be remembered that these people were not chance-takers. They were more like the peddlers who follow an army, not fighting themselves, but living on the men who do. The freighters and cattlemen, and the men from the range, were a different race; the range itself was a strange element; and they were too small to have much curiosity about either. The women were the smallest. It was they who backed the movement to ship Old Man Isbell out of town.

II

Old Man Isbell lived in the cow-town because there was no other place he could live. He had ridden the range, at one job or another, for more than fifty years, and the town would have been strange and foreign to him, even if it had made him welcome. It did not. For one thing, he was not a townsman, but a member of the race which they preyed on. For another, he was eighty-five years old, slack-witted, vacant-minded, doddering, dirty, and a bore. It took an hour to get the commonest question through his head, and another hour for him to think up an answer to it. He never tied his shoes, and he had to shuffle his feet as he walked, to keep them from falling off. Nor did he ever button his trousers, which fact was cited by the women as indicating complete moral decay. He ought to be sent away, they said, to some institution where such cases were decently taken care of.

The clerk in the general store agreed with them, and perhaps he, at least, had a right to. It was his job, every day, to sell Old Man Isbell a bill of groceries, and the old man could never remember what it was he wanted. Sometimes it took hours, and while he was there ladies couldn't come in the store, on account of his unbuttoned trousers and his pipe.

His pipe was another just ground for complaint. It was as black as tar and as soggy as a toadstool, with a smell like carrion and a rattle like a horse being choked to death. To get it lit took him hours, because his hand shook so he couldn't hold a match against the bowl. It was his palsy, no doubt, that was to blame for his unbuttoned trousers, his dangling shoestrings, and the gobs of food smeared on his clothes and through his whiskers. But that was not conclusive evidence that he was feeble-minded. Even a sane man would have trouble tying a bow-knot or hitting a buttonhole if his hands insisted on jumping two inches off the target at every heart-beat. The ladies added it to their evidence, but it should not have been allowed to count. Old Man Isbell's chief abnormality was of longer standing. He was simply, and before anything else, a natural-born bore.

The dullness of his speech was a gift of God. He had lived his eighty-five years through the most splendidly colored history that one man could ever have lived through in the world—the Civil War, the Indian campaigns in the West, the mining days, the cattle-kings, the long-line freighters, the road-agents, the stockmen's wars—the changing, with a swiftness and decision unknown to history before, of a country and its people; yes, and of a nation. Not as a spectator, either. He lived in the middle of every bit of it, and had a hand in every phase. But, for all the interest it gave to his conversation, he could just as well have spent his life at home working buttonholes.

"I remember Lincoln," he would say. "I drove him on an electioneerin' trip, back in Illinoy. Him and Stephen A. Douglas. I drove their carriage."

One would sit up and think, "Well! The old gabe does know something good, after all!" Expecting, of course, that he was about to tell some incident of the Lincoln-Douglas debates—something, maybe, that everybody else had missed. But that was all. So far as he knew, there hadn't been any incidents. They electioneered. He drove their carriage. They rode in it. That was all that had impressed him.

Or he would remember when there had been no Military Road, and no cow-town, nor even any cattle; only, instead, great herds of deer pasturing in grass belly-deep to a horse. A herd of over a hundred big mule-deer trotting close enough for a man to hang a rope on, right where the town was. But when you tried to work him for something beside the bare fact that they had been there you struck bottom. They had been there. Hundreds of them. He had seen them, that close. That ended that story. I asked him, once, if he remembered anything about Boone Helm, an early-day outlaw and all-round mean egg. He considered, sucked his pipe through a critical spell of croup, and finally said, "They used to be a road-agent by that name. He cut a feller's ears off."

It was not a prelude, but a statement of what he remembered. Some old men remember more than what actually happened; some remember things that never happened at all. Old Man Isbell remembered the exact thing, and, that being done, he stopped. He ought to have been writing military dispatches. Or had he? It never came into his head to tone up or temper down the exact and religious truth, and amplifying what he had seen simply wasn't in him.

To events that went on in the town he never appeared to pay the smallest attention. Indeed, he paid none to the people there, either, and, though they laid that to the condition of his wits, it irritated them. Yet it was no more than an old range-man's indifference to things which he considers immaterial. He was sharp enough when anything was going on that interested him—cattle-branding in the corrals below town, or the state of the water on the range. South of town was a long slope, with a big spring almost at the top, ringed with green grass except when the spring went dry. Then the grass turned brown. The old man never failed to notice that. He would. stop people in the street and point it out.

They laughed at him for it, behind his back. What did it matter to him whether the cattle had a dry year or not? He had an Indian War pension to live on, and he would get it whether the cattle throve or died to the last hoof. But, of course, he remembered what cattle looked like when they died of thirst, and swelled and popped open in the unmerciful heat, their burnt tongues lolling in the dust. It excited him to think of it, and he made a nuisance of himself about it. Sometimes he would stop strangers to tell it to them, which gave the town a bad name. Beside, his critics added he smelled bad. Not being able to wait on himself, and never having been particular about washing or laundry, he did smell bad. The place for him, they agreed, was in some nice home where he could be waited on decently. He needed looking after.

In that they were right. He did need looking after. The trouble was that their plan involved sending him away from the sagebrush country, and that would have been the same thing as knocking him in the head with an ax. He was an old sagebrusher. To take him out of sight of his country—the yellow-flowered, silver-green sage, the black-foliaged grease-wood, blossoming full of strong honey; the strong-scented, purple-berried junipers, and the wild cherry shrub, with its sticky, bitterish-honied flowers and dark sour fruit; the pale red-edged ridges, and the rock-breaks, blazing scarlet and orange and dead-black—to lose them would have killed him. By these things, an old sagebrusher lives. Out of reach of them, silly as it sounds to say so, he will die. I've seen them do it.

Old Man Isbell, incapable and slack-witted, helpless with age, and, so far as anybody could tell, without any suspicion of what the townspeople were thinking about him or that they were making designs against his life, did the one thing that could save him. He had nobody to take care of him. It was to see him taken care of that they wanted to send him away; and, surely without knowing it, he stumbled on the way to head them off. He got married.

The wedding threw the town into a perfect panic of delighted horror. This was one of the things that made life a fine thing to live. Other people, other communities, had diversions which the cow-town did without; this made up for them. The justice of the peace, having performed the ceremony, put out for home on a gallop to tell his wife the news. Hearing it, she came out with her hair down, and canvassed the houses on both sides of the street, knocking at every door, and yelling, without waiting for anybody to open. "Old Man Isbell's got married! You'll never guess who to!"

III

The bride alone would have made a rich story. She was about twenty-eight years old, Old Man Isbell being—as I've mentioned, eighty-five—and the rest of her was even more incongruous than her youth. She weighed close to three hundred pounds, being almost as broad as she was tall, and she had to shave her face regularly to keep down a coarse black beard, which showed in the wrinkles of fat where a razor could not reach.

As Old Man Isbell was the town nuisance, she was the town joke. Even in that scantily-womaned place, where only the dullest girls lived after they were big enough to look out for themselves, she had never had a suitor. The men were not too particular, but nobody dared pay court to her, for fear of getting laughed at. She was so fat that to walk downtown for Old Man Isbell's order of groceries took her almost an hour. It made one tired to watch her. Even the Indian squaws, riding through town, their matronly bellies overhanging the horns of their saddles, drew rein to admire Old Man Isbell's bride for an adiposity which laid theirs completely in the shade. They were fat, all right, but good heavens! They cackled and clucked to each other, pointing.

Housewives ran to peep through the curtains at the twenty-eight year-old girl who had been hard up enough to marry an old, dirty, feeble-minded man of eighty-five. Store loafers perked up and passed remarks on her and on the match. But in spite of them all, in spite of the tittering, and the cruelty and the embarrassment, and her own exertion, she carried home the groceries every day. She cooked and cleaned house, too; and kept it clean; and one of the first things she bought after her marriage was a clothesline. It was full every day, and the clothes on it were clean. So were Old Man Isbell's. He sat on his front porch, wobbling matches over his black gaggling pipe, without a thing in the world to bother his mind except his pipe and the spring on the slope south of town. His trousers were fully buttoned, his shoes tied, and his beard and clothing washed, brushed and straightened, without a speck upon them to show what he had eaten last, or when.

Town joke or not, the fat woman was taking care of him. She was being a housewife, attending to the duties of her station exactly as the other married women in town attended to theirs, and that was something they had not expected. There wasn't any fun for them in that. They wanted her to remain a joke; and they couldn't joke about her housework without belittling their own. They took it out on her by letting her alone. There was no woman in town for Old Man Isbell's wife to talk to, except my mother, who, being the school-teacher's wife, didn't quite belong to the townspeople, and would probably have repudiated their conventions if she had. Across the back-fence she got all of the fat woman's story—not all of it, either, but all its heroine was willing to volunteer.

The fat woman had come to the country with her father, who took up a homestead on Tub Springs Ridge. But he got himself in jail for vealing somebody else's calf, and she moved into town to live till he served out his time. For a while she lived by selling off the farm machinery he had left. But it didn't take very long to live that up—"not that I eat so much," she hastened to add, "I really don't eat as much as . . . as ordinary folks do . . ."—and when that was gone she was broke. That was what induced her to listen, she said, to Old Man Isbell, when he first began to talk about getting married. She was desperate. It seemed the only resort, and yet it was so unheard of that she hesitated.

Finally, she borrowed a lift from a stage-driver, and went to the county jail to ask advice from her father. He knew the old man. It would be all right, he said, for her to marry him. But not unless she realized what kind of job she was taking on, and was game to live up to it. She mustn't bull into it and then try to back out. The old man would have to be tended exactly like a small infant—the work would be just as hard, and just as necessary—and, in addition, he was uglier, meaner and dirtier. If she wanted to undertake the contract, all right; but she must either stick to it or let it entirely alone. When Old Man Isbell died, she would get what money he had saved up, and his Indian War pension. Enough to keep her, probably, for life. But it was up to her to see that she earned it.

"He made me promise I would," she told my mother, "and the Lord knows I have. It's just exactly like pa said, too. He's just like a little baby. To see him set and stare at that spring for hours on end, you wouldn't believe how contrary and mean he can be around the house. All the time. He'll take a notion he wants something, and then forget the name of it and get mad because I don't guess it right. I have to pick up things and offer 'em to him, one at a time, till I manage to hit the one he's set his mind on. And him gettin' madder every time I pick up the wrong thing. Just like a baby. And his clothes—they're the same, too." She sighed into her series of stubbly chins. "It keeps me goin' every minute," she said. "It's mighty hard work."

"You do keep him clean, though," my mother said. "He was so dirty and forlorn. Everybody's talking about how clean you keep him now."

"They talk about how I married him to get his pension," the fat woman said. "How I'm just hangin' around waitin' for him to die. I know!"

"That's only some of them," my mother said. "They don't know anything about it. You work right along, and don't pay any attention to them."

"None of the ladies ever come to call on me," said the fat woman.

"I shouldn't think you'd want them to," my mother suggested. "You must be so busy, you wouldn't have time to bother with visitors. They probably think you'd sooner not be disturbed at your work."

"I do want 'em to, anyway," said the fat woman. "And they call on all the other married ladies, whether they're overworked or not. They call on Mis' Melendy, across the way, and she's got teethin' twins."

"Well, I wouldn't care whether they came to see me or not," said my mother.

"I do, though," the fat woman insisted. "I've got a house, and a husband, just the same as they have. I do my housework just the same, too. I'd like to show 'em all the work I do, and what a care it is to keep things clean, and how clean I keep 'em. If they'd come, they'd see."

My mother assented. There was no earthly chance that any of them would come, and she knew it. But the fat woman didn't know it, and it was the one thing in the world that she had her head set on. Everything else that women take pride in and nourish conceit upon she had given up; and for that very renouncement she stuck all the more fiercely to the idea of being visited by the neighbor ladies, of being received as an established housewife, like the rest of them. There might not be any sense in the notion, but she wanted it. No matter how they came, or why, she wanted them. Even if they came prying for things to discredit her with, to trot around and gabble about, she wanted them anyway. When other women got married the neighbor ladies came to call. Now she was married, and they didn't.

The worst of it was, there was no way of breaking it to her that they weren't going to. My mother made several tries at letting her down easy, but got nowhere. She wanted it too much to give it up. Some days she would come to the fence elated and hopeful, because one of the ladies had nodded to her; sometimes she would be depressed and glum.

"I know what's keeping 'em away," she told my mother. "It's him!"

She yanked a fat arm in the direction of her husband, sitting in the sun with his mouth hanging open.

"Oh, no!" my mother protested. "Why—"

"Yes, it is!" the fat woman insisted. "And I don't blame 'em, either! Who wants to come visitin', when you've got to climb around an object like that to get into the parlor? I don't blame 'em for stayin' away. I would, my own self."

"But you've got to take care of him," my mother reminded her.

"Yes. I've got to. I promised pa I wouldn't back out on that, and I won't. But, as long as I've got him around, I won't have any visitors to entertain. I might as well quit expectin' any."

She sighed, and my mother tried to console her, knowing how deep her idiotic yearning was, and how impossible it was to gratify it. She had tried to persuade the neighbor ladies to call. There was no use wasting any more time on them. Yet, to come out bluntly with the fact that they had all refused would be silly and cruel. My mother was incapable of that. Concealing it, she did her best with promises and predictions, taking care to be vague, while Old Man Isbell dozed, or poked matches at his choking black pipe without any thought of human vanity or hope or disappointment, or anything but the Winter stand of grass on the range. Nobody could believe, from his looks, that he could have asked the fat woman to marry him. It was much more likely that she had hazed the notion into him. Some day, I thought, we might find out, when he could forget the range long enough.

But we never did. He died before the Winter grass got ripe enough for the cattle to sample.

IV

It was on a morning in October that my mother was awakened, about daylight, by yelling and crying from the Isbells' house. She got up and looked across, and saw, through their window, a lamp still burning, though it was already light enough to see. As she looked, the lamp went out—not from a draft, but because it had run dry. That meant that something was up which was keeping them too busy to tend to it. My mother dressed, and hurried over.

Old Man Isbell was dying. The fat woman had been up watching him all night. She sat beside the bed, while he plunged and pitched his thin hairy arms and yelled. Across her knees lay an old, heavy Sharp's plainsman's rifle.

"Watch 'em, watch 'em!" yelled Old Man Isbell. "They cut sagebrush, and push it along in front of 'em to fool you while they sneak up! If you see a bush move, shoot hell out of it! Shoot, damn it!

The fat woman lugged the immense rifle to her shoulder and snapped the hammer. "Bang!" she yelled.

"That's you!" approved the old man, lying down again. "That's the checker! You nailed him that time, the houndish dastard! You got to watch 'em, I tell ye."

"He thinks he's standin' off Indians," the fat woman explained. "He's young again, and he thinks he's layin' out on the range with the hostiles sneakin' in on him. I've had to—All right, I'm watchin' close," she told him. "Bang!"

My mother got her something to eat, and built a fire, so that when the neighbor ladies came to help they could have a warm room to sit in. Their resolution to stay away held good only in life. When anybody was dying, social embargoes collapsed. Beside, a death was something they couldn't afford to miss. They came; all the women whom the fat woman had set her heart on being friends with; and nobody thought to remark that, instead of being responsible for their staying away, it was Old Man Isbell who had the credit of bringing them there, after all.

But the fat woman was past bothering about whether they came or stayed away. Even their remarks about the cleanness of her house went over her unnoticed. She had livelier concerns to think about. The old man was driving stage. He was going down the Clarno Grade, and a brake-rod had broken. The stage was running wild, down a twenty percent grade full of hairpin switchbacks. He was flogging his horses to keep them out from under the wheels. He yelled and swore and pitched and floundered in the bedclothes, screaming to his wife that she must climb back and try to drag the hind wheels by poking a bar between the spokes.

"And hurry, damn it!" he yelled. "Drag 'er, before that off pointer goes down!"

The neighbor women gaped and stared. This was something they had never heard of. They didn't even understand what kind of emergency the old man was yelling about. But the fat woman paid no attention to them, and did not hesitate. She climbed along the edge of the bed, reached a broom from the corner, and, poking the handle down as if into a wheel, she set back hard. Her mouth was compressed and firm, and she breathed hard with excitement. She appeared to be taking the game almost as seriously as the old man did, crying back to him that she was holding the wheel, as if it meant the saving of both their lives, though hers was in no danger, and his was burning out like a haystack flaming in a gale.

The women brought food and put it into her mouth as if she was something dangerous. They weren't used to games like this, except in children and dying men. Being neither, the fat woman had no business playing it; and they poked buttered bread into her mouth sharply, frowning as if to show her that they saw through her nonsense, and considered it uncalled for. Neither their buttered bread nor their disapproval made any impression on her. The old man was yelling that she must hold the wheel, and she, with her chins trembling with fatigue and sleeplessness, cried back that she had it where it couldn't get away.

In the afternoon he had another one going. He was in a range-camp at night, and there was a herd of wild mustangs all around his fire, trying to stampede his pack-horses. The woman pretended to throw rocks to scare them off.

"There's the stud!" he mumbled. "Where in hell is that gun of mine? Oh, God, if it wasn't for bringin' down them damned Siwashes, wouldn't I salivate that stud? Don't shoot! Don't you know them Injuns'll be all over us if they hear a shot? Hit him with a rock! Watch that bunch over yon! Look how their eyes shine, damn their souls! Throw! Do you want to lose all our horses, and be left out in Injun country afoot?"

All day, and till after dark, the neighbor women watching her, she threw when he ordered; and when, at dark, he switched to heading a stampede of cattle, she charged with him to turn them, swinging an imaginary rope with her fat arm, yelling and ki-yi-ing as he directed, and jouncing the bed till the whole house rocked.

About midnight he had burned his brain down to the last nub, and there the fat woman was no longer needed. He lifted himself clear of the bed, and said, "Well, hello, you damned old worthless tick-bit razor-back, you! How the hell did you get out to this country?" He sounded pleased and friendly. It had never occurred to the townspeople that he had ever had any friends. Even as it was, the fact was lost on some of them, for while he spoke he looked straight at one of the visiting women, as if he were addressing her. Somebody tittered, and she left indignantly, banging the door. Everybody jumped, and looked after her. When they looked back, Old Man Isbell was lying on his pillow, dead.

The fat woman did not want to leave him. She was dull and almost out of her head with weariness, but, when they took hold of her, gently, to put her to bed where she could rest, she fought them off.

"He might come to again," she insisted. "You can't tell, he might flash up again. And he might think of something he'd need me for. You leave me be!"

They explained to her that it wasn't possible, and that, even if it was, she must have some sleep. She mustn't kill herself to humor a man out of his mind.

"I want to!" she said. "I want to do that! All them things he's done, and been in, and seen—he never let on a word to me about 'em, and I want to hear 'em! I never knew what an adventured and high-spirited man he was. I like to do what I've been doin'!"

She fought them until they quit trying, and left her. When they came back, she had gone to sleep by herself, beside her dead husband; a fat woman, twenty-eight years old, beside the corpse of a man eighty-five.

V

She came to call on my mother after the funeral. Her mourning habit had come from a mail-order house, and, though there were yards of it, enough, I judged, to make three full-size wagon-sheets, it needed to be let out in one or two places, and she wanted advice.

"How to fix it so I can wear it, right away," she explained. "I could send it back, but I don't want to wait that long. I want to show 'em that my husband was as much loss to me as theirs would be to them. He was, too. He was a sight better man than any of theirs."

She rubbed the tears out of her eyes with the back of her wrist. My mother consoled her, and mentioned that now, at least, everybody knew what care she had taken of him.

"I don't care whether they know it or not," said the fat woman. "None of 'em come to see me, and they can all stay away for good, as far as I'm concerned. The way they acted the one time they did come settled 'em with me."

"But they helped out during your bad time," my mother said. "They meant kindly."

"Yes. Helped out. And then they come smirkin' and whisperin' around how I ought to be glad my husband was out of the way. How I must have hated takin' care of him, and what a mercy it was to be rid of him. I told 'em a few things. They'll stay away from me a spell, I can promise you that!"

She sat straight in her chair, and dropped the mourning dress on the floor.

"I was glad to take care of him," she said. "Yes, sir! I was proud of my husband. The things he'd done, and the risks he'd been through, when the men in this town was rollin' drunks and wrappin' up condensed milk. . . ."

She drew a breath, and, forgetting that my mother had been there, began to tell about the time when he had been surrounded by the Indians, creeping in on him with sagebrush tied to their heads. He fought them back and out-gamed the whole caboodle of them; and her voice rose and trembled, shrilling the scenes she had enacted with Old Man Isbell when his numb old brain was burning down through the pile of his memories, spurting a flame out of each one before they all blackened and went to nothing.

She shrilled the great scenes out defiantly, as if it were her place to defend them, as if they belonged to her, and were better, even at second hand, than anything that any of the townspeople had ever experienced. None of their common realities had ever touched her. Beauty had not; love had not, nor even friends. In place of them, she had got an eighty-five year-old dotard and the ridicule of the townspeople. Watching over the old man when he died was the one time when she had come anywhere within reach of heroism and peril and splendor; and that one time, being worthy of it, she passed them all. And that one time was enough, because she knew it.

"The hostiles a—prowlin' around," she cried, her voice blazing. "The houndish dastards! . . ."

Hell to Be Smart

I

There never was a more powerful indictment of the general scatter-brainedness of humanity than in the steamboat travel on the Upper Columbia in late Autumn when the ice was threatening to run. As long as the headwaters stayed open, the stern-wheelers kept on going, and there wasn't a single trip when any of them carried enough passengers to fill one lifeboat. But the moment they went off the run and tied up at Deschutes Landing for the Winter, there would come the blamedest stampede of travelers for Idaho that had been registered for months, all insisting that the boat ought to make one last special trip for them because their business couldn't wait another day. You'd have thought, since it was all so imperative, that some of them might have kept tab on navigating announcements instead of waiting till the whole fleet was snubbed in and logged up with no chance of getting out except on orders from the War Department; but you'd have thought wrong. I watched them when I was steamboat engineer, and I watched them earlier, when I worked with young Flem Oliver peddling horses on the beach; and I never saw an annual tie-up that failed to fetch them in droves.

Supplying equine transportation for travelers who couldn't come a day sooner or wait a minute later was what kept our horse dispensary flourishing. It wasn't a genteel trade, but there was nothing dull about any enterprise that Flem Oliver was mixed up in, and it did keep us in touch with economic trends in the upper country of the late '70s. The people to whom we sold horses in one day represented every kind of trade that the Rocky Mountain region under the Hayes administration could have the least use for—mine-drillers and mine-timberers and powder-men and prospectors and promoters, freighters and packers and loggers and wagon-smiths and wheelwrights, wool-pickers and scourers, sheep-dippers and herders and lambers, cattle-markers and trailers and dehorners, horse-trappers and hostlers and breakers, spurriers and saddlers and harness makers, town developers and land speculators and professional hunters and labor contractors, people who operated matrimonial bureaus and people with new doctrines like flower worship and the milk cure that they wanted to try on the Indians. That was only one morning's haul, and the last of the run was a theatrical troupe that included a string band, a child soprano about thirteen who shot a horse with a blank cartridge pistol and got a case on Flem Oliver, a man who did hypnotism and glass-eating, and a big friendly woman with two wooden crates full of snakes which she claimed were pets and begged me to cinch on the pack horse easy so they wouldn't brood about their confinement and start biting one another.

Packing the horses was my job. Flem Oliver sold and demonstrated them. His father owned the business, and paid us, when there was no possible chance of putting us off any longer, a dollar a day apiece—cheap enough, considering that he bought Indian ponies for five dollars and turned them over for a profit of from four hundred per cent up. There was nothing spontaneous about the service we furnished, but the big woman thought it was all sheer benevolence. She remarked that the Landing seemed a desolate place to live in, and didn't we sometimes get starved for company?

It wasn't exactly a garden spot, being mostly sand and rocks; though what bothered me was not the scenery, but the horses. I'd worked with the brutes all my life, starting with a racing stable in Missouri where I ran the steam pumping plant and had my leg torn half in two by a playful stallion; and I didn't like them. But I told her that the place suited me all right. It was fine. She looked a little disappointed to hear it, but she stuck to the job of spreading a more cheerful prospect for us anyway. "There's going to be some nice company up here to visit you," she said, trying to make her pony stand up under her. "There was the prettiest girl asking about you down at the . . . Eva, keep that dratted horse away from me or I'll whip you!"

The child soprano was crawfishing her horse around experimentally, seeing how many things she could make him bump into. Flem Oliver caught hold of her bridle, and introduced himself into the conversation by asking the big woman to tell him some more. "What kind of girl was that?" he asked. "Did she come up from Portland with you? What complexion was she, and what did she look like?"

I had known all along that the good news wasn't for me. The only girl I knew well enough to hear from lived in Battle Mountain, Nevada, and liked it. But Flem Oliver knew girls everywhere, and the big woman was delighted at the rise she got out of him. This girl, she said, had been on the Portland boat. She had lightish hair done in a big knot, and a number one complexion and plenty of it, and a wonderful line-up of clothes—to all of which Flem Oliver listened inattentively. The child soprano grabbed his hat and threw it over the fence among the loose horses. It was to punish him, she said, for not telling her his affections were attached elsewhere. She was certainly advanced for her age, this little Eva. "So that's another girl you've lied to, is it?" she said, poking her finger at him. "Well, she's coming up here to find out the truth about you. I heard her say so on the boat. You know who she is, too, don't you? You're afraid of her, ain't you?"

It almost looked as if Flem was. He turned her bridle loose and told both them good-by so pointedly that it was insulting. The saddle train had started, so they went bouncing across the sand and fell in line with it. It was a clumsy run thing, with all the men stopping to cock and prime whenever they sighted a stray Indian, and the pack horses with the snakes and musical instruments breaking loose and having to be chased back. The way it was handled, I doubted if Idaho would ever see it; and Flem Oliver had the gall to remark that it made him feel restless, and he believed he would catch up a horse and join it. "A day or two on the march might quiet my nerves," he said. "You tell the old man I'll straighten up the horse money with him later. It don't come to much, tell him. We let a lot of those skates go cheap."

I knew how much it came to. Flem Oliver's father made me keep tally on every horse we sold, and he could spot a ten-cent shortage in the till with an instinct that was almost witchcraft. "You can go if you want to," I said. "But you can't take any of that money, or any of those horses either. They're not yours, and your old man would jail me as an accessory if I let you get away with them."

"Perhaps it might worry the old gentleman unduly," Flem said. That was putting it insanely low. The only good thing you could say about the elder Oliver's thrift was that it didn't run in his family. Flem was a money-slinger when he got hold of any to sling. "Here's another suggestion," he said. "I'll leave the money with you, all except twenty dollars. He owes me that for wages, so he can't have any kick coming if I take it."

He might not have a kick coming, but I knew he would make one. The old man acted as his own paymaster, and he would certainly hold me for every cent that turned up short in my hands. He would probably throw me out to boot, and I liked the scenery. Rivers always made me feel at home, and I never saw a river that suited me so exactly as the Columbia did when the wild swans and snow geese were coming over late in the year. It was even lively, on account of Flem Oliver. He had seen more action without ever getting out of Eastern Oregon than I had by coddling barn loads of horses over half the United States. I'll never forget hearing him tell about going out to run in a rancher's livestock that his father had a mortgage on, and running blind into a hostile Indian horse herd on the march in the dark. The Bannocks had jumped the ranch, killed the rancher, and burned the house on top of him; and Flem bumped into them as they were running off all the stock he had called round to collect. He worked ahead through the herd without knowing what was up until a bunch of squaws burst out singing so close he could have slapped his reins on them. The rancher had put up a fight before they got him, and they were singing a death song for their killed men as they moved out. Flem didn't dare turn back because it would have started the herd milling, and he couldn't turn out because the canyon was too narrow. He kept his head down and his face covered, and rode with them nearly all night before they climbed into open country where he could sneak away. What bothered him most during the trip, he said, was regret that his father hadn't come along. The old gentleman's emotions at watching a foreclosure escape him without even being able to complain about it would have made one of the most dramatic episodes of all time.

There were plenty of such incidents that Flem Oliver had told on himself, and plenty that he hadn't, apparently, from the way he acted about the girl coming to visit him. I tried to make him tell why he was afraid of her, but the best I could get out of him was that it was none of my business; and then the little portage locomotive came snorting up through the sand and routed him right out of my hands. It didn't run but one trip a day, usually, and he thought, with the modesty which rarely failed him, that it was making a special trip on his account. "Never mind what this is about," he said, getting down from the fence. "You won't let me take the money that's coming to me, so I'll have to do the best I can. If there's a girl on that train, tell her I'm not here. Tell her I'm somewhere she can't get to. Tell her I'm on Cabin Creek. Watch the horses for me."

He loped down through the sand to the dock. Some steamboat call was coming in over the dock telegraph, and a couple of men slid back the freight door of the old *Tilkun* as Flem got there. He ducked in through it, and went in the stern under the walking beam. You'd have thought, the way he got himself out of sight, that he expected a heavily-armed file of stern-faced men to march off the train and tell him the game was up, though he wasn't in any game except the horse business, and they couldn't do anything to a man for swindling non-residents.

II

There were heavily-armed men on that train, though—a whole pink-cheeked platoon of infantry recruits, with lumpy new blue uniforms and a brand-new implement to shoot with—a stubbed-off little cannon on cartwheels that they called a Gatling gun, and a young first lieutenant with field glasses and a sword and a red silk handkerchief around his neck to make him look jaunty and superior to his heavy responsibilities. There was a steamboat complement, too—a pack of firemen they had scratched up in Lower Portage, and old Simmons, the *Tilkun* pilot, looking as if he had been pulled out of bed without breakfast; and old Joab Aintree, the steamboat superintendent who had come along as acting captain, wiggling his big stone-colored beard and looking tickled because military business paid high and stood good for all damages in service; and there was the girl. She was tall, with a kind of level-eyed look to her; she had lightish hair done in a big loose knot like one of these exhibition twists of brown taffy in a candy store window; and she had the young lieutenant so enslaved that he couldn't stop looking at her long enough to unship his munitions of war.

I don't know how many beauty prizes she could have run away with. Fashions in looks change, I suppose, along with everything else; but it was a shock, seeing her. From the way Flem Oliver had acted, I expected some king of buzzardish siren with, maybe, a set of bejeweled brass knuckles in her reticule. The actuality was hard to get adjusted to. She came over to the horse corral, the lieutenant trailing her, and asked for the young Mr. Oliver who owned all the horses. "You work for him, don't you?" she said.

Any fool, given such an inquiry and such a girl to go on, could see why Flem Oliver hadn't wanted to be found. He had given her to understand that he possessed one of Eastern Oregon's large independent fortunes, and he hated to have her catch him handling the old man's scrub ponies on the beach for a dollar a day, payable seldom. I could reconstruct the whole case, and I couldn't altogether blame him. That girl would have made anybody want to show off. She had the lieutenant so overpowered that he walked into a wire pile trying to give orders and watch her at the same time, and she got me all mixed up trying to explain about Flem Oliver without unsettling her faith in mankind. The best I could manage, after several stabs at something elaborate, was what Flem had told me to tell her. "He's gone up the river on a business trip," I said. "Probably he'll stay the rest of the winter. He's on Cabin Creek, filing on a homestead." "Cabin Creek?" she said, alarmed, and turned to the lieutenant. "That's where it's dangerous, isn't it?"

The lieutenant said that it wasn't precisely the spot he'd recommend for a hermit's retreat. "Cabin Creek happens to be our destination," he told me. "A Walpapi raiding party is supposed to be riding to cross the river there, and we're ordered to turn them back. Naturally, if they run into any lone homesteaders . . . You're sure that's the location?" He waited, giving me a chance to change it, but I decided not to. After all, if he was going there anyway, the idea that he was rescuing somebody might make his trip more interesting. He looked at the girl. "What you'd better do is come along with us," he suggested. "You can't stay here without somebody to look after you. The boat's comfortable, and there's scenery and chairs with cushions and . . . " He eyed the steamboat, but there was nothing very prominent except the Gatling gun on the foredeck, and he decided not to enumerate that. "You'll know sooner about this friend of yours, too," he said. "And I'll take care of you. It's—I mean you'd—I think you'll like it."

He was all stuttery and anxious, though I didn't think he needed to be. She wanted to go, and, unless I was a bad surmiser, it wasn't entirely on account of her uneasiness about Flem Oliver. The lieutenant wasn't forbidding to look at, himself. "I'd like to go," she said. "Only, if there's men getting killed, and soldiers going crazy and stabbing bayonets into people, maybe I'd better not. I don't want to see that."

"There won't be any of it to see," he said. "My men are under my orders, and they know it. These Indian skirmishes never last over a few minutes, when they come off at all, and those Walpapi sucker-eaters can't hit anything. I'll guarantee that you'll feel perfectly safe."

He wanted her along, good and plain. It struck me he was guaranteeing one or two possibilities that he lacked authority to speak for, but that wasn't his fault. It was the girl's. There was something about that girl that simply compelled a man to lay claim to virtues he wasn't entitled to. It worked even on me. Old Aintree came poking across the sand and said he was looking for a young man from Nevada who had worked with stationary engines. The rickety old pump rig I'd worked on had about as much to do with steamboat machinery as riding a stick horse has with being a jockey, but the girl looked at me, and I stood out and said I was his man.

"So I judged," he said. I knew well enough who had told him about me. "We came off without a second engineer. This Upper River for the present is under martial law, so we'll declare you drafted. Get your traps and go aboard."

I'd probably have gone without a word, but the girl decided to trust the lieutenant's guarantee and go aboard herself. The lieutenant went with her, and I got back enough ethical scruples to explain what kind of engine it was that I had actually worked on. Aintree didn't look surprised.

"I'm glad you didn't blurt that out in front of the military," he said. "He has to report all this truck, and if we start without a second engineer and something busts, the War Department will bring out that we were running short-handed and make trouble about paying us. I'll show you all you'll need to know. Your friend is going as a fireman, and he said to turn your horses over to the dock telegrapher."

I stopped. Flem Oliver had signed up on the steamboat without knowing that the girl was going to be aboard. "He won't want to go up-river now," I said, "so I can leave the horses with him."

"Not this time you can't," said Aintree watching me close. The Lord knows I had no objections to steamboating with him. "I told you the Upper River was under military administration during this Indian rumpus. You and your friend are in exactly the same fix as these soldiers, and if either of you try to jump ship you'll get cinched for mutiny."

It was going to be comical, I thought, for Flem Oliver to be throwing eight-foot cordwood on the boiler-deck to get away from a girl who was being entertained on the saloon-deck right over his head. One thing was certain, you didn't have to go far to find suspense and excitement when that young man was around. He attracted them like some trees do lightning, even when he was trying his best to avoid them.

III

It didn't take much expert knowledge to understand why old Aintree wanted a full engine-room complement in case of accident. He expected to have one, and when I looked at his line-up I didn't blame him. The chief engineer seemed to know his business, but he must have learned it under somebody else, for he didn't know as much about handling men as a Chinese fish-cleaner. He was a big roundhead with a roan complexion and marbly-looking pale blue eyes. I judged that they must have brought him out of a several weeks' jag with cold water, and they hadn't put on quite enough. His notion of making his men work was to yell in a hoarse rattle, and then grab and shove the first man he could get his hands on. Most of them took it as if they were used to that kind of treatment in the saloons they had been sleeping in, but I made up my mind that he wouldn't push me more than once, and then I tagged around with old Aintree to improve my experience with engines.

They certainly had it over any machinery I'd ever been up against before. There were gauges to register every least thing that happened, and valves to regulate it, and the engines themselves were the treat of a lifetime. When they ran, there was nothing except a low hum, and the walking-beam went so easy it reminded me of a cougar slipping up on a cottontail rabbit. When you wanted to back, you pulled the reverse lever, and she turned over and backed. Every single time. It wasn't like a horse, where you had to take what you wanted him to do, add what he felt like doing, and divide by two, with fifteen per cent off for luck and bad feed. With that engine, you called for what you wanted and got it. I got so interested watching it work that I didn't notice how fast we were traveling until we got away up under Horseheaven Flat, and I totally forgot to warn Flem Oliver about his girl being aboard till he laid off heaving cordwood and came over to talk about her.

Her name, he said, was Diana Owens. Her parents got her name out of Pope's poems, and he met her at their house in Portland in the Spring when he had a few hundred dollars from the state bounty on coyote pelts. There were flocks of young men around the place all the time, and her habit of looking as if she believed every mortal thing they told her had led Flem Oliver into a material overstatement of his resources. That was all their acquaintance had amounted to, and the only reason he shrank from renewing it was that he didn't want her to discover that he had lied to her. "It isn't that I expect to profit by her good opinion," he said. "I've got no designs on her hand, or anybody else's, for that matter. I've got a lot of country to look at before I get married. But I would have felt like hell if she'd caught me roust-abouting the old man's horses with eight cents in my jeans. She would have, too, if I hadn't had a mess of luck."

I was about to tell him how much more of a mess his luck was than he imagined, but the chief engineer poked in between us and grabbed Flem. "Get up and work!" he said. "Lay to that woodpile before I wear a post out with your carcass!"

It was bad business to open relations this way with Flem Oliver, and the engineer made it worse by dropping his hands. Flem hit him right on the bridge of the nose, and his head knocked back against the deck beams with a crack like splitting an oak stump. A man of ordinary intelligence would have been laid out stiff for an hour. The engineer wobbled at the knees, wiped his eyes with his thumb, and hauled out a gun. "I want a detail of soldiers," he said into the speaking tube. "Hurry up, a man's mutinied! . . . This is going to land you in a military court, bub," he told Flem. "You hold still or I'll kill you."

He was soreheaded enough for anything. Flem didn't wiggle, except to loosen the heel of one boot with the toe of the other, like a school kid bluffing at the blackboard. Then he kicked the loose boot into the engineer's face, slid out through the freight door into the river, and hung on the guard outside to yank off his other boot. "This is the first installment, greasy," he said, and threw that too. "I'll wait for you up-river with a gun."

He dropped off into the water in time to miss old Aintree and the lieutenant and the soldiers. Aintree had brought a pair of rusty handcuffs, but he hid them under his coat when he heard what had happened. "Shucks, if that's all it is, it's nothing," he told the lieutenant. He was smart, that old man. If he had let on it was important, the lieutenant might have landed men to fetch Flem Oliver back, and the War Department wasn't paying the steamboat company to retrieve its fractious firemen. "Some youngster lost his temper and decided to go home and sulk. No use bothering about him. The engineer's face will heal, and he can run this boat with the men he's got. Can't you?"

The engineer said he guessed so. The bridge of his nose was swollen all the way across his head, and you could see he didn't feel very gay about leaving Flem Oliver at large, even on orders from his boss. But he kept still till they were gone, and then he called me over. "I hated to be rough with that friend of yours," he told me, all confidential. "But when I give a man orders, I expect him to mind 'em and no back talk. Does he carry a gun?"

"Usually," I said. Even the engineer ought to have known a man couldn't swim that river with a gun hanging on him. "It wouldn't make much difference though. There's ranches along here where he can buy all the firearms he wants. He had about fifteen hundred dollars on him."

The engineer looked genuinely shocked. By his way of figuring, anybody with that much money was special. "Why the hell didn't you tell me?" he said. Then he brightened. "Anyway, he's afoot, and we can out-travel him."

"Not if he gets a horse," I said. "Any of these ranches will find him something to ride. We follow the bends of the river, but he'll cut straight across to one of these old landings up ahead. He'll hang out a landing flag, probably, and when the boat heads in he'll step aboard with a gun and blow out your light. I'd be careful, if I was you."

The engineer got up and shut the freight door. There was nothing he could do about the windows, and the forecastle door was shut already. He went over and sat against it for awhile, and then got up and said he was going on deck. "You can't see anything out of this blamed cellar," he said. "Them soldiers get paid to protect the public, and they might as well be watching out for that bushwhacking young hound as not. You run things for awhile."

He went above, and I felt a little uneasy for fear the soldiers would send down for me to explain what kind of haunted house yarn I had been loading him with. Afterward I found out that he didn't mention our conversation at all. He told them that they were running for the biggest Indian crossing on the river, and that they might find the Walpapi raiders using it instead of Cabin Creek. The lieutenant was too busy to listen to him, and the soldiers were too new to such expeditions to chase him back where he belonged. Not that I missed him. It was a lot more agreeable below without him, and I couldn't help thinking how unjust it was that Flem Oliver couldn't have stayed to enjoy it. He hadn't done a thing that I wouldn't have done under the same circumstances, and, simply because the engineer had grabbed him instead of me, he was afoot in the rock flats with no shoes and wet clothes, and nothing to eat if he stayed out, and a military trial hanging on him if he was lucky enough to get back. There was no use talking, excitement had an affinity for Flem Oliver. The only reason there were quiet places in the world was that he could only be in one place at a time.

IV

By this time the engineer had the soldiers edged up, and they were finding signs along the bank that needed investigating Almost every hundred yards, down would come a bell to slow up, or hold her steady, or drop back easy, or something. The Gatling gun crew was all crouched, ready to cut loose on anything, and the lieutenant kept telling the girl that there wouldn't be a particle of danger and then warning her that in case there was, she must go straight to the companionway and wait on the stairs till he got through crushing it. He had her pretty well excited and scared, and his men were as bad. Every gun in the bunch was cocked, capped, and pointed, and it wouldn't have taken much more than snapping a match head to have touched off the whole broadside. Old Aintree was acting captain in the pilot house, wiggling his big stone-colored beard and watching the engineer without letting on, and old Simmons, the pilot, was dodging the first drifts of loose ice, when, for a ten years' wonder at that season, there actually was a landing flag. It was stuck in the sand at the edge of a willow thicket, with nobody in sight. Simmons had no right to pay any attention to it, being on a special run, but habit got the best of him. He whanged the bell and turned in. A couple of loose ponies jumped up in the willows, and the engineer, with bad temper and a bad hangover and a bad conscience all working on him at once, yanked his pistol and shot.

"There he is!" he yelled, and banged loose a couple before old Aintree could get down to grab him. "That's the bush-whacking hound that's laying to get me! Smoke him, damn him!"

The soldiers were too high-strung to need any persuasion. Everybody turned loose at once, and the way that Gatling corn-sheller hove lead was a treat to the traveler's eye. Not that it hit much. The smoke was so thick after one whirl of the crank that you couldn't see the bow of the boat, and it fogged over the pilot house so that old Simmons might as well have been steering with his head in a pillow case. Below decks we could see under it. There were people in the willows, all right. The brush was too thick for us to tell whether they were Indians, but we could see packs and blankets, and a couple of figures jumping down behind a sand dune. Nobody got hit, as far as I could make out, but a couple of horses did. I saw them cave down and start kicking. I don't go a cent on horses, but when you've worked with the brutes long, some instinct makes you remember every individual one you've ever had your hands on; and I knew I had handled those two dead horses somewhere. It didn't help much, because I couldn't remember where or when. I gave up trying, and, since the pilot house signals had gone dead, I took a peek on deck to see what the firing line was up to.

There were several things that hadn't registered above the noise. The Gatling gun jammed up about every two bursts, and half the crew unjammed it while the other half pointed and shot it. Old Aintree had the engineer flat on the deck, sitting on him and trying to work the rust out of that old pair of handcuffs so they would fasten on. Soldiers were shooting all along the rail, mostly without bothering to aim, and young Diana Owens sat huddled on a deck bench, holding it tight with both hands. The lieutenant wanted to get her inside, but he couldn't make her listen and he couldn't pry her fingers loose. She was literally struck stiff, and her eyes, instead of being dark blue, were wide open and completely black. Plenty of women go into a kind of rigid fit when there's unexpected shooting. It isn't so much fear of getting shot as pure instinctive dread of an unnatural kind of noise. Realizing it, the lieutenant got up, patted her hands, and blew his whistle to cease firing.

That was where he lost his claim about having control of his men. All of them had gun fever, and they had to shoot it off, no matter who told them to stop. They paid no attention to the whistle, and when he ran along the deck knocking down their guns, they simply leveled back and started walloping off Government ammunition again. He pulled the men away from the Gatling with his hands, and they pushed him back and fogged up noisier than ever. He gave that up. The thing was not to make them resist temptation, but to get them away from it. He jumped for the companion-ladder and started up to the pilot house to order the boat turned out.

Nobody had realized that the outfit ashore was doing any return shooting. The lieutenant was halfway up when a slug got him in the right shoulder, and he keeled off backwards and came down head first, all spread out and stunned in a big patch of blood. The combatants didn't even look around, but most of the fireroom men edged down the companionway past me to get in behind the boiler. I stayed another half a minute to see what the girl did, and it was worth it. The noise had only paralyzed her when she had nothing else to think about. When she saw that the lieutenant couldn't take care of his men, or of her, or even of himself, she got up and ran to him, propped his head on her knee, and began ripping up his shirt for a wad to plug his shoulder with. Nobody offered any help, but she didn't need any. I went below, and saw, under the smoke, that the boat was still headed for the landing flag, and that another thirty feet would put us in the rock-reef in front of it.

I never went through a harder job of deciding what to do. One thing that Aintree had told me, plain and unmistakable, was that nobody in the engine room was ever to have anything to do with deciding where the boat should go. That was the pilot's job, and nobody else's, and there weren't any exceptions or yes-buts about it. The trouble was that old Simmons, either on account of the smoke or absent-mindedness or excitement or something, wouldn't send down signals or answer the speaking tube. There wasn't time to go above and poke him up. The boat was about to hit bottom, and it was either mind the rules and let her smash, or break them and take her out. I broke them and backed the paddles with every lick of steam she had. We went clear out into the main current before I eased her down.

I couldn't see that I'd hurt anything doing it, either. It kept the boat under us, and it did what the lieutenant had got shot trying to do. The shooting petered out and stopped. The Gatling gun jammed, and the men, once they were clear of their own smoke and could see that they hadn't piled the shore with savage corpses, looked sheepish and crowded around the lieutenant to see how bad he was hurt. Aintree got the engineer handcuffed to the rail for safekeeping, and old Simmons came out of whatever trance he had been in and rang for steam ahead. Nobody appeared to have any notion that they had really been shooting at people until a man came out from behind the sand dune and picked up the landing flag and waved it. He was bareheaded and barefooted and wrapped in a yellow blanket, but he was white, and I knew him. He was Flem Oliver.

Nobody could decide whether to turn in and pick him up or not. The lieutenant, who had the real say about it, was stretched out limp in the main cabin, and Diana Owens wouldn't let anybody disturb him. Getting shot had made a different man out of the lieutenant. He looked like nothing but a badly bunged-up kid, and she treated him like one. She didn't remind him of any of his claims or guarantees, and she seemed even glad to have found somebody who was past making any more of them. I couldn't help thinking what a lot of unnecessary trouble Flem Oliver had gone through to keep his misrepresentations from her, she took the lieutenant's so calmly. Of course, Flem Oliver hadn't enhanced his youthful appeal by getting himself shot. He was a whole lot too smart for that.

He showed his smartness in getting the boat turned in again. Nobody was willing to take the responsibility of landing for him, and he turned around and waved at the sand dune. A whole mob of white people came flocking out from behind it—women among them, which was a class of passengers that any boat on the river had to stop for, orders or not. I didn't have to look at them more than once to remember where it was I had seen those two dead horses before. It was the outfit of snake charmers and glass-eating talent we had helped pack at Deschutes Landing in the morning. They had been moseying along the rock flats when Flem Oliver swam off from the boat, and they loaned him a horse and brought him along, counting on his experience with the country to make their trip easier for them.

He could hardly claim to have lightened the path for them, though none of them was hurt except little Eva, who had tried to shoot live shells in her blank cartridge pistol and burned herself in the eye when it backfired. The sand dune protected the rest of them. When the shooting started, they simply bushed up behind it and stayed there, agreeing if they ever got out, they would hang Flem Oliver for getting them in such a fix. Flagging the boat for a lift had been his suggestion. Nobody said so, but I suspected that shooting back at it had been his suggestion too. I never saw his equal for raising excitement out of everything he touched.

V

The engines needed watching, so I didn't go on the saloon deck to greet the pilgrims. The soldiers brought all their baggage below, and we ran along without anything happening except to little Eva, who tried to let a lifeboat down the falls with herself in it, until we had left Cabin Creek and finished scouting for Walpapi raiders without finding any. Then Flem Oliver came down and sat on an ammunition box without saying anything, and Aintree followed him to look things over. I was doing all right and I knew it, but you couldn't have got him to say so. "You backed that wheel without signals from the pilot, didn't you?" he said. "What for?"

I told him it was because there weren't any signals, and the boat was about to rip her hull off.

"Simmons laid down to dodge bullets, and forgot," he said. "That's his fault, and he'll hear from it, but it doesn't excuse you. You knew the rules. I wish you had a regular engineer's license, because I'd take it away from you. Maybe we can get one for you by Spring, if you learn to keep your men at work and learn your engines. I've made good steam-hogs out of worse timber than you, when I had to."

He left, and Flem Oliver pulled himself out of his thoughts. "You didn't tell me that girl was on the boat," he said.

I hadn't, but I was too pleased over old Aintree's promise to feel very remorseful. After all, what did Flem Oliver have to complain about? He had squared his count with the engineer, and he certainly wasn't likely to have the girl paying him any more unexpected visits, the way she'd looked at that lieutenant. I told him so, but, instead of his humor improving, it got worse.

"She's going to marry that blamed coffee-cooling shavetail," he said, glaring at his bare toes. "You know yourself that he bluffed and swelled and put on more dog in front of her than I ever did. The difference was that he got caught at it. I was smart enough not to, and what happens? She feels sorry for him because he's so boyish and helpless, and so she's going to marry him. She just got through telling me. Hoping I'd buy her an expensive wedding present out of my large fortune, I suppose.

... No, that wasn't it, of course, but can you tell me why parents always want their children to be born with brains?"

Both bells rang, and I cut steam to let some drift ice go past. It was a luxury to mind signals with that engine, though for genuine speed she needed another row of steam pipes.

"Other people manage to live without that girl," I said. "You claimed you didn't want to marry anybody, and you ducked out on her after she'd come all the way from Portland to see you."

He scratched off a kind of before-hanging laugh. The girl hadn't come to see him. She was on a steamboat picnic, and she remembered that he had asked her, if she ever got to his country, to let him show her around. It was nothing. Little Eva, the side show brat, had pretended it was to bedevil him, but it wasn't and never would be.

"And I didn't want to marry anybody anyhow," he said. "Hell, I never decide what I want till it's too late to pick. I wouldn't take the job of punching this mud-sucking old steamboat, because I'd be afraid I was missing something more interesting. You're lucky enough to like it, and sensible enough to grab it. I'll bet you could work here for twenty years without ever getting tired of it."

I hoped I could. People differ, of course, but I couldn't see anything extraordinary about liking a nice-acting engine or feeling at home on that river. As for getting tired of it, that was out of the question, because it wasn't the same river or the same country any two days in the world. The water changed speed and level, and the hills changed color all the time; there were always new clearings coming in and old ones going back to grass, old towns growing and new ones building; herds of mule deer coming down from the hills with new fawns in the Fall, and flocks of wild geese moving out about the time camps of Indians moved in. Not very monumental episodes, any of them; but when you like a place, changes in it that a man like Flem Oliver would consider nothing but monotony, interest you. It was the same way, I knew, with Diana Owens. She wasn't marrying the lieutenant because he was smart enough to keep his promises, but because he was man enough to stand by them, and because she liked him.

But there was no use trying to make Flem Oliver understand that. I tried to, but it only made him meaner and madder. I gave up, and told him to work off his indignation on the woodpile. He grabbed it and pulled the whole end of it down on top of himself and smashed a couple of crates with it.

"That's nothing," he said, getting up from under the logs. "Hell, if wood-slinging is all I'm good for, get out of my way!"

We got out of his way. He had smashed the two crates with the big friendly woman's collection of reptiles, and all the bull snakes and rattlers came crawling out to get close to the warm boilers. The heat made them so lively it took the big woman most of the afternoon to toll them back into captivity so we could run the engines.

There wasn't any use talking, that Flem Oliver could raise more excitement with fewer ingredients than anybody I've ever read about in history. People who knew him used to blame all his tribulations onto his smartness, the same as he did, and the same as I did as long as I worked with him. But you couldn't really give his case the study it deserved while you were around him. He kept you too busy dodging and keeping yourself from getting drowned, shot, tomahawked, ship-wrecked, snakebitten, or arrested as an accessory to some apparently simple stratagem that turned out to be indictable after he got halfway through it.

It was only when you thought him over at long range that you began to see his real talent wasn't smartness. He was pretty smart, but where he really glittered was in being able, every single time, to build ten cents' worth of timber into a generous seven hundred dollars' worth of hell. It was a good thing he didn't marry that Diana Owens, because she couldn't have felt comfortable alongside a gift like that. I didn't feel comfortable myself, sometimes, but I'm glad I stood it. He was the only proof I've got that the country, even at that early day, had started to raise geniuses. He wasn't much use to anybody, but he was a genius.

A Town in Eastern Oregon

The early settlements in Oregon have had enough books written about them to patch the Oregon Trail its full length. Some of them are first-class reading; many are feebleminded puling; but nearly all of them make, either explicitly or by implication, the mistake of crediting the whole keelwork of Pacific Coast civilization—such as it is—to the pioneers who crossed the plains to farm.

Such an injustice needs to be corrected. For one thing, farming lacked a great deal of being the pioneers' fundamental lust. It was, in general, their trade, but only in the most hopeless simpletons did it amount to an ambition. The true explanation would do the early settlers more credit, and would reveal, no doubt, a connection with the propaganda of Senator Thomas H. Benton, who was far-sighted enough to see the West as the gateway to the Orient, and to arrange that, if it came to a plebiscite on sovereignty, the United States should count enough heads to win it. There were, of course, other and deeper motives. The pioneers were not fools. Indeed, they averaged higher than any men the West is ever likely to see again, and to circulate the impression that they were a set of simple-minded, big-hearted goofs is to plaster them with an insult which they do not deserve. It is wrong, also, to give them credit for a structure on which other men did part of the work. In Western Oregon, the French-Canadians of the Hudson's Bay Company had laid down settlements before any of the emigrations started. The pioneers, when they did come, merely took up the job where the *voyageurs* had called it a day.

In Eastern Oregon, they did even less. The country was wild, arid, lonesome as death, and swarming with strong, hostile tribes of Indians. More, it was 200 miles inland, and what the emigrants wanted was the gateway to the Orient, which lay along the coast. They went through the sagebrush without stopping. Civilization came to Eastern Oregon, not by farms, but by the institution of the town.

Towns jibed with the country. Even the Indians preferred to gang together in villages, and one of their *wickiyup* communities, in the gorge of the middle Columbia, has existed longer than any white man's town in America. Not even Saint Augustine or Santa Fé is older. The inhabitants look it. There are old Indians in it who appear to be not a day less than a hundred and twenty years old; and there are smells that can't possibly have started later than five centuries ago. Both smells and centenarians could, no doubt, be done away with by the use of chloride of lime, carbolic soap, and kicks in the trousers. But the Indians haven't the ideal of betterment. To them, both stinks and dotards mean something more valuable than a shiny outside: to wit, permanence and stability. They prefer to let things alone. That is why they have become a subject race. Ideals would probably have saved them, as they have so often saved the town of Gros Ventre.

Gros Ventre is a town on the south bank of the Columbia River, at the foot of the middle rapids, where the deep cliffs of the river-gorge break southward into low, pleasant hills. The amount of devilment and cussedness that its citizens have succeeded in whipping out of its corporate limits since it was founded would line Hell a hundred miles. From 1835 down to the present, it has been one long war for righteousness, and in that war the winning of a victory has meant only the opening of an offensive against something else. Just now, the fight is against allowing youths under twenty-one to play pool.

They will win that, as, of course, they ought to. Not that they have always won. The betterment campaign of 1835, which they undertook before they had learned to measure their meat, ended in defeat, because the job was too much for them. It would have been too much for anybody, for it was no less than the conversion of the Indians to Methodism.

The missionaries themselves were not to blame. It is true that they banked a good deal on journalistic veracity, but worldlier men than Methodist missionaries have fallen for sob-stuff about the Land of Opportunity, even in our own time, and in less reliable journals than the *Christian Advocate and Journal and Zion's Herald*, where, in the issue of March 1, 1833, an artist signing himself G. P. D. honed his quill and let himself go upon the subject of the Flathead Indians, who, he alleged, yearned for religious instruction.

They were so desperate for a dose of the true doctrine, he proceeded, that it was pitiful, and almost an impediment to travel. A delegation of them had even hiked all the way from Oregon to St. Louis to try to find a preacher who would expound the divine mysteries unto them. The worst of it was, they failed to locate one. To anybody who has ever trusted an Indian with an errand in town, that part of the yarn is entirely convincing. But the readers of *Zion's Herald* did not stop there: they swallowed the whole thing, and, in three weeks after the story came out, the Methodist Mission Board had begun to investigate where the Flathead Indians lived, and to receive applications from clergymen anxious to go there. In 1835, the Gros Ventre Mission opened for business, and found that there wasn't any. Indians there were in plenty, but their thirst after the Gospel had been all in the eloquent G. P. D.'s head. They did not hanker to be freed from "the chains of error and superstition." They did not want a preacher, or any number of preachers, and the assurance that they would go to Hell when they died made them laugh.

The Gros Ventre missionary was a good sport. He looked over the flock which he had been appointed to lure into the fold, and decided that, after all, if they didn't want salvation, they probably weren't worth it. He was ahead of his time, and he was also out of step with the tradition of improvement which Gros Ventre later took up and stuck to. The other missions which went into Eastern Oregon at the same time took their disappointment harder. At Lewiston and at Waiilatpu, where the savages showed equal obstinacy in running behind the dope-sheet, the two emissaries of Christianity went so far as to beat the Everlasting Mercy into their unwilling disciples with a cowhide. The disciples stood it as long as they could, and then hit back. They killed all the white men—there were fourteen of them—at Waiilatpu, and carried off fifty-three women and children as prisoners.

The avaricious and unchristian Hudson's Bay Company ransomed them, rescued the whites at other threatened missions, and managed to cool the Siwashes down; it is not unlikely that a fresh missionary would have been able to take up the work in perfect safety. But the divines of the Mission Board had been scared, and it was they who were putting up the money. They now called in all their men from all the missions, Gros Ventre included, and put Eastern Oregon on their blacklist as an apostolic field. When they next appeared in Gros Ventre, it was not to call souls to repentance, but to bring suit for damages against the United States War Department for putting a fort on part of their abandoned mission.

They got judgment for $24,000, for, even without them, the town had got over its setback, and was headed once more down the pathway to perfection. The pioneers were coming through, the government had garrisoned Gros Ventre to guard them out of Eastern Oregon, and with the soldiers came a class of men who were to bring to success the job at which the missionaries had failed; merchants, traffickers and money-changers, peddling at the heels of the army, were started at their task of boosting Gros Ventre to its final eminence in civilization.

II

The War Department, in garrisoning Gros Ventre, did only what diplomacy and strategy made compulsory. The Indians, who had taken nearly ten years to work themselves up to killing the strong-armed missionaries at Waiilatpu, had passed from the control of the Hudson's Bay Company to that of the Indian Bureau, and the change made them nasty. The district Indian agent was an ex-clergyman who, it appeared, still believed the unlucky piece in *Zion's Herald*, and so set out to provide the simple savages with a decalogue, a set of ethics, and the proper machinery of enforcement. The Hudson's Bay Company men had controlled the tribes by playing sub-chiefs one against the other. The new Indian agent got rid of all the sub-chiefs, who now spent all their time talking instead of making their tribes live up to his new code of laws, and, in their place, furnished each tribe with a despot, who, he figured, would get action.

Action was what he almost immediately got. A chief strong enough to keep his subjects out of mischief was also strong enough to force them into it, and all the new appointees took their men out to hunt for trouble. They shot up and butchered small emigrant trains, raided prospectors' camps, and even talked of crossing the Cascades to loot the Western settlements and run all the whites into the ocean. They needed, perhaps, to be well thrashed; but, for that, there were not men enough. The best the War Department could do was to garrison a point which commanded the Cascade passes and the emigrant trail to the East, and the deserted mission at Gros Ventre filled the bill. With a fort and two companies of infantry, the town once more loped forth upon its career of lofty destiny.

The soldiers, however, turned out to be the least important ingredient of the place. They were, of course, a kind of assurance that the Waiilatpu episode would not be repeated; but, beyond merely sitting around and looking ugly, they contributed nothing to the life of the municipality. The real civic bonanza lay in the camp-followers who had tagged into Gros Ventre with them—sutlers, peddlers, card-slickers and horse-holders, who, setting up their counters and chuck-a-luck tables as usual, found themselves distinguished and looked up to as propertied men. Not by the military, of course, but by the emigrants, to whom the sight of established business was like a piece of home in a country where everything else was against them. Gros Ventre became an emigrant rest-station, where they fattened their teams, patched their harness, boiled their bedding, and nerved themselves for the last lap of their trip across the Cascade mountains. It was a tough and dangerous road, and they regarded the Gros Ventre men, who didn't have to travel it, much as a hobo regards the proprietor of an eating-house.

It is not of record how much time it took for the ex-sutlers to get over their modesty and decide that the emigrants were right. It can't have taken long, however, for they next appear in history as signers of a petition to the War Department, asking that the soldiers be sent out to whip the Indians. As customers, the boys in blue had lost their standing. What was wanted now was not their trade, but their services. Why didn't they get out and do something? Why, instead of lying around a comfortable fort, stuffing themselves with government grub, didn't they go out and prune a horn or two on the Siwashes? How could a town ever hope to amount to anything with hostiles yanking off scalps practically at the city limits?

It was the spirit of Community Betterment speaking, for the first time in its own voice. Perhaps they were not yet conscious of an ideal. It was enough for them that there were other towns where a man could run a business and bring up a wife and children without the risk of having them tomahawked, and they wanted their town to be the same. The Army officers, however, lacked sympathy. They alleged that the Indians would mind their own business if the whites let them alone, and that, if they wanted to have wives and children, they had better go somewhere besides a frontier post to do it. The merchants' legitimate business dealings with the Siwashes were rudely termed swindling; they were always getting themselves into a private war, and then expecting the Army to finish it for them. This time they would get fooled.

The merchants took no notice of these ignoble charges. Instead, they went back upon Washington again, to get the department commander thrown out of his job. The whole campaign, up to the time hostilities actually began, lasted almost fifteen years, and even then the new commander, though he fought the Indians willingly enough, didn't tie into them to suit the citizens' notions. He wanted merely to thrash them into good behavior. The business men cared nothing about their behavior, good or bad, but wanted them exterminated. There were controversies about that, and a particularly vicious one about the regulars' objection to killing Indian women; but, in the end, idealism prevailed over squeamishness, the single standard of redskin-slaughter was enforced, and the hostile tribes were thrashed into helpless, starving mobs, and shipped off to distant reservations to die of homesickness. Except strays, and a few inoffensive fish-eating colonies along the Columbia, no Indians remained. Gros Ventre had made its first Civic Improvement.

The one flaw in the triumph was that the pacification had gone farther than it needed to. The Army had whipped the Indians from Gros Ventre, which was all right; but it had whipped them out of all the rest of Eastern Oregon, too, and that was not so good. The town's chief value had been as a refuge, and now there was nothing to take refuge from. Travel fell off. Since one road was as safe as another, the settlers took the Southern line, which was the least rutted. Gros Ventre lost out. Bad luck bred its like, for, on top of this, the soldiers packed up and left for good, under orders for a less peaceful section of country. It was a tough Winter in Gros Ventre without them; but the tide was on the turn, and those who stuck and starved it through came in for their reward. For the settlers took the Eastern Oregon country almost at a grab; and the sternwheel steamboats of the Columbia began to unload for the freight-roads at Gros Ventre.

III

Neither the steamboat men nor the long-line freighters picked Gros Ventre for an unloading-point out of benevolence. The steamboats could get no farther up the Columbia, on account of the unnavigable rapids; and the low-sloping hills behind the town were the only ground for miles where one could take a freight-wagon from the high country to the beach, except by lowering it over a cliff. At the head of navigation, commanding all the roads south and east, Gros Ventre was the commissariat for a country as big as the German Empire, and a whole lot livelier. Its population had been under 500; the steamboat hands alone numbered 2,000, and the freighters, horse-handlers and roustabouts came to half as many again.

The town had not been organized to handle such a mob. Not, perhaps, that its citizens wouldn't have been glad enough to try, but they didn't get a chance to. A report that a town has turned good is like news of a gold-strike. Men came crowding into Gros Ventre to cash in, and the town built back over the hills so rapidly that a string of freighters, returning from the southeastern sheep country, wandered for two days among the new houses trying to find the way downtown.

It would seem natural if the old established citizens of the town had hated the new arrivals who came to claim a share in prey that was none of their killing. But not at all. Instead of opposing each other, they settled down as friendly as buzzards on a strychnined cow, to work on the freighters and rivermen. From that common bond they worked down to one more fundamental, namely, improving the social tone of Gros Ventre.

The freighters were the biggest drawback. For one thing, they charged high for their freight, and hauled slow, which hindered business with outside communities. What was more serious, they were a mob of rough, ill-mannered savages, almost as injurious to a City of Homes as the Indians had been, and far harder to deal with. The most respectable citizens were not safe from insult around them. They got drunk, picked fights, staged runaways down the main business street, shot off guns, broke windows, and, on one occasion, threw lighted kerosene lamps at each other and burned down half the town. One skinner had paralyzed church-goers by parading the street on the Sabbath morning with nothing on but a red flannel undershirt. No city could hold up its head while such persons infested it, and Gros Ventre was determined that, whatever else happened, its head should be full high advanced. The citizens chipped in, helped by the interior country, on subsidies to lure railroads to their city, and got two main lines and eight branches.

The main lines were, in all likelihood, inevitable, though two of them were more than they had any use for. Gros Ventre was so located that no east and west railroad line could miss it without wasting a fortune on grading and bridging. But the branches were something extra, which the citizens had angled for with all their art. It didn't seem possible that they could pick any other terminus than Gros Ventre. The freight roads hadn't, and a team could pull a harder grade than a train. Yet, when the steel went down, Gros Ventre was not the terminus of a single one of the entire eight. The people had trusted too much to their natural advantages, and they had been let down.

In one thing, at least, they had succeeded. They were rid of the freighters, for good and all. Yet, without them, business appeared to have fallen into slack times. The money wasn't coming in the way it used to. The trouble, they decided, was in their not having improved things enough. There were natural resources which needed to be worked over, and the citizens entertained suggestions about them which ranged all the way from a theological seminary to a set of factories to manufacture something. It didn't particularly matter what. For raw material, the country was a very skinny prospect; but the factory idea sounded so good that they built one, anyhow, announcing that they would make glass in it. There was plenty of sand, but something, it turned out, was wrong with it, and the factory became a place where, before the motoring age, Gros Ventre youths took their girls to neck. Their elders decided to put their improvements somewhere else, where they would show. It seemed a pretty good idea to go to work and fix over the Columbia River.

This was carrying Betterment into an entirely new field; for, up to now, the stern-wheelers had gone about their business without much caring where Gros Ventre bloomed or blighted. The railroads had touched them very little, for they were able to underbid almost two-thirds on way freight, and the Big Bend and Palouse wheat countries made up for the cargoes which they lost to the new branches. Gros Ventre was no longer a distributing point, but a *portage*, where the lower river steamers transferred their freight to another line of vessels above the rapids.

It was against this *portage* that the town began to plot, wire-pulling for a congressional appropriation to build a canal around the rapids. They got it. It cost the government $8,000,000, and killed Gros Ventre, as a steamboat terminal, as dead as a hammer. Why they should have wanted it is beyond the power of man to figure. They can scarcely have been infatuated enough to think it would help their commerce to send freight somewhere else, instead of handling it themselves. Nor could it have been a Spirit of Helpfulness, for Gros Ventre didn't think very much of the steamboats, nor of the men who worked on and with them.

Indeed, it may have been mere hatred of the steamboat men, who, like the freighters before them, did not belong in a quiet, respectable City of Homes. They were tough, loud, roughnecked and quarrelsome. They fought each other in the streets, and regarded murder as merely one of the unlucky episodes of a high old social evening. They were too wild to control, too numerous to whip, and, by a very slim margin, too human to shoot. A war like the one that knocked out the Indians would have been the very remedy for them.

Whether intentionally or not, the canal got the same results, for it took away their jobs, and they had to move. Relieved of their hell-raising ruffianism, the town gained in respectability almost as much as it lost in population—about one-fourth. Yet, the canal-builders seem to have been moved by a deeper cause than mere exasperation with a set of loud-mouthed roisterers. Perhaps that started it, but the direct motive was surely something more mystical. Neither profit nor propriety, I should guess, knowing them, but an instinct for fixing things over; for making their town, not what humanity at that stage of the West needed, but what they themselves could live in most comfortably—something safe, mild and predictable.

They wanted a city for home-lovers, in the midst of a country of high-rollers and wild-horse-peelers; and they could only make their town feel as if it belonged to them by making it over. The things they altered might not be any better, but at least they wouldn't feel that they owed them to the wild country in which, after a half-century, they were still actually strangers. I remember a magistrate of the place, to whose court I was hauled as a witness in a case of mayhem. A roistering cow-puncher had chewed a comrade's ear off, and the magistrate, before imposing sentence, explained sternly that what passed for high spirits in Three Notches might be a penitentiary offense in Gros Ventre.

"It's time you out-of-town men found out who this town belongs to," he informed us, as if he suspected us of having divided the ear among us. He was very stern, and the town reporter took notes. "This town belongs to us law-abiding citizens. It ain't yours at all. . . . Huh?"

He glared at the ear-chewing defendant, who had muttered that he didn't want the damned place for a gift, and who now protested that he hadn't said a word, and that it was probably his stomach rumbling.

"It'll have something to rumble about before I'm through with you," replied the magistrate. "This ain't your town. It's ours. We let you use it, and you raise hob around and think you're smart! You!" He glared at all of us, and breathed hard with indignation. "You whip the police, hey? You carry concealed weapons, hey? You buck a cayuse through the main business part of town, hey? You—"

The prisoner had done none of those things. He had merely yielded to momentary impulse, before he noticed what his teeth were clamped on, and he said so. Besides, he ventured, the ear wasn't city property. The crack raised a giggle, and drew him a sentence of six months in the brig. Even that didn't satisfy the Gros Ventre sense of justice. Although we had done nothing except testify, he gave us one hour to leave town.

One of the punchers brought our obvious innocence to his notice. But he was set as granite.

"Maybe you ain't done anything," he admitted. "That ain't sayin' you won't! No, sir! You go somewhere else for your hob-raising! The people of Gros Ventre don't intend to put up with it any more!"

The reporter had taken it down, but, at the time, we presumed that the magistrate had delivered it merely to hear his head roar. But, as the papers informed us within a fortnight, we had done him an injustice. He had been reading us an official bull. The people of Gros Ventre were cleaning house, and hob-raising, of even the most furtive kind, had gone on the death-list. Two companies of militia had appeared, surrounded all the brothels in town, and arrested everybody in them.

IV

The news of the raid filled all the newspapers in the State, but only in Gros Ventre itself was it received in anything but a spirit of levity, which was not unmixed, in the stock country where I worked, with thankfulness that the raid had caught somebody else. Not even the fact that the arrests turned out to have been illegal made any difference in the general self-congratulations. To be arrested was tough luck; but to be pinched in a wenching-house was horrible, because it was funny.

Gros Ventre, everybody agreed, was a good place to stay away from. If they had raided the red-light section once, they would very likely do it again, and it was too much of a chance to take. There were too many other places where people were not so pernickety. The ladies, it turned out, felt the same way, for they all pulled up and left Gros Ventre as pure as the lily in the dell. It could not be learned that any of them even objected to leaving, for their business had not been paying interest on their preferred stock since the steamboat men left. As far as they were concerned, being run out of Gros Ventre was a favor, and not a defeat at all.

Indeed, it seemed that nobody had lost on the affair, except a few scattering individuals. The mayor of Gros Ventre got his name in all of the papers; the militia got credit, which they deserved, for having done what they were told; the men in the stock country were pleased that it had happened before they took their vacations in town; and nobody appeared to feel badly about it except the Gros Ventre bankers, who noticed a falling off in deposits and clearings, and three members of the Anti-Vice League, who had been snared by the militia while gathering evidence, and herded forth to public ridicule until churchmen could rush down and order them turned loose. True, the town had lost population, but the improved tone of cleanness and refinement more than made up for it, and, so far from repining, the citizens made ready to bounce out a few more, on the issue, naturally, of Prohibition.

Up to now, the rum-handlers of the town had managed to hold themselves in place by voting all the cow-punchers who hit town just before election, and by running in hoboes, section-gangs, and all members of the dry party who liked beer, but didn't like to pay for it. All told, these reinforcements gave them just enough of a lead to win with. The dry party used to try to keep even by hauling in the inmates of the poor-farm, but there weren't enough of them. Now, with the cow-punchers gone, and the beer-lovers chastened, the odds were lost. I had been accustomed to make a little side-money from the wet election committee by hauling in stray buckaroos and swearing them in to vote; but now they were so confident of defeat that they wouldn't even authorize me to try. The whole thing was shot, they said, and putting up a fight would only make their licking look worse.

Since they were licked already, I didn't try to argue with them. But I thought then, and still believe, that they could have run Social Betterment a closer heat than any of them imagined. They had lost votes, it is true, but so had the drys, for, odd as it may sound, the bawdy-house inmates invariably favored the side of temperance, and voted it with strength and persistence. Their idea, of course, was not reform, but to remove competition. They sold whiskey, whether a town was dry or not, and the removal of the grogshops, which were more law-abiding, never failed to build up their trade with a boom.

Whether they had counted their votes correctly or not, there was one omen which they had figured right. That was the sudden acceleration of improvement and reform. Hitherto, changes had come only after years of fighting. Now there was almost one new one a day. Prohibition went over with a rush, most of the liquor interests disdaining even to vote; and a system of paved highways carried before the bootleggers had time to agree upon rates and prices.

The highways were Gros Ventre's first purely commercial improvement. They were intended to bring travel into the town, and give the merchants something more to live on than the distinctly waning population. The results from them were a little bit disheartening, for nobody had considered that the same road which brought trade into town would also carry it out. Even the farming population motored to the big city, instead of stopping, as of old, to make the Gros Ventre cash-registers jingle.

From this improvement, they proceeded to the soil itself, and undertook the job of turning their wheat lands into orchard. The bank which financed the project went broke; the land, which was worth $75 an acre for wheat, was worthless as orchard, and couldn't be put back in wheat without pulling out the trees, which could not be done except at a cost an acre of $90.

They tried stratagems to lure back their lost population. A Chamber of Commerce expert sat in, installed a full stock of wheat-samples, pamphlets and form-letters, and succeeded, before they fired him, in fetching upon the town some hundreds of indigents who straightway applied to the county for support, got it, and wrote to all their friends. Then they tried industries again, and subsidized a fruit cannery which had to shut down for lack of any fruit to can; and a sawmill which never ran because there was nothing to saw. Do these stunts sound like stupidity? They were something far more dignified and pathetic—the desperation of a people who, having whipped a wild corner of the earth into a gentility pleasing to their hearts, find that the process has stripped it of anything to live on.

No city in the West could count so many advantages to start with, and they cleaned off every last one of them. How could they have kept them? Indians, freighters, steamboat men, saloons, bawdy-houses—they had to destroy them, for with them life in their town would be too loud and uncomfortable to be worth living. They didn't, it is true, foresee that the consequence would be death, but it is altogether likely that they would have gone ahead with it, even if they had. It was the same instinct that operates in a soldier on the firing-line who, having turned down a hundred chances to rush a machine-gun and be a hero, will straighten up squarely in the line of fire to scratch a place on his leg.

Yet, admitting that their ninety years' campaign for home, fireside and family tranquillity accomplished enough bad to balance every good, it cannot be denied that, without it, they would lack strength for the work before them still. It is not Betterment, in these days; they are even past trying to get back what they have lost. It is hard enough to hang on to what they have left. The population is down to 3,000, and nothing but the fiercest kind of work has held it there. A golf links has kept a lot of them satisfied to put up with the town until times get better; there is an athletic stadium to keep the young blood steady against the same eventuality; an up-to-date water system so the place won't burn down at the threshold of its reward, as it has several times threatened to do. These things came hard, because they cost money, and money is scarce.

The trouble is in the improvements voted when the town had a population of 10,000, and paid for, unluckily, with bonds. Up-to-date schools, $500,000; public auditorium (for receptions and speeches), $150,000; police force and commodious jail, so much; paved streets and highway system, so much. Ten thousand people could afford them; but, now that the bonds are beginning to come due, there are only 3,000 left to pay them. In 1910, the city's tax rate was 1 1/2 cents on the dollar; in 1929 it was four times as much, and the actual increase was twice that, on account of book values having been boosted to make further bond issues look safe. I estimate that the privilege of remaining faithful to Gros Ventre this year will cost every man, woman and child inside its corporate limits about $1.50 a day in taxes. It wouldn't be so bad if they were making anything to pay them with; but nothing comes in. Their trade is almost entirely with each other. If past experience had not strengthened them to hope and endure, they wouldn't be able to stand it.

That, however, is their platform—to hope and endure, to tough the thing through, to hang on and wait for the boom which, after every improvement heretofore, has always turned up to save them. Somebody may strike petroleum in the hills; maybe a syndicate will come along and build a ten-million-dollar power plant on the rapids; the climate, experts say, is as nearly ideal for moving-pictures as that of Hollywood. Things will get better. Times have been hard before, and they always picked up and took a surge. Why leave, when every day, even at $1.50 a head in taxes, is certainly bringing the good streak that much closer? Why go to some other town, where the job of Betterment might have to be done all over again?

Team Bells Woke Me

The wagon-freighters into Eastern Oregon in 1906 had a night-camp on the Upper John Day River, in a country which, having since turned its population over to the payroll towns on the Coast and all its land to the Federal Farm Loan banks, now has neither freight-camps, freight-haulers, nor freight-users. Economic progress has made it merely another hole in Nature's pants; but it was a paying section in the teaming days. Prosperous and dissatisfied farmers worked every creek-bottom, putting up hay for the freight-teams at $50 a ton, and the freight-camp at dusk in the Spring wool-hauling season, with all the cooking-fires shining through the wagon-spokes like a Chicago jail burning down, made me uneasy the first time I saw it. I was eleven years old, playing hookey from the bucksaw detail at home to help Tamarack Jack Pooler haul wool, and the animation and racket in the freight-camp made me feel that humanity had already jammed the country till it popped at the seams. If they kept on coming at this rate, I thought, they would crowd the open country out of existence, and I didn't want them to.

Unharnessing, Tamarack Jack told me that I needn't worry. The willow flat did sound like payday at a cavalry post, with fires, arguments, whiskers, bedclothes, tinware, stray dogs, sucking colts trying to locate their mothers, and chorded copper team-bells plunking as a late string wheeled in to feed up and spread down; but there were only about thirty outfits in the camp. They covered considerable ground, on account of the sixty wagons and three hundred horses; but they were nothing to compare with the crowds that he had seen there. In the '90s, the place had camped sixty outfits a night regularly. In the Indian outbreaks of the '70s there had been more life on this one road than there was now in the country. Counting Indians, of course. An old Piute buck who hung around the freight-camp to panhandle the left-over scraps had once headed a village of twenty wickiyups. Now he claimed title to four, inhabited by a bunch of cavernous-gutted grown sons who stayed with him because he rustled their victuals for them. They weren't worth killing, and the old buck, who would undoubtedly call on us before the evening was out, knew it, and boarded them anyway.

"Because it makes him feel like he's still a chief," explained Tamarack Jack, spreading out harness, "even if it's only over a set of bums. . . . I'll tie them horses. Some of 'em fight, and you don't know which ones to keep separated. Tag around and learn things, that's what a boy your age ort to do. You study about Indian fightin' in school, don't you?"

Tamarack Jack was one of the best freighters on the line. He caught his teams straight out of the wild bunch on the range, and broke them to work by dragging them into harness and working them. The blacksnake whip around his neck was merely a badge of office: he never whipped his horses. If their gait needed correcting, he threw rocks at them. Heaving from the saddled near-wheeler, on the go, he could hit as many as three with one rock. He never apologized for taking a drink of whiskey in the presence of a youngster, or volunteered long explanations about how it was only good for elderly men broken by exposure and sorrows. Instead, he always reached his flask back as if offering a swig, and then corked it and put it away, pretending solemnly that it had been refused. All the kids liked him in spite of the interest he affected in their schooling, which came either from politeness or because he had never had any schooling himself.

"This old Siwash can learn you things about Indian fightin' that I'll bet that school-teacher of yourn never heard of," he said. "I'll poke a couple of drinks down him, and you prop your ears and pay attention. You'll learn some history to take home with you. *Klahowyam*, Spencer!"

The old Piute was wrinkled and skinny, with two braids of gray hair end-bound with drugstore twine. He was all faded except at the eyes, which were black as obsidian. The Mother Goose conceit about beggars on horseback couldn't have been among his memory gems; but he was a beggar, and he not only rode a horse, but led two pack-ponies to take his plunder home on. His saddle had been inherited from the United States Army, and he ate a two-handed piece of apple pie with enjoyment until Tamarack Jack winked and stuck up one thumb. Then he dismounted, stowed the pie on a pack, and started the two pack-ponies home with a cut of his quirt. His people, it seemed, were fussy about getting their meals on time. Was there any brandy? For four drinks he was willing to do a scalp-dance with genuine scalps. For a bottle, he would—

"To hell with your scalp-dance," Tamarack Jack told him. "I'll give you two drinks, and then I want you to tell this kid about Indian fightin'. He's studyin' it in school, and it'll help out with his education. There ain't anything historical about watchin' you get drunk and jump around with your clothes off. Come around back of the wagon where everybody can't see us."

Whiskeying an Indian had to be done on the sly, because of the law which, in those days, was respected even when it wasn't obeyed. The old Piute came back, wiping his chin and breathing deep, and sat down. "White man *kultus*," he announced, after a little thought. "Bad! Me kill 'em—shoot 'em, cut 'em, stick 'em—" He ran through a list of other things he had done to them in the days when he had his strength. It was pretty stout stuff. I hadn't imagined that Indian hostilities ever took quite such a personal form. The only Indian stories I had heard were from people the hostiles had failed to catch. Of the Indians, I had seen only a hard-riding, good-natured set of berry-peddlers who embarrassed townspeople by nursing papooses and settling family rows in the middle of the business district. Here was a new side to the subject. I stopped feeling uneasy about the country's waning wildness. There was such a thing as having a country too damned wild.

I must have looked shaky, for the old buck went back again to his table of premises, which he had laid down as a kind of ethical foundation to excuse his enormities. All white men, he reminded me, were bad. Columbus had been bad, for not staying at home and minding his own business. The freighters were bad. He waved his hand to take in all the men whose large-handedness with cooking measures kept him and his whole gang from starvation, or, worse, from having to go to work. They were all *kultus*, all lowdown sons of leglifters. Murders, mutilations, rapes, tortures and unnatural abuses were too good for them. Shoot 'em. Cut 'em.

And so on. The two drinks were beginning to take hold and talk up. The freighting trade was pretty well mangled by the time Tamarack Jack appeared from behind the wagon, about two-thirds drunk, and explained that he was going to leave us two to entertain each other. "I'll go over and borrow a piece of fresh beef for supper," he said, standing over us with one foot in the fire. Among the wagons, somebody sang "The Dying Ranger" to a fiddle, while a couple of his audience threw rocks at the dogs so they wouldn't howl and spoil it. Tamarack Jack took his foot out of the fire and put one hand on my head benignly. "Spencer'll tell you about this history business," he assured me. "Once he gets started, all hell can't stop him till he's finished. All he tells you is gospel truth. All them freighters got exterminated, just like he's told you."

He had, of course, mistaken Spencer's ill-natured spouting for historical reminiscence. Still, he was merely a few years ahead of time, for, though it wasn't history then, it is now. All the freighting traders did get exterminated, just as the old Piute who lived on their extravagance hoped they would.

II

Tamarack Jack claimed freighting as his profession, but he made most of his money out of his genius for horse-breaking. Of his string of ten horses at the start of a trip, six would be wild, new-shod cayuses that had never before felt iron or leather. At the end of three hundred miles of road, they would be honest, well-broken work-horses, worth from $50 to $80 apiece; and he would sell them and run in another bunch of fence-breakers from the bunch-grass. Three days in a dark barn, and they would step into the collar for him as if they had been doing it for twenty years, without a spark of meanness except to strangers and to one another.

He named them after public characters, probably because it gave a flavor to their habit of fighting on the picket-line. On the trip I went with, Frances E. Willard couldn't be staked with the rest of the *caballad*a because she insisted on biting big hunks out of William Jennings Bryan; Laura Jean Libby and Susan B. Anthony got along excellently with the Great Commoner, but they bit each other, and would also slip their halters to chase off after any barefooted stallion that came within wind of them; and Alice Roosevelt and Emilio Aguinaldo had a mortal feud on, which ended with Emilio caving in three of Alice's ribs so that she had to be shot.

The name, it is gratifying to add, didn't perish with her. Tamarack Jack changed his horses a dozen times a year, but he never changed the names at all. His off-pointer, regardless of sex, color or disposition, was always Alice Roosevelt, and all the other monickers stuck as inflexibly. The horses didn't mind, and it saved Tamarack Jack the trouble of inventing and learning a whole set of new names every time he sold his string down.

Freighting and horse-breaking wasn't a usual combination on the road, but there were personal marks by which each freighter could be remembered. Big Simon and Little Simon Madance were father and son who looked alike, ran opposition lines to a little watertrough town in the Lava Beds country, and hated each other with a fury all the deadlier because neither was able to give any reason for it. They could neither stand each other nor let each other alone, and they ended along in 1909 with a challenge race down the old Sherar toll-grade, which Big Simon won by hubbing his firstborn, outfit and all, over a three-hundred-foot pitch to die under his pile of tangled horses. The only thing about it that the other freighters appeared to mind was that it hadn't happened sooner, and that it hadn't killed both of them. Sociability died wherever they were, as it did around Big Foot Larsen, who, loyal to his racial tradition of Scandinavian gloom, had married a squaw and then eaten her during a hard and lonely Winter.

According, that is, to the story they told on him behind his back. It may have been merely their way of accounting for his expression, which was so Strindbergian that even squaw-eating seemed scarcely an excuse. I didn't believe he had eaten her, because he didn't look bright enough to have thought of it; but I was afraid of him anyway. I wasn't afraid of Greene Tucker, though he was even meaner on account of having been an Indian war hero. He had held a stone milk-house full of women and girls against a Shoshone war-party in 1877, and whipped the whole band with a neckyoke and two kettles of boiling water, fighting most of the set-to with a knife-rip across his abdomen.

It crippled him for life, for the rescued women all got sick when he called on them to sew it up, and he had to do it himself. Unused to needlework, he sewed too deep. The muscles drew up, and the only reward his heroism got him was a life long stoop, like a man looking for a four-leaf clover, and a lifelong grudge against creation for not doing something about it.

His sour temper would have made him a continental pest, if it hadn't been for the rip-staving set of tunes he could whack out of a fiddle. Nothing could have been a more compact study in overlapping humors than old Greene Tucker bowing it up on a wagon-tongue, his eyes set in a gall-shot glare as if he hoped his thrums and double-stops would poison everything they struck, while the tune itself—usually a slippery old hoe-down like "Leather Breeches" or "Hell Among the Yearlings" —cackled to his face that he was a liar, and that he didn't hope anything of the kind.

It would have been easy to have played badly if he had sincerely wanted people to feel badly; and it would have been impossible to heave himself into a mere piece of dance-music if his arteries had really contained as much bile as he pretended. I never heard him play any tune coldly or indifferently. Probably he never realized that his perkiness leaked out on him through his fiddling; probably he didn't even know that there was any perkiness in him at all. Good humor, it seemed, didn't always lie at the surface of the mind, nor bitterness always among the profundities; and either, if it set deep enough, could be involuntary and incurable.

Frank Chambeau was the only example, in the entire Eastern Oregon freighting country, of a man who babied his horses. Not merely to work them humanely and see that they got enough to eat. Everybody did that, for the same reason that a carpenter takes care of his tools. Chambeau hugged and kissed his horses, carried pones of bread to deal out to them every two miles, rubbed them down with expensive hair-tonic, and bought silver harness-studs, conchas, spreader-rings, hame-knobs, and even a full set of silver-alloy team bells with housings of bright orange goatskin.

An ordinary team, strung with such a Siwash get-up, would have run away, out of self-consciousness. Chambeau's horses had no run in them. They were overfed, grizzle-headed old strawbellies that couldn't be left standing unwatched for ten minutes for fear they would all go to sleep and fall down. Resting them at the foot of a grade, he would distribute bread and endearments all round, and then address the string of dozing, limp-lipped old plugs with a personal appeal.

"Now, babies," he would explain, "here's this hill, and here's papa dependin' on you to pull it for him. You're goin' to do that for papa, ain't you?"

They did it for him, even over humps that other outfits were double-teaming to get over. He claimed it was because they appreciated sentiment and hand-holding, which I didn't believe then or thereafter. Yet he must have had some tap on them, or why should they have held his wagons dead still on the steep Shaniko grade for eleven hours while he lay drunk in the road with his head a foot from the wheel? No other horses would have done that, petting or not.

Windy Missou was the biggest-built man on the line—six feet seven, three hundred pounds with his shoes off and his pockets empty, and strong enough to dehorn a bull barehanded. He was also the biggest coward. He slept in his wagon because he was afraid of snakes on the ground, and he kept a lantern burning all night because he was afraid of the dark. He ended by killing a young feed-yard hay-peddler who had tried to shut him into an unlighted granary for a joke, and never came back from the penitentiary. Big John Payne had served in the Philippines, and carried a collection of dark, gristly objects which he claimed were dried ears of the gu-gus whom he had personally dispatched for Civilization and Liberty.

Uncle Ike Bewley had been a lieutenant in the Civil War, had buried seven wives—nearly all of them white—and he chafed with uneasiness for fear his manly fires might cool before he could land an eighth. There was some excuse for feeling nervous, for he was seventy-four years old, and he had proposed to every girl in the country so often that they had all stopped being polite to him. His persistence was a regional joke; and yet there was a lot more to him than mere senile obsession. Uncle Ike had seen enough of death, between his wives and the Civil War, to know it well. Knowing it would land on him, he wasn't in the least afraid of it; only of life, for fear he wouldn't manage to spend the little he had left of it as he wanted to.

Those were freight-camp men. Not all of them, nor a just impression of any as I saw them in the clearing around Greene Tucker's fiddling-stand. They had unloaded a keg of whiskey from a saloon shipment, and, with a gimlet to tap it and a straw to imbibe it through, had given the place a tone shading from camp-meeting exuberance to camp-meeting prayerfulness. The keg helped the effect. It had become, because of the kneeling position in which they had to tackle it, a kind of sacramental altar, theological, compelling, and awful. The liquor was low. To reach it, each man in turn knelt, pressed his forehead against the keg-staves in a long, breathless fervor, and pulled loose with a soul-riven gulp that would not have disgraced any experience-meeting in the land.

Minors, however, were not welcome. Tamarack Jack wove over and ordered me back to our wagon. I embarrassed the men, he explained. They couldn't cut loose with me around, for fear it would be a bad influence. I had better go back to the old Indian, who, besides being educational, needed to be watched so he wouldn't prowl around and steal loose property.

"Go on back, now," said Tamarack Jack firmly. "Cook yourself a feed, and put enough in the pot so the old Siwash'll have something to take home with him, and give him what's left of the small bottle. It's in Alice Roosevelt's nosebag on the trail wagon. Give him that, and he'll tell you some things that'll help with your schoolin'. You learn about Indian fightin' in school, don't you?"

I went back, feeling misused. Nowadays, I would treat a ten-year-old kid about the same way he treated me; but I would still deny that there was much sense in doing it. The freighters were, it was true, a little off-color in their merriment, and they played one game with a row of ten-cent pieces laid out on a wagon-tongue that was certainly no treasure to describe to the home-folks.

But the Indian wars had run through stuff that made even the freighters' little sub-surcingle competitions seem as harmless as anteyover. Why bar me from one and ram my nose in the other? I hoped the old Indian would have stolen himself a load and left with it.

He hadn't. He had found the small bottle, and had been bitten through the hand fooling around the horse-line in the dark. But he had no notion of quitting me with his homicide record half-told. With the tooth-marks red on his skin and whiskey dripping from his breath, he told me about Indian wars, past and to come, in a long, blurred monotony of murders and manglings that ended when the first team bells jingled for the road at daylight.

III

The one season of the year when freighting was pleasant, with the happy, busy importance of peace-time maneuvers at an Army headquarters or protracted meeting in a cracker settlement, was the Spring rush of wool-hauling. Then, with the roads springy and dustless, new grass and water, and a sure cargo both ways for every rig that could carry one, the wagons packed the road with a close, double-columned line, flowing between horizons like a river. The team bells shook out their first clatter at daylight, tolling dry goods, groceries, fence-posts, spring millinery, and Cyrus Noble's Favorite Prescription from railhead to the Shoshone deserts, with cow-town kids from the home bucksaw to tag along and see where they landed. The freighters welcomed company, or pretended to; and the bells, ringing so far out on the road that one could only locate mid-column by the far drift of vapor the teams shed into the sky, were too much to hold out against.

They were not the common bellyband castanets that one sees in pictures of sleighing scenes. Freight teams were too tony for such fifteen-cent-store tinware. They carried real music-making bells, with the same accuracy of tuning and much the same range as the chimes of a modern orchestra. Mostly, they were cast in thin bronze, and set five bells in a strap which fitted over the hames to ring in time with the horse's shoulders. Each set of five struck one major chord, as C, E, G, C, E. To protect them from the weather, and to prevent them from sounding harsh or tinny, they were muffled in a housing of goat's wool. It made them ring sweet and delicate and woody, like water dripping in a barrel spring.

All the freighters belled their teams, but no two of them ever gave the same reason for doing it. Tamarack Jack explained that the tone and rhythm enabled him to keep track of the team's action with his eyes shut. No horse, he pointed out, could drag back or fall out of step without registering the irregularity on the bells, and also identifying himself, so that Tamarack Jack, by noticing which chord was acting queer, could tell where to administer correction with his rock. Frank Chambeau, who never threw rocks at his horses, claimed the bells helped the teams gait themselves together; somebody else thought they were there to keep the driver from going to sleep, and somebody else that they were a kind of warning signal to notify stations ahead that a freight outfit was coming, so the girls would have time to find their hairpins and get downstairs before it pulled in.

That jibed with an old cow-town story about a freight-horse stampede in the night, which, old-timers related, had been headed by a quick-thinking citizen who wrapped a red bandanna around a lantern and tittered girlishly until the horses, thinking they were up against a red-light house, stopped meekly to wait for the boss to come out and pass around the nose-bags. But both story and explanation seemed a little too pointed to be true. The team bells were part of freighting because they sounded pretty and gave style and ceremony to the business.

To the whole country, for that matter. There was never a wool-hauling column that all the towns didn't turn out for, yelling at the lead-wagons to ask where their freighter was, and mobbing his wagon when it wheeled out of line to weigh in and unload. Between towns, lying on the trailwagon out of range of Tamarack Jack's conversation, watching the sky turn round the earth like a flywheel around a slipping driveshaft, I would hear the smooth, even-toned beat of the team bells break, cast off, and swing into a sharp-stepped drum time, which meant that the horses had sighted country people and were putting on dog to give them an eye-full.

If it was a ranch, Tamarack Jack would put on dog too, stiffening to sit straight and light in the saddle, left hand to hat, right hand on the brake-rope as if he expected his whole outfit to light off at a run any minute. The small kids would be lined along the fence by the watering-trough, the big girls by the front-gate, the women bareheaded by the house, shading their eyes and flapping their aprons in welcome, not merely to new dress-patterns and canned goods and phonograph records, but to the whole United States after a Winter of homesick separation. It was a dry line into that Duck Valley section, and there were times when the homestead watering-troughs looked mighty tempting; but not one of the horses ever spoiled the dignity of the occasion by trying to snatch a drink. They arched their necks and hoofed high and went thirsty to give those people the ceremonious parade their enthusiasm deserved.

They showed off the same way in front of the Indian camps, which Tamarack Jack never straightened up for except when some elderly buck made the recognition-sign of slapping himself open-handed across the mouth. Even then his response was only formally polite. The Indians came out to look at us, exactly as the farm women did; but the farm women came because seeing us meant something. To the Indians, we meant merely another object to gawk at, or, if it was a big day, to cheat in a horse-trade.

We meant that much to the other wild life of the country. Little herds of antelope skirmished along the skyline to look us over, pitching back their heads to get our wind, and snapping their tails nervously, all cocked to run if we acted too interested. Coyotes hung out of range, sociable, but cautious, hoping we would lose something they could eat; and bald eagles dawdled along overhead watching for the jackrabbits that our team bells scared up out of the brush. Wild horse-herds drifted along the line sometimes, closing in after dark when the stallion could try his sales-talk on the picketed mares without getting himself shot. If the camp was small, the ground clear, and the mares responsive, he was likely to push his courtship along by stampeding his herd across the picket-line to destroy the peg-ropes. The weight of such a charge would destroy them, all right, and usually it destroyed the mares along with them.

The freighters didn't bother much about wild-horse scares. In open country they always corralled wagons; but none of them ever lost anywhere near as many horses to the wild herd as they got back from it. The wild horses, indeed, were one of the biggest assets the country had. Without them, the Indians, tied to their camps, would have become objects of charity fifty years earlier than they did; a cowboy could no more have afforded to own a saddle-horse than an airplane; horse-breakers like Tamarack Jack—and there were plenty of them—would have been stuck with a talent as unprofitable as writing poetry. Homesteaders would have been hurt even worse. In their lives, the wild herd was as essential as the sago palm to the South Sea Islanders. Broomtail horses were their hog-feed, chicken-feed, dog-rations, garden-compost; the hair made riatas, hackamores and mattress-stuffing; the hides were chair-bottoms, floor-coverings, water-buckets, belt-lacing, and cold-weather vests. Babies in the High Desert were born on horsehair, raised on horse-milk, blooded on horseback, and, pretty regularly, hanged from the neck of one horse in a noose braided from the hide of another.

There were beautiful nags in the wild bunch. The good ones, of course, were the hardest to run down, which accounts for the general notion that all wild horses were hammer-headed scrubs. Only the riffraff got caught. Runts and runners, they are all gone now, fenced out by the wheat-farmers and either starved or else sold in bunches to fertilizer-factories at $3 a head. The country can't be the same without them, and it doesn't deserve to be.

It can't be the same without the old side-hill Indian burying-grounds, either. Even in the freighting days, they were going to pieces fast; but the spots where the dirt shoveled easiest all had them. They were dug shallow and skimpy, probably because the Indians enjoyed manufacturing corpses better than getting rid of them; and the old skeletons, washed out of the earth and wind-polished among the old burial trinkets—grinding-stones and fleshing-knives for the women, bowstaves and horse-furniture for the men, and little toy saddles, papoose-carriers and grass-stuffed buckskin dolls for the children, with big cylindrical stone beads for everybody—had so little of the ordinary graveyard unearthliness that we youngsters would have looted and wrecked them ourselves, merely for curiosity, if the freighters hadn't prevented.

Robbing graves, they explained, was bad luck, and we could either let them alone or else get off and walk. If it had been a fenced-in plot with white posts and epitaphs, money couldn't have tempted us to disturb even the rusty wire of an old wreath. We weren't callous about dead people. Only, they had to keep their skeletons out of sight and show certain conventional trimmings, or we simply couldn't tie them up with the fearful and spooky objects which, instinctively, we believed that death turned people into.

IV

The years 1905-1907 brought the West its heaviest spell of rainfall in recorded history. Draws and gullies flooded, cattle mired on the range, clothes mildewed, and crops, planted mostly by newcomers in ignorance and with a prayer for the deserving, boomed and bore enormously. Momentarily, the anomaly was a nice little stroke of luck. Its eventual effect took longer to work out, and played hell; for the crop-raisers, exultant over their big harvests, refused to listen to old settlers' forecasts for future precipitation, and sat right down to write back East to the folks about the bonanza in sagebrush farming.

The folks, also disregarding warnings, rolled in. Mostly, they didn't stay very long; but there were enough of them to mill heavy while they lasted; and they killed the freighting business colder than a wedge before they left. Crops were poor from the start; but they overlooked that, and concentrated their uproar on the right of a settled farming section to decent communications; and their combined thunderings brought in the branch railroads.

They brought plenty of them. The Shaniko branch, the Condon branch, the Heppner branch, two Deschutes branches, a stub-line East to Prineville, and a narrow-gauge north from the Humboldt River Basin, all piled in as if answering a riot-call; and the freighters jacked up their wagons, rolled the big wheels down to soak in the creek, turned their teams out to the wild bunch, and went out dismally to hunt for jobs.

Curiously, the improved communications didn't help the rainfall of the country at all. The weather turned dry, and, as had been its off-and-on habit for several thousand years, it stayed dry with the completest indifference to all the preparations that had been made to have it wet. The High Desert turned into a nest of hide-outs and cattle-thieves, the Wagon-tire and Owyhee sections into a God-forsaken, do-as-you-please waste. Neither faith, complaints, petitions, nor farmers' protest-meetings helped a particle. The railroads were there, and there was nothing to use them for. A late-started line, rushing steel east across the Cascades from the Rogue River Valley, got scared to a standstill after it had built about twenty miles. Ten years after the rush an auditor for one of the Deschutes lines told me that his company was going behind $15,000 a mile annually, and wishing that it had never been born.

The clamorers had all gone by that time. Their miracle hadn't happened; and their scheme of making it rain on their fields by the Indian system of informing God that it ought to, had worked as badly for them as their doctrine had for the Shoshones, the Bannocks, and the Northern Piutes of 1877, in the outbreak about which old Piute Spencer told me his stomach-turning stories in the freight-camp on the John Day River.

It had been a medicine-war, he told me. A lot of tribes went into it that year—the Sioux, the Utes, the Comanches—everybody. On account of an idea which their theologians had swiped from the white man's ghost book that a man holds up in front of you when they intend to put you in jail. The idea—he had fallen for it along with the rest of them—was that a man could get killed and then come back to life again.

None of the medicine-men claimed credit for inventing such a notion. They admitted that a white man appeared to have done it first, but they argued that, if a white man could do that much, an Indian could do more and better. All that was needed, they promised, was faith. With that, they could lick the whites, restore to life all the warriors who got killed doing it, and bring back all the buffalo herds that had been slaughtered and crowded out by the cattle. Transubstantiation figured in the campaign, for they were ordered to slaughter all the cattle they could, so that the buffalo would have some kind of integument to come back to. For six months, old Spencer bragged, he had lived on nothing but the tongues of slaughtered cows, leaving the rest for the buffalo to inhabit. It was plenty of fun, but it hadn't worked out. The buffalo hadn't showed up. None of the casualties had been restored to health. A lot of them, trying to swim the Columbia ahead of an infantry column, had run into a gatling-gun detail on a steamboat and got cut all to flinders. When the enthusiasm started, he was chief of a big village. Now it kept him humping to stay chief of anything.

He went over a list for me of the men of his village who had got killed and crippled on false expectations, but he didn't mention, except to brag drunkenly, how many white people his witch-doctor plagiarism had got tortured and outraged and murdered.

It was the same with the freighters, driven out of their livelihood by the settlement-rush and railroad-splurge that ended in 1910. The financiers and farmers felt sorry for themselves, but none of them ever mentioned the freighters except to brag about having got the country rid of them. Things hadn't panned out, it was true; but, if they had done nothing else, they had brought modern communications to the sagebrush, and that was something.

It was a whole lot. Merely to have taken away the team bells at morning ought to be enough to get them all immortality. I hope it will.

The Homestead Orchard

The patch of sagebrush which young Linus Ollivant's charge of six hundred lambed ewes had selected as a bed ground for themselves and their progeny was an old starved-out homestead halfway down the slope of Boulder River Canyon, with a few broken-down sheds, a naked slope of red conglomerate that had once been plowed, and a slow trickle of water, small, but holding its flow steady in spite of the drying wind that had driven most of the country's water supply off into the unknown, and a considerable proportion of the country along with it.

It lacked a good deal of being an ideal location for a range camp, being altogether too far from pasture. The sheep, in the three days they had been there, had put in most of their waking hours plodding out to feed and trudging back to water, but they refused to omit either end of the circuit; and Linus, trying to handle them alone until an extra herder could be raked loose from a boxcar and sent out from town, shoved his old herding horse along behind them in the hard glare of a windy twilight and pulled up on the slope above the bed ground to count them into camp before going down into the shadows after them.

The intense blackness of the shadows in that clear air made the camp so dark that even the white tent looked ghostly against the gloom. There was one clear patch of light where the sky reflected in the pond of water, and the mass of dark-wooled old ewes and white-fleeced and inquisitive lambs trailed down into it and stood patterned against it clear and distinct as they drank and crossed to their bed ground for the night.

When they had all crossed, Linus strained his eyes back over the naked rock ridges of the canyon, hoping, because he was too inexperienced at sheepherding to know that it contained no pleasant surprises, that some tail-end bunch of late feeders might still come moseying along in time to bring his count up somewhere near where it belonged.

As might have been expected, he saw nothing except the ridges, ranked one behind another, as frail-looking as if they had been shadows in the pale red sky, darkening to gray at the edges where they touched it. The country's lifelessness was a new thing to Linus. His family had homesteaded on the divide back of that river canyon in his childhood, and one of his few pleasant recollections from that time was of standing on high ground at dark and counting the lights of other homesteads where families had settled to grow up with the country. Now there were no signs of life visible anywhere except in the range camp, where the sheep fidgeted themselves into position for the night and where Linus' father, suffering from a case of dust blindness from the alkali flats back in the desert, fumbled matches into a pile of greasewood in an effort to get a fire started for supper.

His fire building didn't make much headway. His eyes were so inflamed that they were not only useless but so agonizingly sensitive that they had to be kept heavily bandaged against the least light or wind or irritation. Most of his matches blew out while he fumbled around for fuel to touch them to, and Linus, seeing that he was about to run a fit of temper over his own helplessness, gave up hopes of the stray sheep and hurried down to help him out. The fire started easily enough, with a little coddling, and old Ollivant settled gloomily back against the tent pole, hauled his bandage down into place as if he were conferring a favor on society by tolerating the thing, and supplied what entertainment he could by offering conversational leads as Linus got their cooking under way.

"It ain't right for you to have all this work put on you," he said. "It looks like them people in town could have raked up some hobo herder to ship out here; if they had any consideration for a man. How did the sheep handle today? It didn't sound to me like there was as many come in as usual. Did you get a count on 'em?"

Linus raked the fire, clattered buckets and said he had counted them in carefully. He didn't mention what his count had come to. He thought of owning up to it, and then reflected that it would be better to hold back until daylight, when he could make sure that the strays were actually lost and not merely yarded up in the brush, waiting to be sent for.

"They pulled in too tired to make much noise, I expect," he said. "They had a long lug in from pasture tonight. Three or four miles, anyhow."

Side-stepping one disturbing circumstance, he ran squarely into another. His father picked on his estimate of the distance to pasture as if it were a dynamiting he had confessed to.

"We can't carry these old pelters where they've got to trail four miles to pasture," he said. "They'll wear themselves to death on it. If I could trust you to stay out of trouble with people, I'd be about in the notion to hold the whole bunch here in camp for a day or two, till you could scout up some better place to bed 'em. You'd probably land up in some fight, though. Blame it, what does a man have to depend on sheep for, anyhow?"

That was something of a dig; it was Linus' fault that he had been reduced to depending on sheep. Ordinarily, he wouldn't have made a point of that, but enforced inaction made him short of patience. Linus knew enough to humor him.

"It wouldn't do any good to scout around here," he said. "There ain't any other place around here where we could camp sheep at all. You'd see that if you could see what this country looked like."

"If I ever get these old buzzard baits sheared and turned off to ship, I'll kill the next man that says 'sheep' to me," old Ollivant said. "There ain't a jury in the land that would cinch me for it, the provocation I've had." He stopped and lifted one hand for silence for a minute. "I heard horses," he said. "If them people in town have sent out a herder, I'll never complain about my luck again."

It was a handsome offer, and Linus hated to sound as discouraging about it as he felt obliged to.

"It can't be anybody to see us," he said. "We've moved camp five times since you sent for a herder, and the people in town wouldn't know where to send one. You heard some bunch of wild cayuses. Maybe it's Indians out to dig camass."

"It was a shod horse I heard," old Ollivant said.

They both listened, saying nothing and even taking care not to rattle the dishes as they ate supper. Neither of them heard a sound, and Linus fell to thinking over their homesteading days up on the ridge, and of the long string of accidents that had led him back to it against his will. His father had come to that country to homestead a likely quarter-section of sagebrush and find out whether high-altitude soil and climate couldn't be adapted to raising domestic fruits, and he had been obliged to give that up, the orcharding and the homesteading together, through a run of misfortune for which Linus was a good deal to blame.

Afterward he worked around a feed yard in one of the river towns long enough to figure that it led nowhere, and finally he allowed himself to be tempted into taking a half interest in a flock of rickety old ewes, on a chance that, given a decent year and careful handling, they might bring in a crop of lambs worth three times his original investment in them, with the wool figuring at enough extra to cover incidental expenses, taxes, and possibly even day wages for his work.

It had been a tempting project, with little risk showing on its exterior, to begin with. But there had been enough risk about it to make it a gamble, and, like most gambles under taken by people who couldn't afford to lose, things had gone wrong with it almost from the outset.

The roster of bad luck began with a feed shortage and a rise in hay prices, proceeded onward into an outlandishly protracted dry spell and a shortening of the country's water supply, and held on into a failure of all the spring pastures at the exact time when the entire country had counted on them as a last hope to keep going on. A vast invasion of cast-off scrub horses used up what little coarse grass the land had managed to hold on to, and old Ollivant's dust blindness had topped off the whole structure of calamities and left, as far as Linus could see, scarcely any possibility of their pulling through to shearing time with any sheep at all.

He had done his best to keep going singlehanded, and though he had been forced to several emergency measures that his father would not have approved of, he had kept the herd up better than most professional herders would have bothered to do.

He hadn't wanted to pasture back so near the scene of his father's abandoned experiments with dry-country orcharding. That was one of the emergency measures he had not been able to avoid. The sheep had wandered down from the alkali desert with no notion in their heads except to move where they could find something to eat, and the line of grass had led them, almost as if it had been set out for the purpose, straight down into Boulder River Canyon and through it to the water hole where they were bedded. It wasn't a good place for them, but it was the only water in the neighborhood where sheep could be held without running into opposition from the resident landowners.

One of the few useful things Linus had got out of his homesteading years on the ridge over Boulder River was a knowledge of the country and its limitations and prejudices. He knew the region well, and he knew there were no open camping places in it that had even as many advantages as the one where they were. One of the points about it was that there were thirty head of his father's sheep running loose somewhere around it, and he couldn't leave until he had taken some kind of a stab at finding them. He roused out of his train of reflections and remarked that it was a cold wind to be sitting out in with a case of inflammation of the eyes. Old Ollivant said morosely that he wasn't responsible for the temperature of the wind.

"It's a blamed funny thing we don't hear any coyotes," he remarked. "This is the first night since we've been out here that there ain't been a dozen of 'em on the yip all around us. They couldn't all have left the country in a day."

"You can't tell about coyotes around these blamed rock piles," Linus said vaguely. The coyotes had not left the country, and he knew the reason they weren't making themselves heard from as they usually did. With thirty head of sheep wandering at large, they had something better to while away their time on than hunkering on a cold rock to howl.

He tried to decide whether to own up about the strays, and heard metal grate on rock somewhere up on the ridge. He held up his hand for silence, heard it again, and let the strays slip out of his thoughts with a feeling of relief at not having to make up his mind about them.

"Somebody with horses," he said. "You'd better fetch out the gun. It might be some of these neighborhood busybodies come to drag us out of here in a sack."

"Guns can make more trouble for some people than draggin' in a sack," old Ollivant said, without moving. "I told you I heard shod horses fifteen minutes ago. It's somebody from town come out to see what's happened to us, I expect."

The wind shifted, and for a long time they heard nothing more at all. Then the hoofs clattered on the ridge above them, and they could tell that it was several horses in charge of one man who was humming a loud mixture of three or four different tunes as an indication that he was not trying to sneak up on anybody. Linus stirred the fire into a blaze, and he stopped his humming, shaded his eyes against the glare, and rode down into the full light, so they could look him over before he offered to dismount.

"They told me in town that some people named Ollivant wanted a herder," he said. He was a large-built man with a saddle a couple of sizes too snug for him, and he had three pack ponies strung, head and tail, behind him. He kept yanking their lead rope to keep them from trying to lie down.

"My name is Dee Radford. I'm a herder, and I ain't ever worked this country before, so I come out to see what your layout looked like. They had this order of groceries made up for you, so I brung it along. This place ain't fit to camp sheep on. I'll bet you've lost a couple of dozen head in the last two days, if you'll count."

Linus didn't consider it necessary to mention what the correct statistics on his shortage were. "How did the people in town know where to send you?" he asked.

"They didn't. I had to work out your trail from the scenery," Dee Radford said.

He dismounted so heavily that he almost pulled the weary animal over on top of himself, and proceeded to unsaddle and unpack in the dark, working as confidently as if nobody had ever told him what a lantern was for.

"When you've been in this business as long as I have, you don't need to know where people are to find 'em," he explained, unraveling a complicated four-way hitch from a pack. "A man that can't find what he wants without help ain't entitled to call himself a herder. This ain't any place to camp a band of sheep like these of yours. They walk off their feed gittin' to water, and they dry out thirsty trailin' back to feed and they're too old to stand it. I picked out a place up on the ridge where they'll handle better. There's an old homestead with a patch of run-down orchard around it, and there's water enough to make out on if we're careful. You can git your camp struck and packed, and we'll move up there the first thing in the morning."

To Linus, it seemed a little high-handed for even a skilled herder to drop into the middle of a strange camp and start issuing orders as if it belonged to him.

Old Ollivant was less touchy and more interested. At mention of a ridge homestead surrounded by an old orchard, he sat up and said he had been agitating to have their camp moved, and that Linus had assured him the thing was impossible.

"It is," Linus said. "That ridge country ain't open land. It belongs to people that use it to feed cattle on. If we move in with sheep, they'll throw us out, and maybe run the sheep to death for good measure. I know the people around here. I know how they act with pasture thieves, and I don't blame 'em for it."

"We won't be pasture thieves, because there ain't any pasture on that ridge to thieve," Dee Radford said. "There's been cattle over every foot of it, and they've cleaned the grass right down to the roots. The only thing about it is that there's a big scatter of grass seed blowed around into horse tracks and under rocks where the cattle couldn't reach it. Sheep can, and there ought to be enough of it to run us for three weeks or more anyhow. We won't be trespassers, because the place don't belong to anybody. I asked some men in the road about that. I told 'em I was a mind to buy it, and they said it hadn't ever been proved up on. We'll move up there in the morning, if it's all right with both of you."

It was not all right with Linus and he said nothing, but his father said there was no use palavering around about a move so plainly commendable and necessary.

"We'll move any time you say, and don't pay any attention to anything this boy says," he said. "He's always balky at the wrong times, and there ain't much you can do with him. He's done well to handle the sheep by himself without any losses, but he's got to learn to listen to other people sometimes, and he can't start any younger."

Linus still remained silent, so he fumbled his way inside the camp tent and began rattling small articles into his war bag to save having to pack them in the morning. They heard his boots thump and the blankets rustle as he spread down in them, and then the noises subsided as he went to sleep.

Dee Radford remarked that they had better be thinking about rest themselves, if they were to make it up to the ridge homestead in a day's trailing. Linus replied that he didn't plan to make it to any ridge homestead, and that he would rest when he felt like it. He tried to sound chilling, but Dee Radford merely sat back and studied him thoughtfully.

"I've seen young squirts act like this when I've pulled into some camp to help through a bad season," he said. "You're a different cut from that, if looks is anything. You don't look like a squirt, and you ought to know that you'll lose all your sheep if you try to handle 'em down here. You don't think I'd be in this business if I didn't know something about it, do you?"

"You know your business, I guess," Linus conceded, a trifle sullenly. "What you don't know about is this country. You've got it fixed to land us all in trouble with the people in it. That old ridge orchard you've picked for us to move to ain't open land. If any men told you it was, they lied. It used to be our homestead. My old man planted that orchard, and I took care of it, and I could draw you a picture right now of every tree in it. We'd be there yet, but I got into a rumpus, so the old man had to sell out his homestead rights and leave to get away from lawsuits. I shot a man, if you want to know what it was. Maybe that homestead ain't been proved up on, but it ain't ours, because we sold the rights to it. If we take sheep onto it we'll have trouble, and people around here will swear I started it to show off. The old man don't know about that, because he don't know what part of the country we've drifted back to. He'll probably claim I sneaked back here to hunt up some more cussedness, if he ever finds it out."

Dee Radford stirred the fire and said that cleared up two or three points that he hadn't understood at first. He added that old Ollivant's dust blindness had looked serious, and that they might manage to get the sheep sheared and off their hands and get clear away from the Boulder River country before he cured up enough to realize that they had been there.

"It would be playin' underhanded with him, but that ain't any business of mine," he said. "Sheep is all I claim to know anything about, and there ain't but one thing to do with this bunch of yours. We can keep 'em alive on that ridge homestead, and we'll try to handle 'em so people won't find out we're there. If they have to stay here they'll die, and if you'd sooner they done that, say so and I'll leave you to handle 'em. You'll go broke, but that ain't any of my put-in. How many head have you lost since you've been here that you ain't told your old man about?"

That was a sharp surmise, and Linus took no risks in replying to it. He nodded toward the tent, and stated in clear tones that he had lost no sheep at all. Then he opened and closed the fingers of his hands three times, traced the course of one setting sun down the sky, and waited to see if Dee Radford had ever stopped long enough in one place to know what Indian sign talk was.

Dee indicated his comprehension with a nod, and remarked cautiously that he would have expected the shrinkage to have run higher and started sooner. If they had dropped out only that afternoon, they might still be alive. Having turned in that reflection, he got up, got his horse out of the corral, and reached down his saddle.

"I'm goin' to show you that a man don't need to know a country to handle sheep in it," he said. "You show me which direction you pastured today, and I'll find them strays for you. You git packed and line the sheep for the ridge the first thing in the morning, and quit this shiverin' around for fear of trouble. People ain't fools enough to fight us over a place as worthless as that homestead. If they do, I'll tend to 'em, and if we damage the premises, I'll stand good for it. We won't hurt your old man's orchard, if that's what you're uneasy about.

"I don't care what you do to the orchard," Linus said. "I put in four years' hard work on it, and all I ever got for it was a pile of trouble, and all I want is to make sure we won't get into any more. Trouble ain't easy to dodge out on in this country."

"Trouble ain't easy to dodge out on in any country that you spend too much of your time in. You ought to learn your trade and travel around with it, like I do, and then you wouldn't have to bother about what people thought of you."

Linus and his father packed camp an hour or so before sunup. Linus getting everybody's personal belongings together into one of the packs, and reflecting that it did look as if Dee Radford's system of short-staking around had paid better than any protracted residence in one place.

Dee's outfit included such show pieces as a leather-faced bed roll, double-lined goatskin chaps, and a hand-carved rifle scabbard, all of which were expensive and none of which either Linus or his father possessed at all. His rifle was a new flat-shooting rig with box magazine, oiled stock, peep sight with micrometer scale, buckhorn tips, and all the trimmings. Linus' father had a common little saddle carbine with iron sights and a squared-off butt, and Linus not only had no gun at all but wasn't even supposed to handle one except under his father's personal supervision.

Except that it showed what he had missed by staying too long in the shadow of his youthful reputation, the contrast in the rifles didn't bother Linus much. The old piece of momentary recklessness that had ended his residence on the ridge homestead had also destroyed most of his interest in guns, and the sight of one was generally enough to bring the whole unlucky episode back to him clearly and painfully.

Its beginning cause had been the old homestead orchard. He had put in an entire spring on it, pruning, cultivating, whitewashing and spraying for insects, and, as he was applying a few final touches against twig borers, a contingent of old Lucas Waymark's cowboys pulled in and camped a herd of starved-out old cows right against a weak place in the fence where they were certain to break through the minute they were left to themselves.

Linus was alone on the place at the time and, not feeling disposed to let a pack of scrub cows grab what he had barely finished rescuing from all the other pests in the country, he forted up behind some baled hay with the family musket and ordered the Waymark minions to begone.

The minions hadn't kept up with their reading sufficiently to realize that they were supposed to slink away in baffled rage, so they offered to spank him if he didn't take the gun straight indoors and put it back where it belonged. One of them straddled the orchard fence to illustrate how they would go at it, and Linus tightened down and cut loose, intending to hit the post under his hand as a final warning. The fore sight of the old gun had got knocked out of line and, instead of jarring the post, he spread the Waymark man across the top wire of the fence with a smashed collarbone.

There was never any general agreement in the country over which of the parties to the incident had been most to blame for it. The homesteaders blamed old Waymark for running his cattle around the neighborhood as if he owned it. The Waymark men blamed their stricken co-worker for trying to walk down a gun in the hands of a frightened youngster. Linus blamed the gun for not shooting straight, Linus' father blamed Linus for pointing it at a man he didn't intend to shoot, and several people blamed Linus' father for keeping a firearm on the premises without making sure the sights were lined up properly.

All the bestowals of blame were probably partly justified, but none of them could clear Linus of the responsibility for injuring a fellow man with a deadly weapon, and old Waymark played that fact for all there was in it. He worked up claims for doctors' bills, wages for the wounded man's lost time, physical suffering and mental anguish, and complaints against Linus for everything from juvenile delinquency to attempted manslaughter. In the end, Linus' father gave up, sold him the homestead relinquishment, and moved away.

The change was no particular misfortune, but Linus' mismanagement in bringing it on was something he never liked to be reminded of. The old gun that had done the shooting was so painful a memento that he stuck it back of a rafter in the homestead cabin, out of sight, and neither he nor Linus thought enough of it to get it down when they moved. They never mentioned the shooting afterward, and there was always a little strained note in their conversation with each other, because they so painstakingly avoided any subject that seemed likely to lead into it.

They both steered around handling the two herding rifles while they were packing up. After Linus had got them wrapped in some bedding and stowed quietly on one of the packs, his father went out and felt carefully over the horses to make sure where they were. It wasn't that he suspected Linus of having stolen them; he merely wanted to see that they hadn't been overlooked, and he preferred to hunt them out rather than open a subject which neither of them took anything but distrust and uneasiness in thinking back over.

Trailing the sheep was slow, but not troublesome. The cold kept them well bunched, and since there was not enough grass to tempt them to loiter, they moved along without needing any encouragement beyond a little rock throwing to keep them pointed right.

Old Ollivant dragged along behind with the pack horses, holding his eye bandage down against the wind with one hand and his reins, trail rope and saddle horn with the other.

Linus pulled into the homestead about an hour past sundown, and found Dee Radford waiting. Dee sat beside a fresh-banked pond, watching it fill up from the spring. He had turned the little quarter-inch trickle of water away from the sink back of the orchard where it disappeared into the ground, and he was storing it for the sheep to drink.

"We may have to ration it out, the way it's runnin'," he said. "We'll know about that after they've watered a couple of times. You notice I collected your strays."

There was probably not another man in the country who could have found those strays in that river canyon in the dark. Linus paid his respectful acknowledgements to the feat, and looked doubtful about the arrangements for conserving the water. The thing that came into his mind, in spite of him, was that the trees must have come to depend on the flow of water into the ground. They looked so wild and worthless, all broken and tangled and killed down by cattle and heavy snows and freezing, that he kept his thoughts to himself, for fear of sounding sentimental. He did remark that the trees belonged to somebody, and Dee took him up hard on that.

"You've got a patch of fruit trees that ain't worth anything and a band of sheep that'll bring your old man ten thousand dollars if they stay alive," he said. "You've got an old orchard that nobody thinks enough of to prove up on, and you've got sheep that your old man has run himself alkali-blind over, besides the work you've put in on 'em yourself. I don't see how you can even argue about turnin' this water. I'd be ashamed to be that big a fool about any place I'd ever lived."

"I ain't any fool about this place," Linus said. "You may have to answer a claim for damages to these trees before you're through here, that's all.

Don't think you'll be able to argue yourself out of it, either. There's harder outfits around here than you might think."

Old Ollivant drew up with the pack horses, and Dee searched his box-magazine rifle out from under the bedding and hung it ceremoniously on a fence post.

"If anybody shows up to be fought, he's mine," he said. "I don't notice any signs of heavy travel around here, so it ain't likely that anybody will. You don't need to look that far ahead for anything to worry about, anyhow. When you've stood a week or two of feedin' sheep on grass seed in these rocks, you'll wish you had a good quiet fight to rest up on. We'll make a herd camp here where we can take turns standin' guard over the bed ground, and we'll put the tent off yonder in the orchard where your father can be out of the wind."

Old Ollivant didn't think much of that arrangement, insisting, with a stubbornness of conviction that turned out to be almost clairvoyant, that Linus would land in some trouble if he stood guard over the bed ground without somebody to stand guard over him. He gave in only when Dee, having pitched the tent in the cove, helped him down from his horse and led him into it, with instructions to stay there until his eyes felt better.

The ridge was not so abundantly supplied with either grass seed or water as it had looked to begin with. It had barely enough of both to keep the old ewes from bawling loud enough to be heard clear down to the road, and even that frugal measure of sustenance didn't last well.

Trouble started one evening when Linus brought the herd in by himself; Dee having gone down to the road to put up a flag for the shearing crew. Instead of bedding down quietly, the sheep milled, changed ground and collected in little bunches, blatting tunelessly and persistently. Linus was too tired to hear them, and Dee, getting back late, didn't discover till daylight that they had run short of water. Some animal—a skunk or a sage rat, by the signs—had burrowed into the ditch between the spring and the catch pond, and the entire night's supply had seeped out into the ground behind the orchard.

He patched up the break, but that was no immediate help. The ditch and pond basin had dried out so deep that getting them primed and getting the pond filled afterward took the entire day. The sheep waited and continued their blatting, and, to get out of listening to them, Linus went out and cut bundles of willow and wild-cherry sprouts as something for them to practice eating on, even though it couldn't be considered food.

Coming back through the high sagebrush behind the camp with his harvest of shrubbery, he heard men talking and Dee's voice rising in an argument which, to judge by the sound of horses moving restlessly, didn't seem to be commanding much attention. He dropped his brush and crept up behind the old homestead cabin for a look, knowing beforehand who the visitors were and what they had come for.

Old Waymark's bad-news committee hadn't changed its membership in the years that Linus had been away. There was old Waymark himself, undersized and savage-looking. Behind him was his foreman, a sandy-haired man with red eyes who kept fiddling with his rope; back of him were a couple of ordinary herders, and off to one side was old Slickear Cowan, who would have classed as an ordinary herder, except that he was the man whom Linus had rimmed with the shot heard round as much of the world as old Waymark could command a hearing from.

The injury hadn't damaged Slickear Cowan's vitality much. He carried a long jute woolsack on his saddle fork, and he kept working his horse sideways, getting, as if accidentally, between Dee and the post where he had hung his rifle. Linus' father was asleep in the tent, out of range of the conference, and Dee was so absorbed in handling the case for the defense that he didn't notice the maneuver being organized against his peace and dignity.

He proved that he was not stealing pasture, pointed out that, instead of damaging the homestead, he had kept it from falling apart, and touched on various phases of the land-title question with so much authority that old Waymark acted apologetic about being there at all. His sandy-haired foreman shook out a turn of his rope and looked thoughtful, Slickear

Cowan gathered his reins and sat forward in his saddle, and old Waymark studied the tent in the orchard as if half wondering whether there was anybody in it who ought to be invited to see the fun.

It was clear enough what they were up to. Dee Radford was about to be taken through the rural ceremony known as a sheepherder's sleigh ride. Slickear Cowan would make a run and snatch his rifle; when he turned to see what was up, the foreman would hang a rope on him and dump him. The woolsack would be yanked over him and tied shut, and he would be dragged behind a horse over the rugged countryside, with special attention to those portions of it that would bounce him highest.

That was the standard treatment for men who ran sheep on somebody else's land, and there was only one way to head it off. Linus tiptoed inside the old homestead cabin, noticing, with a little half-homesick feeling, that a worn-out pair of his own shoes were still on the kitchen floor where he had dropped them on leaving, and how woebegone they looked with the strings trailing loose and the dust heavy on them.

He had not been tall enough to reach the rafters the day his father hid the old rifle back of them. Now he put his hand up to it without even having to stretch. The rifle was dusty and the action was rusted shut, so it wouldn't work, but that didn't disturb him. He didn't intend to shoot, and it added something to his confidence to know that he couldn't, even if he felt tempted to. He tiptoed to the back door, kicked it open and stood in it with the rifle trained, in involuntary deference to the past, on the fork of Slickear Cowan's collarbone.

"Pull up that horse and drop them reins," he ordered. "Put your hands under your belt and take your feet out of the stirrups. Now move out of here, the whole bunch of you."

If he had appeared draped in a sheet and clanking a chain, he couldn't have quenched the delegation's high spirits more completely. Everybody stared, and nobody moved. Linus motioned Dee Radford toward the rifle on the post, and Dee roused himself, got it and backed off, still staring.

"Where in creation did you find that gun?" he asked. "You ain't robbed any Indian graves, have you?"

"It didn't come out of any Indian grave," Linus said. His voice, with the empty house backing it up, sounded so spooky that he hardly recognized it himself. "We left this gun here when we moved away, and I remembered where it was." He turned apologetically to old Waymark. "I don't want to shoot any of your men. All I want is for you to let us alone. We'll pay for any damage we've done here."

Old Waymark edged his horse sideways, picking up his spirits a little.

"You're that young Ollivant hoodlum that like to killed one of my men once before," he said, as if he expected Linus to deny it. "You ought to have gone to jail then, and I'll see that you do go now. I bought this place from your father, and I want these men to witness that you've ordered me off of it at the point of a gun. You'll hear from it, you and your father both."

He picked up his reins, and Dee asked him to hold on a minute.

"There's a point or two about this trespass business," he said. "This boy has told me that his father moved out of here before he got this homestead proved up on. What you bought was his relinquishment, wasn't it?"

Old Waymark conceded that it was, and said that had nothing to do with the main issue. "One of my men went down and filed on it. You'll find that out plenty soon, if you've got any doubts about it."

"I've got a few," Dee said. "There's a residence requirement about homesteads, and your man ain't ever lived here. This boy's father left that gun in the house when he moved out, and it ain't been touched till now."

Old Waymark's whiskers pointed slightly astern again. It was not unusual for people in remote districts to be a little neglectful about residence on their homesteads. The fact that his man had followed the general custom was the main reason he had come there. There was nothing on the homestead worth squabbling over, and he wouldn't have cared how many sheep camped on it if his title had held a little closer to legal standards, but a counterentry on the place was worth going to some trouble to head off. He said an old gun being overlooked in some hiding place meant nothing, and picked up his reins again.

His men were all staring down into the orchard. The tent had come open, and Linus' father came slowly up from it, holding his bandage clear of one tortured eye, so he could see his way between the tangle of neglected old trees that he had set out to be a light and a beacon to horticultural expansion in the sagebrush. He drew up and fixed Linus with a glare that was all the more impressive because it was so obviously agonizing to him.

"This is the kind of high-handed thuggery you've sneaked in on me, is it?" he demanded. "You tore loose with a gun once, and got yourself in trouble till I had to sell out and leave here to get you clear of it. A man would think that would have been enough to last you, but here you're back for more. You wait till I get my eyesight crippled, so I can't see what you're up to, and then you gallop straight back to the same place to do the same trick all over again. You promised me never to touch a gun unless I was around to watch you, and you know it. You know we ain't got any right to be here too. You know this old skunk bought this place off of me, and you've got no right to order him to leave it. Put that gun down."

Linus leaned the gun against the wall outside the door. The Waymark men watched thoughtfully as he stood back from it, and Slickear Cowan lifted his hands clear of his belt. Dee Radford advised him to avoid rashness, jiggled the safety catch on his rifle to indicate that he was serious and told Linus' father to cover his eyes from the light and show a little sense.

"You didn't sell anything to this outfit but your homestead rights," he said. "Nobody has ever used 'em, and we can prove it. This homestead is open to anybody that wants to live on it the legal time. This boy of yours has got a right to occupy it and he's got a right to use a gun on anybody that tries to run him off of it. He may intend to file a contest on it himself, how do you know?"

"It was on his account that I sold it to start with," old Ollivant said. He did cover his eyes from the light. "How would it look if he come back and took it away from the man I sold it to? It wouldn't be honest."

"You didn't sell his rights to it, because he was too young to have any," Dee said. "He's old enough now to file on any open land he wants to, and it ain't anybody else's business. It ain't even yours."

Old Waymark started to say something about principles, and Linus put in ahead of him, seeing that the argument was reaching a little too far into metaphysics to be practical.

"I don't want to file on any homestead and I wouldn't file on this one if I did," he said. "I've put in too much time in one neighborhood already, and I don't aim to do any more of it."

That was a sentiment that Dee Radford had done a good deal of arguing in favor of, and yet he seemed disappointed.

"I'll be blamed if I'll see this place go back to this outfit, after the way they've acted," he said. "I'll file on it myself, if I have to. I want you men to take notice that there's a contest to be entered on this claim and you can keep off of it till the law settles it. Now move, before I shoot up a few of your horses for you." He watched them until they were a little distance away, and then turned to Linus. "Pick up that old pacifier of yours and touch it off somewhere over their heads. I'd like to hear what it sounds like, and I'd like to see how they take it."

"It won't touch off," Linus said, feeling a little foolish over having to admit it. "The breech is rusted shut. I didn't bring it out to shoot with. Them men was about to drag you in a sack, and all I wanted was to head 'em off till you could get clear of 'em. It come out all right."

Linus' father pulled his bandage clear of one eye, looked the old gun over and tried unsuccessfully to budge the hammer. He put it down again and looked at Linus. The light and wind must have been agony to him, and yet he didn't appear conscious of any particular pain.

"It did come out all right," he said. "Not but what it took a blamed long time to it. I've distrusted you all these years, and the Lord knows how much longer I'd have kept on at it if you'd got hold of a gun that would shoot. You've turned out dependable in spite of me, it looks like. If you've got a mind to take this homestead for yourself, I've got no right to forbid you. It used to be a sightly place, when it was kept in shape."

"I don't want it," Linus said. "There never was anything to it except that patch of orchard, and the trees is all killed out. I whittled into some of 'em, and they're as dry as a wagon spoke."

"Not any more," his father said. "That was what I started up here to tell you, and then I heard them men. There's been a funny kind of a noise outside that tent ever since the sheep blat let up. It got so loud I couldn't rest, so I went out to see what it was. It was bees. Them old fruit trees has all come into bloom. You didn't waste all the work you put into 'em, after all."

"I wouldn't call it wasted, even if them trees all dried up and fell down," Dee Radford said. "If you hadn't recognized them men and remembered about that old rifle, we'd have lost them sheep sure. It would have been the first herd of sheep I ever lost in my life, and I wouldn't want that on my record."

The breaking up of that drought was not especially beautiful in itself, but it ended the long monotony of dust and dry wind and cold sun, and its contrasting mildness and silence made it seem one of the most beautiful things imaginable. A night rain laid the dust, the sky clouded over, the air was so still that the sheep shearers didn't even bother to anchor their burlap corral panels down, and the sheep, having come through their pasturing season, turned from a care and a burden into a salable asset that strange workmen labored over and strange buyers bid for and strange feed yards were almost embarrassingly gratified to advance wagonloads of hay on.

Dee Radford knelt outside the old herding tent, packing up to leave the sheep he had half killed himself to save from the buzzards. That was an old ceremony for him, and he took it tranquilly. Linus couldn't feel quite so lighthearted about it. He detested sheep, but there seemed something unnatural about working so hard over something that had to be given up afterward, with nothing left to show where his work had gone. There were wages, but they were the same for bad work as for good.

He walked down into the orchard, thinking about that, and saw, in the scrubby tangle of old trees in bloom, something he had worked hard on that had not disappeared afterward, but had lived and developed courage to bring forth its clumps of perfect flowers, pink apricot and apple, green-white plum and white pear and cherry, through all the tangle of dead and broken and mutilated limbs that showed how hard it had been to live at all. That much of his work had not been wasted, since it had helped to bring into life a courage and patience and doggedness in putting forth such delicate beauty against all the hostility of nature and against even the imminence of death.

Linus' father was sitting under one of the trees with his bandage lifted from one eye, and Linus sat down beside him. "I've decided to try this old homestead for a while," he said. "It's—"

He didn't bother to finish.

His father nodded. "I know how you feel," he said. "I know how it feels to have something you've raised turn out better than you expected."

Puget Sound Country

The Puget Sound country, which lies about as far to the northwest as you can go in the United States, used to stir up one peculiar reflex in the writers who wrote about it seventy or eighty years ago. All of them, no matter what else their accounts included, always managed to mention that it was like the Mediterranean area of Southern Europe. It is probably a little late to hunt for an explanation of this unanimity now—some early touch of Western hyperbole, maybe, or it could have been merely that they wanted to convey something of the new country's size and spaciousness, and picked the Mediterranean because it sounded impressive enough to do it.

Whatever their reasons, it was not much of a comparison. Puget Sound does spread out over a considerable area—from its southern extremity at Olympia, it is 150 miles to the Canadian boundary at Blaine and 200 miles to the village of Neah Bay, on the Juan de Fuca Strait—but it would be more accurate to compare it to some smaller tributary sea in the Mediterranean rather than to the whole thing: The Dalmatian coast of the Adriatic, maybe, though that would apply only to size. In everything else, it is like nothing except itself. Its cities, big and populous and pushing, reach to the very edge of the wild country from which they were carved, mostly within the memory of people still alive. Bears still raid poultry farms within sight of some of these cities, and there are sixteen Indian reservations within a day's drive of Seattle. The climate sometimes blazes into midsummer in late May and sometimes strings out a cloudy and overcast late February so far into the summer that some of the trees only begin coming into leaf in July. The rainfall, for which the region has always been famous, varies according to location. In Seattle it averages around 58 inches annually. On the western slope of the Olympic Peninsula, less than a hundred miles away, it reaches 180 inches annually. Sometimes, however, it can vary even in its variability. There are years—1953 was one—when Seattle and Tacoma stay chilly and rainy through two-thirds of the summer, while the side roads west along the coast are dry and dusty, the little creeks low and half-choked with leaves falling early.

But Nature holds on hard in this country, and its powers of readjustment and renewal are probably higher than anywhere outside of the tropical forests of Central America. When I lived on Bainbridge Island, roughly opposite Seattle on the western side of the Sound, some twenty-five years ago, there was a retired sea captain a few houses away who took it into his head to keep the trees cleared off the hundred-foot strip of land in front of his house so they wouldn't interfere with his view of the shipping moving back and forth from Elliott Bay across the Sound. Since cutting them would merely have brought up a wilderness of sprouts from the stumps, he used a portable capstan to pull them out by the roots and be done with them for good. He spent most of his time pulling and sawing them up, with a Japanese houseboy helping him. When I left at the end of three years, the trees were more than keeping even with him. Looking from any distance at the handsome stand of young firs and madroñas crowding against his front windows, it was difficult to see where any had been pulled out at all, though his whole back yard was piled high with cordwood. All the towns around the Sound have grown bigger in the years since I lived there, but, though the sawmills have also got bigger and log trucks are everywhere, the timber has kept up by growing bigger too.

It is hardly likely that the wild life of the country has fallen behind the timber in holding its own. A few years ago at a party in Hollywood, I got to trading reminiscences about the area with a woman who had lived for a couple of years in a beach cabin somewhere along the southern end of the Sound, west of Tacoma—Carr Inlet, or some such locality. She remembered so many of the same things I did—grouse, pheasant, bear, deer, wild blackberries and raspberries and red huckleberries, windfall apples from the abandoned homestead orchards, clams, oysters, salmon, fishing for sea perch from the dismantled old lumber docks, dipping out candle smelt from creek inlets with a bucket (some people preferred a wire bird cage) when a run was on, hunting for wild strawberries under the upland bracken in the late spring—that it was hard to believe our dates of residence had been as far apart as they turned out to be. She had lived there in 1951-52. I had left in 1932. Twenty years seems a long time for any part of the West Coast to have remained as much the same as we both remembered it. There are places that have struggled up from savagery to a passable degree of civilization in twenty years; or down, depending on how one looks at it.

It is not that the Puget Sound country resists change more stubbornly than the rest of the country. Things change here perhaps faster than in most places, only the changes tend to work both ways, so that a loss in one direction is apt to be made up by a gain in another. Twenty-five years ago, Tacoma was primarily a sawmill town, with the red glow of giant sawdust burners lighting the main north-and-south highway through it like a bank of outsize exhaust pipes valving off fire from hell. Now the town has spread out into such things as wood-pulp and fiber-board mills and the smelting of copper concentrates from mines in Mexico and Central America and the Philippines. Twenty-five years ago, anybody in Seattle who had ventured to hint at the possibility of a slump in Alaska salmon fisheries and export trade with the Orient would probably have had to leave town. Now, though Alaska canneries are running only one week out of the year and trade with the Orient has dwindled to a shadow of itself, nobody seems to mind, and the town goes barreling along bigger and livelier than ever. Merely the expansion in aircraft manufacture has more than made up for the loss. The Boeing statisticians estimate that their company furnishes employment for one out of every six persons in the entire town. Twenty-five years ago the proportion would have been less than one in sixty.

The countryside keeps the same balance. As late as fifteen years ago, a man with a small skiff and some fishing tackle could move into some deserted lumber-camp shanty on one of the back reaches of the Sound and live fairly comfortably merely from fishing and clam-digging and berry-picking, possibly filling in with a moderate infusion of out-of-season hunting and log-stealing if he liked such non-essential trimmings as a radio and outboard motor and store-bought cigarettes. A man could still do that, probably, given a certain amount of doggedness, a thorough knowledge of the country, and the ability to spot neighborhood game wardens at long range, but it would be harder. It would mean living monotonously and going without a lot of conveniences most people find it hard to dispense with for any long period of time. Living close to Nature for a few weeks every year or so is an excellent spiritual restorative, but having to depend on Nature for a livelihood year in and year out takes the fun out of it. The wild country has changed, of course, the same as everything else, but the real changes may be in the way people look at it.

Nevertheless, monotony in diet doesn't mean as much in this country as it might in other places. Variety in food becomes important when the food itself is insipid or low in nutritive value, but the food of this coastal region is the best in the nation. It was not because of ignorance or lack of enterprise that the local Indian tribes, living in one of the finest big-game countries on the continent, never bothered with hunting. Their community houses and high-prowed seagoing canoes show an understanding of functional design that an ignorant people would be incapable of, and several of the coast tribes—the Makah and Quillayute, for instance—killed whales from their canoes in the open sea, which is hardly a sign of a lackadaisical temperament. They abstained from hunting, evidently, because they had weighed the inevitable work against the probable returns, and had decided that the percentage was not good enough. The food from the rivers and the sea and the beaches was all anybody could possibly need—halibut, candle smelt, crabs, salmon trout, oysters, clams (one species of clam grows as big as a pie plate), ducks, geese, blackberries, salmonberries. With all that at hand, why should anybody spend his time trudging through dripping underbrush in search of deer or bear or elk, which not only took work and patience to track down, but had to be dressed and carried home afterward?

The reasoning holds good for the country today. The food is still the best to be found anywhere. Some of the more highly skilled logging-camp cooks in the old days, according to legend, used to balk at working in Puget Sound camps because there was nothing in the available provender that they could show off their artistry on. All the victuals needed, they complained, was to be walloped onto a hot stove and then shoveled into a plate.

The most important thing in the Puget Sound country is the Sound itself. The water is more a part of everybody's life and consciousness than anything else in it. Its mountains and woods and inland river valleys are all well enough for a weekend of fishing or skiing or hunting or flower-picking, but what happens on the Sound is the thing that really counts—the deep-sea shipping, the halibut fleet, the ships on regular run to and from Alaska, the ferries to the islands and across the Strait to Canada, the trade with the Orient, lumber ships from Europe, ore ships from Latin America, cannery tenders and trading schooners from the north, houseboats where people live, tugboats inching laboriously through the rough water of the Strait bringing log rafts from Neah and Clallam Bay to the mills at Port Angeles, stylish yachts and cabin cruisers flitting through the island channels past swarms of dingy Indian trolling skiffs, little single-masted canoes, gleaming plywood speedboats, freight scows, outboard dinghies salvaging drift logs from the beaches. There is every kind of craft on the Sound, big and little, old and new, slow and fast, handsome and ugly. Name it and they've got it.

The log rafts are scarcer and smaller nowadays, but they are still to be seen sometimes along the Strait and the waters to the north. A full-sized seagoing log raft beating out through the Strait on a clear day, with the dark blue water rolling half over it, used to be something to remember—the great spread of round-backed logs lying almost motionless in the rough water, the smudgy little tug straining and fretting so far ahead that it seemed headed out to sea all by itself except for the tow cable whipping a track across the waves. Sometimes, when a tide was running up the Strait and a raft was being towed out against it, a man could watch the tug laboring and the cable whipping and sawing water and the logs washing under and lifting for two or three hours without being able to see that it was moving at all; but, like the hour hand of a watch, it did make progress even when it didn't look it.

Unionization of the Northwest logging camps has had several long-range consequences that could hardly have been foreseen when it first started. One has affected the Seattle and Tacoma newspapers. At least half their classified advertising used to be announcements of logging-camp jobs—rigging slingers, doggers, choker setters, buckers, fallers, donkeymen, peavymen, cat skinners, swampers, bull cooks, a long string of lively and colorful-sounding occupations. Now there are no such advertisements at all, and the classified ads run mostly to real estate and used cars, the same as everywhere else. Another has changed Seattle's old employment-agency square, once known as the Slave Market, where loggers out of work used to congregate to watch the daily blackboards being hung out with men-wanted lists—a picturesque place, like nothing anywhere else, surrounded by odd little hole-in-the-wall shops dealing in tattoo work and restoratives for waning virility and dream books and paper-backed copies of Cornelius Agrippa's treatise on black magic. It is all quiet and respectable now. The shops are gone, the loggers do their congregating somewhere else, if at all, the neighborhood has become as sedate and decorous as a church cake sale. Civilization is probably to blame. It always smooths out regional peculiarities such as these, given time. One can't help feeling sometimes that it might find more important things to smooth out, if it looked around a little, but that is daydreaming. It never does.

Tacoma and Seattle are the two big cities on the Sound, though some of the others, like Olympia and Everett and Puyallup (some note should be taken hereabouts of the awful place names in this country: Not only Puyallup, but Humptulips, Skykomish, Duckabush, Enumclaw, Chuckanut, Mukilteo—and there are even worse ones), are coming along fast and it may very well be that in time they will grow together into one solid urban area, as has happened with the towns around San Francisco Bay and Los Angeles, and with most of the small outlying villages around Seattle.

Tacoma lies farther south than Seattle, on an arm of the Sound not far from its extreme southern tip. It has one of the most important harbors on the West Coast, though its clear, warm days and the open grasslands around it, usually sear by midsummer, make it seem like an inland town rather than a seaport. It has always been a working town, and still is; and it has always taken its coloring from the work it has had in hand, and still does—sawmills, ore smelters, railroad yards, deep-sea shipping, plywood and fiberboard mills, and the big Fort Lewis Army and air-training bases all add to the feeling of restlessness and movement about it. Work impregnates the very atmosphere; the smelters and the big sawdust burners around the sawmills used to do most of the impregnating, but they have been backed into the wings in recent years by the fiberboard factories, which contribute not only color but smell. It is not an especially disagreeable smell; people brought up around the Chicago stockyards would consider it beneath their notice, and the local residents are probably right in maintaining that one can become so accustomed to it as to find ordinary back-country ozone a little flat and wishy-washy. They are also undoubtedly on sound ground in defending it as a heartening sign of prosperity. Still, it is a smell, and one can't help feeling that if prosperity had to have a sign, it might have done better at picking one.

Nobody seems able to pin down what there is about Seattle that gives it so much more the feeling of a seaport than any other seaport town in the Northwest. The location and topography have something to do with it, probably. It is built on a series of hills which rise on the west from the long half-arc of deep sea docks and ferry slips and lumber wharves facing the Sound, and slope down eastward again to the twenty-six-mile sweep of Lake Washington, where the yacht bases and Naval Air Station and the University of Washington are located. Across the lake are a few villages, still small and scattered, and beyond them the high timbered backbone of the Cascade Mountains that make the divide between the coastal rivers and the Big Bend of the Columbia River.

It is impossible to go more than a block or two anywhere in Seattle without catching sight of open water and deep timber in some direction. It adds something to a city to be able to look out of it into natural countryside—not an imitation of it, as parks always are, but real forests and canyons and mountains and expanses of water reaching somewhere out of sight.

Landscape counts in the character of a place, but people count more. It may be because of its early Alaskan background that Seattle has always run heavily to colorful characters. Let me mention a couple of them to show at least what contrasts the town has been capable of. One was an old Chinese who first came to Puget Sound as part of a shipment of coolies to work in a salmon cannery. He worked himself into the business of contracting laborers to the canneries on commission, installed a corps of expert gamblers to take the laborers' wages away from them on payday, and wound up a multimillionaire. He made regular inspection tours of all the canneries where his laborers were employed, and it used to be one of the sights of the country to watch the old boy disembark from the cannery boat accompanied by a retinue of a dozen or so armed bodyguards, valets, masseurs and umbrella holders, all marching two by two behind him down the gangplank. The other was an old Danish captain of a coastwise lumber steamer who spent most of an afternoon once holding forth about the decline in standards of seamanship brought about by modern progressiveness. He wound up a long string of illustrative anecdotes by relating that, back in the old days, the shipping company he had worked for showed its appreciation of his services after an especially hazardous voyage by keeping a taxi cab waiting for him in front of the best red-light house in town for three days, with the motor running. Such things didn't happen any more, he said, and he was undoubtedly right about that.

Seattle's cultural antecedents are predominantly Scandinavian, though there is not much to show it outside the names on store signs and a noticeable tendency to fair complexions among the people on the streets. There are a few smörgasbord restaurants and a few shops displaying Swedish furniture and Danish housewares and such things, but not as many of either as there are in San Francisco or Los Angeles. The general tendency is to shy away from Scandinavian traditions rather than to cling to them. An architect in Seattle told me once about being hired to build a country house on one of the islands in the Sound for a client, a member of an old New England family, who wanted something patterned after the traditional farmhouse in Sweden. The carpenters, being mostly from Sweden, were delighted to be put to building a kind of house they could remember from their childhood, and pitched in with wholehearted enthusiasm, contributing suggestions and adding extra touches and dropping around after hours and on Sundays to admire and argue about it as if they had a proprietary interest in it. But their own houses, which they had built and mostly designed themselves, were all perfectly ordinary Midwestern frame-and-weatherboard-and-gimcrack structures, uncomfortable and unsightly and badly lighted and worse ventilated, the kind one sees on back streets all over the United States. They were enraptured over the idea of an American wanting a Swedish farmhouse to live in, but when it came to living in such a thing themselves, they went blank. They would as soon have thought of arraying their wives in blue woolen stockings and five or six knitted petticoats apiece. They wanted the things around them to be American, even if the result was uncomfortable and a trifle ugly.

When I lived in Seattle, I used to fritter away the afternoon sometimes at the Pike Street Market. I revisited it recently and discovered that it is nothing like what it was in my time, but at least I had fair warning about it ahead of time from the taxi driver who took me there.

"I remember about 1908 or '09, when the farmers used to drive their wagons in from the country full of truck they'd raised," he said. "They'd back 'em up along the street and sell out of 'em to people on the way to the docks. Climb up in the wagon and pick out what you wanted and bring your own paper sack for it, that was the way it was then. Towards evening, when it was time for 'em to be heading out in the country to milk the cows and get the stock fed and they didn't want to haul all their truck back with 'em, you could buy things pretty reasonable. It's nothing like that now. The stuff they sell and the prices they want for it ain't any different from an ordinary chain grocery store. Things change. A lot of 'em have changed around here."

The rain was coming down so hard his windshield was blurred in spite of the wipers going full blast. He slid down a hill and through a crowded intersection on his brakes, leaning out of the window to see where the openings were.

"You can get used to anything," he said, wiping the rain out of his eyes. "Some people complain about it sometimes. The people that run the ski resorts up around Mount Baker claim they lose business on account of all this rain. No use driving all the way up there to look at scenery if it's raining so you can't see it when you get there. Still, when it don't rain there's brush fires, and smoke so thick you can't see a hundred feet anyway. It's nice when there's a clear day. They've been scarce around here lately."

I said it seemed a little early in the year to expect any run of clear weather. He agreed absently, and observed that things weren't as easy as they used to be. The fault, he thought, was airplanes.

"I'd think airplanes would be more help than harm around here," I said. "The Boeing plant keeps a lot of people at work, doesn't it?"

He conceded the point readily enough. It was not exactly what he had in mind. "The people that work for Boeing are mostly outsiders," he said. "Came in here from the Middle West, Texas and Kankakee and Dakota and places like that. It's all right for them, I guess. Any place is better than where they came from, probably. The people that belong here, they can't do as well as they used to. When things got a little skimpy in the old days, a man could always move up some river and peck around fishing and prospecting and one thing and another, and if he needed money he could cut cordwood and sell it to the steamboat for enough to tide him over. You can't do that any more. They run airplanes into all the back country now. You can't run an airplane on cordwood."

Since there are no rivers in the Puget Sound country navigable for steamboats, and no airplanes into the immediate back country that I knew of, it was not too hard to figure out that he was following the old residents' habit of lumping developments in Alaska with those of Seattle as if they were one and the same. To the old residents, of course, they always have been the same: a sort of back-yard-and-front-parlor relationship that has kept the two regions mutually complementary and permanently inseparable. For at least the past fifty years, anything that happened in Alaska has registered a more immediate impact on Seattle than any event in its own back country possibly could; something like the St. Louis merchants and bankers of the 1850's, who knew more about events in Santa Fe and the California goldfields than about settlements in Missouri forty or fifty miles from their own city limits. With them, it didn't last long. In Seattle, obviously, it had.

The taxi driver was right about one thing, at least. The Pike Street Market had lost originality and color in the twenty years since I had last known it. Some of the stalls had a few out-of-the-ordinary things on display—salmon trout, barrels of rainbow trout, inkfish, codfish tongues, salmon-egg caviar—but the general level, as he had remarked, was not much different from any chain grocery. There were the same things on the shelves, similar prices, the same vague semiboredom about the people looking them over and the clerks watching. One thing that may explain the general listlessness and flatness is the disappearance of the Japanese who used to run most of the cut-flower and vegetable stalls. They always showed a sense of decoration in arranging their merchandise, and I had not realized before how much it helped. I was sorry they were gone, and that I had never bought anything from any of them when they were there.

Some people do keep up with the Puget Sound back county, but it usually has to be forced on them. One was a man who had a house across the county road from me when I was living in a small community on the north end of Bainbridge Island, facing across Agate Pass toward Hood Canal and the Olympic Peninsula. He was an Icelander, and he used to make running translations of modern Icelandic poetry from memory during the long winter evenings when there was nothing else to do. In the summer he used to work as second mate of a salmon-canning steamer working the Alaskan inlets, besides picking up additional income from gillnetting and trading knickknacks to the Eskimos when the steamer was tied up putting away salmon. That was all done and over with now, knocked in the head by the falling off in the Alaska salmon runs. Now he spent his summers working with the Forest Service in the Olympic Mountains, helping to cut fallen trees out of the trails after a windstorm, mending telephone lines, packing supplies to lookout stations, helping to spot fires when there was a long dry spell, hunting for summer tourists who got themselves lost, things like that. None of it amounted to much, but it filled in.

He told of going out once on a Forest Service patrol plan to look for fires after a lightning storm, and of flying low over one of the rivers where four or five bears were out on a long mudbank waiting for salmon that got washed ashore after spawning. One old she-bear saw the plane coming, and reared up and hauled back to slap at it, apparently taking it for some species of predatory bird. She miscalculated its speed and, trying to correct her bead on it, overbalanced and fell off the bank backward into the three feet of thin mud.

The other bears all sat watching curiously as she hauled herself out, mud-plastered and mad, and she drew back and slapped one of them over the bank into the same mudhole, probably suspecting him of wanting to snicker at her. He crawled out, also mad, and slapped one of the smaller bears into the mudhole, whereupon the whole pack of them piled into a free-for-all, clawing, cuffing, biting, gouging, and filling the air so full of sand and mud and hair that it looked as if the whole river had exploded. The Icelander didn't know how it had come out. The plane moved away while the fight was still going on, and when it turned and flew back all the bears were gone. None of them had been hurt much, apparently, or they couldn't have got themselves out of there so fast.

"It must have been worth watching," I said. "You wouldn't see anything much livelier than that in Alaska."

"You'd see bears, if you wanted to," he said. "They're big up there too. These bears around here, there's lots of 'em, but they're little. They don't amount to anything."

"There's salmon around here, and they're not little," I said. "They're not running short, either. I've seen people catching them."

"Tourists," he said. "They play at it. In Alaska, catching salmon is work. I like it better when it's work."

A new highway connects Bainbridge Island with the Olympic Peninsula on the west by a huge and imposing high level bridge across Agate Channel. It comes out on the mainland in approximately the middle of the Port Madison Indian reservation, and then leads south though Bremerton to pick up the extreme inland tip of Hood Canal at a little roadside station called Belfair.

None of the Indian reservations in this country have anything about them that looks particularly Indian. The difference between them and ordinary back-county landscape, usually, is that there are no isolated houses or clearings on the reservations: the people live in villages. It is only white settlers hereabouts who live out in the wild country by themselves. The Indians have always preferred living clustered together, and still do. The Port Madison reservation does have a few scattered shanties and hayfields bordering the highway near its southern boundary, but they may not be Indian: I noticed that the hay, which had been cut, was draped across the fences to dry like a Monday's wash, as is sometimes done in Finnish communities in the Middle West.

From the reservation as far south as Bremerton the country is mostly small hay and dairy farms. From Bremerton on south to the point of Hood Canal, it is wilder: clumps of small second-growth fir, bordered with vine maple and wild lilac and hazel between openings of redtop grass and bracken. The wild flowers in this part of the country run so much to white—marguerite daisies, dogwood, elderberry, vine maple, chokecherry, wild lilac, thimbleberry, wild blackberry, bear grass—that the outcrops of pink rhododendron and wild roses and yellow buttercups seem to have wandered in by mistake and to be trying to work their way out again. This type of cut-over brushland is always a better place to find wild game than the deep and untouched timber. I jumped three deer in a willow swale a couple of miles out of Bremerton, and a covey of a dozen or fifteen ruffed grouse flew up from the roadside into some alders and sat peering down inquiringly as I drove past. From the point of Hood Canal on north, where the timber was heavier and there were no stumplands, I saw nothing except a few chipmunks.

Hood Canal is something of an oddity of Nature. It is really not a canal at all, but a natural salt-water arm of the Sound, some eighty miles long and half a mile wide, so straight and uniform in width that it is difficult to believe it was not laid out with engineering instruments. It is a beautiful body of water, clear and bright and tranquil, with beautiful country bordering it: dark firs lifting above a wall of pale-green underbrush, brightened underneath with thimbleberry and tall spikes of pink and white foxglove.

There was not much traffic along the road except a few logging trucks, but a woman at one of the roadside lunchrooms said it was about average. There was never what could be called a rush season; still, there was never really any slack season, either. She had kept her lunchroom open through November and December, and people dropped in at about the same rate as during the summer months. She wouldn't want them to come in any greater numbers than they did, because it was impossible to get help. The loneliness seemed to be the main objection. Hired help nowadays didn't like to work too far from a town.

"I'd think you'd find it lonely sometimes yourself," I said. It seemed a little isolated. She said no, there was too much to keep busy at: berrypicking, keeping things up, one thing and another.

"It looks a lot more isolated than it really is, anyway," she said. "There's people living all along this road. They leave the trees standing so you can't see their houses, but they're almost as close together as in a town."

I asked if there was someplace around where they worked. She said no, most of them were retired people who had come there to live because they liked it. That was all they did, she thought.

"A lot of them are from California," she said. "I'm from California myself. I ran a tourist camp in San Rafael for several years before I moved up here."

If she had been looking for something different from San Rafael, she had certainly found it. There could hardly have been a more complete contrast. "What made you decide to leave it?" I said.

"Several things, I guess," she said. "Too much to do all the time. Too crowded. I got sick of looking at all those swarms of people."

All mountain lakes are beautiful—that is their business, as Heine remarked about something else—but Lake Crescent, up near the northern edge of the Olympic Peninsula, outdid itself for me under the gray morning light, with mist tatters drawing loose from the dark timber after a night drizzle. Its surface was like glass, black-green in the deep shadows, almost blinding white where the clouds moving across the sky reflected in it, though the sky itself was only a watery pale gray. Some mallard ducks waddled down past the hotel flower beds toward the water, picking things out of the wet grass as they went. The young man at the hotel desk said they didn't belong to the establishment. They were wild, and had merely picked it as a place to spend their summers. They didn't go in the water much, though they spent most of their time hanging around it. We talked about the fishing. He said there were plenty of fish in the lake—Beardslee and Crescenti trout, which were found nowhere else, and rainbows and cutthroats—but that the fishing never amounted to much when it was cloudy. In clear weather they would usually come after a fly: a flying ant seemed to work the best on them. There was steelhead fishing in the creek that led out of the lake, though he hadn't tried it for a long time; the creek was brushy, and there were log jams along it.

I asked about a cutoff road that could get me to the shore of the Juan de Fuca Strait. It showed on my map as unimproved, but the young man said it had been graded and hard-surfaced in the last year or so, and would probably be all right in spite of the rain.

"And the log trucks," he said. They're pounding it pretty hard, I hear, getting out logs for the pulp mills and the shingle mills around here. Still, they haven't had time to beat it to pieces yet. It takes two or three years for them to ruin a hard-surfaced road completely, and they've only been at it since last summer."

I took the cutoff road and ultimately came to Neah Bay, the principal village of the Makah Indian Reservation: a small place or the northwest tip of the Olympic Peninsula facing across the entrance of the Juan de Fuca Strait a few miles in from Cape Flattery and the open sea. It has a Coast Guard station, one or two gasoline stations, a few shops that sell or rent fishing tackle to tourists, and a dozen or fifteen blocks of small wooden houses, some unoccupied and most unpainted, where the Makah Indians live. There is a long sand beach where two or three huge flocks of sea gulls roost and a few people wander around hunting agates and digging for clams, and a long shallow harbor filled with motor launches, mostly for rent to people who come to troll for salmon in the Strait. The history of Neah Bay goes a long way back, for a place so small and so little known. The Spanish viceroy of Mexico established a military post there in 1789, giving it the official name of Puerto Nuñez Gaona. Until 1795, when it was abandoned under pressure from Great Britain, it seems to have been a fairly busy port, with trading vessels putting in from such far-off places as Macao, Canton, Bengal, Boston, Bristol, and Portsmouth. Afterward it dwindled away to nothing, and now it has grown back into an Indian fishing village, so small and so far from anything that most people have never heard of it and few have ever been there.

Nobody could call it a pretty town. Still, the sun was out all along the road into it, and the light on the weathered old houses and the white gulls and the rough water in the Strait gave it a brightness and sparkle that was almost as good. There were clumps of pink wild roses on both sides of the highway that looked as if they had been planted as a hedge, and big bushes of yellow lupine and Scotch broom in the open fields.

I turned down one of the side streets to take some photographs, and opened the luggage compartment of the car to hunt for a wide-angle lens. A couple of little Indian boys came out of one of the houses and stopped to watch.

"You are moving here?" one of them said finally.

They were nine or ten years old, probably. Their English had no definable accent, but there was a painstaking stiffness about it, as if they were having to think of the right words as they went along. The luggage compartment did look a little like moving day. There was everything in it, as the saying used to have it, except the kitchen sink and the lens I was looking for. I said no, and thought they looked a little disappointed. A new resident in town would have been something to talk about, at least. They tried again.

"You are selling something?" the other one said.

It seemed too bad to disappoint them a second time. I explained about taking pictures, to temper it down a little. Then, to change things around, I asked what kind of fish people were catching out in the Strait.

The two boys looked at each doubtfully, probably feeling that any question so useless must be loaded somehow. The first one finally decided to risk it, and said that they were fishing for silvers, meaning silver salmon.

"Does your father rent boats to people, or take them out to fish?" I said.

They looked at each other again. "Our father don't rent," the first one said. "He catches."

"Not around here, though," the second one put in. "He catches out. Away out, a hundred miles out. He don't fish like these people."

They had stopped looking at me. They were looking out past the gray houses and the pink masses of wild roses and the gulls and the swarm of little fishing boats rocking in the bay, toward the bluish outline of Vancouver Island in the distance and a long black-hulled freighter hammering in against the rough stone-colored water of the Strait. It was as if the ship were using some thoroughfare that was theirs. The people who belong here have always been like that, I thought, the Makahs and Quillayutes driving their high-bowed canoes west to their whaling and north to their sealing grounds in the spring, the old residents dreaming of Alaska and its rivers and of prospecting and salmon fisheries and steamboats. The country keeps its own life so well because they have never taken time to bother with anything so close to home. For them, it has always been a place to look out from at something far out—Macao, Bengal, Canton, the Alaskan rivers, anywhere.

The Kettle of Fire

The kettle of fire story was told to me at different times during the summer when I was eleven years old and working at typesetting for a patent-inside weekly newspaper in Antelope, Oregon, though it didn't end with the telling and, I think, has not ended even now. The man who told it to me, a rundown old relic named Sorefoot Capron, held the post of city marshal except when there was somebody loose who needed to be arrested, and also managed the town water system, because he was the only resident who had been there long enough to know where the mains were laid. He used to drop in at the newspaper office sometimes when things were dull around town, which was often, to borrow a couple of dollars to get drunk on, and he would kill time by digging up experiences from his youth while he waited for the editor to show up and open the safe.

As he told it, he had run away from a respectable home in Ohio in the early eighteen-sixties, out of disgust with his parents because, after he had beaten his brains half out winning some prize in school, they had merely glanced coldly at it and reminded him that he was almost a half-hour late with his milking. The war was beginning then, but the enlistment boards turned him down because he was only fourteen and slight of build even for that age. He castigated his itinerary on west to St. Louis, where he supported himself during the winter by gambling at marbles and spit-at-a-crack with the colored youngsters around the stockyards, and by running errands for a Nevada silver-mine operator named Cash Payton, a heavy-set man with a short red beard, a bald spot on top of his head like a tonsure, and a scar across the bridge of his nose from having mistimed a fuse, who was hanging around waiting for the Overland Mail route to reopen so he could freight some mining machinery west over it.

He had two partners who were waiting in St. Louis with him, one a blocky little Cornishman with bow legs who talked in a chewed-up kind of bray, the other a long-coupled German with a pale beard and gold earrings, which in those times were believed by some people to be a specific against weak eyesight. They were both pleasant-spoken men, though hard to understand most of the time, but Cash Payton was not the kind of man to let his good nature stop with mere pleasant-spokenness. He took a special liking to young Capron, believed or let on to believe all the lies he told about being homeless and an orphan, and made plans to take him west with the mining machinery as soon as the road got opened up. When it turned out that the road was apt to stay closed for several months longer, he arranged to sign young Capron on as a herder and roustabout with a train of emigrants from Illinois and Missouri who were organizing to sneak past the frontier outposts and head west for a new start in unspoiled country, and also, though none of them brought the point up, to get themselves somewhere out of reach before they got picked up in the draft.

Travel across the plains to Oregon was forbidden at the time, because the military posts along the emigrant route had been abandoned and there was no protection against Indian raids, but the train managed to work its way out into open country while the border garrisons were busy with some rebel foray, and it rolled along on its westward course without any sign of trouble until it struck the Malheur Desert, not far from the line between Oregon and Nevada. It had moved slowly, and summer ends early in that part of the country, so it struck bad weather and had its horse-herd stampeded by Snake and Bannock Indians, who also killed a couple of night-herders by filling them full of arrows. The emigrants had hired some mountain man to steer them through the bad country, but the killings made them scared and suspicious, and they talked so loud and pointedly about hanging him for treachery that he picked up and pulled out in the night, leaving them stalled without any idea where they were or any draft-animals to haul them anywhere else.

It was a doleful place to be stuck in with bad weather coming on: merely a little muddy water-hole at the bottom of a rock-gully with nothing in sight anywhere around it but sagebrush and greasewood and rocks. They had vinegar to correct the alkali in the water, but several of the women got sick from drinking it, the dead sagebrush that they picked up for fuel was so soggy they couldn't get it to burn, and when they tried starting it by shooting a cotton wad into it they discovered that all their powder had drawn damp and got unusable except what was in the guns. They didn't dare squander that, and some of them opposed shooting of any kind for fear of drawing more Indians down on them, so they held a meeting and decided, since young Capron was not of much use to them and had nobody depending on him, to send him down toward the Nevada mining settlements for help, if he could find any. In any case, and whatever he found or did, he was to bring back an iron kettle full of live coals with which they could start a fire in damp wood.

It was a risky mission to put off onto a youngster, and several of the men, all elderly and in no danger of being let in for it themselves, dwelt with some sarcasm on the idea of selecting anybody so young and inexperienced for a job that they were all willing to offer advice about but not to undertake in his place, but nobody came up with anything better, and as far as young Capron was concerned he didn't in the least mind being picked for it. He was tired of the whole pack of them by then, and would have welcomed anything, dangerous or not, that could serve as an excuse to get away from them. He was not especially uneasy about the risks, or about the chance of finding any fire to bring back. His only difficulty, all through the time when they were arguing back and forth about sending him, was trying to decide whether to come back and expose himself to them again even if he did find it.

The strain and solemnity of starting settled that for him. He knew, even before he had finished saddling up and had climbed on the saddle-pony they had caught up for him, that he would have to come back. They had made him wait till after dark to start, and he couldn't see any of the men around him, though he knew that they were all there. From the ground, he had been able to make out their figures against the sky, but looking down at them from the saddle was like trying to keep track of a foam streak after it had been swept under in a deep rapid. One of them reached out and clattered the kettle-bale over his saddle-horn, and he heard them all draw back to leave the way open for him. Except for that, they were all silent. There was no sound in the camp except for the herd-ponies shifting to keep warm, and a child blubbering listlessly in one of the wagons, and the choking sound of a sick woman trying to vomit. A curious apathy comes over people facing death when they know it and know what form it will take, even when they still go through the form of refusing to admit that they know any thing about it. Afterward, when the reality begins to show itself, they are likely to fall into a panic and do things too disgusting to bear telling or thinking of. Young Capron knew that he had to get back with the fire, and that if he failed to get back with it before they reached that point it would be useless. Saving the lives of people who had made themselves unfit to live would be work wasted, and possibly worse than wasted. It would not help merely to keep on going, either: that would mean carrying the sounds of the camp along with him, the woman choking, the child blubbering, the silent men shuffling as they drew back in the dark, through all the years that he could reasonably expect to live, and maybe even beyond them. He had to find fire, and he had to get back with it while they were still able to hold themselves together. They might have been wrong and selfish in picking him, and they might be hard to like or live with, but there was nothing else for it. With that in his head, and with the kettle on his saddle-horn and a sack of food strapped on the cantle, he rode out between the wagons into the sagebrush.

Getting out of the gully into open country was slow and precarious work. The Indians turned out to have an outpost line drawn all the way around the camp a half-mile back from it, and he had to keep to the draws and move cautiously, leading the pony and inching along in places a step at a time, to dodge them. The pony saved him once, by balking and refusing to move even when spurred. He got off and crawled ahead to investigate, and discovered that he had been riding straight into a watch-post at the top of the ridge. The Indians had dug a hole and covered it with a blanket to keep the warmth in, with a head-slit cut in the middle to look out through. It took him over an hour to back-track, find the pony in the dark, and circle around it. Afterward he heard dogs yapping in the Indian camp, and he put in another two or three hours edging around that, dismounting and putting his ear to the ground every dozen yards or so to keep from running into squaws out rummaging firewood.

Toward daylight the desert around him looked clear, and he dropped down into a creek-wash and slept in a little thornberry thicket while the pony filled up on salt-grass around a mudhole, but when he got saddled up to start off again he saw mounted Indians casting around in the sagebrush for his trail a couple of miles away, so he kept to the draws, crawling and hauling the pony along by main strength where the thorn-bush grew heavy, until almost noon. Then he mounted and struck up a long lope and held it, stopping only to rest for an hour when he struck a water-hole, all day and most of the night and all through the next day, with no sleep except when he forgot and dozed in the saddle and no food except a sage-hen which he knocked over with a rock and ate raw. Toward nightfall he made out some scattering pine timber with shadows that looked palish blue as if smoke were coloring them. He headed for it, hoping to find some camp that was burning charcoal for the Nevada mines, or possibly a dead tree smoldering from being struck by lightning. Night came while he was still a couple of miles away, but he kept going because, in the darkness, he could see that it was a real fire, and that the reddish pine trunks lit up and darkened as it flickered back and forth across them.

He dismounted, playing it safe, tied the pony to a boulder and hung the kettle from his belt, and crept forward on his hands and knees, keeping the sagebrush clumps between him and the light and stopping behind every clump to sight out the ground before inching on ahead. It was a good thing he did, for he saw when he got close that the fire had men around it. The light was too fitful and uneven to show what they looked like, but he could make out a wickiup behind them, a round-topped basketwork structure covered halfway down with skins and tattered pieces of old canvas. It was enough to make him hug the ground and peer through the tangle of sagebrush instead of looking out around it. Only Snake Indians built basketwork wickiups, and the Snakes were the most warlike of all the tribes in that part of the country. He felt pleased at being able to remember about wickiups at such a time, and started looking for more signs that the men really were Indians, ignoring whatever evidence there was that might have hinted at anything else.

The fire itself was a clear sign that they were Indians. It was not the kind of towering holocaust that white travelers always set going when they were camped for the night in wild country, but a wan little flicker of only three or four small sticks, so puny and half-hearted that he wondered how its light could have been visible so far out in the open desert. It was not nearly big enough for the men to keep warm by, but it seemed what they wanted, for they kept piling ashes on it to hold it down, and once one of them picked up a stick that was beginning to blaze up and quenched it by sticking it into the dirt. Only Indians would have gone to so much trouble to keep a campfire low, and when the man who had quenched the stick stood up to rake the coals back together young Capron saw that he was wrapped in a blanket and that there was a gleam of something whitish as he turned his head that looked like an Indian headband.

There might have been other signs, if he had looked for them, but they were not needed, and he didn't dare wait any longer. The smallness of the fire had led him to miscalculate his distances, and his pony was tied close enough so that they might hear it if it started stamping or pawing. There was nothing to hold back for, anyway. Indians were Indians. They had not wasted their time arguing about killing the emigrant train's two night-herders and running off its livestock, and the train needed fire worse than they had needed wagon-horses. He rummaged out his pistol, poked it carefully through the middle of the sagebrush clump, and waited till the man with the blanket stood away from the fire so he would have the light to sight against. He drew for the center of the blanket a handbreadth below the man's shoulders, leveled up till the foresight filled the back notch, and let go. The smoke of the black powder filled the tangle of sagebrush like gray cottonwood-down settling from a wind, but he lay and glared through it and through the smoke still dribbling from the pistol muzzle without even noticing it.

The man stood motionless for a long second while the blanket slid from his shoulders and piled up around his feet. Then he swayed, flapped his elbows and tipped his head back as if getting ready to crow, and fell face-down across the fire and plunged the whole camp into pitch darkness. He must have died falling, by the slack-jointed thump his body made when it hit in the ashes. If he had still been conscious he would have tried to avoid the fire, and he didn't; he merely let go all holds and whopped down and gathered it to his bosom like a hen covering her chickens from a hawk.

The other men jumped up and legged it for cover. Young Capron could hear brush cracking and dead branches ripping at their clothes as they galloped off into the timber. He waited till the light from the dead man's clothes taking fire showed him that he had the camp all to himself. There was something faintly worrisome about the smell of the clothes burning. It was like wool, and Indians never wore anything except cotton cloth and buckskin. Still, it might be from a corner of the blanket burning, and there was no time to speculate about it, whatever it was. He scrabbled in the dead sagebrush needles for the kettle, had an awful moment of thinking he might have lost it, and then found it by the clatter it made against his pistol, which was still clutched in his hand. He grabbed it and scrambled up and ran in, flubbing the pistol into his holster between strides, and rolled the body clear of the ashes and stirred the blackened embers together and began scraping dead pine needles from the ground to pile on them. They were almost out. He had to pile on small twigs and fan up a glaring blaze to keep them from dying on him, knowing that every twig that caught would make him an easier target for the men who had taken to the timber, and not daring to stop feeding in more sticks to make it flame up stronger.

Ministering to the flame and strained between dread when it gained and panic when it sank, he did some wondering about what the dead man looked like, but when it finally took a solid hold and burned high enough to see by, he decided that he would rather not know, and moved back into the shadows and sat with his back to it, except for one moment when some sound, possibly of tree limbs rubbing together, made him glance around to see if it had moved. There was no sign that it had, but he didn't turn away quite fast enough to keep from noticing that what he had taken for an Indian headband was a bald spot and that a stiff beard down one side of the face had been burned to a pale gray ash that the draft from the fire kept crumbling into powder so that it looked, in the slanting light, as if it was twitching.

The sight was unnerving, though he had hard work to hold back from looking at it again, and its significance was not much help, either. Indians did not have beards or bald spots. The smell of wool had been the man's flannel shirt scorching. He had been white: possibly some Indian trader, or gun-peddler, or mining promoter; possibly somebody with political influence, and friends, and relatives; even possibly—

There was no use running possibilities all the way up the string. It was done, and there was no help for it and no use in thinking about it. It was not even certain that there was anything about it to regret. There were white men in the country who needed salting worse than most of the Indians, and a man shacked up in a Snake Indian lodge in that remote corner of the desert must have had some business in hand besides organizing classes in Bible study or quilt-piecing. Still, shooting him had been overhastiness, and young Capron was sorry about it, and scared. He scooped half the fire into the kettle, though the bigger pine sticks in it had not yet burned down to coals, and hung it on a dead tree-limb and ran for his pony. He was thankful that he had his errand to hurry for. Without it, his excuse for hurrying would have had to be something less dignified: fear that the two men might be creeping up through the trees to bushwhack him, fear that if he stayed any longer he would not be able to hold out against looking once more at the dead man's face.

The fire on the ground had burned low when he rode back, but the pitch-knots in the kettle were flaring up so the pony refused to edge within reach of it, even with spurring. Finally he got down and covered the kettle with a piece of bark, and then rode past at a trot and grabbed it from the limb before the bark had time to take fire. He moved up in the saddle, raked the pony down the ribs, and lit back into the desert with the kettle held out at one side and the flame from the bark caressing his hand and arm as vengefully as if the dead man had prayed it on him for a parting retribution.

When he got a couple of miles out, he reined up to let the flame burn down, but he heard hoofbeats from the trail behind, so he merely dumped a couple of the hottest knots out into the sagebrush and shoved on. Afterward, looking back at the glare they were making, he could have kicked himself for leaving so plain a marker for the men to steer by, though the truth was that it didn't matter much. Uncovering the coals he had kept made them flare high enough to be visible two miles away, and when he tried holding the kettle low they scared the pony into a paroxysm of rearing and pinwheeling that threatened to scatter all the fire out of it.

He had to go back to holding the kettle at arm's length before the pony would move ahead at all. It looked like trying to flag a steamboat, and the foolishness of it started him to reflecting bitterly on the things he should have done and had lacked the sense to think of till too late. He should have hunted out and stampeded the men's saddle-horses while he was waiting for the fire to get started. He should have picked greasewood for the fire instead of pitch-pine. He should have covered the kettle with dirt instead of bark. He should have used his brains instead of letting them run to imagining things that merely scared him. He should have kept his nerve, figured things out ahead, made himself into something steadier and more far-sighted than he ever had been. He should not have been in such a hurry to play the hand Providence had dealt him to establish his future on. It would have been better if he had held back and tried to change the spots on the cards by making faces at them, or possibly by crying over them. A man had to live up to what he was, weaknesses and all. Finding out what they were was probably not worth shooting a man, for, but it was a gain. The kettle had returned him that much for his trouble, at least.

He held the pony to a high trot for a couple of miles, and then pulled up to let it catch its wind. He could no longer hear hoofbeats back of him, so he took time to pull off his coat and wrap it around his hand as a protection against the heat from the coals. Then a rock clattered back in the distance, and he knew the men were still coming, and closing the range. The pony heard it too, and he had to rein back hard to keep it from breaking into a run and getting windbroken. It would have been easy to lose them if his hands had been free: he could merely have walked the pony down into some gully and laid low till they passed. The kettle killed that possibility; they could line him in by the light from it, no matter which way he turned or what track he took. He thought of covering it with gravel, or with a sod from some mudhole, but decided against that for fear of smothering the fire completely.

At the end of six or seven miles more, he realized that it was not far from going out all by itself. The coat wadded over his burned hand had kept him from noticing how much the kettle had cooled down. One welcome part of it was that the light had got too weak to be visible at a distance, but he was too much afraid of losing the fire to take comfort in its debility. He slowed to a walk for awhile, and then turned sharp away from his course down a long draw, dismounted and tied the pony in a thicket of giant sagebrush, and felt his way down the slope hunting for dead roots that could be used for kindling. There was nothing dry enough until, in the low ground where the draw widened out, he bumped into some stunted junipers. Juniper wood is too light and porous to be much use as fuel, but the trunks were run through with dead streaks from which, by gouging with his knife, he managed to pry loose a handful of splinters that would take fire easily, even if they didn't hold it long.

The kettle was cool enough to touch by the time he finished collecting them, but with careful blowing they condescended to flicker up so that he could lay on heavier fuel from the dead branches. When that caught, he rammed the kettle down into a badger hole, piled whole branches over it to make sure the fire would last, and went on down the dry watercourse to find hardwood that would burn down into coals. The light from the branches glared like a haystack burning, and he had no trouble finding greasewood roots and a dead chokecherry tree and loading himself up with chunks from them. The flame behind him filled half the sky by then, so he circled back cautiously and hid under a low-branched juniper fifty or sixty yards from it, in case it drew anybody to come investigating.

It happened quicker than he had counted on. He had got himself settled among the juniper boughs, which smelled bad, and was smearing his face with wet dirt to blend with the shadows when two men came down the slope from his trail, stopped where the sagebrush thinned out, and stood watching the fire and shading their eyes against it. They were a hundred yards away, and they looked unearthly tall in the sheeting glare of the fire, but he could see that they were white men. They had on ordinary work clothes, and they wore hats and had their hair cut short. That was nothing much; he had expected that they would turn out to be white, and he was not afraid of them except for a slight feeling of strain inside him. It gouged harder to see that one of them was blocky and reddish and bowlegged, and that the other was tall and thin and pale-bearded, with earrings on which the light sparkled when he moved his head. Young Capron would not have noticed the earrings at such a distance if he had not been expecting them. The men were the sawed-off Cornishman and the tall German who had been Cash Payton's partners. He had liked Cash Payton better than both of them, better than anybody else, as far as that went, but he had liked them. Because he had shot Cash Payton, he dared not move for fear they would pick out his hiding place and kill him. They stood peering across the firelight into the junipers, the German wagging a long army cap-and-ball revolver and the Cornishman holding a rifle as if he were fixing to rake hay with it, all primed and set to open up on anything that moved.

They loomed up against the shadows like clay pipes in a shooting gallery. If they had been strangers, if the firelight had not outdone itself to show who they were beyond the possibility of a mistake, he could have cleared his way back to the emigrant train with two cartridges, besides acquiring possession of two unjaded saddle-horses which he could have used very handily. What they had been doing camped in the timber so far from anywhere he didn't try to guess. Nothing to their credit, likely, or they would not have gone to so much trouble to run him down. Catching Indian children to sell as slaves in San Francisco was a flourishing business then, and if it was that, they deserved shooting for it. So did Cash Payton, except that points of ethics no longer counted. All that did count was knowing that the man who had befriended him and kept him alive over a whole winter was lying dead back in the pine timber with half his face burned off, all because of a scary young squirt's clubfooted foolishness. Bad or good, right or wrong, he had deserved better than to be shot down from cover when his back was turned. Young Capron shut his eyes and buried his face in the dirt, wondering, to end a painful train of reflection, whether he could ever smell juniper boughs again without getting sick, as in fact he never could, in all the years afterward.

When he looked up, the men were leaving, probably having realized the sappiness of standing in the full glare of the fire when the man they were hunting might be lurking somewhere close enough to take advantage of it. The tall German stopped at the edge of the sagebrush and examined the caps in his revolver to make sure they were all in place. That meant that they were not giving up, and that they would probably post themselves somewhere along his trail, figuring to knock him over when he came back to it. If it had not been for the shooting they would have been glad to see him and, if they could, to help him. If it had not been for the fire kettle there would not have been any shooting. Of course, he could leave it where it was and ride after them and let on not to know anything about it, so they would blame the shooting on somebody else. They would probably take his word for it: foreigners were trustful about things they didn't understand very well, in contrast to Americans, who were always the most suspicious in matters they knew the least about. He could go with the two men and be safe, and be rid of the emigrants and their sniveling and domineering for good.

The only trouble was that he couldn't bring himself to do it. It would mean that Cash Payton had died for nothing, for mere foolishness, because a streak of light hit him in the wrong place. The only way to make his death count for anything was to get the fire back to the train. He shook loose from his seesawing and went into the tall sagebrush for his pony.

The fire had burned down when he came back with the pony, and the juniper boughs were falling into coals that the stir of air fanned into flaky ashes. It was hard to lose time building them back, but he had to have some kind of fire that would last, and the pony would hold up better for being left to graze and rest a little longer. He piled on the greasewood and wild cherry, waited to make sure it caught, and then lay down upwind from the junipers and slept until the glare of the new fire woke him. He fished the kettle out with a forked tree-limb, left it to cool while he caught and bridled the pony, and scooped it full of new coals and tried to mount with it.

The pony had recuperated too well. It shied back and fought so that he had to put the kettle down to keep from being yanked off his feet. He tried covering the coals with ashes, but the glow still showed through, and the pony fought back from it till he set the kettle back on the ground and climbed aboard without it. He rode past it and tried to pick it up from the saddle, but the pony shied off so he couldn't reach it. Finally he found his forked tree-limb, circled back, and hooked the kettle at long range and hauled it in. Even then it took all his strength on the reins to keep the pony from pinwheeling and running away from the heat and light following along even with its off-shoulder.

He had held his feelings back too long, probably. He was crying by the time he got the kettle hoisted up and felt the heat on his burned flesh again. He got angry with himself for crying, and his anger made him forget about the two men waiting for him somewhere along the trail ahead. He remembered them after he had ridden a few hundred yards, and swung back along the draw on a wide circuit to keep clear of them. Half the coals in the kettle had got spilled out in his manipulations with the forked tree-limb, and he had no idea how he would manage about renewing them when they burned low again, but there was no use killing snakes till they stopped hibernating. He put it out of his mind, along with what seemed a lifetime of other useless reflections and apprehensions, and rode on.

The coals burned low about daylight, when he was crossing a long level plain on which even the sagebrush grew so thin that he was in plain sight of anybody two or three miles away in any direction. Sagebrush roots burned out almost like wadded newspaper, but there was nothing else, and he got down and gathered an armload of them and nursed the fire back to life. They were damp, and the smoke from them rose in a whitish column that could be seen for miles, but at least the open plain made it impossible for anybody to sneak up on him. It was about fifteen miles across, and he could see anything that moved on it. A man on horseback would have loomed up like a steeple, even at the edge of it.

Nothing came in sight. The plain was lifeless except for horned toads. With the daylight, the pony had got over its fright of the kettle, and it struck up a trot when he remounted, as if it were as anxious to see the last of the place as he was. The plain broke into a long ridge, speckled at its base with little rusty junipers and with a tangle of mountain mahogany marking the line of a dry gully. He halted and broke some of its dead boughs for fuel, since they were hot and slow-burning. They took away his anxiety about the fire for the moment, and it began to be brought home to him that he had circled into country where nobody had ever been before. A herd of antelope came out of the junipers as he passed, looked after him with their back-tufts twitching with inquisitiveness, and then followed along after him, edging downwind to catch his scent and then moving in to gawk at him from such close range that he could have hit them with a rock. The pony watched them uneasily and stumbled over so many rocks and roots trying to keep out of their way that he was halfway tempted to do it, except that it would have meant having to stop and dismount to find something to throw.

Beyond the ridge, he lost them. The ground leveled off into a long expanse of naked earth, pocked and honeycombed with sage-rat burrows. It must have been a mile across, and the country around it for a half-dozen miles was stripped as bare as if it had been plowed and harrowed. There were sage-rats all over it. Some sat up and stared at him as he passed, and then dropped almost under the pony's feet and went on about their business, whatever it was. Some scurried for their holes as if scared, but then they sat up and stared too, and finally sauntered back where they had come from, evidently feeling that whatever was happening at the pony's level was no concern of theirs, and that, when all was said and done, the proper study of ratkind was rats. There was nothing anywhere near their ground that could be used for fuel to keep the fire up, and the ground itself was treacherous because the pony kept breaking through it where they had tunneled it for their nests.

They were not much company. The worst of it was not their strangeness and preoccupation with themselves, it was the loneliness of the country that made young Capron adapt himself, without being aware of it, to their values and scale of living. A few more miles of them, he felt, and he would find himself growing feeler-whiskers, squeaking, and rearing up on his hind-legs to watch himself ride past and try for a second or two to figure out what he was. He turned down a dry gully to get clear of them and the waste they had created, and came to a long scarp of low gray cliffs, broken into rifts and ledges for its entire length. Every rift and every ledge was occupied by great pale-gray owls. None of them moved as he rode past. They sat straight and impassive, hooting to each other briefly sometimes with a hollow sound like blowing into an empty jug, their blank yellow eyes staring past him into the sun without seeing it or him and without knowing or caring what he was. They could see objects only in the half-dusk or in the dark. Nothing that passed in the sunlight made any impression on them.

The cliffs fell away, and the gully spread out into a wide flat covered with stubby clumps of old weatherstained rye-grass. The ground between the clumps was dark and water-soaked, but it was covered so densely with jackrabbits that it looked gray and moving like a spread of water. The jackrabbits moved sluggishly, some of them waiting till they were almost under the pony's feet and then dragging themselves barely out of the way and settling down again. Their trouble was one that usually hit jackrabbits in the years when they had run themselves down by overbreeding. They were swollen with wens from bot-flies, and so weakened by them that they couldn't have moved fast if they had wanted to.

A curious thing about it was that though disease had undermined their instinct for self-preservation, it had left their appetites unimpaired, or only a little slackened. They were still able to crop all the green sprouts out of the dead rye-grass clumps, and they had not lost their interest in copulation, whatever might have happened to their ability. They were not noticeably energetic about it, but they stayed with it faithfully, working as the pony picked its way among them at the absorbing task of perpetuating their kind, botflies and all, and regarding nothing else as deserving of notice.

The flat fell away into a long rise and fall of stony desert, and then to a broad grass-slope that reached down to a bright-green little alkali lake, with dark wire-grass in the shallows and patches of willow on the damp ground back of them. The slopes and the shallows were covered solid with wild geese, mottled like a patched quilt with their different colors—brown Canada geese, white snow-geese, dark little cacklers, blue honkers, ringnecked black brant—rocking placidly on the bitter water or crowded solid along the swell of short grass overlooking it. Young

Capron would have liked to avoid them, but the fire was low in the kettle, and there was dead wood among the willows that would make good coals and no way of getting it except to ride straight through them.

Of all the forms of life the country had put him up against, they were the worst. They held their ground till he could have reached down and touched them, and then rose with a horrible blast of screeching and banging of wings, darkening the sky overhead and spattering him and the pony and the kettle and the fire in it with filth to show how much he had upset them by turning out to be something they had not been expecting. Then, as the next flock went squalling and clattering up with a new shower, the one behind him settled back onto the grass as unconcernedly as if nothing at all had happened, as, no doubt, in the tablets of their memory, nothing at all had.

They should have quieted down and gone back to resting when he dismounted and went to work preparing the dead willow limbs for his fire, but they seemed unable either to stand him or to let him alone. Every few minutes, though he moved as little as he could and the pony scarcely stirred out of its tracks, some of them would stalk close to him, rear up and look him over again, and then let out a horrified squawk and put the whole flock up to spatter him with filth all over again. It was not hostility so much as indignation. They were outraged with him for being there, without having the ghost of an idea what he was doing or the slightest interest in finding out.

Getting clear of the wild country took a long time. He had circled farther than he realized, and crossing the long swells of ground beyond the lake took up the whole afternoon, counting two or three times when he had to skirmish up dead limbs of cottonwood and service-berry to stoke the kettle. There was one more small flurry of wild life, a little creek bordered with short grass that was being stripped off by huge wingless Mormon crickets. They were slippery for the pony to step on, but there was nothing else to them except appetite. Some little darkish rattlesnakes picked languidly at them around the edges, without any great show of interest in doing it. Young Capron spurred away from the place, feeling with some self-pity that a man had to fall low to be siding with rattlesnakes, but wishing them well even in wanting to be rid of them for good.

He would have liked to keep going when it got dark, but the pony was sunken-flanked and laboring on the slopes, so he turned into a little stand of cottonwoods and unsaddled and turned it out to graze. He found some half-dead wild plum and dumped the coals from the kettle and built up a fire with fuel from it, first dead sticks and then bigger green ones, which burned slower but made long-lasting coals. When the fire took hold, he ate some salt pork that the emigrants had given him, downing it raw because cooking wasted it, and spread out on a patch of dampish ground and slept.

Something brought him awake along in the night. He didn't know what it had been, but he could tell by the waning fire that he had slept for several hours, and he noticed that the silence around him was deeper than it had been when he was going to sleep. Building the fire back, he realized that what he missed was the sound of the pony grazing. He piled kindling into the kettle for a light and went out to see what had become of it. The grass showed where it had been grazing, but it was gone. He tried farther out, remembering gloomily that Indians always ran the horses off from a camp that they were getting ready to jump, and found a shallow mudhole that had been trampled all around by horses. The tracks were fresh, which disturbed him for a minute, but a smoothed-down place in the mud where they had been rolling showed that they were running loose. Not all of them were Indian horses either; some of them were shod, and the calk-marks were big enough to have been made by wagon-teams, possibly from the emigrant train, not that it mattered. The pony might have been scared off by some cougar stalking the herd, and it might still be hanging around. That didn't matter either. All that mattered was that the pony had gone with a loose horse-herd, and that there was no use trying to get it back on foot and burdened with a kettle of fire that it had been scared of from the beginning. One from one left nothing, no matter what had been responsible for it.

He ate salt pork again, hung his saddle and bridle from a tree limb, filled the kettle with new coals and cut a stick to carry it by, and started on afoot without waiting for daylight. In some ways, traveling was easier with the pony gone. There was no worry over having it snort or stamp or whinny at the wrong time, or over having to find grass or water at the stopping places, or having it shy and fight back when he tried to mount, and being able to carry the kettle close to the ground made it less easily seen at a distance. More than that, he was freed from the temptation to throw it away and head out for himself. Without a horse and without food enough for another day, the emigrant camp was the only place he could go. Having to concentrate on one thing instead of see-sawing between lurking alternatives made everything simpler: not easier, but easier to summon strength for.

In the afternoon, plodding down a wide valley that opened into draws where there was small wood and water, he found the first sign that he was nearing human beings. It was not a brightening one, merely a dead horse spread out on a patch of bare ground with some buzzards lined up waiting for the sun to burst it open, but it did show that he was headed right and that he was making distance. It turned his thoughts to the emigrant camp, and he began to notice, thinking of the emigrants waiting for him, that the dead sagebrush tops were drying out and that the ground underfoot was strewn with little chips of black flint. He refired the kettle and hurried on, driven by fear that the emigrants might have run into the same thing near their camp, that they might have found dry kindling and lighted a flint-and-steel fire for themselves.

Thinking of that possibility and discovering what his own feelings about it were opened a new area of self-knowledge to him, and not an especially comforting one. He tried to think how much suffering and fear and despair they would be spared if they had thought of trying it, and could get no farther than the reflection that it would make his own suffering and fear and despair useless: a man dead, and his pain, terror, weariness, humiliation and hunger all gone for nothing. He took more consolation from thinking that, if his knowledge of the emigrants was a sign of anything, they wouldn't have sense enough to think of hunting for flints to start with, even if they had the courage to venture far enough out to find them.

It was humiliating to realize that his values had all been turned upside down, when he could welcome seeing a dead horse with buzzards around it and be downcast to think that people he knew might be keeping warm and cooking food and drying out their gunpowder, but the fear held on in spite of him. When he looked down from the last rise of ground on the Indian camp he had skirted around in starting out, he saw a smoke rising from beyond it that appeared to come from the emigrant train, and it set him shaking at the knees so that he had to sit down to keep from collapsing. It was near sundown by then, and when it got dusk he crept on through the sagebrush and discovered that it was not from the wagons at all, but from the hole where the Indian watch post had been on the night he left camp. The hole had been abandoned, it appeared, and the Indians had made a smudge of damp sagebrush roots in it to scare the emigrants into staying where they were. He took time to pile wet earth on he smudge, to keep the emigrants from finding out how easy it would have been for them to get fire if any of them had thought of it, and he felt relieved and uplifted in spirit to think that none of them had.

The camp seemed dead when he came stumbling down into it, but after a few minutes he began to hear sounds from the wagons: children whimpering with the cold, a man praying in a loud monotone under a wagon, the sick woman still trying to vomit. He remembered that the sounds were the sweetest music he had ever listened to. No ninety-eight-piece orchestra in the land could have come within flagging-distance of them. Even after so many years and so many changes, remembering it still stirred him inside, something like jumping off a barn-roof after swallowing a half-dozen humming jew's-harps.

That was all of the story. He used to build up different parts of it at different times while he sat waiting in the printing office for the editor to arrive, but at the first telling he told it all straight through, and he ended it, as he was right to do, with the concluding emotion instead of stringing it out into the subsequent events that dulled it all down. I asked what had happened afterward, and he said nothing worth telling about. The emigrants had scraped up nerve enough to go out and run in their teams, or most of them, and they were so pleased with themselves for doing it that they forgot all about his fire that had given them the necessary courage. Then they had moved on, and finally they had come out at a river-crossing that took them into the old Barlow Road. They were not worth much, on the average, any of them.

"They made me pay for the pony I lost," he said. "And the saddle and bridle, too. Took it out of my wages, what little there was of 'em."

"It don't sound like you'd got much out of it," I said. At the time, it didn't seem to me that any story with such a frazzled-out ending was worth spending all that time on. "It sounds like everybody had come out ahead except you."

"That was what they all thought, I guess," he said. "They're welcome to their notions. None of 'em come out as far ahead as they thought they had, and it's the only thing I've ever done that I got anything out of that was worth hellroom. It's the only thing I'd do over again, I believe, if I had to. Not that I'll ever get the chance. Things like that don't happen nowadays."

He was wrong about that, of course. Such things change in substance and setting, but they go on working in the spirit, through different and less explicit symbols, as they did through the centuries before emigrations West were ever heard of, and as they will for men too young to know about them now and for others not yet born. There will always be the fire to bring home, through the same hardships and doubts and adversities of one's life that make up the triumph of having lived it.

Poems

Davis began his writing career as a poet, winning a national award, *Poetry* magazine's Levinson Prize for 1919, when he was twenty-five. He spent most of the next ten years writing poetry until H. L. Mencken encouraged Davis to try prose, which the young writer did. He published no poetry after 1933, but collected many of his earlier poems in a 1942 book, *Proud Riders and Other Poems*.

After Davis's death in 1960, his friend and a celebrated western poet himself, Thomas Hornsby Ferril, brought out and wrote an introduction for *The Selected Poems of H. L. Davis* in 1978. Ferril joined other notable American poets like Carl Sandburg and Robinson Jeffers who had earlier praised Davis's work. In a letter to Harriet Monroe, editor of *Poetry*, Jeffers wrote "He is a great person, his rhythms, his vision, his manner, like no one else's. The people moving like wistful ghosts, with such vivid gestures, through so intensely real a countryside: it gives one the oddest feeling of the grass being permanent and humanity only a poignant episode: perception the more startling for being implicit and not expressed." (Ridgeway, 1968.)

Northwest writer and critic George Venn, in an important article, "Continuity in Northwest Literature" in the anthology *Northwest Perspectives*, recognizes the signal importance of Davis's poetry to the region's literary development, explaining how Davis was revolutionary for bringing a sense of the actual Northwest flora and weather and day-to-day human life and language into the region's verse. The poems that follow include one, "Witches," which, for reasons of the more rigid censorship standards of the time, was not published in Davis's lifetime.

The earliest Davis poem in this selection is "The Rain-Crow," published in *Poetry* in 1920. "Counting Back," written on February 4, 1959 and included in *Selected Poems*, appears to be the last poem written by Davis to be published.

James Stevens submitted "Witches" to the *American Mercury* at the request of Davis. Mencken turned it down, but asked to see Davis's work that would not risk censorship. According to Stevens, Davis then submitted his fiction to the *American Mercury* and other publications, and so "it was 'Witches' that opened the way to freedom for him from that dismal desk job in a ramshackle, poverty-stricken county courthouse."

The Rain-Crow

While women were still talking near this dead friend,
I came out into a field where evergreen berry vines
Grew over an old fence, with rain on their leaves;
And would not have thought of her death, except for a few
Low sheltered berry leaves: I believed the rain
Could not reach them; but it rained on them every one.
So when we thought this friend safest and most kind,
Resetting young plants against winter, it was she
Must come to be a dead body. And to think
That she knew so much, and not that she would die!
Not that most simple thing – for her hands, or her eyes.

Dead. There were prints in the soft spaded ground
Which her knees made when she dug her tender plants.
Above the berry leaves the black garden and all the land
Steamed with rain like a winded horse, appeared strong.
And the rain-crow's voice, which we took for a sign of rain,
Began like a little bell striking in the leaves.
So I sat in the rain listening to this bird's voice,
And thought that our friend's mouth now, its "Dead, I am dead,"
Was like the rain-crow sounding during the rain:
As if rain were a thing none of us had ever seen.

Crop Campers

Not now,—she says,—but maybe, when you're out of work,
Bereaved, in trouble, or mending from a sickness—then
You'll think your wheat country is too much lived in.
Then come.
Come live with us, maybe for a Summer . . . . If you will?
If you like us enough to want to live with us? . . .
At first
You'll ride in the wagons with us women. Oh, but still,
That isn't a bad way to travel. You can sleep;
You can foot it ahead, and find water, and quench your thirst,
And sleep till your wagon catches up. We would sing songs.
You'd sing to me, riding in the wagon that I have to drive;
You could handle the brake-rope, and sing to me over the reins.
I've wanted to learn some of your songs . . . Then, later on,
We'll find you a saddle-horse to ride on.—If you come.

This is not a good camp. We're camped here to be near the grain.
Most often we camp better—among alders, among white
cottonwoods,
Or quaken-asp shivering beside water. Those draw wind.
There's a wind in the quaken-asp always, in the stillest heat.
Still, even this grain-camp looks nearly beautiful at dawn.
The stars dissolve out, and the black sky bleeds full of light.
The stiff grain crosses and beats together . . . . It's half beautiful.
You'd think so. Yes. But make me no promises to come.
. . . If you liked, you could work with our men, harvesting.
But no need.
They gamble, and waste all the crop-money that they earn.
It's the work of us women that buys us what we eat.
Of course, here there is nothing we can work at. We work in Autumn.
From late Summer till the end of Autumn we pick fruit.
You could either tend camp or follow us pickers. That's more work,
But I think you would follow us pickers . . . .

Because, in camp,
Are all our old people, incapable of work, sick, blind.
They have to be tended, and listened to. Mine are dead.
—My people are all dead, I haven't got even any man.—
But there's plenty of others have, and you have to watch them die.
They think they're not dying, that it's something we pity and make
right,
Could cure, if we wanted to. . . . Blind people come fumbling at your
head.
One old man's got syphilis in his head, and whines with pain—
All during your sleep, whimpering. When you cry out,
Because his voice hurts you to listen to, he'll stare
And sleep and begin whimpering again. It's griped his brain.
Sometimes he mumbles for his dead sons, calling them by name,
Arguing, begging. . . . His voice and his lips hurt you.
Hearing him,
His helpless half-habit and half-agony, any length of time,
You'll begin to wish that you were deaf. You'll stop your ears,
And unstop them fearing he has died. You'll think, what way,
Since I have to listen, can I listen and not hate his tears?
You'll think, maybe you might in passion. Might hear his voice,
Plainly, and yet be lifted by passion to a strength
That would make his hard agony, and his loose-mouthed whimpering
a song,
A strong great harmony of music. Yes. Rejoice,
Not deafening ourselves to his bleating, to his shame and wrong,
But sharpening our ears to hear all of it, every sound
Building the laughter of our passion high and strong.
Oh, maybe we shall, then! We'd be hard-spirited with love.
We'd deafen it to nothing, not pity, not grief, nor fear.
We'd put our memories and senses, our hands and feet
And tongues and minds in the dark hopper, and all we own,
Our bodies and our work, to thicken the muscle of our love,
That might break and digest agony, and still be sweet.

. . . You will teach me your songs then, some time? If you decide!
—But make no promises; for, after I am gone,
You'll remember me better without promises of any kind.
Remember some things—maybe they'll come back to your mind,
Days off and on–the wheat-dawn; quaken-asp wind.
You may wish you could be in my camp-wagon and see the dawn,
Even among the crying of our old people, our cracked and blind,
After some pitiful fierce passion, side by side.

Witches

The old ranch grandma climbed out of bed,
And tottered to the chuck-room, and she said:

"You young harvest-hands, you're mighty fiery-gaited;
You're as high-lived a bunch as was ever congregated.
You get drunk, you yell around the yard after dark,
You pester all the kitchen-girls a tryin' to spark.
I want to warn you now, before you mouth another bite—
There's witches a-bewitchin' us every blamed night!
They bewitched my son, and they rode him with a quirt
From here to Camas Valley in his undershirt!
They rode him all a-lather, and they spattered him with mud,
And they dug him with their toenails till his ribs run blood;
When they wanted him to gallop, they twisted on his private!
He says he never knew how he managed to survive it!"

Well, as long as she believes him, that's all right.
Anybody's liable to get a little tight.
Any drunk'll get his shirt muddied and tore,
And be a little vague how his reuben got sore.

She came over to the bunk-house, and she said,
"Take keer!
There's mighty deathly doin's a-goin' on here!
We've made the witches mad, and they're castin' down a spell
That's a-liable to kill us to a fare-you-well!
Why, a witch has cast a spell around this bunk-house, damn her,
And she's killed my purples grape-vine as dead as a hammer!"

Which, as long as she believes it, seems O.K.
Most harvest-hands, just before they hit the hay,
Get caught short and have to take a squirt.
You can't traipse to the privy in nothing but your shirt.

What do you do, then? Why, generally, this:
Get in against the grapevine and take a piss.
And, with all the harvest-hands' urine there spilled,
Most anybody's grapevine might get killed.

She came out after dark, where we was unhitchin',
And she said,
"Them witches is a ha'ntin' and a-witchin',
Lordy knows what spell they're a-castin' on the wheat!
Most likely they'll bewitch it so it ain't fit to eat!
I'll swan to God, if a witch ain't turned
And witched the evenin's cream till it can't be churned!
There's young Pheemy Halfpapp's been a-poundin' and a-bangin'
Till she's all out o'breath, with her front hair hangin',
And her knees a-knockin', and her face like a beet,
A-scared of her shadder, and a-shakin' like a sheet;
And she's pumped that churn since long about noon,
As steady as a hound a-diggin' out a coon!
I don't know what in the nation to do.
I'm a-lookin' every minute that they'll witch me too."
Which is all well and good, if the facts don't hinder.
I'd noticed Pheemy sneakin' out the milk-house winder,
To meet some feller, pretty early in the day.
And they spent till sundown in a stack of hay.
If she done any churnin' in that old haystack,
It was done without a churn, and a-layin' on her back.

She said:
"When I was little, in East Tennessee,
The witches come and witched a young sugar-maple tree.
All of its leaves turned bloodish red
And hung all winter, when the other trees shed.
Long about spring, when the bugs broke shell,
We hired a witch doctor to kill the spell,
He took green locust, and he whittled out a stake

And marked it with a thing that looked like a snake;
And he set the stake on the maple tree's side
And drove it with an axe. And the maple tree cried.
The tree screamed and whimpered like a full grown woman.
Then it tried to say somethin' and its breath died, hummin'.
The witch-doctor said, 'Well! There's your witch!
I reckon I fixed that son of a bitch!'
And there ain't been a witch on the place since then."

Well. That sounds pretty good for witch-doctor men.
Still, I know lots of things I'd rather do.
I'd rather punch header on a threshing crew,
And live between harvests on the bum, than dream
Of spikin' a live tree and hearin' it scream.

The River People

Gray and white sea-gulls, we own tight-rooted grass
Haired over with frost, and wild leaves that women rake
To cover their bulbs from frost—as when I watched and might ask,
Being a child, why she raked them, and why she laughed
At wild geese crying to pass the sharp apple-pruning smoke
Which shut them from the river. She wondered of the sea.
And that she taught me to make little of women, and of all but death,
Is not my debt. Yet in the hard fields of the river I build speech
Till I say: "When I saw the sea-tide I remembered how you lived
When I was a little boy. I helped you, and cleaned grass
From your wind-fallen apples, and I have seen the sea,
Which in that cold autumn you wished for—not level water,
But higher than your head and like a smooth hill
On which the grass turns the light. Wind presses a man's mouth,
And cuts furrows in that sloped water where dark combs run
And bloom white, and bloom like the black-barked limbs of apples in
rain.
As wild cattle break from the counting-pens, with what dust
The low-headed leaders raise blowing on the packed ground –
When the press lay their horns back and mount plunging with sharp
feet,
And low quaking-asp-boughs whip them on the naked eyes."
And she: "We tasted of waves when we were children gathering mast
Under the myrtle-trees whose broad leafage takes
The bitter taste out of the air. They shook the ground."

And I: "Children on the beach play cattle with myrtle-nuts.
They are Finn and Russian children, who have white hair
And cross the mountains in fall to pick hops. They have cried
When the train passed the hopyards, from ignorance.
They graze cattle on the cliffs for milk. Their hay
Grows wild, seeds, but never ripens. Fine-petalled purple flowers
And late spotted snapdragons fall to the scythe."

"Are they green all year?
We used to race before light when they were burning straw.
We called out for cold of morning. Is there never smoke
Raising the wild geese that glean our hulled wheat? No birds
Like ours that flock twitching the wheat-stems and their sharp
Changing ground when the smoke turns?"
"Not those."
"I'll keep here
And not owe my daughters, but lie against the black ground
Till sand come and weigh down my hands, until birds come close
Having long observed me. I know how much I came
Surely out of the round hills, those that are in grain
Or white stubble against winter; and out of that sound
Of blackbirds changing stand, let that return.
And you also, son, when you described the sea, took your words
Out of cattle-counting and out of river-hills rounded with wind."

Steel Gang

The boss came over and called us out a little bit after dark,
He said, "I don't want you boys to think your work ain't up to the mark,
But Paddy Duffy goes bragging around, the steel his Mex can lay—
All how that spiggoty gang spikes down two miles and a half a day,
And how two miles and a half is more than any man's gang can tap.
So I want you men to help me out to make him shut his yap.
No matter what record a Mex gang makes, I claim white men can trim it.
What I want you to do is, prove I'm right—for one day, go your limit.
I want you men to go tomorrow and make that record climb.
You put it where these damn spigs can't reach, I'll pay you triple time."

We counseled it over and said we would. We hit the deck at three,
And the engineer whistled, "Let's go!" before it was light enough to see.
The tram rolled up to the head of steel. The ties came sliding off
And we had 'em laid and the steel half spiked before a man could cough.
The tram rolled over the spikers' work, and they never missed a lick.
Right under the wheels, they spiked right on, and drove 'em tight and quick.
When the surfacing-crew came up at a run, to raise and level track,
The tram was a dozen rails ahead, and never a man looked back.
We swung those hundred-and-ten pound rails like a grocery-clerk flips matches.
We grabbed those damned ties four at a time, and dealt them out in batches.

At half-past eight o'clock that night, the boss said, "Pull the cord!"
Said, "Call 'em off! Christ, four miles and a half! There's a record, by the Lord!
Call in the men and let's go in—they've earned a feed tonight.

You can boost for your goddam greasers, but I'll string with a gang that's white!"
The snipes let go their tools in the dirt, the hogs climbed down from the tram,
And they flopped in a heap in the outfit-train, too tired to give a damn.
Too tired to talk, too tired to wash, too tired to even eat.
The cooks had a feed shook up, supposed to be a special treat;
But victuals didn't have any taste. The men dragged off to bed.
Some had too much of an edge to sleep, and lay and gaped instead,
Their eyes half-shut and their mouths ajar, too dead to fight the flies
That stuck and bored in the sweaty places, and crawled around their eyes.

For that day's work they paid three days; and then, they paid full pay
For the following day, when none of the men would budge out of the hay.
Then, for the day that followed that, they offered us double jack
Because we had all lost heart in the work, and they wanted to bring us back.
So we worked that day for their double time, and then pulled up and quit.

The spig gang stayed and finished the job after us white men lit.

Clearing Old Stones

Best the indifference of the stones, the hill
About these old graves, my own. A cure, a mending
From sickness of spirit in raking up dead burrs
And dead weed-stalks that have matted all the ground
Since the old farms fell vacant. Raking dry stems
Of old lupin, hollyhock, sunflower, lean milkweed
Blown from neglected fields, from fraying stubble
Long abandoned and left leaching in light and wind.
Under these, chaff of old harvests, stems of flowers
Carried once from some backyard garden long since gone,
And scattered among these stones. Cut twigs come last,
Sprays of wild plum that people brought and spread
To hide a grave till our first grief was past,
Before their own grief struck or these weeds came, cold emblems
Of lives here wasted, hiding the earth from light.

It is like a deliverance to see the dead stalks, raked and piled,
Burn and blow skyward into light upon a flame
Stretching and flapping again silence, and at last
To clean the earth bare again, to bring and scatter
Armloads of wild grass, bright and hard-stemmed and innocent
That grew here before flowers or any mourning came.

Proud Riders

We rode hard, and brought the cattle from brushy springs,
From heavy dying thickets, leaves wet as snow;
From high places, white-grassed and dry in the wind;
Draws where the quaken-asps were yellow and white,
And the leaves spun and spun like money spinning.
We poured them on to the trail, and rode for town.

Men in the fields leaned forward in the wind,
Stood in the stubble and watched the cattle passing.
The wind bowed all, the stubble shook like a shirt.
We threw the reins by the yellow and black fields and rode,
And came, riding together, into the town
Which is by the gray bridge, where the alders are.
The white-barked alder trees dropping big leaves
Yellow and black, into the cold black water.
Children, little cold boys, watched after us—
The freezing wind flapped their clothes like windmill paddles.
Down the flat frosty road we crowded the herd:
High stepped the horses for us, proud riders in autumn.

New Birds

Now all of the snow's gone from the high desert, now the frost
Lets go of the ground except in the deep draws, we find
And recognize and enumerate new birds.
The blue bird's the first comer back to the dead grass range.
Out of some waterless grey rock-break, his low voice
Utters a song almost tuneless; but his blue wings
Are bright like gay innocent music. The brown thrush,
Colored like old hay weathered in the rain, then sings
At evening, when all's darkened except water. Then, concealed
Among dark pastures of the desert, he sings his hurt.
The loud-voiced little yellow-hammers shine by day,
The color of new sagebrush blossoms. Red-winged black-birds
Blazing at the wing-joints with scarlet like the blaze
Of naked red willows in the black creek-beds, flock and talk.
The thorn-brush jolts with hundreds of bright black-bodied
Birds joking over their new country. Then come swans.
Dark wild swans come from the cane marshes in the south,
And pass, long-throated and still-mouthed. Then white geese
Trail, reaching across the dark sky, broad-winged as eagles,
But flapping their broad wings. Silence follows them.
No other new birds follow after these.

That ends our discoveries. Having noted them,
I go back to noticing the bird that wintered here,
That lived out winter in the desert, when I wintered
With them and the cattle for company. Birds that came
To scratch in the hay for a little scattered grain.
Those birds were colorless and songless. Without their presences,
I'd have been too lonely to live on this bare plain.

It is the same with my beloved as with new birds.
Old thoughts, that were my company when I lived alone,
Under her beauty's and youth's energy, have been lost.
I strive to recover them, to put them all in words,
Thinking they'll help me again, when she is gone.

Counting Back

Counting back over the things that, during a long sickness,
Cast shadows deep enough to hide in from the pain
That kept blazing through me like light (for knowing deserts,
One comes to know light as an enemy, a punishment) I remembered
Some wrens that nested in the broken window-frame of a house
I lived in as a child. Sometimes they would fly into the room
And pick crumbs from the tablecloth: solemn, brisk, purposeful,
When I was alone in it. Never for anybody else,
Not even for my mother, who loved birds.

And once, in Nevada,
In the Rabbit Rocks Desert, when I had followed rabbit-trails to a
spring
And lay down to drink from it, clouds of pale-colored little birds
Swarmed over me, perching on my hat, and on my hands.
Everything except the birds and the water stayed motionless:
The course grass and gray willows motionless. Overhead, a hawk
Stood printed on the sky like something cut in smooth blue stone.
Only birds and dark water and my heart moved.

In the Malheur Desert
In Eastern Oregon once, an abandoned homestead: a half-wrecked
Board shanty among half-dead poplars. A trickle of water
Pushing through matted dead leaves. Twists of rusty barbed wire
On fallen fence-posts; beyond them, lines of gray rock-buttes
With light glancing from them, and gray sagebrush lifted toward the
sky,
And a stray dog, abandoned like the cabin, at a distance,
Circling, watching, avoiding me, that ventured close
After a long time, and brought out two week-old puppies
From some hiding place under the house, and watched anxiously
As they came wallowing through the dead leaves to see what I was:

Watched for a few minutes while they played, and then took them
back,
Hid them, and went away herself.

Long after, in Mexico,
In the rainy season, in a village in the mountains, a tree-toad
No bigger than the tip of a man's finger, almost transparent,
That when it rained at night, squeezed under the closed door
And came into the room where I was working, into the light
To take shelter until the rain stopped. Little and fearless,
Knowing that nothing within reach could wish it harm.
Crossing the floor, it would let out a shrill little whistle,
At every few hops, lest I might step on it, not seeing it—
So small, so near transparent—and then settle itself
On the work-table papers, where the warmth of the lamp struck
And wait till the roaring of the rain passed. Then, whistling,
Go out under the door as it had come.

Once, in California,
In a place in the mountains, in the timber, two small king-snakes
That came every evening toward sundown, hunting for crickets
And grasshoppers, in the small space where the stone of the terrace
Met the boards of the house. Too busy, too absorbed
With their hunting, even to notice that I was there. Sometimes
They would pass within inches of me. When they had finished
They would go back where they had come from. Always toward
sundown.
Always absorbed and busy and indifferent to me.

Then, once,
In Mexico City, late, in an all-night restaurant
Packed with men yelling and arguing, mostly half-drunk,
A girl in her mid-twenties, overdressed, made up badly,
Breathless and a little scared, who stopped at my table
And asked if she could sit down till the mob thinned out.

It was only that she was afraid of being grabbed at
By some of the drunks, and possibly fought over, and of having
Her clothes ruined. If they saw she was with a man,
They would let her alone . . . .
                                                            I said, "Of course, sit down.
Have a drink."
                                    She laughed and said "Having a drink
Would be swindling you. I am one of the girls here,
And if I should order a drink, they would bring burned sugar
And water, and then they would put it on your bill
As cognac. No, it will be better if we just talk
Or pretend to be talking. These drunks will be leaving before long,
The shows will be out, better people will be coming in.
Some of them will be looking for girls, and perhaps among them
Will be somebody I would like. You have to move fast
Or the other girls get in first. But it has happened
More than you might think, and it might. What do you think?"

                                                                        . . . Counting back,
I think I preferred animal and birds. Their indifference
Pleased me, and pleases me to remember. It did not leave me
As hers did, feeling half slighted and half relieved.

Letters

H. L. Davis's letters make lively reading, and along with his journals, deserve publication in a volume of their own for what they tell us about the man and his times. Less guarded and crafted than what he intended for a public audience, Davis's letters are studded with moments of insight, outrage, humor, and irony.

This short selection of letters focuses upon three periods of Davis's life: First, the early years, and his friendship with James Stevens, resulting in their joint publication of *Status Rerum*, their fiery manifesto against the sorry state of Northwest writing. Davis discovered Stevens with a shock of recognition. Here was another rough-cut Northwest country boy whose writing talent (first encouraged, like Davis's, by H. L. Mencken) lifted him up from a hard-knocks life. Also representative of this early period are Davis's letters to Walter E. Kidd, an aspiring young Davis admirer who later became a writer himself under the pseudonym Conrad Pendleton.

The second, middle period of Davis's letters is represented here by his letters to Mildred Ingram, a Tennessee author and friend. In this period, after the success of *Honey in the Horn*, Davis was an established writer, publishing stories, essays, and novels, and occasionally being drawn—by the money—to Hollywood to work on film scripts. A third period, Davis's last decade ending with his death in 1960, is represented by letters written during his return to Oregon and the Northwest to gather material for the place-centered essays that were collected in *Kettle of Fire*, and while he was living in Oaxaca, Mexico. The last letter in the selection here is to Ralston Bridges, his relative and fellow-townsman of Oakland, Oregon.

The Dalles, Oregon,
19th April, 1927.

Dear Stevens: The trees here are in flower too, and go cavorting in the wind—but a good deal more like a bald eagle caught in a steel trap. The limbs rise and strain, there's a desperate spasmodic struggle; and they fall inert, and glare spitefully at the earth. A 60-mile gale is blowing from some iceberg in the North Pacific—cold, O God! And I've been riding that flat east of Shaniko for 3 days, and feel as if I'd been given a thorough workover with a good stiff stable-broom.

Your visit was an event I've already begun to date time from. I keep remembering with amazement other discoveries we collaborated in, which I'd previously overlooked—we made so many! It was so easy to make them! How we tightened on the old doubletree, and pulled! And what we discovered is of far less moment than that we were able to gouge these things, at last, from their holes; a man could feel a sense of power. Ha! Nothing was difficult!

It has simply got to happen again. The balcony of the Empress Hotel in Victoria, whether the management know it or not, is due for a literary rapport that can not fail to go down in history. – Express pleasure over a man's poetry, and he's ready to hand over his watch. Mine is at your service. How will you have it sent?

Unhesitatingly, I give you free leave to mention me to Knopf with all the pomp you care to embellish the subject with. Perfect candor obliges me to state that I have been, heretofore, in negotiation with Alfred Harcourt and with Henry Holt & Company; but I made no promises to either, and Harcourt (Sandburg recommended me) is not, I gather, particularly wild about publishing poetry at all. Neither he nor Holt make much of a spread of such books—and if I can't have a spread, I'll be damned if I wouldn't just as leave not pewee the dice at all. At any rate, I may get 'em bidding against each other? . . .

So please do point me out to Knopf, and, whether they feel called upon to fall for my stuff or not, I'll be very grateful. Let me hear from you, when you think of it! *Vaya 'sted con Dios.*

Yours,
H. L. Davis

Wednesday, 13th Dec. (about)

Dear Jim—JERKLINE plumb tipped me over. She's a real meat-gitter, believe me! The dope is there, and yet it isn't pushed at you—and the two freighters are distinguished with an amazing sureness and certainty. It is much more definitely a *conte* than the first version. And how splendidly well done the horses! And that very thing shines its light on the yarn without weighting it—his team was the freighters main conversational topic—the strain coming up to *them*, and their going through with the pull—There is one small point of detail—the snow, you say, had gone from Shaniko Flat, but the roads would be good till it rained. But the snow—remember, there's usually 3 ft. of it—the bottom fell out of the roads the moment it thawed. All the draws were—and are still—roaring floods whenever the Chinook bears down. Rain would merely be a little on top of a lot. But that's picayunish. The story does everything.

I got an entertaining and heartening little note the other day from the lady librarian at Blackfoot, Idaho. Haven't got it here, will send it from the house. About Status R. "The gods be thanked," says she, "that somebody has had the nerve to tell the truth about this drivel . . . We poor devils of librarians have to collect it, and are expected to like it, and rake it together for club ladies' papers on 'Idaho in Literature.' They might as well talk about edelweiss in hell!' . . . A most untypical servant of the Carnegie Foundation, I fear.

* * *

More later. —Davis

Thursday p.m.
[August 1928]

Dear Jim – Great Jehoviacal powers, what a week! I ought to have written sooner, for you must have been wondering whether I was being held for ransom, or undergoing a shakedown at the hands of that blonde manicurist, or what the hell. But that's part of the story. Attend!

It began with the reception of a sunny little message to the effect that there was an attachment against the Davis barouche, done and dated in the State of Oregon, and that I had laid myself liable to incarceration in a dungeon by pulling out and leaving it. Great suffering Lucifer! thinks I, in rage and injury, how in hell can there be an attachment against a car that Wasco County paid all of the expenses on? Ah! That was the catch! They hadn't. Furthermore, one of the minions informed me, they knew nothing about it, and wouldn't pay it if they did. I phoned The Dalles, and nobody knew anything. I phoned the bucko who bought my house & lot, and then wired him. He was out, evidently being a bit better prepared to dodge collectors than I was. I threw fits, cussed and foamed, and thought of going down and setting fire to the whole town. Then I wired you. Ah! Snatched from the claws of justice! Raked from ruin! Then I called up Kenney, in Portland, and talked $4.30 worth about bringing suit against the county, for breach of contract, mental anguish, mayhem, personal injury, character damage, and I don't know what all else, and he swore he would do it. The weak point is, that the contract was oral. My idiocy again! It's always causing me inconvenience, one way or another. But he thinks he can fetch 'em round, anyhow, as they've paid former claims of the same kind, and we can show papers for that.

Well, to proceed. I pushed your cash into the claws of the gent in Seattle, told him how much I'd enjoy slapping him, and got back to Seabold at 1 a.m. Dead beat! My gosh, I had to take both hands to turn the doorknob. I lunged out of my clothes (this is to be remembered) and fell across the pallet like a tenpin. At dawn, thumping at the portcullis. A 12-year-old Paul Revere, on a lathered Shetland pony (this is the God's truth!) shrieked that the island was on fire, and for the sake [of] our wives and mothers I must hop over and join the brave fire-laddies in putting it out. I looked, and he had told no lie. It was on fire, about an eighth of a mile away, and coming like hell.

Hastily drawing on shoes and pants (never let anybody talk you into fighting a forest-fire without 'em) I staggered over and fought fire. I packed water in coal-oil cans, from a windmill. The windmill quit, and I manned a hand-pump inside. The pump-house caught fire, and we threw dirt on it, hammered it with wet sacks, and ripped it to pieces with our hands. When we got it put out, the well went dry. All of the water had to be lugged a quarter of a mile, through a ten-acre field of peas—ever try to hurry through 'em?—and across four barbed wire fences. I packed water till I broke down at that, and then hove dirt with a shovel. Anon, came a sad-looking senior with a Scandinavian accent and a spray-pump—the kind they spray fruit-trees with. Being the owner, he held the hose, while I worked the pump. It didn't kill me. More, I can't say. My back feels like I'd been walked on by a horse yet. A clump of fir-trees caught, and the flames ascended straight into heaven, burning off my front hair and eyelashes and setting fire to the dry grass. We fought the grass-fire. I took station in a burned-over place, and fought until I noticed that one of my shoes was burned full of holes. It seemed time to knock off a bit, and, as I strolled drunkenly behind the lines, I ran into my bride, come with succor and sustenance for her fainting spouse. She'd just come over from interviewing somebody at Port Madison, and she wore a white silk dress, trimmed with scarlet; white silk stockings; gold-buckled slippers; and a red summer-hat. Imagine tripping through a forest-fire in that rig! What I looked like, I don't know. Whatever it was, I doubled it when I found what she had brought, to revive my failing spirits. It was a quart thermos bottle, full of—God is my witness that I speak truth—pure, cold water! And I'd pumped water, pulled water, packed water, thrown water, splashed water, and breathed water, and nothing but water, since 6 o'clock that morning! I felt that another look at anything even the color of water, would founder me. Ah, well, this love! I drank that pure, cold water, and then clasped my arms around a tree and stood on tiptoe to keep myself from running over at the bilge. Would you hear more? Would you imagine there could be any more? Read on!

The car, she remarked casually, refused to run. Something was probably the matter with it. I might just run over and fix it, if the fire was safe to leave. Well, I thought, why not? Kind of taper off on the day with a nice little exhibition of skill and adroitness. So we came over, very idyllically, arm-in-arm, and I made the car run.

No, not like that. Not that there was anything wrong with the mechanism, really; only, she had run the hind-wheels into a ditch, 6 feet long, 6 feet deep, and 3 feet wide. Of course, since the hind-wheels failed to touch the ground by some 3 feet, she hadn't been able to move it. She knew, of course, that it would be child's play for me.

I carried rocks, and built up under the wheels. Then I jacked up, and blocked, and jacked up again. Hours of that. Somewhere past midnight, I got it to where it would pull out by itself, and I fell in and pushed the starter with the last ounce of strength I had. The last twist of the knife! She had thought of that starter, too; and, working it gallantly, trying to save trouble for her husband, she had run the battery down till it didn't have a single squeak left. Nothing. Dead.

"But you can crank it, can't you?" she inquired; and then, everything went dark. She tells me that I fell over on the ground and went into hysterics. I don't believe it. The things she lays onto me are simply impossible. She swears that, laughing like a fiend, I cranked the car with one kick, and hove it out of the ditch with another, and then walked over and tried to jump down into the well. I couldn't have. I was too sleepy.

I still am. The two hundred bucks was a life-saver. I'd send you the car, by return post, to cinch the obligation; but that would be something one might do for a practical joke, never in acknowledgement of friendship and favor. I'll hear from my real-estate interests pretty quick, and may have to make a trip down there, anyway, unless Kenney succeeds in extorting something out of them. Anyway, I'll fire it right along when I get my hands on it, with the earnest wish that I'll be able to shoot a rattlesnake off your Adam's apple one of these times, or something large like that, and all my gratitude.

Harold.

Wing Point, via Winslow,
Bainbridge Island,
Washington.
9th February, 1929.

Dear Walter—Many thanks for both your letters, and apologies for delaying so long to answer the earlier one. Mails here are slow and clumsy. Everything turns up a week late, and can't be answered until another week later. So I keep way behind with everything.

What I want in writing is emotion—the faculty to realize, in writing, all the emotions which human beings can feel. If I can manage to give an account of all of them, I shall have succeeded in writing a record of humanity as this new country has conditioned it. Character is secondary to that, but it can't be dispensed with, for to make an emotion real, you must also realize the man who had it, just as you make a weight realizable by putting it on a set of scales. Though I don't practice this as a formula, it might be reduced to one. Three elements are necessary——the character, the emotion, and the incident which produced it. One could, I imagine, take any two elements and make the third. Thus, given character and emotion, it would be possible to invent the incident which would move one to feel the other. Or, with character and incident, one could calculate the resulting emotion. And so on.

That, of course, is the very broadest kind of generalizing. But all the other things are corollary merely. To realize a character, for instance, one may cite an incident to which the run of people react in some particular way, and exhibit one's hero as cavorting differently. Or one may do it by adducing the emotions which he provokes in the narrator. As long as you do it, it doesn't matter how. But the character is only there to make the emotion real.

I mean that for poetry as well as prose. And even the things I do in and with poetry are for that purpose. Unconventional or irregular rhythms, for instance, I resort to because I imagine they reproduce the rhythm of the country itself—no traditional metre has the combination of swiftness with weight, which, to my notion, the landscape, and even the speech of the people, have.

I'd like to give this a much longer spiel, and not stick to such vaguely fundamental principles. And it is a fact that, in practice, I haven't stuck very firmly to even these, and that, most likely, I never shall. But they are sound, they are inclusive enough to admit almost every kind of known writing, and, even when I violate them, I do it obsequiously and reverently, with the hope that God may make me a better boy.—I shall be deeply and sincerely pleased—need I say?—to have such a review of my stuff as you have in mind. And there's an article of mine in some forthcoming *Am. Mercury* on homesteading in Oregon in 1907 which has some good spots in it. Within the next month or so, I imagine.

To finish—I've been trying to puzzle who in Antelope could have reminded you of the dotard in my story. Doc Kimsey? Enoch Dickson? John Hanley? None of them quite hit. The old man came, really, from Prineville. The fat girl from Fossil—she was a morphidite, they claimed. But that would have spoiled the story.

So long.
H. L. Davis

Thursday, 19th Sept., 1935

Dear Walter—
Many thanks for your note, and don't always be so blasted modest about yourself. The novel hit a lucky number, and I know as well as anybody else that I could have been a lot better and that I can write one a damn sight better, given time and a chance to work back over the whole business once it's done.

The ring of Portland fictionists are all pretty much upset over this thing, I understand. By now they've no doubt figured out an explanation for it. Nobody cares anything about those flatheads outside of Woodlawn, so what they invent about me won't hurt a speck. I'm not bothering about 'em and they needn't bother about me. Let me hear more about yourself next time; what the hell, I know all about my stuff already, so why write about that? Mail care Harpers will always get me. I leave St. Louis tomorrow. England next Spring if at all. Problematical.

Sincerely,
H. L. Davis

COLUMBIA PICTURES CORPORATION
1438 No. Gower Street
Hollywood 28, California
Hollywood 3181
Wednesday 23 April 1947.

Dear Mildred: If you are tempted to regard this as official on the strength of the letter-head, you'd better take a peek at the end first. It ain't anything but us chickens, and I am dotting it off mostly on general principles, not knowing how many communications from what people there may be waiting for me away up yonder in Point Richmond, and not knowing enough about my tenure down here to risk having them forwarded. I came down here on a rush-call to help with a script that had been moved from the quickie class to a high-budget job; as such, it was considered to need a hasty infusion of (a) literature, and (b) historical verisimilitude. Hence me, considered a ready and inexhaustible source of both. The understanding was that it was to take me about two weeks: certainly not more.

* * *

We went to work a week late. It was still only to take me about two weeks. I might have managed to get it done in that time if I had done a little figuring ahead. Unfortunately, it was a studio I'd never been in before, and I thought it might be different. As it turned out, it wasn't. So I am well into the third week and have given up setting any date to finish. It may be for years, I tell myself resignedly, and it may be forever. I expect I have got a lot of mail waiting for me, and probably some of it is pretty frantic. I don't care. I wish I could, but I've got other things on my mind.

It's a pleasant enough spot to work in, as far as that goes. The difficulty is that it's too blamed pleasant. The producer, me, and a ferociously industrious girl named Matilda, who draws pay as my secretary and insists on consulting me about mysterious movie-terms that I don't know anything about, occupy an upstairs wing of the studio office-building, all to ourselves, with a side-entrance where you can sneak in or out without anybody checking on you. The producer is pleasant, intelligent and entertaining: the only one of his calling in the whole outfit who is. Hence, all the dull-eyed slaves from the writers' wing always duck out and sneak up to our suite when they want to forget their troubles. So they sit and visit, and time goes by, and when one leaves another comes lurking in, and all of a sudden it's quitting-time and you realize that you haven't done a goddamned thing all day except sit and swap dirty stories. Nice enough, only the script is scheduled to go into production next month, and if you imagine Columbia Pictures is the kind of outfit that would wittingly pay anybody a thousand bucks a week to sit around swapping dirty stories with the hired help, you just don't know 'em.

At any rate, it'll be over before much longer, and I don't mind admitting that I'll be rather glad of it. The work is rather interesting in spots—it isn't easy, by a whole hell of a lot—and entertaining sometimes, and I did need a change. But I've gone about as far as I want to with it now, and there's a lot of things about it that do wear on you: some irritating, some just plain insane. If I were doing it for a living, or as a permanent career, it would probably end by driving me nuts. Today was fairly typical. They all run about alike. The same things don't happen on all of them, but equivalent things do, infallibly. At around 9:45 a.m. I lumbered panting into the main lobby and checked in with the switchboard-operator. You have to do that; you're supposed to show up at 9:30, but they give you a little leeway if you're agreeable. Of course I can't write a lick that's worth reading before 11:30, but what do they care about that? They pay you to be there on time, not to write stuff worth reading. If it was worth reading, they wouldn't know it, because they can't read. Well, up to the second-floor suite I bound, plunk down in a chaise-lounge (I don't know why chaise-lounges; they look faintly immoral in an office, somehow, but they're there, and you have to sit on something) and haul out the script and sharpen four or five pencils, getting up nerve to start. In comes Matilda, bearing yesterday's sheaves, with a question: set 92 don't say what kind of a shot you want, short, long or medium. Also, is it interior or exterior? I don't want any kind of a shot, they're all alike to me; all right, medium. It sounds harmless, anyway. As to the interior-exterior business, the directions say "A grass hill-side looking over an expanse of desert." Would you be apt to encounter anything like that indoors? Exterior, I guess: now please go away. She goes, unsquelched. The producer comes in, very sociable. He sits down, relates the good one he heard downtown last night, and proceeds to explain about the production-problems of "Antony and Cleopatra" and the flotation-process for extracting gold from low-grade ore. (He was formerly with the Theatre Guild, and also a graduate from the Harvard School of Mines.) He's a nice guy, and very entertaining. It is 11:30, and you haven't written a line.

You start ferociously. You keep at it for maybe half an hour, and there enters the director. He also is an exceptionally agreeable person, and he installs himself in a chaise-lounge, closes his eyes restfully, and tells a couple of Sam Goldwyn stories: both very funny. He then opens a discussion of why, when he gets paid $500 a week and goes without everything except the bare necessities of life, he is always flat-broke. He hasn't the faintest idea what becomes of his money; all he knows is that he gets it, and when he goes to reach for it, it ain't there any more. He finally gets up and leaves; it is now 1:45, and you go out to the studio lunch-counter and eat; the company consists of 8 stage-hands in overalls and two actresses from a set. One is a housemaid, the other wears a pale-pink formal gown with rhinestone trimmings and is trying to eat a hamburger without dripping gravy on herself. The housemaid is more cautious; she sticks to chocolate-doughnuts and an ice-cream cone. They would probably both be quite pretty if their faces were washed; they are painted a kind of dark mauve, with black lipstick. They look as if they had been greased. It's 2 p.m. and you've written about a page and a half.

Well, you start again, and there enters a workman, bringing something to install and hammers and wrenches to do it with. What he brings doesn't much matter; it's something different every day, and he never misses. If it's hotter than hell, he comes in with a dingus that has to be attached to the gas-heater. If it's freezing cold, he lugs in an electric-fan and wires it up, hammering lustily and knocking plaster all over your desk. Or it can be a water-cooler, or a set of Venetian blinds, or any damn thing at all, as long as it raises hell with what you're trying to do. Well, he gets through and goes, thank God. You no longer feel like working. It is 3:15 p.m. and you look out the window and wish something would happen. A man from the publicity department comes in, sits down, and tells about a row he has been having with the boss, and what he told him. He wants sympathy, gets it, and leaves, feeling better. He has taken up three-quarters of an hour at it, but after all, it's lightening a fellow-mortal's burdens, and the company is paying for it, I hope. It's 4 p.m. A young writer from the downstairs staff comes up, dark and morose and ready to end it all. A year or so ago, he wrote a dog-story. It made money. Now he is under orders to write a sequel to it so the company can make more money. He has lost interest in dogs; he hates dogs and everything about them. He loathes the stuff he is doing; the mere sight of it turns his stomach. He hasn't eaten anything except benzadrene-tablets for four days. He talks about how terrible he feels. His secretary comes up looking for him, and also sits down and helps with the conversation. Since she's pretty, the producer comes in and likewise sits down and takes a hand in it. It's all great fun, and everybody has a gorgeous time. It's a quarter to six. No use starting work that close to quitting time. All right, we stall for the remaining fifteen minutes, slink out and check at the desk, and so home. What you'd call leading a full life.

It's been a change, at least, and some day I'll be glad I agreed to do it just when I did. I'm glad it turned up; I'll be still gladder when it's over.

* * *

So long for now—
H. L. Davis

Klamath Falls, Oregon.
1 May, 1952.

Dear Mildred—
This is a sort of interim job, like the apparitions Prospero contrived while waiting to be shipped back to Milan, where he really belonged. I came up North a couple of weeks ago to skirmish up background for an article on Oregon for *Holiday* magazine. Everything went fine. The magazine was paying all expenses, the country was lovely and full of things that look well in writing (it can be one and not the other sometimes) and people along the way loaded me down with delightful and illuminating stories and reflections. By the time I got to Klamath Falls, I had ten times as much material as I needed, and my deadline for the article was miles away, no need to start worrying about it for a long time yet. So, losing my head completely, I let some forest service boys talk me into a side-trip down into the mule deer country along the California line. What the hell, it was either that or go home and go to work, and who wants to work?

What might have been expected to happen happened. It was a hard trip, the weather turned bad, we almost froze and had to fight muddy roads for miles. I got back here frazzled out and ill, and had to go to bed for three days to get over it. When that was over with, my deadline for the *Holiday* article had moved up so close that I didn't dare put it off long enough to get back to Point Richmond, for fear it would run me too close for time. So I buckled down and wrote it here. Got it finished this morning, 11, 500 words (they had told me to take all the room I needed and not to skimp, and I took them at their word) in 5 days, including history, tradition, folklore, flora and fauna, landscape, geography, ethnology, narrative movement, philosophical background, and a few vagrant interludes of individual biography, improvised for the occasion.

I had promised to have it in by the first week in May. It's on the way by airmail now, and a well-written little decoction, if I do say it, and nothing could exceed my thankfulness at having it off my hands so I can stop worrying about it. But it has left me exhausted. There is really nothing in Klamath Falls worth hanging around for (though it's a beautiful little town on a big mountain lake, very picturesque, and of a high cultural level: the bookstore had 5 copies of *Winds of Morning* in stock) but I am going to stay over another 3 or 4 days, because I'm still too tuckered out to face driving 600 miles till I've recuperated a little.

So this is a sort of stage in the recuperative process; a transition between having to work and not feeling like it and not having to work and feeling vaguely that I should. It really was a grand trip. A lot of it was in the lake country of the Great Basin, east of here. The migratory waterfowl are on their way north, and the lakes are a resting point for them. There were mallard ducks floating serenely on puddles a couple of feet from the road, and wild geese feeding in a meadow all mixed up with a flock of sheep, and horses and cattle diving for grass in a pond (really they were: their heads were completely submerged, and they were eating the most gluttonous relish) while some Canada snow-geese gloated around among them, pecking at them to make the move over; and on one of the lakes about sundown a flight of black-headed trumpeter swans, gigantic things that looked like seraphim descending and sounded exactly like French taxicab horns in a traffic-jam. And I thought hopefully, well, maybe the Day of Judgment will be enlivened by some similar incongruity, and why not? It would be a nice touch.

* * *

Well, it's over and I am glad of it. It really was tiring. This is (you may have noticed) a new typewriter: Italian, portable, no bigger than a lady's handbag, fitted with 18th-century Bodoni type, and a beautifully made little trinket. I got it from London, out of some (I hope) English royalties. Looks imposing, I think. Exotic.

Adios –

H. L. D.

Apartado Postal 196,
Oaxaca, Oaxaca.
Mexico.
10 February 1955.

Dear Mildred—The above address doesn't signify a change. Merely that the suburb where I inhabit has mail delivery only once a week and I have been having my mail sent to Oaxaca Courts because it gets picked up there every day. The trouble was that I had to go there and get it. So one of my neighbors (a nice young man, retired bullfighter, runs a lumber yard) said why not have it put in his box at the postoffice, and he could bring it out every day so I wouldn't have to go after it? So I decided to try it, and it has worked very well. Hence the Apartado Postal: that's his postoffice box and its number. Things always fall into some kind of working order if given time.

Since you bring it up, I will explain about Oaxaca a little, to make up for D. H. Lawrence failing to. I had forgotten that he was ever here. He was, of course, and didn't get much out of it. He didn't get much out of most of the places he visited except disappointment, as I recollect. Expected too much, maybe. He seems to have started himself out in the world with a set of emotions forty feet high taken from some adolescent nightmare, and to have spent the rest of his life trucking around in search of a place where it all might actually have happened; never found it and always blamed the places for his failure. I suppose you are right about Frieda being necessary to him—morally more than psychically, probably. German or not, she was a real blown-in-the-glass Baroness with a coronet engraved on her stationery, and it bolstered him to feel that the scion of a coal-mining household could have risen to so close an association with the quality folks. There were a lot of problems involved, but he would have been unhappy without problems, and it saved him from having to look for them or make them up.

But to Oaxaca. It is a town of about 50,000 people, mostly barefooted Indians. Capital of the State of Oaxaca, has a university, a penitentiary, an army garrison of one infantry and one artillery regiment, three or four brass bands. Excellent hotels, bookstores, municipal auditorium, baseball park. It is a very old town, colonial architecture dating back to the 1500s, a trading center for a dozen or so outlying Indian tribes who speak totally different languages (but not Spanish) and wear different regional costumes, some very picturesque. It is within an easy drive of two beautiful prehistoric ruins, Mitla and Monte Albán—20 miles from one, 5 miles from the other. Both are impressive and unforgettable. At least they used to be. I haven't laid eyes on either of them since I was here 20 years ago, but they were impressive then, and if they had managed to last out 1500 years they won't have lost much in a mere 20.

Where was I? Oaxaca is on the Pan American Highway, 350 miles South of Mexico City (hour and a half by plane) and some 3 or 4 hours by car from the line between North and Central America. It is in a valley closed in among very high mountains, mostly heavily timbered, oak, fir and pine. There is considerable logging done, and the Indians of the hill villages live by cutting cordwood and burning charcoal, bringing it down on trains of pack-burros to peddle in town. There is a large gold mine 30 or 40 miles up in the hills: has a payroll of some 1000 men, owned by some Spaniards. There is a large coffee-growing area in the valley below town, and all the coffee-growers are rich because of the boom in U. S. prices. They are looked down on a little as parvenus, but don't seem to mind. A large colony of Confederate army officers moved down here immediately after the Civil War, under the leadership of General E. Kirby Smith. Most of them moved back afterward and took government jobs under the Hayes administration; General Smith, of course, went back to become President of Sewanee University. One of his sons, also E. Kirby Smith, stayed on, married some Indian woman and begat a considerable family, and died here only a few years back. He has something of a sprinkling of descendants scattered around Mexico City still; I bought a radio set from one of them when I was in Mexico City a couple of weeks ago. There are none left in Oaxaca now, apparently. Oaxaca and Sewanee seem an odd tieup. At least neither of them show any effects from it.

Your account of the Nashville reaction to your book brings back old times. I know what it must have been like, I have been through it all. These things blow out of nowhere, like the wind in the Scriptures, and dwindle back to the same place. When you think they are not there, there they are, and when you have accustomed yourself to taking them for granted, they ain't. When *Honey in the Hor*n first hit the bookstores up in Oregon, it raised the biggest literary hellabaloo the Pacific Northwest had ever seen. All the papers ran indignant editorials about it; there were whispering campaigns, abusive and threatening letters, the American News Company (the wholesalers for the area) refused to stock the book at all. The people who did all the yelling about it obviously hadn't read it, so, lacking anything to argue about, I was compelled reluctantly to let them holler. It all died down and I supposed the whole thing had been forgotten, the book along with the indignation, until the reviews of *Winds of Morning* began to come out a few years back. Then I discovered that all the hollerers had disappeared. The book had rolled on over them. The newer generation of book reviewers in Oregon accepted *Honey in the Horn* as gospel, as revelation. They invoked it reverently when they wanted to prove anything.

It was embarrassing. *Honey in the Horn* wasn't as sacrosanct as all that. There were plenty of inaccuracies and cheap spots in it, some deliberate, some mere sloppiness. It had not deserved all the fury piled up against it, but it didn't deserve to be received as gospel, either. I did wring a little consolation out of reasoning, after considerable worrying about it, that the controversy hadn't been between the early reviewers and me at all. It had been between them and the book. I had been on the sideline all the way through. It was the book that had beaten them, not me. One against the world will always win, as some poet noted, but you can't always be sure which one it will be.

* * *

Oh, well. I could go on and on.

Adios—

H. L. D.

H. L. DAVIS
Apartado Postal 127
Oaxaca, Oaxaca
MEXICO
8 May 1960.

Dear Ralston—
Your letter was waiting for me here on my return from being poked and pawed over by a bevy of doctors in Mexico City—a little routine I have to go through occasionally these days, to show them that there are no hard feelings. So I am late in answering it, but that has got to be so chronic with me that I am thinking of having a general apology for tardiness printed on my stationery. You are quite right that I mentioned wanting to drop in on you in Oakland back in 1953. I even had a spot worked out to do it in: an assignment for a magazine article in Puget Sound that I thought I could squander a few extra days on. But the magazine got in a hurry for it and I had to go up there by plane; and then I had to do one on Palm Springs, and then I had to go to Texas to get married (second time—my wife's from San Antonio) and then back to Hollywood for a writing contract with Paramount Pictures. Then I got another magazine assignment in Mexico City and stayed to finish a novel. When that was over I was sick, and got hauled to the Institute Naciońal de Cardiología with a case of acute arteriosclerosis that took me through a series of operations lasting, all told, something over eight months.

It would be overdecorating things to say that I'm all well again. I still have to get around in a wheel chair, as I have been doing for the past three years. But the doctors agree that I am getting better, and that beats getting worse, I suppose, even if it does take a lot longer. Mexico City is huge and inconvenient to live in, so we've got a house with a big walled-in garden in Oaxaca, a medium-sized old town (50,000 population) in the high mountains about an hour and a half away by plane—fir and pine timber, a pleasant climate, no hot weather (I can't stand heat), with hired help plentiful and cheap. We've got four servants, all very good, and their wages for a month all put together come to less than we paid a cleaning woman in Hollywood to come one day a week. It's beautiful country. I hope to get back to the Northwest some time when I can stand a long spell of travelling better, but for the time being it fills in well enough.

Your project of working back through Old Oakland is completely fascinating to me; all the more because almost everything you have dug up about it is completely new to me. Of course I remember the place as it was when I lived there, and even what it looked like—the old blank-windowed houses and gigantic overgrown shade-trees and tottery picket fences, and the one resident who still lived there, Aunt Polly Eubanks. There was nothing much about her to remember, except that she kept several dozen parrots: for company, I suppose. She was entirely normal and wholesome and friendly (a lot more so than some of the old ladies in the main town) but it always made me uneasy to be around her, because I kept feeling that she had no business being normal and wholesome in a spooky place like that. The Dr. Cozad you mention might stand some looking into; it seems to me (I've got it in a book somewhere, but it would take too long to root it out) that a French doctor of that name came in with the 1843 emigration, and that he had served in Napoleon's Grand Army on its march to Moscow. He died, I think, in the middle 1870s.

Two things strike me in thinking this over as material for a book—a story, since that's what it would have to be. One is that you would either have to limit your work to the old town and stop where it stopped, which would mean doing it deliberately as a costume Western, or else you would have to carry it on into the period after it got moved and aim at making it an out-and-out literary undertaking. Carrying it on may seem like a lot more work, and probably it would be, but the results would be worth it. The town itself would have to be the real core of the story, and bringing its origins out through all their color and strength to an end in something familiar and universally experienced would be more to work for than merely showing how colorful and picturesque it all was and letting it rest with that. The other thing (I said there were two) is that you are probably making the whole job infinitely harder by piling up so much material on it that it will founder you to get any clear and sharply drawn story line dug out from under it. You need interesting characters, but you have to be ruthless about slapping down the subsidiary ones when they threaten to get too interesting. You even have to be coldblooded about throwing things away; it can be very painful sometimes, but it can't always be avoided.

I remember almost all of the people you mention who lived in Oakland, and even a lot more. Odd, maybe, because we lived there rather less than two years—1906-07, I think it was. I was born in October 1896, at Roane's Mill (the community was called that) on Hinkle Creek. The Roadmans (one of them killed somebody, I seem to recall) are right about my father's marksmanship. In his time he was the best rifle shot in Southern Oregon. I am truly sorry to hear that Annie Kruse is ill, and will be anxious to hear how she is doing now. She got written up in the Book Section of the *N. Y. Times* last Fall, I noticed. It was pleasant to see, even if they did spell her names Crews . . . . The book, to end on that, could be something really superb, and I hope you go ahead with it.

Sincerely, H. L. D.

Davis (center) with friends at Dick Malone's ranch, around 1925

Winds of Morning

Of the four novels that Davis published following the success of *Honey in the Horn* in 1935, *Winds of Morning* (1952), a Book of the Month Club selection, may be his best. The first-person narrator of the novel, Amos Clarke, is its main character, a young deputy sheriff of an eastern Oregon town on the Columbia River in the 1920s, as Davis himself had once been. Clarke finds himself journeying through the back country with an older man, Pap Hendricks, and his herd of horses. Both men are following their own obligations, which for the young man involve a murder investigation and a love relationship with a young woman, Calanthe. Old Hendricks has returned to the region after a long absence, to see what has become of his former country. But his deeper motive is revealed as a wish to confront his own troubled past, and his relationships with his children, now grown and scattered over the local countryside.

The story depicts ordinary post-frontier western lives lived in the shadow of failed frontier expectations. Still, neither of the main characters has closed off the chance for love and hope, even in a diminished time and place. Davis's astonishing feel for landscape and weather and animals and country talk and behavior has never been stronger and more distinctive, as the following selection reveals.

Describing *Winds of Morning* as in some respects Davis's best novel, critic Dayton Kohler says, "Within its compact framework, he brings together the themes which have previously engaged him: the West, the past, the world of nature, the groundswell of history, the ironic contrasts between appearance and reality, the imperatives of love, the necessity and consequence of moral decision." (Kohler, 1952)

CHAPTER FIVE

The noise of a late-lingering flock of wild geese going out to its day's feeding in the wheat fields woke me the next morning. The sky was already beginning to fill with light, and there were a few cold yellow sun streaks on the high ridges, but it was still too dark in the camp to make out anything except the pond and the spaces of a few leafless bushes patterned black against it. The sky's reflection in the pond water made the darkness around it deeper and more impenetrable. The cold bound down like rawhide contracting, and scythed up through the cracks in the floor as if the straw and dead leaves old Hendricks had spread down for bedding didn't count in the least, though they may have slowed it down a little. The air felt frosty, but it was impossible to be sure till I reached one hand outside the shanty and felt the hoar frost, deep and bristly and searing cold, on a pile of old boards.

As usual in such places, the first appearance of light in the sky touched off noises. Animals began wandering in to the pond to drink, and the horses in the corral roused up and moved over to the near fence to watch them. Horses could see in the dark. They were ahead of me on that, but the sounds were plain enough, and the animals around a waterhole in the early morning were always pretty much the same. The laws of the Medes and Persians would have looked like a flea on a hot griddle in comparison to the solemn and unimaginative regularity of wild animals in that country. Some cottontail rabbits came and drank. A couple of porcupines came and drank. A family of skunks came and drank. A covey of grouse came clucking down from the cottonwoods and drank, and were followed by something that sounded like a deer, though it was not deer country. Then a big waterfowl of some kind hit the pond with a splash that scared everything else away and made the horses shy back from the fence with a thudding of hoofs and rending of fence poles that always sounded as if they were tearing the corral to pieces and always turned out, when you got up and looked, not to amount to anything at all.

The waterfowl rose after a minute or two, and flapped away to the north: a wood duck, maybe, or some lone snow goose that had got left behind by the main flock and was hurrying to catch up. The ripples in the pond smoothed out again. The light overhead was strengthening steadily, swelling the sky out like a bubble being blown thinner and thinner. The darkness outside the shanty changed from black to a wavering gray, like a river fog at nightfall. There was light in it, but it was no easier to make out objects in than the full dark had been. The pond was no longer bright and sharply outlined; it looked like merely a place where the dimness had worn threadbare. Some quail whistled from the cottonwoods, and went suddenly still, as if something had startled them. The horses in the corral moved restlessly, and one let out a loud whinny. A rock clattered, something splashed in the pond, and I could see that there were horses crowding down to it and drinking. They were coming down from the dead-grass pasture on the ridge. There was not enough light to see what any of them looked like, merely their bulk as they came out of the grayness and stretched down to drink from the pond. Behind me, old Hendricks finished hauling on his shoes and went out, wrapping his bedding around him like a toga, to start a fire. He walked lightly, as if the cold hadn't crippled him any, old though he was. His kindling caught and flamed up, and he turned to reach some heavier wood from the pile and saw that I was getting fixed to join him. He dropped some boards on the fire and got up.

"Well, yonder they all are, as big as life," he said. "It's funny how a man is. Here I put in all last week swearin' to God that if I ever got the dratted brutes off my hands I never wanted to see 'em again, and then I laid awake most of last night stewin' for fear they might have stampeded on us, or got stole, or something. It don't look like any of 'em had, but they might try to stray when we hit new country with 'em. By God, there ain't many places left in the world where a man as flaxed out and stove up as I am can come into a herd of livestock overnight, and I'd hate to lose any of 'em right at the start. If Busick's give up his title to 'em, that brand he's got on 'em won't count any more. Maybe we ought to counterbrand 'em before we strike camp. By God, this is a morning with feathers on its legs, ain't it?"

I let that go as it stood. It was a morning, for what it might be worth, and putting counterbrands on fifty full-grown horses without any branding equipment was more of an order than I had any authority to tackle. "It would take too long," I said. "You've got no brand to put on 'em. Even if you made one up, it wouldn't count unless you had it registered with the county clerk. We'd have to have a branding iron made in town, or else use a running iron. It would take us a week to get done with it either way. There's not feed enough to carry these horses another week here, and they're not worth that much trouble."

Old Hendricks set a bucket of water on the fire and looked sideways at the pond. "We could put on hair brands," he said. He was set on showing off his ownership somehow, and he was away behind the times. Hair branding had been a device resorted to in the old days by horse thieves. It was not really branding at all, merely crimping a horse's hair into a brand pattern by scraping it with a sharp knife blade so that, when finished, it appeared as if curled back from a brand scar. It was painless and plausible looking, but there were drawbacks. The pattern vanished completely when it got wet, and it was five times as much trouble to put on as an ordinary iron brand was. Old Hendricks turned back from the pond and stirred the fire with his foot. "Hell, it don't matter," he said. "It would be foolishness to waste time brandin' all them horses, and it wouldn't be right anyway. This country's treated me right, the same as it always does anybody that meets it halfway, and I got no right to haul you in on a brandin' job that wouldn't mean a damned thing when we got it done. It's this property business that's the trouble with me, I can see that. Property can make a plumb idiot out of a man if he ain't careful."

"We could put the hair brands on a few of 'em, if you want to see how it'll look," I said. "Five or six wouldn't take long. We can pick out some that are scrawny and not too rambunctious."

His reasonableness had seemed to call for at least that much of a compromise, but he wouldn't have it. Once he got a case worked down to its underlying principle, he played it straight through. "I wouldn't waste two minutes of my time on it, or anybody else's," he said. "It wouldn't mean a damn thing. Everybody would know it was childishness, and that I was back of it. Right's right, and there ain't any halfway business about it. I've done enough halfwayin' in my time, and I'm through with all of it now. You're wrong about them horses, though. There ain't any right-down rambunctious ones in the bunch, and no scrawny ones, either, except that they're all gaunted from poor feed. Look 'em over when the kid gits 'em strung out. You'd better tell him to drop off and eat before we pack up, if you can handle his lingo. I've been havin' to swing my arms at him when I wanted anything."

The Mexican youth sat on his horse at the edge of the pond, waiting while it drank. He kept his blanket bunched tight against the cold, and he had fixed a pad of gunnysacking with a halter rope cinched around it for a saddle. He nodded when I translated the message and rode out to head the horses down the draw as they left the pond. Old Hendricks was right about the horses. They weren't anything like ordinary range ponies; not skimpy little cat-hammed Indian cayuses at all, but square-built American farm stock, with solid shoulders and bone structure and even some space between the eyes for a few brains, if a man wasn't too exacting. The explanation was simple enough, when it was worked on a little. The war boom had infected the country with a fever for tractor cultivation, and the introduction of tractors had resulted in all the regular farm horses being turned out into the sagebrush to run wild. Some of them had the marks of old harness galls on their shoulders, and a few still had nail marks in their hoofs where they had been shod, though travel and rock pastures had fixed that for them long since. They were better than I had expected, even if they weren't worth owning.

"They oughtn't to be hard to handle," I said. "Some of 'em have been worked. They made money for these back-country scissorbills when the boom was on. This is what they get for it: turned out to rustle or starve. It's a great country we've got here. Fair treatment's the watchword."

Old Hendricks said stiffly that there were bound to be few natural-born thunder mugs anywhere. Property ownership had raised his spirits in spite of him. He acted as if any criticism of the country was a reflection on him personally. "I've seen 'em splurge around like this when I was runnin' sheep out here in the old days, and I've seen 'em bawl their heads off about it afterwards. There'll be fair treatment for these horses before I'm through with 'em, I'll promise you that. Does that blamed kid know he's supposed to come in and eat before we pull camp?"

I said he did if telling meant anything. The truth was that country-raised Mexicans didn't bear down much on breakfast: a bun and a few swigs of half-burned coffee usually covered it for them. "How did he ever get signed on here?"

"The same way I did, or right close to it," old Hendricks said. "He got throwed off of a freight train down at the water tank. I was down there tryin' to run some of the horses off of the railroad track, and he come over and took a hand at it. I was mighty glad he did. One man can't do much with a bunch of loose horses."

"It's funny you didn't know enough Spanish to talk to him, if you used to run sheep out here," I said. "All the shearing crews have always talked it, and most of the herders used to be Mexicans or Basques."

"I never got around to learnin' it," Old Hendricks said. "Some of the kids got so they could handle it. Kids pick up things like that. And a hell of a lot worse ones sometimes, too."

That was heading the conversation into ticklish territory. The sheriff's instructions to dump him on some of his progeny probably didn't hold any longer, since he appeared able to look out for himself, but it was safer to have some understanding about it. "You said you had children scattered around the country. Maybe we ought to hunt up some of 'em, if it won't take us too far out of our way. They may not even know you're out here."

The Mexican youth rode past and dismounted to wash his hands at the spring. Old Hendricks watched him absently. "You're damned right they don't," he said. "They don't any of 'em know where I'm at, and they wouldn't thank anybody to tell 'em. All they'd think was that I needed help, and it would scare the livin' peewallopus out of 'em to think they might have to furnish some. I don't need their help."

"Some of them might need yours," I said. "I heard Busick say something about one that might. She had her husband murdered out at South Junction last week. Some crazy young Greek from a railroad gang did it. She's been laid up from it ever since, and she's got a big place on her hands and nobody to run it for her. It's the old Farrand place. Her husband's name was Farrand."

The Mexican youth helped himself to a piece of bread and coffee in a tin can, and went back with it to his horse. Old Hendricks said he remembered the Farrand freight station. "It was back in the big cove above the Upper Camas River. This would be the old man's son, I guess. I don't know which one of the girls was married to him, though. There was some that hadn't got married when I left here. I never heard who any of 'em got married to. They figured it wasn't any of my damned business, and they was right. One thing I can't git through my head is how a thing like that would lay any of 'em up for a week. It don't sound like 'em. You say this Farrand left a big outfit?"

"It's supposed to appraise at about a quarter of a million dollars," I said. "It wasn't the killing that laid her up as much as the way it happened. It was in the middle of the night, and she was alone. This Greek shot her husband almost in front of her, and then tried to rape her. She ran outside and hid in a ditch to keep him from finding her, and then walked to the railroad station and got help. She was almost froze when she got there. That was partly what laid her up. She was scared half to death, though."

"I can imagine," old Hendricks said. There was no sympathy in his voice. It sounded slow and thoughtful, and a little shaken. "Yes, I can imagine it. It must have been enough to lay anybody up, havin' to hide outdoors at night, as cold as it's been, and then walk through the dark barefooted and with nothing on but a nightgown. Have they caught the Greek that done it?"

"Not the last I heard," I said. His imagination was vivid. I hadn't mentioned her nightgown or her being barefooted. "The sheriff's out after him. The trail we've got to take the horses over will come within a couple of miles of the Farrand place, if you want to stop in."

He picked the coffee bucket from the fire with a stick, and stood holding it. The steam from it made a sort of veil before his face. "I'll have to see about it. Maybe we ought to, if it's close to our trail. I don't know what for, but there might be something. I might be some help. I hate to git into it, but maybe I ought to. There might be somebody out there that needs help. I'd better find out, I guess."

"You'd find out which one of your daughters it is, anyway," I said.

He moved the coffee bucket so the steam blew away from him. There was a hardness in his face that made me wonder whether I hadn't been right about him in the beginning. The old cuss could be dangerous, if he took a notion. "I know which one of 'em it is," he said. "I know which one it is now, good and well. By God, if I didn't know another damned thing in this world, I'd know that! That's one reason I'd sooner not git mixed up in it. We'll see. I wish you hadn't told me about it. Hold your cup, and I'll pour some of this gumboot juice into it. We've got to git packed and git out of here."

Packing didn't take long. Except for the groceries I had brought and a small pile of bedding, there were only a few cooking utensils to pack, and we had canvas packsacks, locally and inaccurately called *alforjas*, so there was not much to it except dropping things in and roping them down. There was no tent, but that didn't make much difference. It would have been a nuisance to handle, especially if it got rained on, and there were old homestead shacks spaced out every few miles along the Camas River breaks that would do to hive up in if a storm hit us. We saddled up, and drove the pack horses ahead of us down the draw to overtake the herd. The Mexican youth had taken down several panels of his fence to let the horses go though. We helped drive them past the wire, which some of them were nervous about crossing, and he rode on ahead to turn them up the river when they cleared the mouth of the draw. It began to dawn on them that they were being taken somewhere after they had got past the fence, and they kept closed up and moved along without even needing to be prodded. Old Hendricks reined up at the flattened fence panels, and looked back.

"I was prayin' the Lord for something to git me out of here a couple of days ago," he said. "Yes, by God and as late as yesterday night. Now I hate like hell to leave. I wish we didn't have to. A man never knows. Maybe he's better off not to know . . . . This saddle of mine's a hell of an out for these times, ain't it?"

It was a little bit dated: an old split-seat army castoff that had been rigged with a high knob-ended horn and a cantle board reaching clear up into the small of his back. The horn, besides being of a model that went out with the free silver agitation, was sprung about three inches to one side so it looked as if the whole saddle was tilted. His sheep-herder rifle, which was tied under one stirrup leather with some ravelings of rope, was a rusty-looking .44-40 that must have been the last word in firearms back around 1876, reinforced in spots with baling wire. His horse was a cumbrous-footed old hide rack with a humped nose and prominent hip joints that worked up and down like a railroad block signal when he walked. I remarked that he might have found something sightlier in the herd than that. He said one advantage about being old was that things like looks ceased to matter.

"This old skate was easy to catch. That's the big item when you're my age. He matches the saddle, anyway. I found that in an old hay shed up at the head of the draw. The rain had warped it forty ways from Sunday, but I limbered it out. It'll carry me all the places I want to go. Yes, and some that I don't, the way it looks now. Damn it, a man can't stick his head into a place without gittin' things piled on him to fix. These horses, and the kid's pay check, and now this business out at the Farrand freight station. Well, right's right, and it don't do any good to dodge around it. The country's still here, anyway, and we'll have a few days that other people can't mix their hell into."

He had some things to learn about what had happened to the country since he had left it, I thought. Some of it was still there; a lot wasn't. There was no use telling him that. He would find it out for himself soon enough, and it might be better to let him. Maybe the other people's hell that he had taken it on himself to fix would seem less forbidding by comparison.

We trailed up the river along the edge of the low hills, letting the horses pick what grass they could find as they went. The Mexican youngster rode ahead because his night herding had got them accustomed to him, and we followed along behind to keep the tail-enders from straggling too far in search of feed. When the big poplar-grove bordering Camas River came in sight, we turned south through some Indian allotment lands bordering the hills, and kept to the high ground till it dropped off into Camas River canyon. There were some fences in the way, but the country was ridgy and broken, so they were not much hindrance. Wherever there was a gully, the fence builders had saved posts by stringing their wire straight across from ridge-top to ridge-top and drawing it down to the low ground by weighting the middle with a big rock. Crossing it meant merely taking the rock loose and driving the horses under the wire when it hoisted up in the air. We crossed half a dozen fields of winter wheat that had been frozen out and left standing, dead and yellowish-brown and unhealthy looking. The horses tried to graze it at first, but it was too much like musty mattress stuffing for even their appetites, and they gave it up and hurried along through the acres of brittle deadness without bothering to look at it.

There was one field where somebody had made a start at reseeding, and had given it up after two or three rounds because the low ground was too wet for a tractor to work in. He had left his seed drill and tractor standing on the edge of a plowed-over gully. The tractor had three of its wheels dug into the soft ground almost out of sight and the fourth slanted up in the air like a man gesticulating for help after a well had caved in on him. The tractors of those years appeared to have been designed for use out on the prairies. They were too unwieldy and topheavy to stand up to the light soil and steep slopes of that foothill country, though nobody discovered it till almost everybody had bought them. Old Hendricks sidled his horse over and nodded at the one iron wheel poking dumbly up at the sky.

"It looks like somebody had got enough of them things already," he said. "There'll be a lot more of 'em like that before long, you wait and see. All it takes is time."

There was no way of telling whether the tractor's owner had got enough of it or whether he had merely got enough of work, but it showed that old Hendricks was feeling in better spirits, and there was no use starting an argument with him. I said that all anything took was time, only a lot of things took too blamed much of it. He rode for a while thinking, and then came up with another one.

"There used to be bunch grass all over these ridges," he said. "Belly-deep to a horse, some of it. I freighted wool through here three or four summers. There was a freighters' camp where we crossed Buck Creek, and a stand of big alders for a couple of miles both ways from it, and prairie chicken thick enough to write your name in, and deer. It ain't like that now, I guess."

I said it wasn't likely that anything was. We had already crossed Buck Creek. There hadn't been much about it that he would have noticed. It was merely a chain of naked mud holes at the edge of a wheatfield, no different from a dozen others we had crossed except that the mud was deeper and juicier. There were no alders, no deer, no bunch grass, no prairie chickens. Civilization in any country meant shifting the balance in favor of people. That was its business. Where people had to live, other things had to die. Someday all other forms of life would be exterminated, and there would be nothing left anywhere but people. Then humanity could settle down with a happy sigh to revel in its triumph. There wouldn't be much of anything else left to do.

"It's always bad when you start a trip like this," old Hendricks said. "It gits better. I've done enough of it to know. I've hatched out some humans that I'd take back if I could, but you never know about 'em till it's too late. It always looks for a while like it was worth tryin'. One thing my old man used to tell me was that you didn't git game with the bullets that stayed in the gun. You have to shoot blind and risk it sometimes."

"If that's the best he could do with his advice, he'd better have kept it," I said, to take his mind off any depressing analogies. "He might have got somebody shot."

"He might have, for a fact," old Hendricks agreed. "Come to think of it, I wouldn't be surprised if he did. Maybe it'll turn out that he . . . No there ain't any use lookin' that far ahead. To hell with it, we're headin' for somewhere new, and that's enough. New country puts an edge on a man."

We held south between the wheat fields and Camas River canyon for four days, making around fifteen miles a day and camping wherever night caught us. There was wind along the breaks, but it stayed clear, the waterholes had not blown dry yet, and the horses herded without much trouble except to keep them from drifting down into the canyon. The wind was cold enough to keep them bunched close, and the rockbreaks had tufts of old grass spaced out far enough apart so they had to keep moving to keep eating. We didn't talk much. At night everybody was too tired to think of anything to talk about, and talking against the wind during the day was too much work to be worth it. Sometimes old Hendricks moved his lips as he rode, but nothing was audible when I edged close to listen, so I edged away again and left him to have his argument out with himself undisturbed.

A storm hit on the afternoon of the fifth day, as we were clearing the wheat fields and entering a long gravel flat grown up to sagebrush and juniper, with blackish outcrops of rim-rock poked out into it like headlands in a gray sea. Like most storms in that country, it began with the wind letting up close to the ground and blowing so hard in the upper air that the hawks had to beat their wings to stay in one place. Big cloud banks came driving up from the west, coloring the ridges with clots of shadow that looked blackish-purple against the sunlit places and then streaking them with splotches of sunlight that looked coppery-yellow against the shadows. Across the wheat country to the west we could see half a dozen places where it was already raining, some blurred dark with it, others blank white with faint rainbows wavering over them. There was a washed-out old wagon road a mile back of us that led down to an abandoned ferry station on the river. I hurried ahead and helped the young Mexican turn the horses back toward it. A yearling coyote jumped out from behind a bush while we were getting them turned. There was a six-dollar bounty on the ratty brutes, so I pulled up and threw a couple of shots at him before he made it to the shelter of a rockbreak. One missed him a country mile because my horse fidgeted while I was letting it go. The second would have nailed him right in the middle of a jump, except that he was digging for cover so hard he didn't take time to jump. I looked around and saw old Hendricks watching me. He had swung his horse to face the on-coming rain, and he had taken off his hat to let the first drops spatter on his face.

"By God, this is something like it!" he said. "To hell with people's troubles! This here's something new for you, the way that rain stomps along the wheat fields, and three rainbows all in sight at the same time . . . No, by God, there's four! You can't expect to hit anything with that pistol off of a horse that's standing' still. He'll always shift his feet or do something to throw your aim off. Put him to a canter before you shoot. Then you'll know what he's goin' to do next."

I held the pistol out to him. "There's four shots left in it," I said. "I've got extra loads, so go ahead and show me. If you can hit anything off of that old plug at a canter, you belong in a circus."

"I ain't as good at it as I used to be," he said, and took the pistol and eased off the hammer to test the pull. "I hope we don't scare that kid to death with all this bangin' around. He's gun-shy sometimes. Well, watch the white mark on that rock yonder."

He thumped his old mount to a lope, and let go the four shots at the rock as he went lumbering past it. The young Mexican pulled up and looked back, but I waved him to go on, and then rode over to see what the rock looked like. The white mark had four lead splashes in the middle. Old Hendricks handed the pistol back and reined around to follow the horse herd. "She's light in the barrel, but she handles easy," he said. "Hell, I've seen the time when I could wipe the drip off of a man's nose with a thing like that. Where are we headin'; down into the canyon?"

"Down to the river," I said. "There's an old ferry down there, and some empty sheds and a fenced pasture. It ain't been lived in for years, so we may have to patch it up some, but it'll beat laying out a storm up here."

"I remember that old rope ferry," he said. "An outfit named Waymark owned it and the land alongside it. If nobody lives there now, maybe somebody ought to. What's to hinder me from movin' in with the horses and holdin' it down? There used to be enough wild hay on that river flat to run a bunch of horses like this the year round. If nobody's usin' it, why ain't it open land?"

"It's been reconveyed to the government," I said. "They bought back the patent, and it's being held in reserve for water-power site, or something. Nobody's supposed to use it at all. We can sneak a few days on it till the storm's over, but you try to move any bunch of horses in on it to stay, and you'll land in the cooler."

He fingered his reins, and pulled his hat down tight. "It used to be like that back in the early days," he said. "My old man used to tell about the times when you wasn't supposed to take any government land unless you paid for it. People moved in and took it anyway, and they kept it, too! By God, I knowed there was places where a man could still git started in this country, if he wanted to bad enough!"

"Maybe there are, but you'd better not try it here," I said. "You can't make much of a start anywhere from inside a jail. The place is all run down, anyway. The buildings are all caved in, and the hayfield's run to weeds."

"Somebody ought to try it, just to show 'em," he said. "If I didn't have this family business on my hands to settle, by God, I would! We'll see what it looks like, anyway."

The rain was coming closer, beating a grayish spray into the air as it hit the ground. He prodded his horse to a trot, and we went shouldering and thumping down the old ferry road into the river canyon.

Afterword: *Exit, Pursued by a Bear*

by Glen A. Love

At his death in 1960 at age sixty-six, H. L. Davis was deeply involved with writing what was to be his last novel. His working title was *Exit, Pursued by a Bear*, after the famously oddball stage direction in Shakespeare's *The Winter's Tale*. The novel was to be concerned only with Davis's early years in and around his birthplace in the foothills of the Cascade Mountains near Roseburg, Oregon. Living in chosen exile in Mexico, far from this birthplace and from the Oregon that was the setting of most of his best work, Davis searched his memory for the matter of his childhood. At the same time he was probing for the means of making it new.[1]

But by the mid-1950s, his body was not making any of this easier. He had increasingly suffered from circulatory problems as he aged. His condition had worsened and eventually led to severe arteriosclerosis and the amputation of his left leg in 1956. A lifelong horseman, he was now unable to ride. Still, he wrote and worked steadily in the late 1950s, seeing his last finished novel, *The Distant Music* (1957) through publication, writing a masterful story, "The Kettle of Fire," for the 1959 Oregon Centennial issue of the fledgling literary magazine, *Northwest Review*, and combining it with his recent Northwest essays to form his final book, entitled *Kettle of Fire*, in the same year. In May of 1960, in a hospital in Mexico City, he underwent major heart surgery from which he never fully recovered. He would be dead by the end of October. His last months saw him writing hundreds of draft pages of *Exit*, or more often, draft pages of arguments with himself about how the new book should be written, a practice that had worked for him with his earlier novels. But from the start, as his notes to himself reveal, this autobiographical approach had him worried:

> Something about the novel that I want very much to get cleared up in my own mind. I am not altogether clear about it yet—about the end, yes, but not the means, which counts the most—and I will put off speculation about it for now, hoping for something concrete to work with later on. The concrete that I have would be a start, but it needs an underpinning—what it really needs is the emotion of looking back on it and seeing, as a new experience, what it amounted to.

More precisely, looking back on it and discovering that it amounted to something, after all. This whole day I have been beating it over as the possible beginning of a list of Things That Have Influenced Me. Essentially, it pains me to realize, some such undertaking as Wordsworth's "The Prelude."

Books of this nature nowadays seem always to fall into a tone of gentle and elegiac mellowness, that is the trouble with them, and it has been the trouble with mine up to now, which I think is why I haven't been able to go with it. What is to run all through it—the narrator and his mind and feeling *as they are*, as he knows and feels them to be, as the life about to be narrated has formed and moulded them—this has to be declared and established from the outset. There has to be the invented incident or scene or person viewed as reality and criticized as reality; ironically when necessary for contrast, and perhaps ironically more than anything else—this certainly more than anything else possible to me—could give the feeling of the narrator being present, and of what he has seen and lived through being used as a living and contrasting background for the text.

God knows there should be some other way of setting up a character behind a narrative—certainly there are types of narrators who manage to register themselves without being capable of the smallest spark of irony—but it is the best out I can think of to line one kind of experience up against another and make them both seem living and active forms of judgment. I am aware that care will have to be exercised in aiming the irony; it is phony and painful to set up some character as ridiculous and then poke ridicule at him; the incongruities and foibles ridiculed must be those that are current and active. It must be holding up examples from the past to show that the absurdities of that time are still current, or that the asininities of the present go a long way back.

. . . (I am completely aware of the risk in laying down these ready-made precepts and then trying to write up to them—it usually looks labored, and nobody ever has the remotest idea what you are getting at.) (Ams, 12-13)[2]

Given Davis's habit of deflating his own good intentions as soon as he announces them, as he does here, he still is clearly aware of the complexities posed by his characteristically ironic narrative voice when addressed to his own childhood, and to the child's capacity for wonder, or dreaming. Irony might well apply from an adult narrator in dealing with the error and confusion of his youth, but it might also be tempered or transformed or otherwise rethought when considered from the viewpoint of an older man in his sixties.

At this point, Davis considers whether his outside reading at the time offers useful ideas for *Exit*. He mentions two current first-person narratives, Nabokov's *Lolita* (1958) and "recent work" by J. D. Salinger (probably "Seymour: An Introduction" [1959]). A reader familiar with the characteristic speaking voice of Davis's prose—Western, rural, laconic—might wonder what he could possibly take from Nabokov's libidinous and exotic cosmopolitan, Humbert Humbert, or Salinger's chatty New Yorker, Buddy Glass.

The sardonic Davis might well have smiled at the earlier Salinger's Holden Caulfield and his rejection of "all that David Copperfield kind of crap" about birth and early life, but Davis was already committed to attempting it in *Exit*. What he could have found relevant in the later Salinger is that writer's efforts to get the reader to understand and feel the narrator's relationship to his material. The same might be said of Davis's interest in Nabokov, and Davis, had he lived beyond 1960, might well have found Nabokov's *Speak, Memory* (1966) of surpassing interest. But breaking down the barrier between writer and reader was Davis's immediate challenge. He devotes many pages of his notes to a strategy that might allow him to go back obliquely to his early self, to tell the truth, but tell it slant. He considers framing his early life by beginning with his present recovery from heart surgery in a Mexico City hospital:

> I don't want too smart an opening, but it shouldn't be too painstakingly literal and detailed, either. Without any of your stream-of-consciousness touches (I don't think anybody has ever noted that there was a fairly well-done s-of-c passage in "Oliver Twist"; and what of it?) to set down the place and the environment as they were impressed on the consciousness of a man coming out from under anaesthesia after a major operation and taking stock of what is around him to measure how much he has come back to himself. (This needs some precise phrase—not a phrase so much as a closer and more complete grasp of what he is doing and why he is doing it; would it be that I didn't know? But I think I did know.)

But the details taken note of would be more than merely establishing the setting and period and bringing out what was picturesque about it. (Or otherwise.) It would go even beyond the record of a consciousness taking stock of itself, taking note of these details to test itself, to find out its range and accuracy and its limits. It would be both of those things for the narrator to establish an accurate relationship with his own mind; and in addition a relationship between the narrative and the reader by showing, in the fullness and accuracy of these details, that he is completely conscious and of sound and disposing mind and memory (memory because he not only perceives the details of the room, but remembers them and knows which are the same—the furniture, the pile of magazines and letters on the invalid-table, the bedside cabinet with water-jar and tumbler, matchbox and ashtray and radio still set on the dial-number where he had been playing it last, the special nurse in the straight chair by the window working absorbedly at the same piece of embroidery, not even much farther along than when I left it—the same bunch of pink flowers in the same corner, with only three or four petals that look unfamiliar. . . . (Ams, 15)

—Continuing, after an interval. I think I have learned (but only recently) that it was necessary to get the foregoing down on paper to keep it from cluttering up a clear and impartial-sounding presentation of the events and reflections in this prelude that are to count. Much of this, in the form it has here, does not count, and I can see now that putting it in at all was the survival of an instinct to show off how much I have been through and how much I know. The saddest part of it is that what I have elected to put down (with a life and a world to pick from) is not even the truth, either of what I know or what I have been through. It is trying to express both through something completely—and I am afraid—obviously invented and fictional.

There does seem, since this is only one of many times that I have gone wrong on this, to be something about spreading out to write a book that sweeps me off my feet and separates me from all consciousness, all I have learned by experience, about what has to be

> done and the equipment I have in hand to do it with. I piddle around at it, and try to repeat effects without establishing the tone and setting on which the original depended. (Ams, 21)

Pain and drugs from his recent heart surgery have caused Davis to experience a succession of "visions" that commingle with his attempts to repossess his early life. The hallucinations interest Davis greatly, and he mentions at one point, "Aldous Huxley's book on the peyote, referred to as mescalin." (Ams, 152) "It stands to reason," he writes, "that [the visions] must all have originated in something that had been remembered from somewhere. A man could hardly invent complete and detailed scenes and people and emotions entirely out of his imagination without having them owe something to reality." (Ams, 22) Davis's mind alternates back and forth between the pain and drug-driven power of these illusions and his rational questioning of them, but he finds their force finally irresistible. As Davis works his way toward a satisfactory start for the book, various visions and his cognitive reactions to them result in a fat handful of handwritten pages, perhaps ten thousand words, all exemplifying the agonies of the early composing process, like a blind man following his cane, as someone once described it, or like Theodore Roethke's speaker in "The Waking," who can only learn by going where he has to go. Sometimes a vision plays to Davis's strengths, to his braille-like depictions of his western Oregon backwoods, for land devoid of people, for the sky and clouds, for trees, flowers, plants, for animals and rough outbuildings, for making the country, in Hemingway's terms, so real you could walk into it, even though, as Davis later claims, he has never seen the place of his vision before:

> . . . night in a wagon camp beside a grassed over mountain road . . . facing an abandoned farmhouse and a half-dead old orchard with deep timber all around it. It is autumn; the dead grass is wet and beaten flat by rain, and the light from the campfire brings out the yellow scattering leaves and the pale gray of the mossed over branches in the orchard. Outside the firelight is darkness so solid and intense that it looks as if it would rub off at a touch; it is impossible to see what the country is like, even where the line of high timbers tops and the sky begins. There are no stars visible and there is no sound except a faint roaring that might be either wind in the treetops or a streak of rough water in some river farther up the road. Inside the firelight, there are the remains of two or three fallen treetrunks lying parallel with the road, their branches all trimmed down close with an axe, with

> tall stalks of fireweed and goldenrod and young vine maple sprouts growing around and over them. Those and all the plant growth in sight are identifiable only by their shapes; some quality in the firelight reduces all colors except its own to the uniform grayish-white of old snow or dead trees in an old timber-burn. A line of pole-fence almost buried under a mass of wild blackberry and sweetbrier and thimbleberry and crowded dogwood and alder separates the orchard from the road, and a footpath matted over with fallen grass leads to a small gate that, if I were to turn back from the whole scene to reality, would be located at approximately the point where the nurse's elbow is moving back and forth over her embroidery. (Ams, 26-27)

Later, the hallucination expands to include people and actions, even absurd actions, like a mysterious woman carrying a presumably significant sack, which, as she takes it into the firelight and carefully, reverently, empties it out, piece by piece, turns out to be a collection of worthless and discarded junk—burnt-out light bulbs, bundles of old wire, used automobile parts, and such. Davis ponders the idea that the attempt to pin down this and other visions to some definite origin is less important than their capacity to reveal something of how his mind works.

Finally, the whole vision tickles his broad realist's sense of the comic: "Seeing the funny side of an illusion usually knocks it in the head, which is probably the main reason, since illusions pay better than reality, for the decline into which humor has fallen nowadays. This one thins out, dissolves into the ordinary daylight delivered ready-sliced by the Venetian blinds [of his hospital room], and is gone." He concludes that he need not burrow further into the illusion that has taken all his attention for the previous seven or eight close-packed, handwritten, four-hundred-plus-words-to-the-page manuscript, because it all is in some way a part of his life. He feels no curiosity about what place this is, or who these people are. "And this is not because these are not interesting points of speculation, but because he knows all about them already." (Ams, 34) Yes, this is just the sort of place and people who are part of his early life, and there is no need to go on frazzling his brain over them, because, like the mundane contents of the mystery sack, they are piled up to remind him of what he didn't know he already knew.

Following this insight, Davis plans to return to the framing structure of the hospital room. But his comic sense of how illusions fade in the light of day—combined very probably with a lessening frequency of hallucinatory visions as his reliance on painkillers diminishes—seems to whet his appetite for getting started on the early memories themselves. Davis frequently voices his apprehension about the way he is structuring his work, about his need to stop writing about what he is going to write, and to actually write the novel. He is apprehensive about all that he has done so far that is "half-baked and windy" and will have to be redone, but tries to convince himself that the "doctoring jobs" of rewriting can be done later. (Ams, 39) The conflict between getting the general plot line down now and doctoring it into final shape later, versus sweating everything out until it's as good as he can make it before going on—this quarrel with himself dogs him to the end.

> Clearly I have not arrived at anywhere near the sureness of tone and of associations that I need. I hesitate too damn much over everything, and if I really had it down it would run off as easily as this orgy of muttering about it.
>
> One thing, anyway. I am not ready yet to back up on it and pull it around where it belongs. Tomorrow I go on with the birthplace and early childhood and it must trust to writing like this—but always and everywhere humility and self-apology and deprecation. Never an opinion set down without some careful undercutting it afterward; never a reference to self without some meek qualification. (Ams, 39)

One cannot be sure of the point in time at which Davis went so far as to commit the several alternative openings of *Exit*—the birthplace and early life just promised—to typescript, but the handwritten page 39 just quoted is followed by a typewritten page marked 39-A, which is one of only a very few typed pages in the three-hundred-and-ten-page main manuscript. It begins with the directions "to be inserted (along with other extraneous afterthoughts) in the King James version of ch. 1." These typed pages are the only typed draft of several possible typed openings for the book that is extensive, containing what might be a fairly complete chapter one and chapter two, and unfinished shorter versions of chapters three and four. The total number of typed pages is something less than the fifty-three numbered on the last page, since some of the earlier pages are missing. So the typed pages represent only a small portion of the 310-page, mostly handwritten, first draft that comprises the unfinished novel.

But what is striking about page 39-A is that it describes a horrific Indian massacre of an emigrant party—an apparent return with a vengeance to the potential jolting effects of the post-operative drug-induced "visions." At the top of the page, Davis has handwritten, "It will have to be cut merely to the scene. The rest is too much." The "scene" is the first paragraph. But what follows is also worth noting. The entire page is reprinted below:

> To be inserted (along with other extraneous afterthoughts) in the King James version of ch. 1. Some illusion—not set down as an illusion, but rather as a visualized simile—of being the little boy who escaped from the emigrant flatboat when the river Indians jumped it in the night; and of watching from his hiding place in the mud and swamp willows while the Indians torture and kill off all the people in the emigrant party; his parents, his sisters, (after first taking turns mounting them)—and of course this should be his father, his brothers, his mother and sisters, after first taking turns mounting them. Of watching while they lead each of them, and then the people from the other emigrant boats, into the firelight (the fire fed with broken furniture from the boats) and of having it slowly dawn on him as they go on leading the emigrants out and killing them in the light of the fire, having first mutilated and abused them, that each of these people being murdered is a part of himself, each represents some streak or neglected thread of character that he had in himself to begin with—some good, some capable of being made into something good and useful, some weak or bad or meaningless, exactly like the men and the women and girls and children that are being led out and killed; and that the country has mutilated and destroyed them in him as the Indians of this visionary country are destroying them in his fantasy.
>
> He knows that this was an old story some of the old people told among themselves: the old people who had been children of the early settle[r]s in the Mississippi Valley. And he remembers what the rest of it was, that the little boy finally got away (stayed in his hiding place until the Indians finished killing all the people and looting the flatboats) and made his way down the river to an American military post, and that afterward he grew to manhood and prospered. No different from any other prosperous landholder of the upper valley country, and even quieter and more temperate in his conduct than most of the others. He would never allow himself to be bantered into a fight or even a mild cussing-match with any of the other settlers of the neighborhood (and they fought among themselves as a regular

> habit) even when they got insulting and accused him of cowardliness. There was not another man in the country who could have knocked under meekly to threats and insults as he did without bringing eternal disgrace and contempt on himself for it.
>
> The difference was that though he never resented injuries from his neighbors, he made it a rigid and unfailing habit to kill every Indian he saw, old or young, male or female, civilized or savage, without the slightest regard for time, place or circumstances. And this has been run much too far.

This gruesome account is noted for inclusion in chapter one, the opening of which is about the Native American community near his birthplace. Now, looking back on the unfinished manuscript, one can question how and where this fearful cautionary tale might fit into the opening chapter, the most developed one of the typed beginning chapters of the planned book. The opening pages of chapter one read as follows:

> The country where I was born was a scattering of small farms and sidehill homesteads strung along a beautiful little creek that reached up from some foothills into the high Cascade Mountains of Southwestern Oregon. It was twenty-five miles from the nearest town, over a road that was knee-deep in reddish dust during the summer and belly-deep in mud through the winter and spring. There was no post office or store or center of any kind that it could be named after, but it was generally known as Roane's Mill, for a small log-stealing sawmill of the early days that had been abandoned for so long that nobody could remember exactly where it had been.
>
> None of the people in the community were in the least alike or wanted to be, but at the time—along in the late 1890s—they did fall into groups that represented a kind of seesaw between new values in process of formation and old ones beginning to wear thin at the bends. Near the foothills where the big timber tapered out into scrub-oak and grassland, they were shirt-tail cattle ranchers, with an edging of new homesteaders who had been squeezed out of places in the Mississippi Valley by the financial colic in the East. Farther up, reaching back into the high fir timber, there was a tag-end remnant of a tribe of Indians, probably of some Athapascan stock to begin with, but so mongrelized by infusions of Negro, Kanaka, gipsy, Chinese, tagalog, Hudson's Bay

French, fur-company Russians, and American riffraff, that they had forgotten what their own origin was, and had no tribal name even among themselves except the collective one of half-breeds. Half didn't begin to describe their genealogical complications, but it did for a name, and the exact fraction would probably have run into too many decimals for anybody to keep track of.

They did keep up a tribal organization, with a hereditary chief and a council of elders, and some vague religious ceremonies once or twice a year that usually wound up with everybody laid out drunk. Keeping their tribal status enabled them to draw government annuities under some old treaty of the 1850s, and also to hold title to their tribal land, which they leased to valley cattle-men for enough to scrape along on without worrying much about working. An old cattleman named Finn Wiro, loaded with wealth and so stricken in years that he had to have a bodyguard to interpret his mumbling and help him on and off his horse and show him where he lived, held the grazing rights to most of the tribal lands up the mountain. He was married, vaguely, to eight or ten squaws from the more influential half-breed families, so as to ensure himself a stand-in with the council when any outsider tried to muscle in ahead of him on their land leases. His herders—he kept eight or ten on his payroll regularly—were middle-aged men with criminal records, which he liked because it made them easy to handle and kept them from stirring up trouble with the neighbors. They got drunk and fought among themselves occasionally, but they always picked some line camp to do it in, so nobody ever knew how it had come out. And even they were so prone to disagree about the final result that they usually steered shy of the whole subject to avoid getting into another fight about it.

The older half-breed men divided their time between hunting and resting. As the settlers told it, the head of a half-breed family would sit in the shade till his butt ached, go out and lug home some venison or somebody else's beef till his back ached, spread out and eat till his belly ached, sleep till his head ached, and then resume his seat in the shade and start the round all over again. It is taking something of a fall out of romance to say it, but it is no more than the simple bedrock truth that, as a means of sinking a people into complete worthlessness, their system was one of the most efficient ever devised by man. All the

> Indians with the slightest spark of enterprise or ambition invariably threw the whole thing over and went out to rustle for themselves; all the degenerates, no-accounts and do-nothings from the white communities for hundreds of miles around moved in to take their places, married into the tribe, begat children, and settled down to take things easy on their cut of the annuities and land lease revenues. Getting rid of them may have helped the white communities they had belonged in, but the improvement was too widely scattered to show much, whereas with the Indians it was too concentrated and cumulative for anybody to overlook. (Tms, 1-2)

Set against Davis's innovative plans for beginning his new book, this opening is disappointing. The idea of framing the story of his early years within his awakening from the anesthetic of his recent heart operation has apparently been shelved, or forgotten, or saved for further thought, as has the Indian massacre story. Davis goes back to his familiar, laconic, I've-seen-better narrative voice, but the Indian depictions, even when laid off to "the settlers," seem presumptive, especially looking back now, and realizing that Ken Kesey's heroic Bromden of *One Flew Over the Cuckoo's Nest* and other Native American literary figures of Leslie Fiedler's *The Return of the Vanishing American* were both to follow in the same decade in which *Exit* would have been published. (I have to keep reminding myself, of course, that nothing in the story is set in stone yet. The manuscript is still in a draft stage, and, unfinished and unpublished at the author's death, it will always remain so, absent some editorial re-creation job of major presumptuousness.) Against the narrator's depiction, steeped in the casual prejudice of its time, of the conditions of his own remembered childhood—a local native population characterized by general sloth and indolence—what is the reason for the (eventual?) inclusion of a nightmarish story of early Mississippi Valley Indian atrocities that the narrator remembers so vividly from his own boyhood, and that he describes as "not set down as an illusion, but rather as a visualized simile—of being the little boy" in the story? Is it motivation for the narrator's sense of the origins of his own attitudes? And if so why does Davis remind himself that only the first paragraph—the rape-torture-killing scene—should be included in his narrative?

Why would Davis exclude the remaining two paragraphs, in which the boy grows up to be the sort of apotheosis (as depicted, say, in Melville's chapter in *The Confidence Man*) of Indian hating, the killer of every Indian, young or old, innocent or guilty, he ever meets? Wouldn't inclusion of these two paragraphs, especially the final sentence, "And this has been run much too far," amount to a renunciation and repudiation of such blind racial vengeance as he has just described, and of the monster that the young boy who witnessed the massacre has grown up to be? Or would "And this has been run much too far," apply not to the murderous advance of Indian-hating, but to overstating the nuanced relevance of the last two paragraphs to his narrator? Omitted, would they not leave the massacre scene to serve as a muted, and thus more rhetorically effective, admission of the susceptibility of his narrator to the in-group folklore of his people?

Or would Davis elect to exclude these two final paragraphs because they are not to be ascribed to his narrator, whom he would portray in the story to follow as a vintage Davis speaker, unimpressed with the general run of human nature, but likely to judge individuals by their actions rather than their race or ethnicity, sizing people up by the content of their character, not the color of their skin, as Martin Luther King would later put it? Would the authorial Davis regard the noun "riffraff' as having been applied to all the racial and ethnic types, including "American," *i.e.*, white, as among those indicted for the decline of the Native American culture? He says as much in his scorn for the whites who moved in to take the place of the ambitious Indians who "went out to rustle for themselves." Wouldn't slothful and indolent behavior be what this narrator can't abide, wherever it is found?

Judging from Davis's characteristic heroes and heroines, including his sensitive treatment of the beleaguered young Stafford, the hereditary chief of the local tribe in the *Exit* story to follow, I think that Davis would claim something like this last as his position. Still, it is worth noting, notwithstanding the panoply of fictional characters throughout all Davis's earlier works with whom he sides for showing gumption, enterprise, ambition, that these traits have their darker aspects. See what happens when one applies these virtues unexamined—doubtless those of the unscrupulous white rancher Finn Wiro and the builders of the "log-stealing sawmill" for whom Davis's birthplace is named—to the fallen condition of the local native people and to the land that they had lived in for centuries and walked lightly on, so that it had remained pretty much as they had found it until the whites arrived. Compare that fair country to Davis's 1950s description of the Roane's Mill landscape in another early draft of chapter one: "The whole spread of country has been ruined since, taken apart and cleaned down and built up and done over to suit the vagrant notions of new settlers and real-estate promoters and loan companies till it is merely another tired and frowsy backwash of overpopulation." (Tms, "Early draft of *Exit*," p. 1)

Davis may be charged with harboring some of the prejudices of his time, including a failure to acknowledge the possible virtues of a people who could live long in a place without destroying it. But, all things considered, his application of his gospel of gumption was about as even-handed as one could ask. See, for example, his story "Extra Gang," in *Team Bells Woke Me*, or his poem, "Steel Gang," in *Proud Riders*, in which a team, or "gang," of white railroad-track layers are goaded by their racist boss into a contest to beat the record, for a day's distance of new track laid, of a rival gang of Mexican workers. The white gang, thanks to extra-pay inducements and an exhausting fifteen-hour day, bests the record of the Mexicans, but are so worn-out and dispirited by their efforts, that they have no more heart for the rest of the work. They drop off, quit, and the Mexican crew comes in to finish laying the rest of the track. For Davis, the important thing is to know to what end gumption is to be applied. If it is to have moral value, it must arise out of a sense of selflessness, of doing the right thing for the rightness of it, under difficult circumstances, requiring sacrifice and courage on the part of the individual, and the stamina to see the task through to the end.

Two central characters emerge from Davis's drafts of *Exit* to face such important moral challenges. One is the narrator's father, introduced in the "King James" version of chapter one, immediately after the pejorative description of the Indian community. He has been hired as a teacher for the local Indian and white youths, on the assumption that he can keep order in this troublesome mix. The other is the young man who is hereditary chief of the tribe, called "young Stafford," or simply "Stafford." "He was around thirty, and handsome, and it showed something of his stiff-backed haughtiness . . . that nobody ever became well-enough acquainted with him to find out whether Stafford was his first name or his last." (Ams, 69) He and the teacher, the narrator's father, have a gradually earned, uneasy bond of responsibility for settling disputes and heading off local conflicts that invariably edge into the groups from which the two men come. Young Stafford enters the story more fully when he joins the searchers called out to find the narrator, Isham, as a young boy of eight who has become lost in the woods. It is Stafford, on horseback, who finds the boy, in the night, and in a threatening environment. In the dialogue between the two, and in their long ride back to the settlement, Davis's notes to himself detail his conception of Stafford's deeply conflicted role in the community.

Both Isham's father and Stafford face demanding challenges, but Stafford's role forces him to preside over a communal tragedy: his people being overwhelmed by a cultural tsunami.

> There are some subtle and important overtones of emotion—not psychology but emotion, and strong ones—that belong in this. They lie back of everything in it, of everything young Stafford says and of the state of emotion that impels him to say it to an eight-year-old kid hanging onto the saddle-strings behind him in the dark and in the doghouse with the whole community for getting himself lost and getting everybody called out to hunt for him. These are all versions for young Stafford's lapse into talking openly about himself and the kind of job he is up against. With anybody of any responsibility, of any weight or influence or maturity of judgment, he would no more dream of doing it than a shot wolf would of letting the other wolves in the pack [know] that he was physically handicapped. And I note that even this must be pinned down more firmly to an emotion at the beginning, and the reasoning about why he is doing it must be a process taken step by step, of drawing away from the original emotion of acute embarrassment that a full-grown man like young Stafford should pick an eight-year-old kid to confide in, and thankfulness that the darkness keeps him from being reminded of the kind of dirty-faced and deplorable urchin he was unloading his innermost doubts and bitterness on.
>
> But again, if reflection on these confidences is to be carried that far, these must be more than merely this mild and rather complacent speech to carry it on from. It will evidently need a little more working up to. There will have to be some rejoinder by Isham that can be used to touch off young Stafford's train of bitter reflections about himself, and his people, and how he is wasting his life standing up for them and settling their squabbles and keeping them out of trouble with white people and seeing that they don't get swindled and that they live up to their contracts when he knows perfectly well that the money they do make will be blown in on getting drunk and gambling and worse. He can't have any friends; if he shows a liking for any of his own people (not that there is any great temptation to) he will be suspected by the others of favoritism; if for any of the whites the tribal soreheads will start telling around that he is fixing to sell them out and that he thinks

> they are not good enough for him to associate with, and the plain truth of it is that for the most part they are not. They lie around and let somebody else do the thinking and deciding for them . . . . It takes all of his time and it will take all of his life; and then somebody else will let them get swindled out of their land and their allotment funds—the less thinking and deciding they do the less they will be able to do—and his work and his life will all have been for nothing. (Ams, 104-05)

Reflecting further on this scene, Davis writes a memorandum to himself that the scene will need to reveal the effect that young Stafford's unburdening of himself has upon the boy.

> [T]hat Isham likes this excursion and the conversation, and hates to think of being landed back at home with his parents; there should be something to bring out the feeling he has about having young Stafford open up to him like this—maybe the contrast between the creek as it shows in the darkness and its remoteness and indifference, as against its closeness and friendliness in daylight; and Isham will reflect that young Stafford has changed in the opposite direction. All his friendly straightforwardness is because of the darkness, Isham thinks; by daylight he will go back to being stern and stiff-backed and short-spoken: all the stiffer, probably, for remembering how he let himself be drawn out in the dark. (Ams,109)

The reader might also speculate from this act of communication between the boy and the man that there is the feeling that the isolated confessor senses in the listening boy a capacity for understanding, and even, one day, for communicating that understanding to a wider world.

Davis's early interest in casting his story in first-person yielded, in the writing process, to his sense that such a restricted point of view would necessarily limit his handling of events either preceding his birth, or in his childhood, such as the scene with young Stafford. Thus, he writes to himself in his notes, "I am more and more tempted as this goes along, to pull away from this first-person business and do it as a commentary and speculation on somebody else. It seems to me that it would loosen the thing up and let [in] a lot of fresh air: not our young hero rooting back through his memories in search of himself, but a world, with its accumulation of thought and feeling and experience, finding out things about him that he may not have suspected and might not be willing to admit if he had." (Ams, 62) A few pages of notes later he writes,

"My protagonist will lug around some plain and unsensational name, easy to write and easy to repeat. The one I dug out for him, mostly because it has no special color or quarterings, is Isham Coffield. It will do as well as any." (Ams, 65) So it is Isham Coffield (the name somewhat redolent of Holden Caulfield, Salinger's famous teen) who is lost in the woods and rescued by young Stafford, and upon whose consciousness, filtered through the perspective of sixty-some years of living, the events of the novel-to-be are presented.

Perhaps the most distinguishing characteristic—that's too kind; call it instead a behavioral tic—of the Roane's Mill people is their contrariness, their combativeness, verbal and otherwise:

> As the early settlers in the country had proved in their lives and conduct a hundred times over, people who have stood together against the bitterest hostility from outside forces will turn around and start backbiting and kicking shins among themselves as soon as it is lifted. The Roane's Mill people had arbitrated themselves out of factional quarrels, but quarreling was so much a standby with them that they turned to doing it inside factions, over such picayune subjects as line-fences and partnership salt-logs and discovery rights on bee-trees and whose son was to take whose daughter to the next play-party, and even, when there was nothing else handy, over such remote abstractions as politics or taxes or religion.
>
> Some of the meanest quarrels were inside families. One of them needs to be set down in some detail. Both for its influence on my early upbringing and because there was a moral to it. There may even have been two or three, and if there were, all the better. Morals in stories have been given scant attention in recent years, and some of them are still constitutional and operative. (Tms, 7-8)

Thus ends the "King James" version of chapter one, raising the curtain on one dispute, this one having led to a murder, and on a number of other "rows" to come. The term "row" (rhymes with "cow," and has nothing to do, in this usage, with propelling a boat) is regionally common enough to appear frequently in Davis's notes as a synonym for a dispute. Davis's claim for the fractiousness of human relations in southwest Oregon is borne out by the fact that the name Row River, a branch of the Coast Fork of the Willamette River near Cottage Grove, remains today as geographic testament to Davis's claims. Its name immortalizes the argument between two local neighbors, also brothers-in-law, who locked horns in a serious row over a minor issue of stock trespass, which ended with one man dead.[3] The rows between Indians and whites, Indians and Indians, and whites and whites are sufficient to bedevil the best efforts of the narrator's father and young Stafford throughout the rest of Davis's notes and plans for the novel.

Conflicts, however, often narrow down to their effects upon the boy, Isham, and his father and mother. The father—noted for his fairness and trusted by the community, cool under pressure, expert rifle shot—is a model of competence for the boy.

Surveying Isham's father from the perspective of Davis's "Exit" notes on his own father, James Alexander Davis, he writes, "there have been at least two books recently in which the author undertook a reappraisal of his father from an adult point of view, and they make it important, I think, that this one should explicitly avoid anything of the kind. What my father seemed to me as a child he seems now, and this is no more than putting down what it was and what the changes in the world around him did to him because of it." (Ams, 211) But for Isham, his father's competence may be so complete as to grate on the boy. "The catch with Isham's father is that he can't stand to think there is anything about the woods that he doesn't know, and he can't stand the thought of having somebody else figure it out before he does." (Ams, 116) At one time, Isham and his parents are in the woods together after a quarrel between the father and mother, and Isham sees a deer that his father does not see. "Isham had half a notion to point it out, since his father gave no sign of having noticed it, but reflection stopped him, and he said nothing. They were going somewhere that had something to do with their quarrel, and there was no use in calling their attention to things by the way that they might not want to waste time on, and that would only drag the unpleasantness out longer if they did. It was better to leave them to the squabble that they had managed somehow to get stalled in, and to keep the deer to himself." (Ams, 81)

Isham's relationship with his mother seems to resemble that of the father with the mother, the father wanting to argue things down logically, and the mother deferring to her feelings, but with her son, the pressures of more fundamental human emotions come into play, and the boy comes to realize something of this after he and his mother quarrel:

> [S]o she gathers him into her arms [as] when he had bumped his head or been flogged by an old hen with chicks; and she says she is not angry, she didn't mean to sound angry, it's only that she wants

> to do what's right and sometimes arguing about it makes it sound wrong; Isham is all she has got, she says, holding him against her and talking over his head so he can hear her voice hum in her chest, and she doesn't want him to think she is out of humor with him; she loves him. It's only that she wants to do what's right, and having him argue about it makes her feel that whatever she does is wrong. And he agrees that it doesn't do any good to make her feel like that, and—not without embarrassment—that he loves her and doesn't want to add to her worries; and then they hear the wagon and break to a different scene with a different background of feeling and different values, not argued about, but opposed. (Ams, 200)

Davis's strong sense of nature's presence as balance and refuge to human cussedness is underscored by Isham's urge to withdraw from parental squabbles to the disregarding nature that lies close to his home. "What is needed," Davis reminds himself, in describing the boy's feelings after such parental difficulties,

> is to bring in the sound of the creek . . . and the wind in the big trees and some of the smaller noises outside not as commonplace and ordinary and meaningless, but as something vast and welcome and reassuring, the presence of a world and life and motion that these spells of anger and misunderstanding and bitterness can't reach out far enough to touch; the deliberate groaning of a horse lying down for the night, . . . the sleepy chucking of quail crowding each other on the tree-limb they have picked for a roosting place. These are things that go on the same every night, the water hurrying over the loose stones, the air moving and the tree-branches swaying and tossing to feel its strength drawing through them; they are still there, unflurried and unchanged and unending; and Isham is as thankful for them as if they were some vast act of open-handed generosity, and less aware than he should be that he might have fallen into the habit of ignoring them without his parents' squabbling and bitterness to drive him into listening for them. (Ams, 79-80).

Davis's keen ecological understanding of what Darwin first made clear as the animal-human continuum is present throughout all his work, as it is in the *Exit* manuscript. Sometimes, it is simply a reminder of how closely we are interested in the lives and behavior of the non-human animals, as in the narrator's simile that "she took to him as fervently as a crow to a cut-glass doorknob" (Tms, 10), or the description of a horse belonging to an ill-favored visitor to Isham's parents: "It was a compact little blue roan gelding with a close spattering of white spots on top of its hind-quarters that looked as if it had been left tied somewhere with its rump sticking out in a wet snowstorm. It was one of the established horse strains east of the mountains, where it was known as the Nez Percé or appaloesie [*sic*], but it was the first of the breed that I had ever seen, and one of the prettiest that I ever did see: clean-legged, intelligent, fearless and sociable with everybody, and as gentle as a dog. Owning a horse like that kept even Mr. Fulton's looks from counting against him." (Ams, 52) In another scene, Davis's dialogue reveals how horses new to the narrator's country can be distinguished from those who are native to it. The newcomers leave bunches of old grass lying around, bunches uneaten and inedible, with the roots and dirt still clinging, while the local horses have learned the trick of nipping off the grass neatly with a sideways jerk at the bite. A wondrous animal that figures heavily in the action is a wild Mexican bull with a huge sulphur-colored head, who terrorizes the region. The "head" is revealed to be the crushed and dried carcass of a dead cougar. "It tried to jump the old bull, I guess," says Isham's father, "and he got it down and gored it so deep it got stuck on his horns. He can't get it raked off, and it's down over his eyes so he can't see. . . . and whenever he hears anything move he charges at it. . . . You'll live a long time before you see anything like that again." (Ams, 124)

Unnatural wonders like the cougar-headed bull show something of Davis's attraction to anecdotes, often very funny, that intrude upon his plotting of the manuscript, and that he cannot resist. One is about an old mountain man and his wife:

> His conversation never gets beyond how he tracked down some kind of wild animal and shot it, and what the hide was like and the haggling and dickering he went through marketing it. His name could be Pinkney Kloster, maybe. And his wife, . . . she will have been a country schoolteacher; she married him when nobody else would, in spite of being warned by everybody that she didn't know what she was letting herself in for and wouldn't like it when she found out. And either from contrariness or because it was so completely different from anything she had imagined or expected, she took to it like wild morning glory to a trashpile, and lived out every one of his trials and triumphs with as much intensity of feeling as he did, from the moment when he lit

> out [on] the trail of something to the time when its hide finally got peeled off and framed and hung in the barn-loft to dry and smell. She had an assortment of books scattered around the house that must have taken some discrimination to get together, though it would have been hard to decide what kind of discrimination it was—Macaulay's "Lays of Ancient Rome," Mrs. Gaskell's "Cranford," Joaquin Miller's "Life in London," Owen Meredith's "Lucille," with horrible illustrations, an English translation of a historical novel by Felix Gras, a biography of Peter the Great, "Rollo in Switzerland," a torn and weatherstained copy of "Indian Wars of Oregon," and a padded-covered edition of "Pilgrim's Progress" that didn't look as if anybody had ever opened it, besides various out-of-date schoolbooks; the best was Barnes' "History of the United States." It had illustrations of all the battles; somebody had embellished the foreground figures in them with overgrown sexual appendages, in India ink, so that Stonewall Jackson, General Grant, George Washington and Christopher Columbus all came out looking like somebody had opened the bathroom door by mistake. . . .
>
> It will not be possible to run all that in here, and perhaps I shouldn't have taken the trouble to note it down in so much detail; but it may be useful later, and nowadays I have to nail these things down before they get away from me: once gone, they are gone for good. (Ams, 113-14)

A natural storyteller, Davis resembles someone herding cats as he tries to move his main novel plot along to some publishable state, while also adding to the menagerie every delightful and vagrant anecdote that runs through his territory. But the thought that must have most preoccupied him was his realization that time watches from the shadows, and coughs when you would tarry, to paraphrase Auden. And Davis had hundreds of pages of drafts—upwards of two hundred thousand words, mostly huge blocks of indirect narration unrelieved by dialogue—that would nearly all have to be redone. The self-rebukes run through the manuscript every few pages, like a Greek chorus of self-warnings:

> I interrupt to put in some memoranda on what has gone before; it will really take some severe overhauling and revising, and perhaps I should go back and attend to it instead of wasting time on this throwaway style of half-doing it, but I resolved at the beginning not to do any rewriting in this draft, which is really only a process of getting

the story and some of its possibilities settled in my mind—a kind of framework in which the general run of the narrative can be worked out and decided on. The tone and the emotions, the things it can be made to touch and illuminate in its passage, will all have to wait till that part of it is settled and out of the way, even though they are more important than it is. (Ams, 64)

Seen in writing on this, I could feel that I was wallowing deeper into irrelevance and triviality with every line, especially the dialogue. Dialogue should be the flag marking something important, the sizing up of what has been narrated through some different mind—or maybe partly the sizing up of the mind through what has been narrated. (Ams, 82)

[I]nserts that belong everywhere except at the point where I am writing keep rearing up and slapping me in the face, and my mind nowadays is such a leaky vessel that I hate to risk losing them by neglecting to note them down. (Ams, 98H)

I am not going to piss away any more time on this. It isn't much of a scene and it shouldn't be made to sound like one. (Ams, 162)

Maybe there should be some dialogue about it to give the exact shade of feeling between them about it. (It's a blessing being able to do things casually like this: really it's shirking doing them, but it's better than nothing at all.) (Ams, 165)

This thing has got its ass hanging out in at least a dozen different places and how they are all to be decently covered and smoothed out, my strength and power of concentration being what they are, the Lord knows and the Lord help me. (Ams, 237)

I am perfectly sure now that my mind is going to pot. (Ams, 265)

Near the end of his manuscript, Davis pulls all his regrets into a powerful realist's summary of the bleakness that now faces him: "What I lack, I lack; it can't be made up by muttering about it or trying to define what it is. There have not been many times in my life when realizing my limitations made me lose my nerve so that I was afraid to keep trying. But this appears to be one of the times, and I can't help it and feel self-deluded and hypocritical in even pretending not to feel it. Going on in spite of it takes courage. Not going on would take even more courage." (Ams, 240A) In the painful self-honesty of these last two sentences, Davis prepares us for his remaining pages, in which the plot of the novel, with which he has struggled so long to this point, is interspersed with thoughts of an approaching end:

> Well. Down underneath all this anxious tinkering and brain-wrenching there is the conviction that I won't last long enough to finish it, or even to get it into anything like printable shape. And in that there ought to be a certain consolation: what the hell, if nothing is ever going to come of it, what difference does it make whether it gets done well or badly or at all? A man does have to have something to work on and something to think ahead to, for the sake of his own self-respect, I suppose; there is always the sneaking possibility that I might drag on longer than the percentage calls for, and I have always had to hold to the precept that defeat or victory is out of my hands, and that what matters is to do my best and keep at it. (Ams, 280-81)

As Davis's plot-patching seems to "striddle out into aimlessness," the ending pages turn more and more to straight memoir, his heartfelt claim that what matters is not the background but that " . . . it happened to me; and no better than what might have happened anywhere and to anybody, except that it was like this and not like the ordinary and received idea of such things, and I can't help it." (Ams, 272) These remembrances from his childhood are often beautiful and moving, as in his description of couples in a country square dance: "Uncle Buck would whack his bow on the fiddle and rake off a double-stopped run on the strings, my father would call out, 'Honor your partners!' and away the whole swad of bright-colored sets would go, circling and scraping and crossing and swinging, with pompadours jiggling and coattails popping and big skirts billowing and side angling like a flowering orchard in a high wind." (Ams, 278) And so the strong memories pour out at the end: his step-grandfather, unrelated to him, but, among his relatives, one for whom he had a strong liking, and in whose company he found in himself "an involuntary and besetting interest in people." (Ams, 291)

As Davis, on his next-to-the-last page of manuscript, looks ahead ruefully to the job of typing it all, and to how much of it will have to be discarded or rewritten, one can imagine his possible sardonic realization that at least the death that watches from the shadows will spare him from that distasteful duty. Anyway, no more typing or rewriting. I think, here, of Edward Abbey, who, on learning that he had incurable cancer and had only a short time left, deadpanned, "Anyway, no more flossing." Abbey, more to the point, was a close next-generation western counterpart to Davis, as was fellow-Oregonian Ken Kesey. All share a characteristic wry humor, as well as an instinctive environmental regard, a feeling for nature, for place and animals, and an understated but no less serious concern for the writer's craft, for the words on the page and the ideas behind them.

Exit, Pursued by a Bear. Whatever literary universals of Shakespeare's *The Winter's Tale* Davis may have originally hoped would reverberate in his final novel, the finality of its incompletion widens the possibilities. Would the tie between the play and the novel still relate to, say, Polixines's brilliant little demonstration, in Shakespeare's play, of nature preceding and thus underlying all such manifestations of culture and art as a novel? Would this suggest that nature, in this case human nature (now revivified by biology and the neurosciences as an entwined nature-nurture) is indeed universal, and thus still allows us to draw pleasure from the human drama of times and people not our own, as in Davis's novel? And can't we still enjoy remembering them as they were, "so that the experience still counts for something in this life and world," (Ams, 281) even allowing for the inescapable pursuing beast of time and death? Or, conversely, would the title serve as analogue to Davis's suggestion in his final pages that the novel's characters were now cultural anachronisms? That they stood for a time and a natural world "that was closer and more manageable and more straightforward, for the very reason that so much of it was less human," and thus were harried off the present stage by the devouring pomo-bear of the un-natural, of urbanism, traffic, and cellphones?

Or is all this putting too fine a point on it? Maybe he had *Exit, Pursued by a Bear* in mind all along as a good line to bow out with, given his failing heart and circulation and the likelihood of his early death. His inability to finish the last job of writing, and of being chased off the task by the bear of inevitability, of death, or time, or revision, just gave the title a little wry twist that would not have been unwelcome to an ironist: "Here Lies Davis, Victim of a Terminal Case of Rewriter's Block." Or as the hipster of the 1950s, Davis's last decade, might have put it, "Sometimes you eat the bear. Sometimes the bear eats you."

But as a Davis admirer, I'd prefer the benison of W. H. Auden for the Irish poet William Butler Yeats, which is a fine one for all writers:

Time that is intolerant
Of the brave and innocent,
And indifferent in a week
To a beautiful physique,
Worships language and forgives
Anyone by whom it lives[.][4]

H. L. Davis lives by the words in his finished works, from which his novels, a handful of poems, and his two collections of stories and essays may be especially recommended.

Notes

1. This essay was originally published in longer form in the fiftieth-anniversary issue of *Northwest Review* (vol. 45-3/2007). Our thanks to *Northwest Review* and to editor John Witte for permission to reprint.
2. Citations to the Davis manuscript of *Exit* are marked with "Tms" (typed manuscript) or "Ams" (autograph manuscript), along with any other symbols used to identify the selection. We are grateful to the University of Texas Ransom Center and Richard Workman, Research Librarian, for permission to use the *Exit* manuscript from the Davis Collection.
3. Lewis L. McArthur, *Oregon Geographic Names*, Fifth ed. (n.p., Western Imprints: The Press of the Oregon Historical Society, 1982), 636.
4. The lines are from the original 1939 version of the Auden poem, "In Memory of W. B. Yeats." These lines are among three stanzas later deleted from the poem.

A Brief H. L. Davis Bibliography

Here is a list of Davis's published books, plus a very limited sampling of criticism on his work. For fuller bibliographical information, Paul T. Bryant's volume, *H. L. Davis* (Boston: Twayne, 1978), is an excellent starting point. Also see *Bibliographical Guide to the Study of Western American Literature*, Second Edition, edited by Richard W. Etulain and N. Jill Howard (Albuquerque: University of New Mexico Press, 1995), and the annual bibliographies of American literature by the Modern Languages Association (MLA). The most extensive collection of Davis materials is at the Humanities Research Center at the University of Texas at Austin. Northwest scholars and readers will also find Davis correspondence and other papers at the libraries of the Universities of Oregon and Washington, and the Douglas County Museum of History and Natural History, Roseburg, Oregon. The quotations from James Stevens in the text are from James Stevens' annotations to the H. L. Davis correspondence in the James Stevens collection, University of Washington Libraries.

Novels

Honey in the Horn. New York: Harper, 1935.
Harp of a Thousand Strings. New York: William Morrow, 1947.
Beulah Land. New York: William Morrow, 1949.
Winds of Morning. New York: William Morrow, 1952.
The Distant Music. New York: William Morrow, 1957.

Collections

Proud Riders and Other Poems. New York: Harper, 1942.
Team Bells Woke Me and Other Stories. New York: William Morrow, 1953.
Kettle of Fire. New York: William Morrow, 1959.
The Selected Poems of H. L. Davis, with Preface by Thomas Hornsby Ferril. Boise, Idaho: Ahsahta Press, 1978.
H. L. Davis: Collected Essays and Short Stories, with Introduction by Robert Bain. Moscow, Idaho: University of Idaho Press, 1986.
Davis Country: H. L. Davis's Northwest. Edited by Brian Booth and Glen A. Love. Corvallis: Oregon State University Press, 2009.

Selected Criticism and Sources

Armstrong, George M. "An Unworn and Edged Tool: H. L Davis's Last Word on the West, 'The Kettle of Fire.'" *Northwest Perspectives: Essays on the Culture of the Pacific Northwest*. Edwin R. Bingham and Glen A. Love, eds. Seattle: University of Washington Press, 1979, 169-85.

Bain, Robert. *H. L Davis*. Western Writers Series No. 11. Boise, Idaho: Boise State University Press, 1974.

Bingham, Edwin R. "Pacific Northwest Writing: Reaching for Regional Identity." *Regionalism in the Pacific Northwest*. William G. Robbins, Robert J. Frank, and Richard E. Ross, eds. Corvallis: Oregon State University Press, 1983, 151-74.

Brunvand, Jan Harold. "*Honey in the Horn* and 'Acres of Clams': The Regional Fiction of H. L. Davis." *Western American Literature* 2 (Summer 1967): 135-45.

Bryant, Paul T. *H. L. Davis*. Boston: Twain, 1978.

Clare, Warren L. " 'Posers, Parasites, and Pismires': *Status Rerum*, by James Stevens and H. L. Davis." *Pacific Northwest Quarterly* 61 (January 1970): 22-30. Reprinted in *H. L. Davis: Collected Essays and Stories*. Moscow, Idaho, 1986, 341-56.

Corning, Howard M. "All the Words On the Pages, I: H. L. Davis." *Oregon Historical Quarterly* 73 (December 1972): 293-31.

———. "The Prose and Poetry of It." *Oregon Historical Quarterly* 74 (September 1973): 244-67.

Ferril, Thomas, and Helen Hornsby. *The Rocky Mountain Herald Reader*. New York: William Morrow, 1966.

Findlay, John M. "Something in the Soil?: Regional Identity in the 20th Century Pacific Northwest." *Pacific Northwest Quarterly* 97 (Fall 2006): 179-89.

Greiner, S. M., Francis J. "Voice of the West: Harold L. Davis," *Oregon Historical Quarterly* 66 (Summer 1965): 240-48.

Kohler, Dayton, "H. L. Davis: Writer in the West." *College English* 14 (December 1952): 133-40.

Love, Glen A. "Stemming the Avalanche of Tripe: Or, How H. L. Mencken and Friends Reformed Northwest Literature." *Thalia* 4:1 (Spring-Summer 1981): 46-53. Reprinted in *H. L. Davis: Collected Essays and Stories*. Moscow Idaho, 1986, 321-40.

O'Connell, Nicholas. *On Sacred Ground: The Spirit of Place in Pacific Northwest Literature*. Seattle: University of Washington Press, 2003, 57-66.

Potts, James T. "H. L. Davis' View: Reclaiming and Recovering the Land." *Oregon Historical Quarterly* 82 (Summer 1981): 117-31.

Ricou, Laurie. *The Arbutus/Madrone Files: Reading the Pacific Northwest*. Corvallis: Oregon State University Press, 2002, 21, 22, 43-44, 87-91, 185.

Ridgeway, Ann N., ed. *The Selected Letters of Robinson Jeffers: 1897-1962*. Baltimore: John Hopkins Press, 1968, 76, 124.

Stevens, James. " 'Bunk-Shanty Ballads and Tales': The Annual Society Address." *Oregon Historical Quarterly* 50 (December 1949): 235-42.

———. "The Northwest Takes to Poesy." *American Mercury* 16 (January 1929): 64-70.

Editors' Note

The editors would like to thank Professor Richard W. Etulain and Professor Robert J. Frank for their early support of this book, and Tom Booth, Associate Director, and Jo Alexander, Managing Editor, of Oregon State University Press for their encouragement and help. Thanks, too, to their Press colleagues: Director Karyle Butcher, Mary Elizabeth Braun, Micki Reaman, and Judith Radovsky.

We also thank Karen Bratton, Research Librarian, Jena Mitchell, Curator, and Stacey McLaughlin, former Director, of the Douglas County Museum of History & Natural History, Roseburg, Oregon; Paul J. Constantine, Associate Dean of University Libraries, University of Washington Libraries; Richard Workman, Associate Librarian of the Harry Ransom Center, University of Texas; James D. Fox, Head of Special Collections and University Archives, University of Oregon Libraries; and Donald Urquhart, Director of Collections Management, Portland Art Museum, Portland, Oregon, and their respective staffs, for their kind assistance.

Brian Booth is grateful once more to his wife, Gwyneth Booth, for her patience and support of his pursuit of H. L. Davis for this book. He extends a special thanks to his assistant, Kathleen Seethaler, for her diligent secretarial services in connection with this project.

The editors also wish to acknowledge the following individuals and organizations for their assistance in matters involving H. L. Davis and this book: Shannon Applegate; Stephen Dow Beckham; the late Edwin Bingham; James Sheldon Brown; the late Elizabeth T. Hobson; Barbara Davis Kroon; Adam Lowry; Charles Lee; Peter London of HarperCollins Publishers; Steve McQuiddy; David Milholland, Walt Curtis, and the Oregon Cultural Heritage Commission; Georgia Nelson; the late Terence O'Donnell; and Margaret Tilbury.

In addition, Oregon State University Press and the editors would like to thank Douglas County Museum of History & Natural History for permission to use the photographs in this book on pages 9, and 275, Oregon Historical Society for permission to use the photograph on page ii (#OrHi 27399); and the late Elizabeth T. Hobson for permission to use the photograph on page 26.

Acknowledgements

The editors wish to thank the copyright holders and publishers listed below for their permission to reprint materials included in this volume. Every reasonable effort has been made to trace the ownership of copyrighted material and to make full acknowledgement of its use. The material in public domain has been listed with the date of original publication for purposes of reference. If errors or omissions have occurred, they will be corrected in subsequent editions, provided that notification is submitted in writing to the publisher.

"Davis on Davis," first published as *Childe Herald* in *Rocky Mountain News* (Denver Co. 1951) and reprinted in *Many Faces: An Anthology of Oregon Autobiography*, edited by Stephen Dow Beckham, Oregon State University Press; copyright 1993 by the Oregon Council of Teachers of English; used by permission of the publisher.

Selection, pages 1-26 from *Honey in the Horn*, Harper & Brothers (1935); copyright 1935 by Harper & Brothers; copyright renewed 1962 by Elizabeth T. Hobson.

"Oregon," first published in *Holiday* (June 1953); copyright 1953 by H. L. Davis; republished in *Kettle of Fire* by H. L. Davis; copyright 1959 by H. L. Davis; compilation copyright (1959); renewed 1987 by H. L. Davis; reprinted by permission of HarperCollins Publishers, WILLIAM MORROW.[b]

"Open Winter," first published in *Saturday Evening Post* (May 1939); copyright 1939 by H. L. Davis.[a]

"Fishing Fever," first published in *Holiday* (May 1954); copyright 1954 by H. L. Davis.[b]

"Old Man Isbell's Wife," first published in *American Mercury* (February 1929); copyright 1929 by H. L. Davis.[a]

"Hell to Be Smart," first published in *American Mercury* (November 1935); copyright 1935 by H. L. Davis.

"A Town in Eastern Oregon," first published in *American Mercury* (January 1930); copyright 1930 by H. L. Davis.[a]

"Team Bells Woke Me," first published in *American Mercury* (April 1931); copyright 1931 by H. L. Davis.[a]

"The Homestead Orchard," first published in *Saturday Evening Post* (July 1939); copyright 1939 by H. L. Davis.[a]

"Puget Sound Country," first published in *Holiday* (May 1954) as "The Puget Sound Country"; copyright 1954 by H. L. Davis.[b]

"The Kettle of Fire," first published in *Northwest Review* (Summer 1959); copyright 1959 by H. L. Davis.[b]

"The Rain-Crow," first published in *Poetry* (June 1920); copyright 1920 by H. L. Davis.

"Crop Campers," first published in *American Mercury* (January 1929); copyright 1929 by H. L. Davis.

"Witches," unpublished poem dated 1927 from the James Stevens Collection, University of Washington Libraries; used by permission of University of Washington Libraries.

"The River People," first published in *Poetry* (March 1925); copyright 1925 by H. L. Davis.

"Steel Gang," first published in *Poetry* (September 1928); copyright 1928 by H. L. Davis.

"Clearing Old Stones," first published in *The Selected Poems of H. L. Davis*, Ahsahta Press, Boise State University, Boise Idaho; copyright 1978 by Elizabeth T. Hobson; used by permission of Ahsahta Press.

"Proud Riders," first published in *Poetry* (April 1919) as "The Sweet Tasting"; reprinted in *Proud Riders and Other Poems*; Harper & Brothers (1942); copyright H. L. Davis 1942; copyright renewed 1969 by Elizabeth T. Hobson.

"New Birds," first published in *Poetry* (May 1933); copyright 1933 by H. L. Davis.

"Counting Back," first published in *The Selected Poems of H. L. Davis*, Ahsahta Press, Boise State University, Boise Idaho; copyright 1978 by Elizabeth T. Hobson; used by permission of Ahsahta Press.

Letter to James Stevens, April 19, 1927; used by permission of University of Washington Libraries, James Stevens collection.

Letter to James Stevens, December 13, [1927]; used by permission of University of Washington Libraries, James Stevens collection.